Praise for *The Forgotten*

'Engrossing, heartbreaking and eloquently written, *The Forgotten* left me breathless. Chamberlain offers readers new perspectives on war, women, espionage and what it takes to survive.'

Lara Prescott, author of *The Secrets We Kept*

'Beautifully crafted, elegantly written, with characters to root for – I loved this heart-stopping tale.'

Saskia Sarginson, author of *The Bench*

'A masterclass in immersive wartime fiction. While Chamberlain is characteristically unflinching in her portrayal of the grim realities of war, *The Forgotten* is so much more than a catalogue of brutality. It is a pacy and compelling story of intrigue and espionage, and of how people can survive and love can endure. I loved it!'

Sonia Velton, author of *Blackberry and Wild Rose*

'Beautifully written, realistic on the human impact of war, with characters I fell in love with.'

Louise Hare, author of *This Lovely City*

'Mary Chamberlain brilliantly explores the devastating toll of war on every side, the price paid by women for survival and the impossible choices ordinary people were forced to make, reminding us that history is never really in the past.'

Sarah Day, author of *Mussolini's Island*

'A riveting drama in the lingering shadows of the Second World War: the inherited, the lived, the choices made and the secrets they bring.'

Cecilia Ekbäck, author of *The Historians*

'*The Forgotten* is a triumph, the kind of novel you hate to finish.'

Carmen Callil, author of *Oh Happy Day*

Praise for *The Hidden*

'A powerful and raw, though elegantly written, character piece dealing with inhumanity and endurance, firmly grounded in real events.'

Alastair Mabbott, *Herald*

'Recent novels, such as *The Guernsey Literary & Potato Peel Pie Society*, have taken the occupation as their subject, but none so potently as Mary Chamberlain's *The Hidden*... The realities of life under a ruthless occupying power are slowly, skilfully revealed.'

Sunday Times

'A heartbreaking yet hope-filled tale.'

Woman's Own

'A powerful story, well told.'

Choice magazine

'Set against the backdrop of the Nazi occupation of the Channel Islands, *The Hidden* is a powerful, heart-wrenching story of deception and guilt, love and loss; I was completely engrossed, seduced by its strong characters and atmosphere, and intrigued by the mystery at the heart of the novel.'

Saskia Sarginson, author of *The Bench*

'Shines a piercing light on the shrouded history of human trafficking and labour camps in the Channel Isles during WW2. A fascinating and powerful story of love, endurance, betrayal and guilt.'

Anna Mazzola, author of *The Unseeing*

'This compelling and heart-rending novel is a potent reminder that the horrors of war aren't limited to the battlefields. Nor do they cease when the guns fall silent. There are those who will carry the scars – emotional, physical and psychological – for the rest of their lives. There is scant justice. But in *The Hidden*, Chamberlain gives them credence and a voice.'

Susan Swarbrick, *Herald*

THE
FORGOTTEN

Mary Chamberlain

ONEWORLD

A Oneworld Book

First published in Great Britain and Australia
by Oneworld Publications, 2021

ISBN 978-1-78607-907-7 (hardback)
ISBN 978-1-78607-908-4 (ebook)

Typeset by Geethik Technologies
Printed and bound in Great Britain by Clays Ltd, Elcograf S.p.A.

Oneworld Publications
10 Bloomsbury Street
London WC1B 3SR
England

Stay up to date with the latest books,
special offers, and exclusive content from
Oneworld with our newsletter

Sign up on our website
oneworld-publications.com

For Kikelomo, and a kinder world

CHAPTER ONE

London: February 1958

Betty was late. She hesitated at the door, in two minds whether to go in. She hated drawing attention to herself, but she'd come this far. She sidled through, stood at the back, spotted a vacant seat, tiptoed to the row, head bowed, squeezing herself along, *excuse me, sorry. Excuse me. Thank you.* Her coat snagged on the armrest. She pulled it free. The man in the row in front turned and glowered at her. *Sorry.* He wouldn't understand why she had to be here, how *personal* this was.

She sat down and fanned her face with the programme. She'd had to run most of the way and even though the February day was frosty, she was sweating. She unbuttoned her coat, wriggled her arms free and rolled to one side and the other, pulling the coat's skirt from beneath her. The man next to her glared and tutted.

'Sorry.' Clenched her teeth, opened her lips. *Can't help it.*

She folded her coat and bent over, slipping it under her seat, took off her hat and scarf, and laid them on the coat. Sat back, lifting her hair off her neck, enjoying the air on her skin. Leaned forward as she rummaged in her bag, pulled out a notebook and a pencil and began to flip the pages, crackling the paper. Out of the corner of her eye she saw her neighbour twist towards her and put his finger on his lip. She pretended not to see, though she felt his eyes on her, monitoring her. She licked the tip of her pencil, sat upright and began to write.

That historian, A.J.P. Taylor, said MPs who supported the bomb should be hailed as murderers. He was about the same age as her father, in his fifties. It's not just young people who think like I do, Betty thought. Middle-aged men do, too. She stood up and applauded. Her notebook and pencil tumbled to the floor so when they sat down she had to crawl between the seats to retrieve them.

'For goodness' sake,' the man next to her said. 'Keep still.'

'Sorry.' She smiled, *forgive me.* He nodded, pursed his lips. He was older than her. There were even a few strands of grey at his temples. He was angry. Was that what happened as you got older? You got moody? Short-tempered? He wore a beige Fair Isle pullover, hand-knitted, out of place among the navy duffel coats and black polo necks. Her mother used to knit her jumpers and cardigans, two ply lambswool which she bought in a skein and called on Betty to hold taut while she rolled it into a ball. Her mother knitted everything, far more than she needed or Betty could use, come to that, chain-smoking as she worked so every-thing whiffed of stale cigarettes and lavender talcum powder. She hadn't smoked until the war. The war had changed everything.

Betty sniffed, as if she could conjure it up, pulled her hankie from her sleeve and blew her nose. She still missed her mother, more than ever. More than her sister, perhaps. It was difficult to know. She knew what had happened to her mother, but her sister had just *gone.* This meeting is for them, she thought. For *them.* She felt the man glaring at her. She tucked her hankie back and focused on the podium. Who was Alex Comfort? She liked what he said though, about Britain's moral bankruptcy and ceremonial suicide. That was a good turn of phrase. She wrote it down. There was more applause. She put the notebook between her teeth so it wouldn't slip away while she stood up again and clapped. It was, she knew, very un-British to behave like that at a public meeting.

Still, needs must. She agreed with every word. She'd sign up, or whatever you had to do, immediately.

She removed the notebook from between her teeth and fanned herself again. The hall was packed. How many people were here? She couldn't begin to calculate. *Thousands*, at least. All of them thinking like she did. Some of them were quite old, too. Nuclear war was wrong. What did it matter if Russia had won the space race? So what if they could fire an H-bomb from a sputnik? Didn't mean the West had to copy them. America and Russia were like roosters sharpening their spurs. Or was it a game of chicken? The first to blink – *bam*! Armageddon. For what?

She couldn't understand why so many people didn't see that, harping on about the Red Peril and world domination, about godless Communism and heartless Russians who'd sent the family dog into space and incinerated her alive. They seemed to care more about the dog than they did about people. If there was a nuclear war there'd be nothing left to dominate, whoever started it. What was the point of that? That frightened her far more than the threat of Russia. She didn't always sleep at night, dreaming of the nuclear strike, the firestorm, the mushroom cloud, the slow invisible blanket of poison. Sometimes she wondered whether she'd take a suicide pill, like Mary in *On the Beach*. Was it cyanide? She couldn't remember.

There was an air of urgency here, in this room. She was breathing excitement, she and all these strangers, linked in this moment. Even the grumpy man next to her was smiling. She'd never felt like this before, part of a vast, unstoppable movement of change. It felt, she thought, like being in love, swept in an avalanche of hope and adventure. Bliss. She listened to the last speaker, a call to action, a march on Aldermaston. Ban the bomb! We will stop it. Yes. *Yes.*

The meeting came to a close.

'Excuse me,' she said to the man next to her, pointing to the exit. 'Would you mind?'

He stood up with a clumsy gesture while she pressed past him, her coat over her arm, hat and scarf in her hand. She pushed to the end of the row, threaded her arms through her coat and, buttoning it up, walked towards the door. She sensed him stand up and follow her. The crowd was pressing in and she had difficulty walking. She had to elbow her way through, *excuse me, excuse me.*

'We're all trying to leave,' a man said.

'I know,' she said. 'I'm so sorry.' She didn't want to talk to the angry man. 'I have a train to catch.'

She pushed out into the open air, stepped into Storey's Gate, and cut into Great George Street. The crowd was less dense there. The February night had turned for the worst so she stood on the corner, tying the belt of her coat tight, clamping her red felt hat to her head and muffling her neck with her scarf. The street lamps glowed soft and yellow and she caught a glimpse of the man she'd sat next to, wrapped up in a dark overcoat, heading in her direction. Perhaps she should apologise, step in before he berated her. Or ignore him. She'd probably never see him again.

She hurried into Parliament Street, crossed the road and walked down Whitehall. There was a gathering in Downing Street with banners, home-made jobs on cardboard. She could make out *Ban the Bomb* in the lamplight. She walked past them, looked back. He was still following. The crowd had thinned by Horse Guards and she sped up, walking fast towards Charing Cross. There was a Lyons Corner House by the post office. It was still open. She had time for some tea before the last train.

Betty could see the man running across the road, entering the shop after her. Oh Lordy, she thought. The nuns at school had warned her about men who followed women, though honestly, what did they know? Still. The café was crowded but there were a few spaces free. She sat at a small table in the centre of the room, head down, rummaging in her bag, and watched as he sauntered past her. *Phew.* Then he stopped and turned.

'Excuse me,' he said. 'Weren't you at that meeting?'

'Which meeting?' She was peeling off her gloves, finger by finger. Poised and sophisticated, not gauche and clumsy.

'In the Methodist Central Hall. The Campaign for Nuclear Disarmament.'

'Oh, that,' she said. 'Yes.'

'What did you think?' He pulled out the chair opposite her. 'Mind if I sit down?' His eyes were a soft green-hazel and gave nothing away. 'Or are you meeting someone?'

She shrugged. 'I can't stop you.' No, she thought, *surely?* Someone at a meeting like that wouldn't be an axeman. They were all pacifists, Quakers. Gentle people. Besides, he didn't seem cross and his face was intelligent.

The nippy came over, young and ill-formed in her black dress and white pinny.

'May I treat you to a cup of tea?' he said.

'If you like.' Non-committal.

'Two teas,' he said. 'And two iced buns.'

The waitress wrote it down. Her writing, Betty could see, was unsure and immature. She was probably called Gladys, or Beryl.

'Actually,' Betty said, 'I'd rather have a Chelsea bun.'

The nippy scowled, corrected the order, let her notebook dangle on its string and replaced the dirty ashtray with a clean one from the table beside it. The man fished in his pocket and pulled out a packet of Weights. He flipped it open and offered it to Betty.

'Thank you.' She took a cigarette and propped it between her fingers, leaning forward for him to light it. He rummaged in his trouser pocket, and the other one, then patted his jacket.

'I'm sorry,' he said. 'I seem to have forgotten my matches. Do you have a light?'

Betty laughed and peered into her bag, pulling out her lighter. She held up three fingers in a Boy Scout salute.

'Always prepared.' She leaned forward and lit his cigarette, and her own, closed the lighter and threw it into her bag. She was in control now, and it made her feel safer.

'Be prepared,' he said. 'That's the Boy Scouts' motto.' He smiled and dragged on his cigarette. 'Did you come by yourself?'

She lifted her face to the ceiling and blew a smoke ring, a perfect circle. She paused, turned and looked at him through lowered eyes.

'Yes,' she said, plucking a strand of tobacco from her lip, flicking it into the air. *So what?*

'What did you think? Of the speakers?' he said, taking another long breath on his cigarette.

'All right.' She tapped her ash in the tray and looked past him, over his shoulder, as if she was waiting for someone. 'What about you?'

'I thought they were first-rate.'

She turned and studied him. He wasn't as old as she'd thought. More like thirty than forty, not that much older than her, and his face was kind, good-looking even. Perhaps there was nothing sinister about him, he was just trying to be friendly. But he was awkward, she could sense, as if he was unused to striking up a conversation. Or was expecting a rebuff.

'I'm sorry if I disturbed you,' she said. 'I meant to get there on time but the bus didn't come for ages. You know how it is, you dither whether to walk or not, and the more you dither, the later it gets.'

'No worries.' He smiled. 'You settled down in the end,' he said, adding, 'Sort of.'

She wondered if he was playing with her. She wasn't much good at small talk either, and wasn't sure what to say to him.

'Did you have to come far?'

'Oh no,' he said. 'Only Bloomsbury.'

She stubbed out her cigarette as the nippy approached with the tea and buns, waited while she placed them on the table. 'Thank you,' she said to the waitress and smiled at her, turning to the man opposite, who sat stirring his tea, concentrating, as if playing for time.

'War is so awful.' She fiddled with the spoon on her saucer, turning it left, right. That sounded naïve and she wished she hadn't said it. But it was true. Even now, she could taste its horror, as if the memories had coated her tongue in a membrane of fear.

'I agree,' he said, nodding, his voice melancholy. He must have been old enough to have fought in the war, Betty thought, so he'd know all right. Buffeted by war, like she was, taking a stand, like her. She wanted to know if he was a pacifist or a unilateralist but didn't like to ask. She bit into her bun, savoured the fruit and the soft, sweet bread.

'My name's John,' he said, leaning forward, his arm outstretched. 'And yours?'

'Betty.' She wiped her hand on her napkin and took his. 'A bit sticky, I'm afraid.'

He laughed, shrugged, *doesn't matter.*

'Betty. Nice name. Do you work, Betty?'

'Of course I work.'

'Let me guess,' he said. 'You're a journalist.'

'A journalist? Why do you think that?' She was flattered. Her guard, she knew, was falling.

'You were taking notes,' he said. 'In shorthand.'

'Goodness,' she said. 'Are you a detective?' She narrowed her eyes, added, 'Or a spy?' He looked the most unlikely spy, or detective, with his Fair Isle pullover and college tie, and she found herself smiling.

'No.' He grinned, the hints of dimples, his eyes alight. 'I'm a teacher. Camden Grammar for Boys. So what *do* you do?'

'I'm a typist.'

He laughed, and it was the gentlest of sounds, like a robin chirruping. 'A typist? Really? I'd have had you down as a pioneer of something or other,' he said. 'Like Vera Brittain. Or Winifred Holtby. A revolutionary.' He added, 'I bet you're a Somerville alumna.'

'Not quite,' she said, relenting. 'Bedford College for Women.' Bedford or nothing, her father had said. Anywhere else was for him a hotbed of Communism.

'What did you study?'

She sipped her tea, broke off a piece of bun and shoved it in her mouth.

'English Literature,' she said with her mouth full. She could feel a small piece of raisin stuck to her tooth. She curled her tongue and licked it clean. 'My father's choice. Not mine.'

'Oh?'

'He thinks education is wasted on a woman,' she said. 'But literature is at least decorative, does minimal damage.' She smiled. 'I had to promise him I'd learn to type when I graduated.'

He laughed again. 'And what would you have preferred to study?'

'History,' she said. 'Or anthropology, perhaps.'

'Why anthropology?'

She shrugged again, lifted her cup. 'I don't really know. I'd like to travel, see how other people live.' She wanted to kick herself. Such a silly answer. What she really wanted was to get away from home, see the world. Nyasaland. Jamaica. Perhaps she'd meet her husband there, bring back a native. The thought of seeing her father's shocked face made her smile.

'So what do you teach, John?'

'French. German.'

'German?' She swallowed. They always spoke English at home – *We must forget Germany*, her father had said. She'd worked hard at her accent, spoke English now without a trace, blended in so no one guessed where she was from, like a talking chameleon. She twisted her mouth. 'Is that a popular subject?'

He shook his head and looked into the distance; she saw his eyes moisten over and his fingers begin to shake.

'John?'

He placed his cup back on its saucer, his hand trembling so the tea slopped and the clink of the china sang out like fallen keys.

'John?' She reached over and dabbed his saucer dry with her napkin.

'I'm sorry,' he said. 'I was miles away.'

She knew she'd touched a nerve, and wasn't sure what to do. Perhaps he needed to be alone. She tapped her lips with the napkin. 'Thank you for tea. I must go.'

'So soon? May I see you home?' he said.

'I can make my own way,' she said, pushing her chair away from the table and standing up. He stood too. He was average height, slender. She had thought he was taller when she'd seen him in the lamplight. Shadows did that. Distorted perspective.

'I'd like to see you again,' he said.

'Are you going on the Easter march?'

'Possibly. But that's weeks away. Perhaps I could take you out? The pictures?'

'Maybe. I must dash.'

She pulled her hat from her bag and tugged it on.

'I work at Barstow's,' she said, holding out her hand. 'Goodbye.'

She put on her coat, walked towards the door. A man stood up as she passed him, tipping over the chair in his haste. She caught a glimpse of him. He looked like someone she once knew but when she checked again, he'd gone. She was imagining things. She stepped out of the door, and waved at John as she ran past the window. It had begun to sleet.

9

CHAPTER TWO

London: February 1958

John let himself into the building, checked the table for post, and climbed the staircase to the rooms he rented on the top floor. He kicked off his outdoor shoes and padded into the bedroom, fishing under the bed for his slippers. He had a stack of marking to do and the flat was chilly. He'd have to light the fire, warm himself up, fill his pen with red ink and coax it into action. It was sluggish in cold weather.

He padded across the linoleum into the sitting room and switched on the wireless. He was used to living on his own, but coming in tonight the silence of his rooms was overwhelming. That young woman, in a way he couldn't fathom, had made him lonely. He hadn't had that feeling for a long time. If ever, really. The dirty plate and frying pan from supper were piled in the sink in his kitchenette, and his upturned cup and saucer were balanced on the draining board. *Bachelor.*

He laid the fire and fished for the matches on the mantelpiece, watching as the flame caught and the coals began to glow. A gentle heat radiated out. The feeling began to return to his fingers and his cheeks started to tingle and sting, and he remembered how the cold outside and the warmth of the hall had flushed her face so it glowed, ripe and lush. Peaches and cream, was that what they called it? A peaches-and-cream complexion, her hair berry-brown, curled like a pageboy's at the back of her head. A nut-brown maiden. Percy's words rang through his mind: *Shall never be said the nut-brown maid / was to her love unkind.* Her eyes, he'd noted, were grey.

Barstow's. He had no idea who they were, but he could look them up in the telephone book and send her a letter, or if it was close, deliver it by hand. It needn't be long, but it would be polite. *I apologise if I appeared a bit forward.* She'd bolted when he suggested meeting again, so he must have moved too fast. He'd made a fool of himself too, when he told her what he taught. Why did he have to get the shakes then? Maybe that's why she left in a hurry. She sensed his instability. *Thank you for your company at tea.* He didn't know her surname but was sure it would arrive, especially if he put 'typing pool'. There couldn't be that many Bettys in a typing pool. *There is a meeting of the Campaign for Nuclear Disarmament in St Pancras next week which I plan to attend. I'll send off a postal order too, as they need the money.* She'd been brittle, non-committal, even strict with him, but when he'd trembled and spilt his tea she'd seemed sensitive, understanding. He'd put ten bob on her writing poetry. *I enjoyed our talk and hope we meet again, perhaps at Aldermaston.*

He leaned back in his chair and laughed. He'd never send the letter. He was far too shy. Was it shyness? Or nervousness? Most men his age were married. He found it hard to make the first move and his job took up most of his time, so where would he ever meet anyone? That's what his mother kept saying, *Why don't you find a nice girl and settle down?*

Would that it were that simple. It wasn't just reticence, or time, he knew. It ran far deeper than that. He stared into the flames, his mind wandering back to Berlin. *Enough.* He opened his briefcase and took out the exercise books, resting them in a pile by the fireplace, glancing at the mantel clock on the shelf. Ten thirty. He'd work for an hour, then go to bed. Do what he could, and polish off the rest in his lunch break. The clock was as silent as the room, no brash tick-tock or tinsel chimes. It sat on its chrome base, reminding him, pain etched in its round glass face, a kind of penance.

He shut his eyes and tried to think of Betty sitting in front of him, cradling her cup in her slender, white fingers, but it was another woman's face he saw, another's hands with broken nails clutching a chipped enamel jug, picking through the rubble of the Adlon, where dusty buddleia and grass were colonising the ruins and where he'd spotted a rabbit the day before. Her hair was a rich golden brown, like Betty's, but streaked with dust. Her eyes were gold.

He picked up the first book from the pile, slammed it back down again.

Betty was serious, intense. Was she just another bluestocking, too unsure of herself to let go? Or was there a deeper reason? She wasn't beautiful, but she was striking, and mysterious. Though, if he was honest, most women were to him.

No matter he didn't have her surname. 'Miss Betty c/o Barstow's' would find her. If he was keen, that is. Otherwise, forget her. On second thoughts, he could play for time by trying to find out her real name. It was juvenile to write 'Miss Betty c/o Barstow's', the sort of thing one of his love-struck sixth-formers would do. He'd write to the boss, or Personnel if it was a big enough company, get her proper name. He didn't need to contact her today, after all. And if he wrote on the school notepaper, then whoever read it would see he wasn't some crank but a respectable citizen. He'd ask the secretary if he could borrow her typewriter. A typed letter would make it more official.

§

The reply came a week later. Miss Bette Fisher. Bette? They must have made a typing mistake. She was Betty, a common-or-garden diminutive Elizabeth.

He found it hard to concentrate these days at the best of times. Found himself setting translations and comprehension tests more than was strictly necessary while he sauntered over to the classroom window and gazed up at the clouds squatting over the city, the tips of the chestnut trees around the playground beginning to glow green with the promise of spring. She worked in Lincoln's Inn Fields. On Monday it would be five weeks since he'd met her, and he'd made no move to contact her even though he thought about her all the time.

A letter had come by second post and was waiting in his pigeonhole. It was marked *Personal*. He slit the envelope along the top with his finger, and pulled out the contents. It was folded over, written on a small sheet of blue Basildon Bond paper, the brand he used to write his letters. *Dear John*. He skimmed to the bottom of the letter. *Yours sincerely, Betty.*

The writing danced and bowed. She had made the first move, beaten him to it. The secretary was staring at him across the teapot. She raised an eyebrow.

'You've gone very pale.'

John could feel the smile climb along his lips and into his cheeks and finally settle around his eyes.

'Have I?' he said. She signed herself Betty. He put the letter in his pocket to read later. He'd relish the moment, like saving the cherry for last. It was double French for the sixth-formers and he let them hold a debate on France and the crisis in Algeria. There was a staff meeting at the end of the day, so it was past six o'clock before he got to his rooms in Bury Street. He could do with a beer, enjoy its bitter yeasty tang while he read the letter. He parked his bike and chained it to the railings, and went into the local opposite.

'Evening, John,' the landlord said as he entered. 'Your usual?'

'Thanks.' He paid, and took it over to a small table by the window and pulled out the letter.

Dear John,

It took me some time, but I finally tracked you down. The secretary at your school was very reluctant to give me your surname. I have no idea why. I had to lie like mad for my reasons for wanting it! If you don't want to hear from me, then please read no further. We met at the rally in Central Hall, you remember, and then had tea afterwards. I'm sorry I had to rush off, but I had a train to catch and was cutting it a bit fine!

I hope you are well and if I am not being too forward, I would like to take you up on your offer to meet again. If you've changed your mind, then please ignore this letter. If not, my address is at the top. It's a work address, I'm afraid, but it's the easiest way to contact me. Write, please, don't ring. We're not allowed to take personal calls.

Yours sincerely,

Betty Fisher

He smiled to himself. If he posted his reply tonight, it would get to her tomorrow second post, or Friday at the latest. That would give her time to reply. Saturday. Or Sunday. He'd collect her from wherever she lived. Or the station. She said she had to catch a train. They could go to the zoo. Animals were a good icebreaker. Elephants, big cats, creepy-crawlies. Monkeys. It was years since he'd been there. Or perhaps she'd prefer the pictures? They'd saunter afterwards to the Corner House in Marble Arch. Maison Lyons, no less. Have a slap-up tea in one of the restaurants there or, if he had enough money, go to the grill. He finished his beer, folded the letter, waved goodbye to the barman, and crossed the road to his buildings.

CHAPTER THREE

London: April 1958

Betty had never seen anything so posh. It wasn't a polite word, *posh*, but sometimes no other word would do. John sat opposite her, his napkin tucked into his collar like a schoolboy. She wondered if she shouldn't do the same with hers. It would be awful to spill gravy or worse down her best day frock. It had taken her a while to decide what to wear before she settled on her choice. Smart, but not flashy, bluestocking-ish with a hint of bohemian. It was red, after all, albeit a rusty red rather than a brash pillar-box. A stain would be too embarrassing. She picked up the napkin, and tucked it in.

She had suggested they meet at the restaurant.

'I'm in town anyway,' she'd said. This wasn't quite true. She'd come in especially to meet him.

They'd shaken hands, and his palms were dry and soft. She'd confessed right away that she hadn't walked all the way to Aldermaston, only to Chiswick really, which wasn't far, but her father had wanted her home at Easter. Had *demanded* her presence, but she didn't tell John that.

'Just as well, though, given the weather on Easter Saturday. Chucked it down.'

'That's further than I went,' he said. 'And for much the same reasons.'

She wondered whether he was a mummy's boy, tied up with apron strings. Was that why he was so anxious and unsure?

'Your work misspelled your name,' he said, after they'd sat down and ordered. 'They put an "e" at the end of Betty, not a "y".'

She looked across the table at him. He seemed nervy, fiddling with his fork, turning it over and over. She took a deep breath, even though she had said it often enough.

'No they didn't,' she said. 'That *is* my name.'

She smiled. Fib, she'd done it often enough, *put him at his ease.* 'My parents called me after some Hollywood star or other.' She looked up, straight at him. 'I hate it. Betty's much nicer.'

'Bette Davis?' he said. 'She's very glamorous.' Betty felt the coarse grip of a blush colouring her face.

'I rather like the name Bette,' he went on. 'It's more unusual. Betty with a *y* seems very Home Counties. Godalming. Gymkhanas and all that.'

He raised an eyebrow, as if to say, *Am I right?* His eyes teased and a smiled edged his mouth.

'Actually,' she said, 'Hatfield.' He looked disappointed, as if his judgement was wrong, so she added, 'At least, that's where we ended up after the war.' And wished she hadn't said anything.

John thought for a moment, his forehead furrowed. 'Everyone was on the move after the war.'

He spoke softly, as if recalling a particular moment. Of course, she thought, he'd probably been there, in Europe. He'd know. She was twisting one corner of the napkin, rolling it in her fingers. The last thing she wanted to talk about was the war. She looked away, spotted the waitress bearing a tray.

'I think our soup is here,' she said, leaning back so the waitress could put the bowl in place. Tomato soup. Betty could tell from the smell it came from a tin, but no matter. It was her favourite. He swirled the soup and made a vortex and she wanted to say, *Be careful, you'll spill it.*

'Where were you before?'

'Before what?'

'Before you moved to Hatfield.'

'Oh,' she said. 'Well.' She hadn't told anyone that. 'Well, everywhere, really. We moved around.' That was the truth. She stirred her soup, took a sip.

He leaned back, dabbed his mouth with the napkin.

'Was your father in the army then? Moving around?'

She looked up, her soup lumping in her throat. 'Everyone was in the army,' she said, feeling her cheeks redden. Well, it was half true. She shrugged, added, 'I was only a child.'

'What does he do now?'

'I don't know exactly,' she said. 'He works with de Havilland, something to do with aeroplanes. It's all very dull and suburban. Shall we change the subject?'

'I'm sorry.' He smiled. 'I didn't mean to give you the third degree.'

Betty shrugged, her shoulders tense. 'That's all right.' She scraped the last of the soup from her bowl. 'I just don't terribly want to talk about it, that's all.'

The waitress removed their plates, brought their main course. Chicken. Mashed potatoes. She wondered whether they were powdered, like the ones in the canteen at work. Carrots. *Tinned.*

'Your turn now,' she said. 'For the third degree.'

She picked up her knife and fork. She was, she realised, hungry.

'I was brought up in Surrey,' he said. 'Purley. Ghastly place. Couldn't wait to leave.'

He sat, chicken and potato poised on his fork. 'Minor public school.' He pushed the food in his mouth, added, 'Very minor. Then I was called up. I was eighteen, never really left home except for a few months when the school was evacuated to Somerset. Straight into the army. They gave me a few tests, said I was officer material. I mean…' He rolled his eyes. 'What did I know about leadership?' He pushed some carrot onto his fork, popped it in his mouth, turned to cut at the chicken leg with his knife. It slipped, splashing gravy onto the tablecloth.

'Sorry,' he said. 'I'd prefer to use fingers, but...' He looked around him, leaned forward. 'It wouldn't be very U.'

Betty laughed. He was an awkward man, intense, but he made her smile. Perhaps, she thought, he's just shy.

'Where did they send you?'

'Germany.' He looked down at his plate, picked at the chicken leg with his fork. It was a while before he lifted his eyes and Betty thought for a moment that they were glassy. He sniffed. 'Enough of this. Listen. Are you free this afternoon?'

'Maybe,' she said. 'That depends.'

'Have you been to the British Museum lately?'

'No,' she said. 'I'm ashamed to say.'

'Then you're in for a treat. There's a whole section on recent discoveries in Ife.'

'Ife?'

'Nigeria.' He held up his two forefingers. 'You'll be interested, as a would-be anthropologist. It includes the Ife head. You must have heard of that? Bronze. Fourteenth century. Phenomenal. They've got other bronzes too. And terracotta. You'll love it.'

'I've heard of the Benin bronzes, of course I have, but I've never seen them, not in real life. Only pictures.'

'Then gobble up your chicken,' he said. 'We can stop somewhere for an ice cream on the way. Call it pudding.'

'I'd like that too,' Betty said.

The years don't matter, she thought, when you like someone.

'Well,' she said. They were standing outside the museum. The sky had been cloudless earlier, the sun warm and welcoming. Showers had been forecast and now the sky was fat with rain clouds.

'Goodbye then. And thank you.' She shifted her weight, switched her bag from one hand to the other. 'I had a lovely time.'

She saw him fiddle with the lip of his jacket pocket.

'Goodbye.' He took a breath, and she watched as a blush swirled round his neck, rushed up his cheeks. Held out his hand and took hers. It was surprisingly large and she felt like a bird in his palm, a robin or canary, with frail limbs and honey plumage.

'Actually, Betty,' he said, 'may I see you again?' She was standing on a magic carpet, holding on to air. 'If you're agreeable, that is.'

She frowned.

'I mean,' he went on, 'I quite understand if you say no. In fact, I probably look a bit of a fool, asking you like this. There'd be no hard feelings. So, just say if—'

'I'd like that, John.'

Betty saw his blush return, circling his forehead and nose.

'I can't give you my phone number,' she went on. 'My father's a bit funny about...' She pursed her lips and twisted her head. 'About people calling and stuff. But I can ring you, if you have a phone.'

CHAPTER FOUR

London: June 1958

The memory of that touch lingered. That she wanted to see him again was a miracle. She would be his healer, he knew, turn his brittle soul into a soft, malleable thing that could fly to a heaven of their choosing.

They spoke every Thursday, six o'clock. There was a shared telephone where he lived, tucked beneath the stairs in a makeshift booth, and he sat on the bottom step waiting for her call, poised to answer at the first trill of the bell. She always called from the same telephone box and he imagined her standing at the other end, holding the receiver to her ear with one hand, twisting the flex with the other. She'd lean against the glass, leg outstretched so no one could open the door, wearing slacks and a jumper. Or perhaps her office clothes, a smart skirt and blouse. She fed in the pennies until her change ran out, and if there wasn't a queue to use the phone, he'd ring her back straight away. He knew the number off by heart now.

He wished he could see her more often but she said her father insisted she stayed at home at the weekends. She didn't talk about him, but John got the impression he was a bully. Or overprotective. She was, he learned, his only child. During the week they were both busy at work, but they met when they could, a squeezed hour here or there, CND meetings in St Pancras, the big march on London at the end of the month. He longed to be alone with her, to wait for the moment when he could invite her home, to his rooms.

The last time they'd met, John thought he'd test the waters, see how she felt about him.

'The thing is, Betty...' He took a deep breath, catching the words before they fled. 'I like you.' He had no thoughts, only a hurly-burly of desire. He had never been here before.

She looked away. 'And yes...'

Sentences half opened, smiles half closed.

'Do you have anyone else?' he said.

'What do you mean?'

'I don't know.' He shrugged. 'I'd have thought half the men in London would be wanting to go out with you.'

She laughed then.

'Don't be silly,' she said. He saw a blush creep up her neck. She looked down, stared at her feet. He couldn't work her out. She gave nothing away that could calm the anarchy rampaging in his soul.

That Thursday, he left the telephone booth, and was climbing the stairs to his flat when the phone rang again. He wasn't expecting her to ring back, and his parents always wrote. His mother considered the telephone for emergencies only. John swallowed hard, his stomach tightening as he turned and leaped the last three steps to the ground. What if it was an emergency? A heart attack? His father drank too much and since he'd retired did little exercise, unless you counted nine holes once a fortnight before a liquid lunch. He grabbed the receiver.

'Bloomsbury 5657.'

There was silence, although John could hear breathing.

'Dad?' he said. 'Dad?'

He could see his father lying by the telephone in the hall at his parents' house, alone, though it would be odd for his mother to be out at this time of night. Perhaps it was her, too distraught to talk.

'Mummy? Is that you?'

He heard a click, silence and then the dialling tone. No. It was a prank call. Perhaps one of his pupils had found his number in the telephone book, rung him for a dare. He put the receiver back on its cradle. His hands were clammy and his heart racing. *Calm down.* How stupid to get so agitated. Or it was a wrong number? That happened. He climbed the stairs again, two at a time. The linoleum was worn and the backing was showing through in places. The landlord should replace it. The phone rang again. John hesitated. There was another tenant on the floor below. Perhaps he could answer it. It could be for him. John peered over the bannister. There was no sound coming from his neighbour's, no light beneath the door. Nothing for it. It could be serious.

He walked down the stairs this time. No hurry. If the prankster was going to do this all night, he'd have to take the phone off the hook. Perhaps they'd give up. He lifted the receiver. There was silence again, echoing, as if the caller were on a party line or this was a trunk call from a thousand miles away.

'Hello?' John said. 'Hello?' He tapped the cradle a couple of times, in case the connection had broken. 'Anyone there?'

Perhaps it was Betty after all. She'd run out of pennies. He rang her usual number. Counted. Twenty rings in all. No one was there to answer. It couldn't have been her. He put the receiver down again and returned upstairs.

It was almost midsummer, and the day was fading into dusk, the clouds filtering the late sun and turning the sky red. He pulled up the window sash and leaned out. The air was warm. A bee buzzed in his window box, a soft muted sound but clear as a bell against the hum of London traffic. Strange how nature could hold its own. He'd spent time in Kew Gardens when he worked at the War Office, curating his memories, filing them away in collector's drawers where they would muster, out of sight, out of mind. The gardens had calmed him, transported him to another world where the vast redwoods reminded him that they had seen it all and were still there and the autumn beeches promised they would return, green and strong in the spring. In the winter, when the hoar frost made lace from spider webs and a single snowflake had a thousand shapes, he'd found refuge in the Palm House, in the lush velvet of the damp air, against the stark axe-cold outside. Once, a robin had ventured in from the frost, sat at the top of an ancient cycad and sang his heart out. He could be heard over the buzz of conversation and the hiss of the humidifiers.

He wanted to share all this with Betty and lay the ghosts of war to rest. He still had nightmares. Running away from something, but never moving forward.

Anxiety dreams, Norman said in the staffroom the next day. 'You know, turning up for an exam on the wrong day. Mine is 3C for a double period on a Friday afternoon.' Norman taught history. He added, 'And no lesson plan.'

'Or feeding the five thousand with only five loaves and two fishes,' the technology teacher said, winking at the vicar from St Michael's who came in to give the RE lessons.

Staffroom banter. It kept them all going while they dipped their Marie biscuits into their tea. The phone rang. John was the nearest, and picked it up.

'Just the person,' the secretary said. 'There's a call for you. I'll put it through.' John could hear her voice in the distance. *Hello. Caller? Are you there?*

'Sorry, John,' she said. 'Whoever it was couldn't wait. The line's gone dead. I expect they'll ring again if it's important.'

'Did they leave a name?'

'No,' she said. 'It was a man, though.'

John wondered who was trying to reach him. The bank manager? Had he dipped into the red? He was careful with money and wasn't extravagant with clothes, had stopped going to his father's tailors for his shirts and bought the new St Michael drip-dry ones from Marks. Perhaps it was someone from the CND, though they were unlikely to ring him at work. Nor would the bank manager, come to think of it. He would write.

Well, if they hadn't left a name or a number, then it couldn't be serious. Perhaps it was the same person who'd rung last night. Besides, why was he so sure that last night's caller was for him?

'Back to the chalkface.' He drained the last of his tea, put the cup and saucer back on the table and picked up a pile of exercise books.

He did his usual detour through Holborn and round Lincoln's Inn Fields. It was, he thought, one of the most beautiful squares in London, with its luscious trees and gracious buildings. Barstow's was on the west side of the square, and he lingered as he passed it. She finished work at five and they could sometimes snatch a cup of tea before she had to head home to Hatfield. Now it was summer the café stayed open long enough, though by that time of day the tea was stewed and the scones gone. He was seeing her in two days, but a glimpse now would be perfect. He didn't like to loiter in case it got her into trouble. Some firms could be funny like that.

Never mind, he thought. He wouldn't see her today. She might even have left work early. They sometimes let her do that, if there was no more typing to be done. He cycled off towards his flat, crossing Theobalds Road and turning right into Bury Place. A man was standing at the far end, just by the entrance to his building. He began to walk towards him. A tall, thin man, with bowed legs and arms looped like cup handles. He walked with a limp, but there was no mistaking him. John pulled at his brakes and shut his eyes, hoping the man would vanish.

'My friend,' the man said, drawing up close to John. 'You're looking well.'

'How did you know I'd be here?' A lame, manufactured response. He should have said, *Get lost*.

The man laughed, looked at the back of his hand, checking his nails.

'You forget. We know everything about you.'

No. That was over. Finished. Kaput. He had expunged the debt that summer in Berlin in 1945. Thirteen years ago, for God's sake. He owed them nothing.

'What do you want?'

The man's face was as pasty as ever, the scars of his acne still visible.

'We have unfinished business, you and I.'

John was gripping the handlebars tight, white knuckles on chrome. He reared the bike up on its back tyre like an angry stallion.

'Two words, my friend,' the man said. 'Bette Fisher.'

'I don't know what you mean,' John said.

'You will find out.' The man smirked and sauntered away, looking over his shoulder once. John let go of the handlebars and the front wheel bounced down on the macadam. He caught the frame before it toppled between his legs, his hands sticky and the sweat clinging to his shirt, those last hideous months of 1945 galloping past, like a drowning man whose life flashes before him.

CHAPTER FIVE

Berlin: late April 1945

Bette could cope with the bombs, with the firestorms and explosions, but this was different. This terror smelled of dread, of stale onions and dried urine, of menstrual blood and unwashed bodies. The Müllers on the floor below had died of dirt, so young Frau Baumann said, but Mutti said it was hunger. Or infection. Suicide, old Herr Baumann said. *Suicide.*

'Is Vati safe?' Bette said.

'Oh yes,' Mutti said. 'He's safe.' She made it sound as if it was his fault.

Their cellar was dark and damp and musty. Earthy mounds of rubble and broken glass and empty mortar shells swept into a corner with the buckets of faeces and vomit. *Careful where you tread.* Even the thin air of the U-Bahn or the bunker in Oranienburg was better than here but with the Russians now there was no warning, no sirens. Just the roar and clatter of the tanks, the thunder of the artillery and the race to the cellar. The nights were the worst. And the stink.

Greta Weber sat next to her. The Webers lived in the back building with their grandmother. Before the war, Mutti had said they were common and Bette was forbidden to talk to them even though Greta and she were classmates. But now. Now was *now*.

Women sweated under blankets in the cellar, front and back building together, hugger-mugger.

Opposite them Tante Winkler, who wasn't a real aunt, just old, sat with her white napkin spread over her lap, cutting half a crust into cubes on a china plate and sprinkling them with pretend salt. She always said grace, again and again, *Bless me, Father, for what I am about to receive…* There was no food, only routines.

Bette was squeezing her hands until the nails left half-moons in her palms. The ground shook as a tank rolled down the street, and she could hear the percussion of soldiers banging their guns against the turret. The tension curdled inside her, slabs of bile and gall that choked in her throat and soured her taste. She wanted to hammer her head against the wall, to fling herself at the ground and roll in the rubble, to feel pain in her legs and arms where it belonged, in bruises and cuts and not in her belly, where it gnawed and churned. She wanted all this to go away, to end. Her lips curled downwards, a whimper building up. She heard a mewling and knew it was her.

Bette saw the tracks of the tank as it lumbered past the cellar windows, close enough to buckle the frames, shaving the outside wall. The ground was trembling, the grind of the engines deafening, the squeak of the tracks like a screaming, tortured beast, on and on until it passed their building and hobbled on down the street, its echo drifting back. The explosion threw them backwards. There was a roar as if the Devil himself had belched. Thick smoke billowed through the broken windows, and Bette could hear the flames crackling, clicking their fingers as the paint outside blistered, *pop-pop-pop*.

Soldiers burst through the cellar door, their machine guns poised at the ready, ash and carbon on their filthy uniforms, searching, searching, eyes left, eyes right. They could shoot us all, Bette thought. That's what they did at Nemmersdorf, it said so in the newspapers and on the wireless. That's what they're going to do. She shut her eyes, screwed them tight, hearing herself breathe in short, grating rasps, hearing everyone else do the same. The soldiers backed out. A woman across the room began to cry. No one moved. Bette didn't know how long they sat, petrified. Stone shapes in the dust.

Two more soldiers entered the cellar. Mutti sat the other side of her with her hand on Bette's knee, pinning her to the ground. Her mother's lips were tight and narrow, her neck taut, the pulse throbbing. Lieselotte was the other side of Mutti, her face hidden by her hair.

Bette leaned forward and retched, right there, thin yellow sick all over her socks and shoes, and over Greta's too, and splattered on the soldier's dusty boots and grubby puttees. The barrel of his rifle pointed down but he moved on, not bothering.

That night it was Waltraud, Greta's sister.

She screamed as the Ivan yanked at her arm, shrill as a wounded raven. Bette had never heard a human cry like that. Waltraud was digging in her heels, struggling. Her mother, Frau Weber, tugged at her daughter's sleeve, *nein, nein.* Another Ivan slapped Frau Weber's face with the butt of his rifle and she staggered back, blood pumping from her mouth. Bette smelled its iron.

Waltraud wasn't as pretty as Lieselotte, but she was plumper.

Bette was forbidden to go out, but that morning Greta had climbed the stairs to the Fischers' apartment and they had stood on the landing outside their door, opposite the Baumanns'. The paint in the stairwell had peeled and in places the plaster had fallen off. The building shook every time the tanks rolled through the street, a slab of brick here, a chunk of masonry there. The stone steps had cracked, the treads become chipped and uneven, the bannisters taken for firewood. The apartment on the ground floor was empty, the windows broken and gaping where the artillery had fired through.

That was where they had taken Waltraud, Greta said, *right there.*

'They rammed her mouth with the barrel of a gun to shut her up.'

Bette was holding the handle on the front door so it didn't slam shut, but the door opened inwards, pulling Bette with it.

'I wondered where you'd got to,' her mother said. 'Come inside now. And Greta,' she added, forcing a smile. 'You go home too.' She pushed Bette indoors and stepped out onto the landing, closing the door behind her. Bette heard her whisper, 'How is Waltraud? And your mother?' She didn't hear Greta's reply.

Mutti backed into the hall, shutting the front door and locking it. She took Bette's hand and led her into the sitting room. Lieselotte was staring out of the window. Three of its panes were missing and the fourth was cracked.

'Black and burnt,' she said. 'Everything black. And burnt. It's like a funeral pyre.'

Bette didn't know why Lieselotte was saying that now, as if she was seeing it for the first time. They were used to it, scorched air thick as dust, smouldering homes, the charred bones of cars. It never ended, the black and the burnt, the ruins and the remains, cratered roads, a flash of curtain like a flap of skin. A piano hanging out of a shattered room, the wind plucking the strings so it played a strange, ghostly melody. They could taste death, grit in their teeth and up their nostrils. There were graveyards everywhere now with makeshift crosses. They could hear the fighting in Wilhelmstrasse or Prenzlauer Berg, explosions that shook the core of the city. *They've flooded the U-Bahn.* Rumours swirled like spinning tops. *They're at the Reichstag. No, the Landwehr canal.* Nobody believed it, anyway.

'Come away. You'll be seen.'

'I'd fight like hell if it were me.'

Mutti glanced at Bette, then Lieselotte, putting a finger to her lip, shaking her head, *not in front of the child.*

'I'm not a baby,' Bette said. 'I'm twelve years old and I know what's going on. What they did to Waltraud. And Frau Müller before that. You can talk about it in front of me.'

'Who told you?' Mutti was shouting.

'Greta,' Bette said. 'But I have eyes. And ears.' She knew she was being cheeky but her mother just said, 'Well, then,' and walked over to Lieselotte and placed her mouth across Lieselotte's ear. 'If you fight, you make it worse.' She spoke softly, but Bette heard.

'What am I supposed to do?' Lieselotte turned to face her mother, not bothering to lower her voice. 'Lie back and do nothing?'

'Yes,' her mother said. 'You don't want to be hurt.' She paused, her words quiet and gentle. 'Or worse.'

Lieselotte gave a strange twisted smile, turned her back to her mother, looked out of the window again.

'Then I'll fight *my* way.' She tossed the words over her shoulder.

Mutti glanced at her, picked up her cigarettes and lit one, faced Bette. She reached over to the table and held up a pair of boy's shorts and braces, and a shirt.

'Try these on. Otto has grown out of them.' Otto was fighting in the Hitler Youth. Frau Baumann and Mutti had sat in the kitchen the day he left, sobbing into their handkerchiefs. *Only a child.*

'You can trust the Baumanns?' Lieselotte said.

'Who knows?' Mutti answered. 'You have a better idea? Come on, Bette.' She held her cigarette between her lips, shook the shirt impatiently. Bette slipped out of her dress and pulled on the shirt.

'The buttons do up the wrong way,' she said.

'Never mind that,' Mutti said. 'Try the shorts for size.'

They were too large, but with the braces they would do. It didn't matter anyway. All the children wore clothes that were too big or too small, the fabric frayed and faded.

'What's this for?' Bette asked.

'Your safety,' Lieselotte said.

'How?' She pulled at the braces. 'What good will this do me?'

'If they think you're a young boy,' Mutti said, 'they might not touch you.' She turned away, coughed into her hand, tapped the arc of cigarette ash into a saucer.

'Everyone can see I'm a girl.' Bette flicked her long plait. 'And everyone round here knows who I am anyway. Besides,' she added, 'the Russians *promised* they wouldn't hurt us, I saw the leaflets, and there's posters everywhere.' She hadn't noticed the comb on the table, nor her mother's dressmaking shears, until Mutti reached over for them.

'No,' Bette shouted. 'No.' She held her plaits and ran to the door but Lieselotte was there before her, barring her way.

'Why don't *you* dress up then?' Bette shouted.

'Because if they think I'm a man, I'll be shot as a deserter,' Lieselotte said, adding, 'Either by the Russians, or the Gestapo.' Her voice was calm and confident and Bette looked from her mother to her sister and knew they had discussed it, and decided. 'Sit down.'

She pulled a chair into the centre of the room and, taking Bette by the shoulders, steered her towards it and pushed her down onto the seat. Her mother undid her apron and pinned it round Bette's neck. The smoked curled from the saucer and Mutti stubbed the cigarette out.

'Please,' Bette said. 'Please don't.'

'Keep still.'

Bette felt the shears mouthing her plait, then gripping and biting at the hair, crunching it again and again until the braid came away in her mother's hands. Her head was lighter, and Bette ran her hand across the back of her neck. It felt cool but her mother was combing through and cutting, combing and cutting.

'Move your hand.'

Bette could feel the cold of the blades against her skull, the sharp edge of the comb as it parted her hair at the side, the snip of the scissors as they trimmed closer and closer. Bette put her hand to her temple. She breathed in sharply.

'Let me look.' She pushed herself up and ran into the bathroom. A shaft of sun was illuminating the cracked mirror, reflecting on the floor. She climbed on the bathroom stool. Someone else was in that mirror, with shaved temples and a flopping fringe. She saw her mother's face emerge next to hers, her long hair pulled back into a bun. She'd always thought her mother's hair was thick, but in the bright sunlight of the mirror she saw a bald spot above her ear where Mutti twisted the hair and pulled it every evening. Worry lines had etched deep valleys into her forehead.

'Come,' her mother said, placing her arms round Bette's tummy and swinging her free from the stool. 'I have to finish.'

Bette sat, her lips quivering until the snapping stopped.

'Let's look at you.'

The sides of her head, and the back, were shorn.

'Will it grow again?'

'Once the war is over, of course.'

'Must I always be a boy?'

'Except when we sleep,' Lieselotte said. 'You can wear a night-dress. We don't have boys' pyjamas.'

She shared a bed with Lieselotte. They did exercises every morning, lying on their backs, cycling in the air, counting the rotations. *Twenty-nine. Thirty.* Mutti did exercises too, one hand on the door jamb for balance as she lifted her leg and touched the lintel. She'd been a dancer before she married, in the corps de ballet at the Lindenoper. They all took it in turns to empty the chamber pots, carrying the slops downstairs and throwing them into the gutter. It had to be done first thing. The soldiers caroused at night, lay senseless in the dawn. Mutti always lit a cigarette. *Takes away the smell.*

The Russians had put up a standpipe in the street and turned on the water for two hours in the morning and afternoon. Mutti took the deep pan that she used for making jam and Lieselotte two buckets, one for Frau Weber. Bette took the big kettle.

'What's my name?' Bette said, as she emptied the last of the water from the kettle into a jug. 'I mean, my boy's name?'

'Bert,' Lieselotte said, without missing a beat. 'It sounds like Bette, so your ear is half tuned to it.'

'It's a horrid name,' Bette said. 'And it doesn't sound anything like Bette.' She thought for a moment. 'Why can't I be something heroic and *heimatlich*, like Heinz?'

'Shut up, will you?' Lieselotte said. 'You're really getting on my nerves.'

'Girls. Please. Bette, put on your shoes.' Her mother pointed to a pair of battered boys' boots, and a pair of darned grey socks.

'I can't wear those.'

'You can't wear your girls' shoes, so put them on.'

Bette scowled and sunk to the floor, pulling at the socks so they stretched beyond her knee. The toes and heels had been darned in a thicker ply and lumped as she shoved her feet into the boots and laced them up. She stood up, grabbed the kettle and stomped out of the door.

Old Herr Baumann was standing on the landing, leaning on his walking stick, as if he was waiting for them. Bette didn't know what was wrong with him, but Mutti said whatever it was had got him out of the Volkssturm, who seemed to take anyone these days. Better not to ask, she'd added. Young Herr Baumann, Otto's father, had died on the Russian front.

'Well, little man,' he said, patting Bette on the head. 'You make a handsome young fellow.' He chuckled, picked up a jug with his free hand, and set off.

'How does he know?' Bette said, tipping her head towards the stairs, where Herr Baumann's lopsided tread echoed up through the well.

'Of course he knows,' Mutti said.

'But what if he tells?'

'Tells who, *mein Liebling?*' Mutti said. 'Who can he tell? Who is in charge now?'

'The Russians,' Bette said. 'He could tell the Russians.'

'There's no danger of that.'

'The Führer. The Gestapo.'

'That man?' Her mother snorted. 'Too busy rounding up the white flag wavers to bother about us.'

They joined the queue for water, shuffling forward, one after the other. It was a slow business. Bette knew not to complain. The routine was the same every day. First the water, then to forage, a turnip or two in exchange for a saucepan, or a pair of Vati's shoes. They had to eat the vegetables raw. There was no fuel for cooking. The soldier who took Waltraud was standing by the water pipe marking the tally. Bette froze, but her mother pushed her forward. She went to place the kettle under the tap but the soldier took it from her, held it in place.

Bette bit her lip and hoped he couldn't see her shaking. He was very young, the soldier, and brown, with slit eyes and bowed legs. He patted her head and smiled at her. She couldn't understand how a man could be kind and cruel at the same time.

Lieselotte followed. She kept her head down, staring at the ground, her hair over her face, not looking at the soldier as she placed her pail under the tap and waited, watching it splutter and splash the sides of the bucket.

'Enough,' the soldier said. It wasn't even full.

The days were getting longer now so it didn't matter too much that they couldn't turn on the lights in the evenings, but she'd have liked a light in the cellar for when they had to go down there. It was spooky enough as it was.

The soldiers were drunk at night, bottles of schnapps from busted distilleries or methyl alcohol from God knows where. The rifle shots were the first warning, then the shouting and the singing.

'It drives them a little mad,' Old Herr Baumann said, tapping his head.

Bette needed the lavatory, right now. She began to shuffle herself up. The bucket was in the far corner but Mutti was pulling her down. The soldiers were in the street outside, cheering, whistling. She could see their boots. One of them started to piss, aiming the urine through the shot-out cellar window. She heard them laugh, then thudding boots on the steps down to where they cowered in the underground gloom. The soldiers knew they were there, knew how to round them up in their shelter, line them up like skittles to be knocked down, one by one. The door smacked against the wall as the Russians flung it aside, the beam of their torches searching, dazzling. Three of them, guns and torches, left, right, left, right. Different soldiers from last night. Bette held her breath. Tante Winkler sat with her linen napkin and knife and fork. One of the soldiers pulled the napkin, waved it like a flag.

'You surrender? Why don't you Germans surrender?'

Tante Winkler was old and doolally but she sprang like a young woman and snatched back the napkin. She fell as Bette heard the shot. Lay on the ground with a hole in her head, blood across the floor and on the stiff white napkin. Bette's trousers grew wet and warm, she couldn't stop herself.

Lieselotte crouched in the shadows, at the back.

'You.' The torchlight went above Bette's head. Bette dared not turn to track its arc.

'You.' A soldier pushed his boot against Bette, shoved past her, his gun jabbing at the air, at anyone. At someone behind her. 'You.'

She could hear Mutti stifle a cry, saw her eyes screw tight, her lips pucker. She sat in silence, trying not to cough, and Bette stared at her as Lieselotte was pulled forward. Was Mutti going to let her go, just like that? Without a cry or a struggle? *No.* This was her *sister.* Bette wriggled but her mother's hand was on her shoulder keeping her still. She was shaking her head, her finger on her lips. They had planned this, Mutti and Lieselotte, *what they would do if...*

The two other soldiers had their guns poised. Nobody said a word. Nobody shifted a limb, rustled a skirt, coughed. Swallowed. Frau Winkler's body lay where it had fallen, the stained napkin in her hand. The silence hung heavy as dirt. Lieselotte tossed her head and braced her shoulders. She shook her arm free of the soldier, gave the same smile Bette had seen earlier. She saw its meaning now, its defiant strength. *I will fight my way.*

CHAPTER SIX

North Germany: late April 1945

The truck jolted over a pothole, threw John against the side so he hit his hip. He winced. The sergeant, a Londoner with freckles and ginger hair, smirked. *He's all we bloody need* written across his face, letters sky-high. *Fucking translator.* The sergeant was battle-hardened and toughened up, John almost half his age, a spoilt schoolboy, wet behind the ears. John pretended not to notice, stared out of the back of the truck. It was his fifth day on the road. France, Belgium, Germany. Nothing but the stumps of war and the stench of death.

'Don't know why they don't just pack it in,' the sergeant said. 'Hitler and that lot. These buggers have given up.' He nodded towards a farmhouse window, where a threadbare pillowcase was being waved.

'It's just a matter of time,' John said. That's what they all said, and John said it too, like a mantra, *a matter of time.* It gave him comfort, put bone in his spine.

'Will we make it to Berlin before the Russians?' John said.

'With all due respect, sir,' the sergeant said, 'not a chance in hell.'

Besides, they were on a different mission, so John had been told. To beat the Russians to a different target. Orders from the

Admiralty. They called it something fancy like reparations. But it was plunder, when all was said and done. Get there first, before the Russkies. And don't trust the Yanks or the French. Two-faced, they were. And keep our lads out of it while you're at it, don't want them rampaging through, destroying evidence. They'd vandalise as soon as look at it. Or loot it. Common or garden looting, not the poncy stuff his lot were up to.

All those secrets. Target Force. T-Force, a giant 'T' plastered on the bonnet of the truck.

The truck swerved, jolted, potholes as deep as craters filled with oily black water, bulbous grey clouds reflected in the surface. A few isolated houses began to appear, to cluster, become a street, a village with a cobblestone square and high-pitched wooden frame houses, not a tile out of place, not a mortared road, not a blackened ruin. A fairy-tale village, like the picture of one in the Baedeker guide to Northern Germany he'd found in the school library. How had this place been spared the war? There were spring flowers in the window boxes, narcissus and primroses, and some of the windows were open, their white lace curtains blowing in the breeze, the shutters secured to the walls. People must have been living in the houses, hiding inside, the streets and the square deserted save for a thin, mangy brown dog that sniffed the gutter, limping.

John sat in the back of the truck, its canvas cover taut at the sides. It was damp to the touch, spat their musty breath back to them in cold, hard droplets, let in the wind through the webbing. He was next to a private with dusty ankle gaiters and shining boots, sitting at the end of the bench closest to the opening, his rifle across his knees, his hand poised over the trigger, looking out. Private Nash, 5th King's. John hardly knew him. He didn't talk much.

'I like dogs,' he said. He put his fingers in his mouth and whistled. 'Here, boy.' The dog looked up, pricked its ears and Private Nash clicked his fingers. 'Here, boy.'

Opposite John was his sergeant and the other men, a ragbag of regimental leftovers in John's charge. Second Lieutenant John Harris. Six weeks at Pirbright brushing up his school German, six weeks square-bashing at Caterham. Commission. What the fuck did he know? He was eighteen years old. The sergeant was twice his age.

'With a bit of luck,' his father had said, 'this bally war will be over and you'll never hear a shot fired in anger.'

Only it wasn't over, was it? John pulled out his cigarettes and, leaning forward, offered one to the sergeant. Arthur. His name was Arthur. Sergeant Arthur Gambol. North Africa. Normandy. Now Nordhausen, with a bit of luck. Pushing his way across Germany with this motley crew. He must have a guardian angel, John thought, some high-up with God's ear because John couldn't see for the life of him how he'd survived all of that. He was married to an infant teacher, John knew, with a son conceived when he was on leave. Arthur took a cigarette, lit it, and sat with it in his mouth, smoke curling into his eyes. They must have developed a second lid, John thought, they never watered once. The other soldiers sat holding their rifles, faces blank, tense.

The dog cocked its leg against the kerb, its ribs and vertebrae jutting out beneath its threadbare fur. The private whistled again, and the dog began to run after them, dragging its back leg.

'I miss my dog,' Private Nash said. 'Bits.'

'Bits?' John said. 'Is that his name?'

'Yeah.' The private whistled for the dog again.

'Why Bits?'

'It's what went into him, isn't it?' He shrugged, grinned. 'Bits of this, bits of that.'

He looked away from the dog and turned to John, smiling. He had a gap tooth. His eyes had brimmed up. 'I miss him. I really do.'

He wiped his eye, stared back at the dog running after them as fast as its lame leg would allow.

'Don't like it,' Arthur said, leaning forward and peering out of the back.

'Orders.'

Arthur gave him a look, *don't 'orders' me, sonny.* John never pulled rank, nor did Arthur parade his savvy, but John knew that in Arthur's eyes he wasn't just green, he wasn't a proper soldier either. He should be in the other truck, with all the scientists whingeing about unpressed trousers and dusty billets, not here with the men, bringing up the rear.

'Bloody liabilities,' one of the squaddies had said to Arthur when they first saw the scientists. 'Reserved occupations, my arse.' Arthur pinched the tip of his cigarette to put it out, then ground it into the earth. He'd nodded. They didn't think John had heard. He should have tackled them on it, there and then. They knew what this mission was about as well as he did, brought together, an army within an army. Top secret and all that. But he hadn't liked to. These were grown men with more battle scars than John could ever count. He needed them far more than they needed him. His job was to translate but till then he was in the army, and don't you forget it, Second Lieutenant, *sonny.*

'You know,' Arthur said, taking the cigarette out of his mouth and looking over the jolting floor at John, 'you never hear the bullet that hits you. You hear the one that misses you. The hiss as it passes, then the crack—'

The hiss. The *crack-a-tat-tat.*

'Down,' Arthur yelled, throwing himself on the floor. Private Nash had fallen against John, blood pumping from his perforated neck, his slumped head pinning John to the bench. John vomited down his battledress, yellow bile mixing with the thick black blood, dribbling on the squaddie's dusty gaiters. He felt someone pull him free, push him back into the far corner of the truck. He heard the thud of Private Nash's body as it fell to the floor, watched the head tumble free.

Arthur had crawled to the tailgate, pointed his rifle, squinting into its sights. John shuddered, retching, heart pummelling, hard, heavy thumps, but he followed the angle, saw the machine gun draped in the white window lace, watched as it lifted and aimed. And fell. Arthur's shot caught the sniper square on. The squaddies were crouched next to him and John could hear their short, sharp breaths, smell their iron sweat. He could taste the metal in his own mouth. The truck had picked up speed, rattling and jolting them as it sped over the cobbles, around the corner, out of the village, onto the open road. And stopped. In front of them was the first truck, with the major and the scientists.

John wasn't sure he hadn't messed himself. His gut cramped and curdled and his underpants felt warm. That bullet was a hair's breadth away from his own neck. He knew his hand was trembling, but the men were looking at him. *Second Lieutenant.* He had to take charge. These seasoned men knew the ropes better than he. But no revenge, no revenge. This was not their target, not their destination. The men were clambering off the lorry, leaving him alone with the dead body and its severed head. He had to get up, walk past.

'Lieutenant?'

John pushed himself onto his feet, walked towards the tailboard, jumped to the ground, saluted as best he could.

'Bloody snipers,' the major said. 'I gather you've a casualty.'

John nodded. 'Private Nash.' He breathed in as deep as he could and tilted his head towards the truck. 'Poor bugger.' He hoped he sounded braver than he felt, in command.

'We'll leave him for our boys to pick up,' the major said. 'We've radioed through already.'

'You don't want us to take the rest out then, sir?' Arthur asked.

'No, Sergeant,' the major said. 'That's not our job.'

Arthur was drumming his fingers against the barrel of his rifle. This was not how war went. John swallowed, caught his breath. *Leadership.*

'You got the sniper, Sergeant, and well done,' he said, thinking fast, remembering the stories he'd heard in the mess of other snipers, other skirmishes. 'For all we know there could be another thirty in the house. They could put up a fight. Or they could all surrender. Either way, there's nothing we can do. There's not enough of us to handle it.'

'Thank you, Lieutenant,' the major said. 'Well said. Arrange for Private Nash's body to be organised for pick-up. Your driver has the co-ordinates. We'll push on.'

They saluted. John watched as he strode towards the first truck and swung himself into it. He heard the engine start and rev, the crash of gears, the chug of the engine as it left, leaving John in charge.

'I've detailed the men, sir.'

He hadn't heard Arthur come up beside him. He fished into his pocket for his cigarettes, pulled one out and offered it. They stood side by side staring at the dark, empty field opposite, their hands curled around the cigarettes, the smoke unfurling through their cupped fingers.

'Thank you,' John said. His voice was thin, strangled.

They rocked on their heels. His father used to do that. Perhaps he'd got the habit in the Great War. Brigadier Alfred Harris. He'd come back with a DSO and a leg full of shrapnel.

'First time, was it?' Arthur said.

John nodded.

'You get used to it, you know. Water off a duck's back in the end.'

John swallowed, took a drag of his cigarette. His throat was parched. Even if he had the words, he couldn't spit them out. He could smell the vomit on his uniform, see the stains on his jacket. There was a clot of blood on his shoulder.

'First time it happened to me,' Arthur went on, 'it sliced him in half. Corporal at the time, like myself, he was. Nice man. Family man, you know what I mean? Never did whores or anything like that.'

John heard him suck on his cigarette, the whoosh as he blew the smoke out and over the field where it hung like a ghost.

'Always one for a lark, he was. Never took the officers seriously.'

John watched Arthur smile at the memory.

'It was his idea to nick the rattan chairs out the sergeants' mess. Thought why should those buggers have all the comfort? So in we went, while they were eating. Took out two, one each. I tell you, sir.' Arthur began to laugh, turned to face John, his cigarette half smoked. He's trying to cheer me up, John thought. He wanted him to shut up, but he couldn't say. 'Running out with them. Bloody awkward, chairs are. All legs. Tripping up the path. Mind you, we'd had a few.' He took another puff. 'Cairo, that was. Ever been to Cairo, sir?'

'No.' John's voice had returned, but it had no force.

'No,' Arthur said. 'I don't suppose you would have. The pyramids are a sight, I tell you. I went on a camel there, too. Just the once.' He sucked at his cigarette, then pinched it dead, threw it on the ground. 'Filthy beasts, they are. Spewing green mulch out of their mouths. Smelly. How that man learned to ride them beats me. You know, sir, the one that liked the Arabs.'

'T.E. Lawrence?' John said.

'Yeah, him. Mind you,' the sergeant went on, 'they can go for months without water? It's all in their hump. Bloody clever.'

'You still think they're foul, though?'

'Well, their breath is, sir. It's because they don't drink enough.'

John smiled. 'Thank you, sergeant,' he said. His cigarette had burned to the end, had singed his fingertips. He threw it onto the ground. 'Have they finished?' He didn't turn round.

Arthur walked away and John waited for his return.

'Won't be long, sir,' Arthur said. 'They're having to—'

John held up his hand. 'I know,' he said. *Collect the body parts.*

'I've given them my groundsheet,' Arthur said. 'You know, to wrap him up.'

'That's kind,' John said. 'We'll have to be sure we get a good billet tonight then.' He smiled. 'No sleeping under the stars.'

'I fancy something soft and fragrant,' Arthur said. 'Clean sheets. Warm bath.'

John felt the tears well from nowhere, his legs tremble. A homesickness so sudden, so acute, so all-consuming.

'Anyway,' Arthur went on, 'two days later I was only promoted to sergeant, wasn't I? Needn't have nicked the chairs at all.'

John swallowed, smiled, and Arthur nodded.

'It's not my job,' he said. 'But when we bed down tonight, in whatever billet we're in, I'll get you cleaned up a bit.'

'That's the kindest offer I've ever had,' John said. He put his hand on Arthur's shoulder, squeezed it. 'But I'll clean my uniform myself.'

He turned and walked back to the truck. Private Nash's body lay by the road, wrapped in a tarpaulin shroud. His comrades had found two fence posts and had tied them together in a rough cross which they'd laid on top of the corpse. It felt wrong to leave him. But their orders were to advance.

'Come to think of it,' Arthur was saying, 'you get VD from them if you're not careful.'

'From whom?' John said. The tarpaulin had fallen open at the top and John could see the top of Private Nash's bloodied, severed head.

'Camels,' he said, moving close to John so John had to peer over his shoulder to see the body. 'Well, at least, that's what you tell the wife.'

John looked away. The dog from the square was there, running towards them. Private Nash would be happy. *Bits.*

'Sir,' Arthur said. John heard the engine start up. 'We have to go.'

The rest of his men were already in the truck. He nodded, clambered aboard. There was blood on the bench and a line of holes where the machine gun bullets had penetrated. He stood with his back to the cab and held onto the roof bar as the truck lurched away. The dog slunk towards the body, began to sniff it, the open end with the private's head.

'Stop!' John yelled. He signalled to one of the soldiers.

'Tell the driver to stop. Now.' The soldier banged onto the glass window of the cab and the truck drew to a sharp halt, tipping John so he stumbled for a moment.

The dog was tearing at the shroud with short, urgent movements. John saw its curled lip and hungry teeth, its shrunken gut and spindle ribs. He raised his rifle. Didn't think. *Crack.*

CHAPTER SEVEN

Berlin: late April 1945

Bette shared Mutti's big bed now. They all did. No one slept alone, not anymore. A drunken Russian had broken the service door to their apartment, and anyone could walk in, loot the place, and worse. They'd wedged a chair under the handle, but even so. Lieselotte crept beneath the covers in the early hours and whispered to her mother for a long time. *Women's things*, Greta said. *That's what they talk about.* When the Ivans came, Greta hid in their ceiling space. It was the best Mutti could do. Frau Weber had gone to pieces, so Mutti said.

'And where does that leave her? And the girls? Or her poor old mother? Just more work for the rest of us.' Mutti clasped her hands to her head. She was irritable these days, snapped at the slightest thing. She couldn't get cigarettes now, and that made her temper worse. 'What will become of us? When will it end?'

Mutti's hair had turned grey in a week, and the bald patch was bigger. They hadn't eaten for days, not properly, some nettle soup cooked on the oven heated by laths and splinters gleaned from the bombed-out buildings. The authorities were rationing the coupons now. Their turn to collect had been two days ago, and wouldn't come again for another day, and even so there was little in the shops and what there was cost a fortune and took all day to

46

buy, what with the queues and the looting. Mutti's cough seemed worse, too, and they had nothing to give her, not even honey.

Bette pulled on Otto's trousers, hitched the braces over her shoulders. Her mother and sister were still sleeping. Perhaps, if she was fast, she'd get back and catch them talking, hear what they said. She tiptoed out with the pot. The gunfire was far away, the sharp shot of a pistol, the rattle of a machine gun muted and muffled by the ruins, but the smoke from the smouldering city hung thick and yellow, clogging her nostrils and coating her tongue so she could taste the soot and grit. The burned-out tank, its frame buckled and blackened, was still lodged in the basement of the building five along from theirs. It had been there for days now, squatting half in, half out, part of the furniture, like the pockmarked street signs and the unlit lamps and the broken cobbles.

Bette placed the old check tea towel over the top of the chamber pot.

'Shame enough we have to use it,' Mutti said. 'But that doesn't mean every Tom, Dick and Harry has to see our business.'

She turned to go back into the house but a small body in a brown uniform was on the steps of the building close to the tank. It hadn't been there yesterday. Mutti always pulled her away from the corpses on the street, placed her hand over Bette's eyes. 'Don't look.'

Some lay as if they were asleep, calm and unharmed, but others were twisted, or blasted, or pumped up fit to burst. You could smell them, all the time, even when they had been buried in graves scratched from the rubble. It was hard not to look, whatever her mother said. Sometimes they hung from a window, feet dangling. No one had gone near the building down the road, not after the tank, and the bodies were still in the cellar, stinking of rotten flesh and bad eggs and faeces.

This one didn't look dead, not like the other corpses she'd seen.

Bette checked no one was peering at her. She put the chamber pot down and wrapped the towel around her nose and mouth. If someone saw her she'd say she was checking to see if he was asleep or needed help. She gulped deep, held her breath.

The street was deserted, the early morning sun low in the sky. Bette felt the hairs rise on her arms, her heart thump in her chest. She tiptoed towards the form, hand over hand on the brickwork of the building for balance, creeping towards the motionless body.

It crouched on all fours, its head twisted to one side, chin down hard on the cobblestones. She saw the face, smooth skin waxy, unmarked. Otto. *Otto*, from next door. She cried out, shut her eyes. Opened them again. There was a small, bloodied hole in the back of his head. Why was he here? Was the war over? Had he been on his way home and something had happened? They'd played together, she and Otto, on rainy days when they couldn't go out. Ludo. Draughts. Chess, until she beat him and he said she'd cheated. How can you cheat at chess?

She put her hand to her mouth, yanked the towel free and placed it over his face. She ran back to the apartment, tearing at her clothes, pulling the buttons of the shirt and trousers. These were Otto's clothes, a dead boy's clothes. She pushed open the heavy outer doors and ran up the broken stairs, two at a time. She knew them well enough now, which ones were cracked, which wobbled, which missed a central step, hammered at the Baumanns' door opposite them on the landing.

'Frau Baumann. Come. Frau Baumann.' She knew she was screaming, but it was Mutti who opened their door and pulled her inside their own flat and slapped her face hard.

'Be quiet. Now.' Beyond her, sitting at the table in the kitchen, were five Ivans. Her mother grabbed her by the collar, pulled her into the sitting room and slammed the door behind her.

'Button yourself up.' Her voice snapped the order. 'And behave.' Bette was trying not to cry, her mouth spluttering. Her mother had never hit her. Never. Ever.

'So what was so urgent,' her mother hissed, 'that you had to yell it out to everyone?'

Bette breathed hard before she spoke.

'Otto, Mutti,' she said. 'Otto's dead. He's lying there. On the street.'

Her mother's eyes grew wide. She nodded, bit her lip. Her eyes softened. 'All right,' she said, glancing at the door. Then she added, 'The chamber pot? Where's the chamber pot?'

Bette looked at her hands, at the floor. 'I left it.' She began to cry.

'You left it?' Her mother was screaming. 'How could you? Find it. Now.'

There was a wildness in her mother's face that Bette had never seen before, fury, fear. She darted past her mother, out of the apartment, down the broken stairs, through the vestibule and onto the street. The chamber pot had gone. Of course it had. Everything was stolen now. Bette looked down the road. Otto's body was still there, but the tea towel had been taken. A pigeon with a missing tail feather strutted beside his body. She ran up the street in the opposite direction. Whoever had taken the chamber pot couldn't be far away. Please, she thought, please let me find it. Her mother's moods were bad enough already. She said it was her nerves. Her nerves were playing up so they were all treading on eggshells. Everyone's nerves were raw.

It wasn't her fault she'd lost it. It was only a stupid chamber pot. Hardly more important than Otto. They'd have to use a bucket. So what? She hated war. She hated the Ivans who crowded into their kitchen, their arms laced with looted watches. She hated that there was no water, no light, no food. Nothing. That she wore Otto's clothes and had her hair cut like a boy. The Führer said they were winning, but the last soldiers she'd seen didn't look like heroes. They didn't even look like men.

Old Herr Baumann was sitting at the table when she came back. She could see him facing her as she opened the front doors.

'Bettelein?' her mother said, her back to the hall. 'Is that you?'

Bette's eyes filled with tears and she stood still.

'I'm sorry, Mutti,' she called from the hallway. 'The pot had gone and I couldn't find it. I looked and looked and—'

'Come in,' her mother said. 'Come closer.'

Bette stepped into the kitchen. Old Herr Baumann was sitting where the Russians had been, Frau Baumann to the right of him. Greta sat like a mouse at the end of the table.

'Where's Lieselotte?' Bette said. She wanted her sister there, in case her mother lost her temper again.

'Asleep,' her mother said. 'Come, sit.'

Bette stepped into the kitchen and perched on a stool her mother pulled towards the table.

'You found my Otto,' Frau Baumann said, her voice flat and emotionless.

Bette nodded. 'I think he was coming home. He was nearly here.'

Frau Baumann's mouth clamped tight and Bette saw the muscles in her cheek ripple beneath her skin. She must have said something wrong, but she didn't mean to. She thought Frau Baumann would be pleased.

'He would not be coming home,' old Herr Baumann said, slapping the palm of his hand hard on the table top. 'Let me be clear. *He* was *loyal* to the Führer, to Germany. He was defending our city.' He spoke slowly, emphasising each word, as if Bette did not understand. He tossed his head towards the empty window. 'Barbarians.' He turned and stared at Bette. 'Are you saying he ran away?' Bette went to answer, but he broke in before she could say a word. 'Otto was no coward.'

He put his hand over his face and Bette saw how twisted and gnarled it was, how the veins pulsed and the knuckles had swollen.

'Don't be hard on her, Herr Baumann,' Mutti said. 'She's just a child.'

'She's old enough for the Jungmädelbund,' he said. 'She should know better.'

'Frau Baumann,' Mutti said, turning towards her, her voice plaintive, pleading. 'We have been neighbours and friends for so long now. You will understand. Bette meant no harm.'

'My son and my grandson sacrificed their lives for the Fatherland,' old Herr Baumann went on. 'This is my honour you talk about. Their honour. *Our* honour.' A dewdrop hung from the tip of his nose. Bette looked at him, at Frau Baumann staring at her hands tucked in her lap, at Mutti who was reaching over and touching old Herr Baumann on the arm, at Greta whose lips had curled and quivered as if she was about to cry.

'The Führer can't know what's going on,' Mutti said. Bette wanted to say, *Has the Führer left us? He wouldn't leave us, would he?* No one moved. She wasn't sure she should speak but she could feel fear rising in her chest. She looked from one grown-up to the next, each wrapped in their own thoughts. She could hear the panic in her voice. 'What will happen to us?' That's what her mother said, all the time.

'Enough.' Old Herr Baumann's voice was rasping, angry. 'Our sons made the ultimate sacrifice.' He groped for his daughter-in-law's hand and stood up. Frau Baumann pushed herself away from the table, tucked her hand in the crook of the old man's elbow.

'Goodbye.'

Bette watched as they walked from the room, along the hall and out of the door, the erect figure of old Herr Baumann, who wasn't so old really and could have been in the Volkssturm as Mutti said, and young Frau Baumann, shuffling like a grandma. Her mother sat at the table, staring ahead. She didn't even get up to see them out.

She waited until she heard the front door click shut, then turned to Bette.

'They are Party members,' she said. 'We must be so careful. The night is at its darkest before the dawn.'

Bette knew the SS went from house to house, pulling out the traitors and the deserters. She'd seen them, even in their street. That's why Mutti covered the chamber pot with an old check towel, grey from use, in case they thought it was white. Surrender. Perhaps they'd shot Otto. On his way home.

Greta pushed her chair free.

'May I leave, Frau Fischer?'

'Not yet, Greta,' her mother said, not even glancing Greta's way, her eyes fixed on the empty food safe on the other side of the table. 'Bette, take Greta into the living room. Don't go near the window. I have to go out.'

Sorry, Bette mouthed, sidling close to Greta and squeezing her hand, walking her into the sitting room where they sat on the floor behind the old Biedermeier sofa, cosy, out of sight.

'My mother says that Frau Baumann was raped by four Russians.' Greta spoke into Bette's ear, covering her mouth with her hand. 'And the old man did nothing.'

Bette opened her eyes wide. 'Mutti never told me.'

Greta shrugged. 'She's too polite.' She picked at her fingernail. 'Your sister has got herself a wolf.'

'What do you mean?'

'A Russian,' Greta said. 'An officer. To keep away the pack. That's what Waltraud said. *A wolf to keep away the pack.*'

One of the Ivans who'd been there in the morning returned that evening, with another, younger soldier. He smiled as he came in, removed his cap and pulled out of the pockets of his overcoat some bread, a bottle of schnapps and a packet of cigarettes. He nodded to the younger man, who carried a knapsack which he put on the table. Bette watched as he opened it and took out bacon, herrings, butter, sugar, a can of milk and some candles. He placed them on the table and sat down.

The older Russian was smiling at her. He had a gap in the front of his teeth and his lip curled into the cavity. He was stocky, thickset, looked like one of the pictures of the Slavs, *die Untermenschen*, in their schoolbooks. His hair was dark and wavy, his eyes pale blue and crinkled at the edges as if he laughed a lot. The younger soldier was taller, and thin, with vile spots and boils on his face and neck. His eyes, Bette saw, were taking in everything, appraising it all – the pictures, the rugs, the furniture. Her sister, her mother, herself. His fellow soldier, watching his every move, like a spy. Or a chess player, Bette thought, calculating his advantage.

'Eat,' he said, breaking into her thoughts, nodding to Lieselotte, and then to Mutti and Bette. Bette thought she must try and save some of the food for Greta, hide it under the table or slip it in her pocket.

'Boris,' the older man added, pointing to himself. 'Boris.' He poked his finger towards Bette.

'Bert,' Lieselotte said, glaring at Bette, *be careful*, tapping her on the head. 'His name is Bert.'

'Hitler Youth?' Boris said.

'*Net*,' Lieselotte said. Bette guessed it meant no. Lieselotte must have learned some Russian words. 'Too young.' She gestured with her hand to indicate shortness.

She was grateful to Lieselotte. She would have forgotten her new name, her boy's name. She'd never had to talk to any of the Ivans before.

The Russian beamed, pointing to himself and to Lieselotte.

'Boris marry Lieselotte,' he said. He, too, had learned some German words. 'Boris love Lieselotte.'

'Here,' Mutti said, pushing between Lieselotte and Boris, placing a board on the table and breaking up the bread. Bette couldn't work out whether it was disgust or resignation on her mother's face.

'Boris is a major,' Lieselotte said, as if this explained everything.

'Very important,' Mutti said. There was no warmth in her voice, no recognition, just a *be careful* in her tone. 'So we will be polite to him in our home.' She nodded at Boris.

'You all come to Soviet Union,' Boris said, pushing the bread board towards Bette. 'Novgorod. Boris, teacher.' He beamed, waved his hand. 'After. Before.' He looked at Mutti. 'Good job.' He smiled at Bette. 'Boris like boys.'

'He means children,' Lieselotte said. 'Boys and girls.'

The younger soldier was opening the tin of milk with his army knife and said something in Russian to Boris.

He laughed, then said, 'Comrade here. He call Vasily. He want good girl. Clean girl. You know?'

Bette swallowed. She was wearing Otto's shirt and trousers, a dead boy's clothes.

'You have friend?' Boris said.

'*Net*,' Lieselotte said.

He pointed at Bette. 'You have friend with sister?'

Bette stared at Lieselotte, shaking her head. She didn't like this talk, and there was Greta in the ceiling space. What if she moved? Coughed? Frau Weber said that they didn't know about ceiling spaces, as they didn't have them in Russia. The apartments in the back buildings didn't have them, which was why Greta was here. Bette looked at the food, at the young Russian slathering butter on his chunk of bread, reaching out for the bacon. She was desperate to eat but dared not grab. She could sense the tension in the kitchen, for all of Lieselotte's smiles and the major's toothless grins. Then the young soldier handed her the bread and butter, and the bacon he had sliced with his army knife. He waved it, *take it*, smiling. Bette remembered the young soldier at the water pump. Kindness and cruelty, but her stomach cramped and she could stand the hunger no longer. She grabbed the bread and shoved the crust in her mouth. In normal times, she'd have been sent from the table for such rudeness.

Boris was passing round the schnapps. Bette took the bottle.

'May I try?'

'*Nein*,' Mutti said, grabbing the bottle and passing it back to Boris.

'A little,' Boris said. 'Like a man.'

'*Nein*,' Mutti said again. Bette could hear the rage in her voice, could see the set of her jaw as she controlled herself. She coughed again, turned away for a moment, calming herself. Boris smiled and passed the bottle to Lieselotte, who held it to her lips and gulped. Bette heard her mother gasp, saw her leap up and grab the bottle, saw Boris's face cloud to anger as he snatched the bottle back. Mutti walked away, into the sitting room. She returned a few minutes later, wiping some dusty schnapps glasses clean on her apron. She placed them on the table. Four glasses. For Boris and his soldier. For Lieselotte, for herself.

'Bedtime,' she said to Bette, adding, 'Take the bucket.'

Bette wanted to stay. The heat from their bodies warmed the kitchen. Even though Mutti had covered the broken windows with old newspaper, the apartment was still cold, and the heating hadn't worked for months. For the first time in weeks, Bette's hands were not frozen and she was enjoying Boris, and his soldier friend who said nothing but cut bread and buttered it and pressed the sawn-off pieces of bacon into its centre before he passed it round, a piece for her, for Lieselotte, for Mutti. It was good to eat, to feel her stomach full. These were not like the Russians they had learned about, the monstrous Slavs with their savage instincts or the ones who'd taken Waltraud, or Lieselotte, that first night.

'He stay,' Boris said, winking at her, then held up his hand. 'Five minute.'

Bette looked at her mother, and Mutti nodded. She picked up her glass and tipped back her schnapps in one. Bette had never known her mother take a drink, even before the war, when Vati was at home, even at Christmas, when they ate the goose, not even when she and the Baumanns held a party to celebrate the victory over France. Boris was beaming again, filled Mutti's glass and Mutti inclined her head and nodded and smiled, cheeks flushed.

'Ballet,' she said, pointing to herself. 'Lindenoper. Ballet.'

'Ballet?' He stood up, knocking over his glass. 'Dance?' He was around the table in two strides, taking Mutti's hand, leading her across the hall into the sitting room. He called to the young soldier, who followed him in with his rucksack. Boris was speaking in Russian, Vasily smiling as he pulled a small accordion out of his knapsack. He sat on one of the hard chairs, opened the bellows, felt for the keys and began. A few slow chords and as the tempo sped up, Boris pushed the other chairs out of the way.

'You.' Boris pointed at Mutti.

'Oh no,' she said. 'I'm out of practice. I need to warm up, I need to do exercises.'

Boris looked confused and Lieselotte said, 'He doesn't understand. Do something, Mutti, please.'

Bette could see the panic on her mother's face.

Mutti had often waltzed round the sitting room, in better days, scooping Bette up as she went, twirling her round. She loved watching her mother, her grace and poise, weightless in motion.

'Waltz,' Bette said. 'Do a waltz.'

'Yes, waltz,' Lieselotte repeated. 'Waltz.' She began to hum 'The Blue Danube'. The soldier shook his head.

'Wait,' Bette said. 'The gramophone.' Mutti had locked it in a cupboard in the attic, with their records, so the Russians couldn't steal them. 'We can play it.'

'No,' Mutti said, frowning and shaking her head. 'No. Not that.'

'You idiot, Bette,' Lieselotte said, her teeth clenched tight.

'Bert,' Bette said, glaring at her sister. *You forgot.* Lieselotte stared like a hare in headlights. This was all a sham, the dancing, the manners, the flattery. Bette understood that now. Humour them.

'It's all right,' Bette said. 'He doesn't understand.' *The wolf doesn't understand.*

'Dance.' Boris had grabbed the schnapps bottle and was shouting, stomping his feet in time with the beat.

Mutti nodded at Lieselotte and walked to the centre of the room with that splayed-out walk that ballerinas have and Bette watched as she rose onto tiptoes, raised her chin so her neck stretched in a graceful arc, and began to dance across the floor, pulling Lieselotte with her, one arm round her waist, one raised above her shoulder, and together they waltzed and polkaed, dipping and rising, graceful as doves, light as fairies.

'Now me,' Bette said. 'Dance with me.' She forgot Boris and the other Russian, rushed towards her mother and sister.

'Teach,' Boris said, striding towards Mutti, arms stretched as if he were holding her already, pushing Bette aside as if she were no more than a mote of dust. Bette could smell the schnapps on Mutti's breath, on Boris's. She slunk away, lay on the floor behind the Biedermeier, watching as her mother and Boris and Lieselotte danced as if there were no war, as if they were not bitter enemies. The sky grew lighter and Boris took Lieselotte and led her into the bedroom, shutting the door. The soldier slumped into a chair, his accordion on the floor beside him.

Bette didn't hear the Russians go, but when she went into the kitchen in the morning they had left what remained of the schnapps, and the food and the cigarettes. Mutti was already up. Bette sat at the table, watching as her mother broke up the bread and soaked it in the milk, sprinkling the top with the sugar and cinnamon.

'Fetch Greta,' she said without looking up, but Bette heard the waver in her voice. Her mother untied her apron, stepped into the hall, picked up the bucket and opened the front door. There were two chamber pots on the threshold, the ones Frau Baumann used to use. She heard Mutti breathe in, watched as she flew to the Baumanns' door, rattling the handle, knocking hard with her fist, calling.

'Frau Baumann. Herr Baumann. Open up.'

She saw her mother lean her head against the wall, coughing and sobbing. Their neighbours' door would not open again.

CHAPTER EIGHT

North Germany: early May 1945

The truck lurched to the left, passing a line of refugees with shabby suitcases and ragged coats.

'So if Hitler done himself in,' Arthur said, squinting at the refugees, against the sun, 'how come the war ain't over?'

He was grateful to Arthur for not showing him up when Private Nash got shot. John respected him, though he wasn't sure this was reciprocated. Still, hours in a troop truck, all jolted spines and spiked nerves, did wonders for camaraderie. Arthur, he thought, tolerated him.

'Search me,' he said.

The tarpaulins were rolled up. John could see the refugees four or five abreast. Their faces were sallow and grim, eyes hollow and fearful, filling the road, thousands of them in a line that stretched to the horizon, like a river coursing through the countryside, rising higher by the moment.

A man in a hat was struggling with a wheelbarrow, an old woman scrunched in its tray. Her ankles hung over the end, her feet bandaged against the chill spring air. Her head rested on a cushion propped against the edge of the bowl. She was covered in a rug. He wanted to stop the truck, jump down. It could have been his grandmother. Perhaps this old woman baked a seed cake every

Sunday, saw her grandson once a week. The man had paused, removed his hat, was wiping his forehead and the woman raised a corrugated finger, whispered a word. The man shook his head, heaved at the barrow. He'd lost his place in the line, but there was no rush, no end to find or deadline to meet.

John knew he wouldn't have survived, wrenched from home, if the boot had been on the other foot. Where would he have gone in England? Tramping to nowhere?

'This will take forever.' John stood up in the truck and peered over the heads of the flow. It was already late afternoon. 'What's the hold-up?'

'Rations, sir,' Arthur said. 'Our boys have set up a station along the way. Water, biscuits, you know. Feeding them.' He rolled his eyes. 'Talk about a miracle. Where's this lot heading?'

John shrugged. 'Anywhere but east. They're fleeing the Russians.' He sat back onto the bench.

'Where's the Green Line bus when you need it, eh, sir?' Arthur said. 'Bremen to Braintree. Nordhausen to Northolt.'

John liked Arthur, with his dry, sly humour, found himself turning round, looking for the familiar transport, just in case.

'After Dunkirk,' John said, 'I wouldn't be surprised at anything.' He fished in his pocket for his NAAFI cigarettes, offered one to Arthur.

'Where are they going to put all these people when they get to where they're going? That's what I want to know.'

People.

John had braced himself for war back home but even so, every sense and sinew reeled from its horror. Death screamed from the ruins, polluted the air, soured the taste, blighted his sight. But the *people.* The life, in all this death. Clinging on. That took his breath away. Wherever he turned there was a frenzy to survive. A kaleidoscope. That's what he saw now. Not a flowing river at all, but a human fractal changing at each twist of its body, a never-ending mosaic of Germans, Jews, Russians, Italians, Poles. Men, women, children.

He pulled out his matches, lit Arthur's cigarette and his own.

The lorry edged to the side of the road, revved its engine hard. The crowd was too dense to move. Above them, scudding clouds and a late spring sun filled the cupola of sky, like a Constable painting, John thought. The same sky had hung over this part of the world when it tore itself to pieces in all the wars that had gone before. The Great War. The Schleswig Wars. The Seven Years' War. Thirty Years' War. Now *that* was a war. Almost wiped out Europe and those it didn't kill it pushed around. *Movement*. People. Refugees. This was what was meant by dis-location, to un-place. Dis-place. Displaced Persons.

'So who's in charge?' Arthur was saying. 'Now Hitler's gone.'

John dragged on his cigarette, his mind away, playing with words. He focused his gaze on Arthur.

'I think his name is Dönitz. It can't be long now, before it's over.' Added, 'They're not in Berlin anymore, so I heard.'

'Who's not?'

'The German government. They left.'

'Then who's in Berlin?'

'The Russians.'

He finished his cigarette, flipped it over the side of the lorry.

They left the refugees behind and the truck picked up speed, skirting the potholes. On either side of the road, the fields and dykes of the north German countryside lay flat and wasted. Now they were moving there was a chill in the air, reminding them that spring still had a bite. But the breeze was fresh and salty, and screeling above them John spotted seagulls. They couldn't be far from the sea.

'So where is it this time?' Arthur said.

'Kiel,' John said. 'Walterwerke.'

'What's that when it's at home?'

'We shall find out more later,' John said. 'They made torpedoes, U-boats. Rockets. Fuel.'

'Oh,' Arthur said. 'Bastards. Especially those doodlebugs.' His mouth twitched, as if he was thinking aloud. 'So do you understand it all? What they're saying, all those scientists?'

John laughed. 'I translate,' he said. 'I haven't a clue about the physics.' He tapped his pockets. 'Have you got a cigarette?'

Arthur pulled out a pack and offered it. John had a twenty a day habit now, more in the hard times, or the bored times, like now, churning over the miles for days on end.

'Still,' he said, cupping his hand around the match flame and dragging on his cigarette, 'the scientists seem to understand each other. It's a kind of code to them, I guess.'

'That makes sense.' Arthur paused for a moment, gazing into the distance, his mouth moving with silent thoughts. 'I wish I'd had your chances. I would've liked to have learned a language. Force for peace, I reckon.'

'Never too late to learn.' John smiled. 'What'll you do when the war's over, Arthur?'

Arthur shrugged, twisted his mouth.

'Find a job,' he said. 'It won't be easy, will it? Six years in the bloody army, fighting this sodding war, then we're supposed to go back to Civvy Street like nothing happened.' He flicked the cigarette stub over the side of the truck. 'My own son won't even know me.' He looked away, wiped his nose on the back of his hand.

'What did you do before the war?'

Arthur shrugged, turned back to face John.

'This and that,' he said. 'I left school at fourteen. No training, no trade. Not like you. I got work where I could, when I could.' He smiled. 'I always liked learning. Great respect for teachers. I even married one. She teaches little ones.'

The truck stopped with a jolt and the driver stepped down from his cab, walked towards John.

'What's up, Corporal?'

'The bridge is down so we have to detour. There's a Bailey bridge a bit further along, but we won't make Kiel before nightfall.'

'Have you informed HQ?'

He nodded. 'They suggested we bivouac somewhere. Commandeer a dwelling of some sort.' He shaded his eyes from the low sun. 'There's habitation ahead.' John nodded, returned to the truck, passed the information on. They'd have to be on their guard, watch out for snipers, a unit or a loner, still loyal to Hitler. The war wasn't over yet. They were sitting ducks.

'Roll down the tarpaulin,' John ordered. It was close to dusk, and with the sides covered the interior was dingy save for the lights from the cigarettes. The truck slowed and stopped.

'All out.' The Bailey bridge was ahead and John watched as the driver manoeuvred the vehicle onto the tracks before ordering the men to follow. Ahead of him, silhouetted against the cobalt sky, were the ruins of a village. They piled back into the truck and drove in silence along the road, alert, charged.

They stopped in a small square in the centre of the village. Half had been bombed out, the walls of the buildings little more than rubble, the ruins picked over for anything worth saving. The rest of the buildings looked uninhabited, save for half a dozen white sheets fluttering from the windows. So far, John thought, so reassuring, but he was jittery, could feel anxiety curl and tighten. He watched as Arthur walked towards one of the empty houses on the square. It was his job to requisition accommodation, but it could be a trap. Any of these houses could be an ambush in waiting. After Private Nash, they were doubly cautious. Behind Arthur was his corporal, rifle at the ready.

Arthur kicked the front door and it opened. He slipped into the building, the corporal at his side. John wanted to shut his eyes, waiting for the explosion, the tripwire, the booby trap. Another soldier guarded the entrance as the others looked around, surveying the side streets. Arthur and the corporal were out of sight. And gone. John checked his watch. Was it ten minutes? Too long. A silent ambush. Garrotted. No sound. Waiting.

The corporal appeared, beckoned to the soldier guarding the entrance. John saw him nod, run across the square.

'Lieutenant,' he called, 'come over here.' He was panting as he drew close. 'A man's injured. Bring the kit.'

John reached in for the first-aid bag and ran across the square. *Please, not Arthur.* He wasn't sure what he'd do without his sergeant to keep him steady. He jumped the steps to the building, over the threshold.

'In here, sir,' the corporal said.

The shutters were half closed. In the gloom John saw a figure lying on a stretcher made from old bedsprings, supported by two chairs. A woman was standing at one end, Arthur at the other. Alive and well. *Thank goodness.*

'*Mein Herr,*' the woman said as John came in. '*Bitte, hilfen Sie ihm.*' Her voice was weak, keening.

'Open the shutters,' John said. The last of the daylight filtered through. The room was bare, apart from the stretcher and a stove covered in cracked ceramics. John stepped towards the figure. A lad, not much younger than John. He lay trembling, his lips blue from shock and cold. His eyes were open, unblinking. The woman was stroking the boy's temple. John wasn't sure if he was conscious.

'*Was ist los?*' John said. *What's the matter?*

'*Mein Sohn…*' she said. She began to talk, too fast for John, her dialect unfamiliar, tumbling.

'Slow, slow,' John said, raising and lowering his hands, conducting the tempo.

The woman nodded.

'*Mein Sohn.*'

She lifted the blanket. One foot hung by its sinews, bones poking through the flesh. The skin was brown, the wound smelly. John clasped his hand to his mouth, afraid he'd retch or worse.

'*Mein Sohn,*' she was saying. '*Ein Schuss. Sein Fuß.*'

'Gangrene, sir,' Arthur said, matter-of-fact. 'Nothing we can do.'

She was holding a handkerchief in one hand, screwing it tight then fingering out an end, twisting it.

'*Gnädige Frau,*' John said, 'he must see a doctor.'

She walked over and tugged John's sleeve, crying, out of control. 'A doctor, please, *mein Herr, bitte, bitte.*' She sank to her knees, rummaging in her blouse, pulling out a wad of banknotes. 'Take it.'

John shook his head. 'I can't,' he said, in German. *Nein.* 'We can't take him to a doctor. Or a hospital.' He turned to Arthur.

'Can we make him more comfortable?'

'What do you mean, sir?'

'We carry morphine, don't we?'

Arthur stared at John.

'That's not allowed, sir,' he said. 'You have to account for every drop used. They'll never allow it, not on the enemy. There'll be hell to pay.'

'We can use as much ammunition as we like,' John said. 'To kill and maim and wound. But not a drop of morphine to help the suffering.' He opened the first-aid box and pulled out a phial and a syrette. 'The War Office have got their priorities wrong.'

'It's for us, sir,' the corporal said. 'The morphine's for us. If we need it.'

'But we don't, do we?' John said. He felt light-headed, as if the weight of youth was lifted and he had grown up, matured, like the rest of them. He stared at the syrette. He knew the theory – shallow angle, into the skin, squeeze the tube.

'I'll take full responsibility for this,' John said. He walked towards the boy, breaking the seal.

'Have you ever done this, sir?' Arthur said.

'I know what to do.'

'I'll do it,' Arthur said. 'I've done it before. That way, sir, we both stand guilty as charged.' He took the syrette before John could protest, turned, injected into the boy. 'He's probably going to die anyway.'

Arthur left the empty phial on the stretcher.

'Sir,' he said. 'I don't mean to alarm you, but look in the corner over there.'

John followed Arthur's gaze to the small, oblong object in the corner, its wings folded close to its body. Even from this distance John could see that the safety cap was off and the launcher was fully loaded.

'Everyone out,' John said, his voice steady. *Don't panic.* He waited until Arthur and the corporal had left. He nodded to the woman and her sleeping son, then crept over to the corner, picking up the anti-tank grenade. He backed out of the room, footsteps seamless across the floor, the grenade at arm's length, gliding down the steps, into the open. The river was not too far away, a quarter of a mile. Maybe less. Slowly, slowly. He could hear the shouts of his men behind him, but not a word of what they said. Steady, steady. One jolt. Blown to smithereens, meat and bone, minced and shredded. John kept one eye on his destination, one eye on the uneven road. Don't trip, don't stumble. Beware the rut ahead, the shell hole. The lights of the truck were switched on, full beam ahead. *Don't move. Stay away.*

He saw his shadow grow longer. Walk to the left, steady as you go, his grip clammy on the handle. Hold firm. Don't let it slip. He could feel the sweat sting as it ran into his eyes, could feel it dripping down his neck, soaking his shirt. The lights faded. Don't follow me, *do not follow me.* A hundred yards. Don't think. Keep walking. A rabbit darted across his path and John jumped, jerking his arm. He stopped, held his breath, his arm trembling. He grabbed his elbow with his free hand. Waited. Nothing. A close shave. *Phew.* Steady, steady. Could he quicken his pace, get this over with? The road looked smooth ahead. He had been good at running. He could sprint, be there in half a minute, half the time. His breath was light, his muscles taut, the taste of iron and blood flooding his mouth. Fifty yards. Steady as you go. Forty. Could he throw it from here? Thirty yards. He'd been in the first eleven, after all, opened the bowling against Whitgift in the Surrey Schools. Take a run and bowl it? Twenty yards. Could he risk it? Ten yards. Five. Four.

He raised his arm, flicked his wrist and released the grenade. Turned and ran. Behind him he heard a splash. And nothing. Running and running, eyes blind, feet flying. *Nothing.*

Arthur was standing by the truck, began to clap as John drew near. They were all clapping. John grabbed the tailgate, sat down on the tailboard, held his head in his hands, his body quivering, out of control.

'That was something, sir,' Arthur said, handing him a lighted cigarette and a bottle. 'We'll have a brew-up, the lads and I,' he said. 'But I thought you'd need something stronger.'

John pulled the stopper, took a swig, expecting a raw, burning liquid to scald his throat, but what he swallowed was warm and smooth. He looked at the bottle. Hermitage. Grand Cognac. 1895.

'Blimey,' he said. His hand was shaking. He wanted to cry.

Arthur stood in front of him, silhouetted against the evening sky. 'We're proud of you, sir,' he said, laying a hand on John's shoulder. 'I want to say, on behalf of all of us. You saved our lives. And what you did for the boy, that was charity, sir. Pure charity.'

John nodded, knuckles pressed against his mouth, the enormity of what he'd done beginning to shape itself in front of him.

'We've agreed, sir,' Arthur went on. 'The lads and me. We'll let them know your bravery. You'll be mentioned in despatches. I don't think any of us could have done that, sir.'

John looked up at his sergeant and smiled.

'None of you would have been so stupid.'

'And, sir,' Arthur went on, 'none of us saw that missing phial of morphine. They must have miscounted it, don't you agree, sir?'

'I can't think about that now,' John said. 'But I won't ask you to lie for me.'

He took another sip of the brandy, filled his lungs with the cigarette. His head began to swim.

'Corporal Lennox here,' Arthur said. 'He's commandeered another house. All clear this time. Not a soul. Not a dicky bird. Not a picture of Hitler or a single swastika. Buried them all, I reckon. They do that, you know, sir. Hide the evidence. Pretend they never swallowed all that rubbish hook, line and sinker.'

Arthur's banter danced in John's head. He was exhausted, a huge wave of fatigue rolling over him.

'I'd like to go there now,' John said.

'Not long been occupied,' Arthur was saying as they walked towards the accommodation on a side street off the square. 'Beds, sheets, the works. Even a cellar. Full of fine brandy. We've decided, sir, that you're to take the master bedroom, with the big fluffy eiderdown.'

John smiled. Arthur opened the door, led John upstairs. He flopped on the oversized bed, shut his eyes, aware that Arthur was taking off his boots and covering him with the bedding.

'I reckon you'll sleep like a baby, sir.'

The pillow was soft, smelled of hair oil, of home.

CHAPTER NINE

Hatfield: July 1958

He was still an athletic man, kept himself in trim, exercises morning and evening. He was on his knees now, poking round the pansies at the base of the old Anderson shelter with a garden fork. Her mother had had pansies in her wedding bouquet, a waterfall of purple and yellow. Mrs H liked pansies too, made posies from them and put them on the breakfast table, like a cheap B & B.

A newfangled transistor radio rested on the grass beside him. She could hear the reverential timbres of John Arlott rising and falling. Her father's lips moved soundlessly, as they did when he was thinking. He'd rolled up the sleeves of his shirt and was wearing his old grey gardening trousers that were once part of a suit. The lawnmower squatted behind him and the grass smelled sweet and freshly cut. She'd grown used to the purr of the blades as they rotated, the steady rhythm as her father pushed and pulled. It was the sound of England. He cut the lawn twice a week, checking for weeds or moss, neat stripes, up down, up down. How little she knew him really. He had never allowed her inside.

'Who's winning?'

'England. Cowdrey going into bat.' He lifted the transistor to his ear. Betty waited a moment.

'No cricket?'

'I've done something to my ankle,' he said. He played cricket on Saturdays and she had the house to herself then. He'd learned to play in the war, so he said, in Sark. *Got the locals to teach us and we formed a team. You didn't know that, did you? That the Wehrmacht had a First Eleven? It was their last Eleven too. We were thrashed. But we took it in good spirit. We played the game, and all that.*

More English than the English. Even in Sark, even in the war. She didn't know whether to be proud of him, or ashamed. He never mentioned what the Wehrmacht were doing in Sark. Never talked about his war. Or his work before the war, except to say it was at the university. She'd asked him once if he'd supported the Nazis. He'd given a lopsided smirk.

'You had to be a Party member, Betty, if you wanted to succeed.'

'Things that were done in your name,' she'd said.

'The guilty ones were prosecuted. Why should I take responsibility for things I had no control over?'

He'd snapped at her. Amnesia was the way he lived with the past, a convenient forgetting.

He pushed himself up and walked towards her, limping. He smiled, and she saw that his mood was warm. She could never be sure whether she'd be sailing with his breeze or knocked sideways by his boom. She'd been six years old when the war started, twelve when it ended. When they'd met again, they were strangers. He was father to her, never *daddy*. Even now, they were ill at ease, the space in their lives filled with silences, with fantasies, a web of *seeming*. She guessed it was like that all over Europe, only her father seemed more remote than most, more absent. Stricter, too, with the power to terrorise with a single word, a sharp tone. A stiletto in her gut.

'You should stand up to him,' Dee used to say, but it was easy for her. She never had to live with a bully, to live to milk the softer moments, like now, to pretend he loved her, and she him, to all the world a devoted family.

'How about a cup of tea?' he said. 'Will you put the kettle on?'

§

She slipped the cosy over the top of the pot and laid the tray with the Royal Doulton cups and plates, the sugar bowl and the cake that Mrs H had left for them. They'd had to start from scratch after the war and this tea set was one of the first new things her father had bought, after the tablecloth. One or two pieces had since been broken, and the milk jug was chipped, but her father insisted on using it.

'So you can be proud when you bring your friends home.'

Who could she bring home? She'd no real friends from school. Who wanted to be friends with a Nazi? That's what they'd called her. *Nazi.* There had been all sorts in her class. Irish, Italians, Poles. Maltese, Latvians, Cypriots. Refugees, all of them, but not a single German. Nor a Jew. When the other girls talked about the war she bore the brunt of their blame. How could she answer back? She kept her head down and worked hard. She and Deirdre O'Cleary, whom no one liked either as her father was a tinker, so they said, only Dee got pregnant when she was seventeen and had to get married and that was the end of that. Besides, he'd banned Deirdre from coming to the house. *Irish.*

She missed Dee. They'd been thick as thieves once but had drifted apart when Dee had her babies and Betty went to college. She should get in touch. Dee's father would have her address. Go out for a coffee. There was even a brand-new Wimpy Bar opened up in the centre of town. Perhaps they could go there, have a bite to eat, catch up on all the gossip. The children must be quite old now. She'd give Mr O'Cleary a ring later on from a telephone booth, so her father couldn't eavesdrop, get Dee's new address. *Hello, stranger, long time no see.* Yes, that would be fun.

She opened the French windows from the dining room, took out the portable card table that doubled as garden furniture, laid out a cloth and placed the tray on top. She fetched two kitchen chairs, poured the tea, passed him the milk, cut a slice of cake and handed it to him.

'Dundee,' he said. 'My favourite. We're lucky to have Mrs H.'

Mrs H had come with the house. She washed the kitchen floor each day, covering the lino with yesterday's newspaper to protect it from dirt. She dusted and vacuumed, washed and ironed. She made their meals, baked their cakes and had tried to teach Betty the facts of life when she'd started her period. 'I know all about it,' Betty had said. She'd run to her bedroom and locked the door. *I know what men do.*

'Why don't you marry Mrs H?' Betty said. 'She'd look after you very well.'

'She's a fine woman,' he said. 'And an excellent cook. The way to a man's heart is through his stomach, so they say.' Her father smiled, but it had no substance. His eyes wandered towards the old Anderson shelter and the purple and yellow pansies clustered at its base, like posies in a graveyard. Her mother's favourite flowers.

Betty broke off a piece of cake and sat with it poised in her fingers. He never talked about the war, about Mutti or Lieselotte. Even now, after all these years. She'd tried to tell him, when he found her, but he'd said, *We do not talk about such things. Nothing will restore the past, or give sight to the blind.* She could see his mouth set, his jaw muscles tighten. She wanted to say, *Or me. You never asked about me.* Sometimes the silence and the pain ballooned inside her, fit to burst.

He picked up his cup. His hand began to shake and the tea slopped into the saucer.

'If you don't mind, I'd like to drink my tea in peace,' he said.

He pulled out his handkerchief and wiped the saucer, gazing at the pansies. Was that a conversation, of sorts, with her mother?

About her mother? Betty thought he cared more for the pansies than for her. Or his work. She didn't even know what he did, except that he worked for de Havilland and built aeroplanes and was involved in the Comet, which he said would be able to fly to New York in less than eleven hours and back to London in just over six. Tailwinds.

She'd leave him to it. Let him sulk. But it hurt, his silence, his denial. She stood up, and a small ceramic CND button fell out of her pocket onto the stone terrace and cracked in two.

'What was that?' her father said. 'Did you drop something?'

'It's all right,' Betty said. 'I can see it.' She reached down and scooped up the broken pieces, holding them in her hand.

'What is it?'

'Nothing,' Betty said. 'A china button, that's all.'

'I'd like to see it.' He held out his hand. 'Please give it to me.'

'I'm not a child,' she said, turning on her heel, but he'd whipped round and grabbed her wrist, pressing the soft bones so she yelped and opened her fist. She could feel her father scrabbling at the pieces. He released his grip and she shook her hand.

'That really hurt.' Her eyes were stinging with tears. Her father was fingering the broken button in his palm, piecing it together.

'Where did you get this?'

'I bought it,' she said.

'Do you know what it is?' His voice was full of rage.

'Of course I know what it is,' she said. 'Why are you so angry?'

He tossed his head back. 'You understand nothing of the world.'

'No.' The valve inside her exploded. '*You* don't understand. Do you know what these bombs do?'

She never shouted, and never at her father. She could feel her heart beat, her stomach knot. 'Look at Hiroshima,' she said, her voice at full pitch. An ordinary bomb was bad enough, and she knew about those, fireballs, everything. '*Hiroshima.*'

She sniffed loudly, pulled out her handkerchief and blew her nose hard.

'Do you want the Russians here?' There was spittle on his lip. 'I thought,' he added, his voice vibrating as he controlled his anger, 'you'd learned your lesson with the Russians.'

She stood, open-mouthed, speechless, a million memories hurtling, burning. Her breath came short, pelting in and out. She picked up her cup and threw it at him. The tea splashed on the ground but the cup flew past him, landing on the lawn, unbroken. She stood, hands clenching and unclenching, expecting him to leap up and shake her, but he sat, his lip curled, silent, superior.

'It's nothing to do with Russia,' she said, after a minute or so. Her voice was low and she was swallowing hard, dollops of saliva threatening to choke her.

'No? Where do you think these ban the bomb people get their money from?' He narrowed his eyes, not waiting for her reply. 'The Russians, that's who. They want us to disarm. And then they walk all over us. Communism is a scourge.' His voice was full of threat, fury. 'Only the Germans saw that, had the courage to confront it.' He paused, shaking his head, adding, 'We were right all along.'

Betty stood, words churning, but no sound came out. She didn't want to hear what he had to say.

'It was Germany who bore the brunt,' he went on. 'But that has been conveniently forgotten.'

She thought she might hit him if he said another word. He'd wiped his slate clean, as if he had nothing to do with the history there'd once been. She stomped past him, picked up the teacup, brought it back and slammed it onto the tray.

'You'll be telling me next that if Germany had had the Bomb, Russia would never have invaded.'

'I think as a matter of fact that they would have thought twice about it.' He held out his hand, beckoning for Betty to come close, to take it. She stayed still. 'Nobody wants nuclear war,' he went on, his voice oily. 'But until everybody destroys their weapons, it's only common sense to be armed.' He patted his pockets, pulled out his pipe and tobacco pouch. 'That's what our government thinks.'

'But they're wrong.'

'Says who? A bunch of scruffy idlers?' He shredded the tobacco, stuffed it into the bowl of his pipe, tamping it down. He pulled out his lighter, sucked on his pipe, drawing the smoke. She wanted to say, *They're not all idlers, they're not all scruffy. They're people like you, too.*

'You will never know the sacrifices I made.' He was looking at her, his grey eyes unblinking, and she saw in him a sharper steel, a ruthlessness she'd not recognised before.

'Is there more tea?' He lifted the teapot, peered inside.

'Make it yourself,' Betty said.

He drained the dregs into his cup. She left him to drink it, grabbed her keys and her bag and left, slamming the front door behind her.

CHAPTER TEN

London: July 1958

Most of the customers were in their twenties, he guessed, Betty's age. It was always packed and everyone seemed to know each other. Did people look at him, coming alone? *Who's that man? What does he want?* He should bring Betty. He wondered if she knew the place. He was sure she'd like it, even if the coffee was undrinkable and the food for the most part weird and inedible. Borscht. What on earth was that? The Partisan Coffee House. He could sit here all day and nobody would care a toss. Goodness knows how it could ever make money. But there was plenty going on, jazz and skiffle, poetry and folk songs, literature and film. Politics, of course. Chess, in the basement. Library on the first floor. And on the top, the editors of *Universities and Left Review.*

He pulled out his cigarettes and lit one. He hadn't been sleeping. Every noise made him jump, put his teeth on edge – a desktop slammed, a bench pulled. He should go to the doctor, get some barbiturates to calm him down. They'd worked in the past.

His name was Anatoly, or so he'd said. John hadn't seen him again since that first visit. Sometimes he thought Anatoly was an apparition, a nightmare made flesh. But it wasn't a ghost that had seeped through John's skin. It was the essence of him, as if Anatoly lived inside him now.

Kneeling down by her side, staring at the lesions on her neck. Her face. He couldn't recollect her *face*, though he knew how cold it felt. In his mind he saw her body, but her features vaporised into the cloud of his memory. He had to remember her, even as she moved away and Betty came closer, became her, like a photograph with a double exposure. A love expanded. No. This was too soon. The shock remained, the touch of her. *Dance with me, John. Dance.* He'd watched as she disappeared in the dusk, as the torn trees of the Tiergarten became skeletons against the pink eiderdown of an evening sky.

John had no idea what Anatoly wanted with him.

He looked out of the window. The bombed-out house at the corner of the street had scaffolding and hoardings round it to keep the children out. The straggling tip of a buddleia could be seen above them, picking up nutrients from the ash. Were there buddleias in Hiroshima now, pushing through the fractured bricks, gorging on incinerated flesh? There'd been plenty in Berlin.

He caught the eye of the stranger who seemed to run the place and smiled. He seemed so very young. They all did. Some might have done national service, but they hadn't fought in the war and he admired them their conviction, envied their innocence. They'd never had their moral universe tested and shattered. Never had to tuck that murky past in their pocket, put on their civvies and pretend it never happened.

He stood up, handing a copy of *Tribune* to the young man next to him.

'Bit old, I'm afraid,' he said, fishing for his wallet. 'I recommend the chilli con carne.'

As if he came here all the time.

He put his hands in his pockets and set off for home, a quiet saunter on a sunny evening. He'd pick up some eggs and milk in the market, perhaps some veg and fruit if they were going cheap. It was the end of the day, after all. He was in no hurry. He'd do some marking and have a nightcap in the pub. He felt calmer now. Funny how his worries surged and drained, like a tidal river.

He paused at the corner of his street and waited. It was empty. He looked behind him. No one he recognised. The museum was shut now, the crowds gone. No Anatoly. He fumbled in his pocket for his keys, but the door swung open. It was on the latch, unlocked. That was not how he had left it this morning. He always made a point of pushing the door after he shut it, to make sure. He'd have to tell his neighbour, *Make sure you lock up.* His bike was leaning against the wall inside the hall and he could hear his neighbour practising. Bob Welham, a flautist, played with the LSO. He must be about to leave for the evening performance. Bob could wangle John into rehearsals at the Festival Hall in the holidays. John would sit in the stalls as the musicians went through their paces, cigarettes propped on their music stands, puffing between bars. John had no idea musicians *smoked*, though he supposed they were human too, even if the music they made was divine. Bob didn't smoke.

'Couldn't blow the bloody thing if I did,' he said. 'Should have taken up percussion. Or the fiddle. They get through a whole packet, you know that, don't you?'

John climbed the stairs two at a time, jumping over the torn lino. He reached his landing, placed his key in the lock, turned it. He could feel his heart begin to hammer, sweat on his neck, the familiar dread. Why now? There was no rhyme or reason to his panic. This was his home, not a stranger's. There was no sniper, no mangled boy, no live grenade. Perhaps his landlord had come in. He had a key, though he usually gave John warning. John took a deep breath, pushed the door wide open. There was an air of occupation, as if a ghost had wandered through leaving a scent of honeyed milk. *Her.*

John grabbed his umbrella from the stand by the door. It wasn't much of a weapon but it could parry a first blow, give him a head start. He kicked the door so it slammed against the wall. No one was hiding behind. He stepped into the sitting room, his umbrella in two hands like a rifle, eyes left, eyes right, scanning, searching. He was a soldier again, boots heavy and soiled. The shade on his standard lamp had been knocked askew, and the reading lamp lay on the floor. The newspaper on the table was crumpled, the books tipped off the shelf. He leaped forward, turned, no one behind, turned again, three paces, kicked open the bedroom door. The bed was as he had left it, the cord of his pyjamas showing beneath the pillow where he'd folded and tucked them. He sidled in, checked behind the door. His work jacket hung on the hook, next to his woollen dressing gown. He bent down, peered under the bed. Shoes, slippers, dust. No crouching form ready to spring.

He walked back through the sitting room. He could taste the blood rust of iron as his stomach churned. He relaxed his hold on the umbrella, gripped it again. The door to the kitchenette was ajar so he pushed it open and let it bang against the wall. The muscles in his legs began to quiver.

A bloodied hand had dragged along the window and over the sink and tiles behind it. It had wiped across the enamel top of his table and there was white stuff dribbled down its legs. John traced the trail across the room, poked it with his umbrella, not sure what it could be. The cups on the draining board had been knocked off, smashed on the floor, curved shards of blue china, a handle smeared with blood. Blood was spattered on the cupboard and on the twisted mesh door of the food safe. John looked behind him. The sitting room was empty. He held his breath, poked at the door of the safe, swung it open.

A large black crow lay inside, its wings spread, flapping faintly. John felt the adrenalin drain, his legs lose their steel, his muscles their tension. He wanted to laugh. How stupid. It was only a bird. He dropped the umbrella and walked over to the safe, scooping the bird up. He could feel its tiny heart beating fast as a clock, could see the terror in its eyes. It was too faint to struggle, its neck too weak for its head. He should put it out of its misery but he hadn't the courage. He cradled it, waiting for it to die. Private Nash's hair had been as black as this crow, his blood and bile on John's uniform, his slumped form held by John's body.

The bird went still. John carried it down the stairs, not sure what to do with it. There was nowhere to bury it, no soldiers coming up behind to take care of it. He placed it in the dustbin down in the area and turned back inside the house, climbing up, his knees trembling. That's all it was. A dead bird. The thing had flown in, beaten itself against the window, flapped around in a panic until it sank into the food safe, exhausted, waiting to die, in pain, in terror.

How had it got in? His windows were shut. Someone must have released it into his rooms. Someone with a key, or who could pick a lock. He groped his way towards the armchair and lowered himself into it. Off course. That's what he was. Blown *off course*. He placed his head in his hands. Who had done this? Why?

Anatoly. The lanky-legged Russian with the pockmarked face had the powers of the Devil.

There was a movement in the grate. John jumped, cried out. He looked again. Soot had fallen on the hearth, feathers. Another bird, one wing jutting at an angle, was scrabbling to move. The chimney. They had come down through the chimney.

A phone was ringing, but it was somewhere else. He was somewhere else.

They made nests in chimneys. One crow took a wrong turning, flew down the stack, its mate following. There would be chicks up there, orphaned. Perhaps they'd fledged already.

The bird lay still, its death throes done. There was always a simple explanation. That's what his father would say. A car backfiring. Fireworks. A motorbike's roar. *Calm down, dear boy. Nothing to worry about. It's all over.*

He'd have to clear up the mess. He reached over to the newspaper and carried it to the hearth, lifting the bird onto the paper, its body still warm, its feathers oily to the touch. He'd put it with the other one. *Sorry, old bird. Nowhere to bury you.* He went into the kitchen for the dustpan, steeling himself to open the cupboard door. There was blood on the handle. He wasn't sure whether to clean the blood off first or fetch the bucket and the Vim. Scrub and scrub.

'John.' Someone was knocking hard at the door. 'John. Phone.'

He walked back through the sitting room, opened the door.

'Bloody hell,' Bob said. 'Are you deaf? I've been yelling for you. You have a call.'

'Who is it?'

'How should I know? Take it, for heaven's sake. I have to go.'

He turned, ran down the stairs. John followed him. He felt sick. Too much adrenalin. It did that. Couldn't disperse, that's what the doctor had said, makes you nauseous. Bob was rushing out of the door, his flute case in one hand, music bag in the other.

John tripped on the torn lino, grabbed the banister to save himself. He was still shaky, anxious. He knew the caller would have gone by the time he got to the phone. Knew it was Anatoly, up to his tricks. He walked into the booth. The receiver had been left hanging, and he picked it up.

CHAPTER ELEVEN

London: July 1958

The telephone booth was smelly and hot and she pushed open the door with her foot. She was sure the operator would butt in at any moment, *I'm sorry, caller, there is no reply.* It never crossed her mind John could be out. She'd run out of the house, her bag under her arm, sprinted down the road, feet slipping in her flimsy sandals. She'd pulled them off, dashed across the road outside the station, bare feet slapping the pavements, her hand brushing a cyclist who pulled up and swore at her. She'd waved her shoes at him, *sorry.* The phone booth was occupied by a woman with curlers and a hairnet who was leaning against the glass, laughing. Betty hammered on the door.

'An emergency.'

The woman nodded. Betty saw her mouth *I have to go*, put the receiver down. She left the booth, glaring at Betty standing barefoot, hair awry, her blouse worked loose from her waistband.

'Thank you,' Betty said, no idea what to do except that she had to see John, be close to him, feel his breath and face, hear his voice. Sometimes he teased her, said her name the German way, *Bette, Bette.* She hadn't told him, not about Germany. One day, perhaps. Not just yet.

She was about to give up when a man answered. She knew it wasn't John, but she said his name, all the same.

'I'll see if he's in,' he said. 'Hang on.' Of course, John had a neighbour.

Minutes ticking.

'Do you wish to continue, caller?' the operator said. Betty had laid out her change on the top of the telephone box. She had one more shilling. Trunk calls were expensive, and John usually rang her back. If he didn't answer now, then what? She didn't want to go home, not with her father in that mood. And *she* was angry. With her father, and his version of the war that held no one to account, least of all him.

It was still early. She could go to London anyway. See a film, perhaps, get the last train. *Dracula*, if she dared. The evening was hot. She wouldn't need to go back and fetch her cardigan. Her feet were filthy.

'Insert more money, caller.' She pushed the shilling into the slot. *Please be there, John, please answer.*

The receiver clunked, as if it was being picked up by the cord and swung.

'John Harris speaking.' His voice was breathy, rushed.

'John,' she said.

'Betty?' He sounded puzzled, distracted, as if he was being interrupted.

'Is this a bad time?' They rang at a prearranged time each week, never spontaneously. Perhaps he was busy, about to go out, meet friends. Her stomach tightened, swallowing her disappointment. What if he had a girlfriend? A proper girlfriend, one he spent the weekends with, not snatched evenings on Mondays and Wednesdays. She hadn't thought of that. She knew so little about his life, when she thought about it.

'No.' His voice was flat, uninterested. He wasn't pleased to hear from her. She was deflated, humiliated even. She'd made a fool of herself. It was nonsense to think of John as a boyfriend. It was based on nothing. He was an older man, a mature man. A fantasy, a teenage crush.

'I'm surprised, that's all,' he went on. 'I didn't expect to hear from you.' Silence. A beat. She'd run out of money soon. She should make her excuses, ring off. 'But I'm thrilled you called. What's up?'

His voice had warmed and lightened, and her spirits rose.

'I…' She hesitated, unsure now what to say, or how to say it. 'I thought I might come into London this evening, that's all. I just wondered…' Was she being too forward? She always let him make the first move, apart from that first time, when she'd written to him. 'Do you fancy a coffee or something?' Added, 'If you're not doing anything, that is.'

'What a great idea,' he said, his voice welcoming, excited even. 'What time?'

'In about an hour? My train's about to leave. Is that okay?'

'Lovely. I'll meet you at the station.'

'Caller, your time is up. Do you wish to extend?'

'By the clock,' she shouted into the phone. 'The clock.' The line went dead.

Perhaps he'd been asleep, woken up by her call, grumpy like a startled baby.

The station was crowded, even though it was a Saturday. Families, mostly, out for the day. Taking the kids to London. Big Ben. St Paul's. The Tower. All the sights. She made her way towards the large clock, searching for him. He wasn't there. She craned her neck, wishing she was taller. She couldn't see him. A small boy darted in front of her, pushing as he passed, catching her off balance. She teetered for a moment, staggered, regained her footing.

'Brian, come back here.' A harassed woman ran past her. 'Sorry, love. Brian. This. Minute.'

She watched as the woman caught the boy, raised her hand and walloped his bottom. The boy pulled a face, pretending it hadn't hurt, pretending he wasn't humiliated. Betty smiled at him, *it's okay*. Shook her head, *but your mum's right*.

Perhaps John hadn't heard the bit about the clock. He knew it was St Pancras, though. He'd seen her off at the end of an evening so many times. He kissed her these days, properly, pressing himself against her, *Betty, Betty*. She'd give him fifteen minutes, get some change at the ticket office, ring him again.

Though what if he was on the way? They could easily miss each other.

She positioned herself under the clock, checked her watch against it. She was a few minutes fast, but she did that on purpose. She hated to be late. She'd never understood this English 'ish'. Come at *elevenish*. Why? Come at eleven, come at ten past eleven. No *ish*.

She felt a movement behind her, two hands cover her eyes, the rough tweed of a jacket sleeve brushing her cheek.

'Guess who?' She smelled him, his signature.

The hands came down, spun her round. He must have been running. He was breathing heavily and there was perspiration on his forehead.

'Sorry I'm late,' he said. 'Have you been waiting long?'

She shook her head. John respectable in his schoolmaster's jacket with the leather patches, a woollen tie. She brushed her finger against his forehead. 'Aren't you hot?'

'Yes,' he said, slipping off his jacket, slinging it over his shoulder, groping for her hand, claiming her, *she is mine*. Why had she thought he could have a girlfriend?

'Come on. What shall we do?'

She braced herself for a moment. Sometimes, she thought, a woman needs to move first.

'I've never been to your rooms,' she said. 'Why don't we go there? Have a cup of tea and then decide?'

He stopped, paused. Her doubts hurtled back. He has someone there. Not just another girlfriend. He's *married*. He could be. She'd never asked, but the arrangement would suit him. What had he told his wife? *Just got to nip out for a bit.*

'See,' he said. 'The problem is…' He moved a step away from her, looked into the distance. Her stomach lurched and she felt tears threatening. Her nose was beginning to run and she sniffed.

'You have someone,' she said. She couldn't help herself.

'What?' He looked surprised. 'No, nothing like that. The thing is, my rooms are in a dreadful state.'

She laughed.

'Is that all? No mummy to tidy up?' It was a spiteful thing to say, and she wanted to swallow it back straight away. Anxiety, that's what it was, made her say silly things.

He looked cross. 'No,' he said. 'I'm very tidy. The thing is, a couple of birds flew down the chimney and made a terrible mess. I thought I'd been vandalised, to be honest. Until I realised what had happened.'

'Are they still there?'

'I've got rid of them but I haven't had time to clean up. It looks like a battle zone.' He looked confused, as if he shouldn't have said that.

'Then why don't I help?'

'Would you?' he said. 'I'm a bit squeamish about blood.'

They hopped on a bus, clambered up to the top. The two front seats were unoccupied and they scrambled forward, lurching as the bus started up.

'I like to sit up top,' John said. 'Childish, I know.'

'Me too,' she said. 'But it has to be the front.'

He squeezed her hand. The evening would be fine.

'So what made you decide to come to London?'

'Spur of the moment.'

She didn't want to tell him she'd had an argument with her father. The row wasn't important. Lots of people shared his views. Most of the lawyers where she worked, for a start. A deterrent, they called it. The nuclear deterrent.

It was her father's attitude. Lieselotte. His own daughter. His *anger*. How many German men had disowned their women once the Russians left? Wished them dead? Her father was one of them, she saw that now. She didn't even know if he'd voted for Hitler, supported the National Socialists. Had he been a willing member of the Party? A fellow traveller? He never spoke about it, what part he'd played in that wrecking ball of history. It was hard to live with a man who gagged his past. She'd been a child in the war. It hadn't been her fault. She had not been responsible. But she felt it, because her father did not.

'Spur of the moment? You've gone very quiet. Did something happen?'

And Berlin? The muteness of the women was thick and heavy as tarpaulin over a corpse. *Nice girls don't talk about that.* Why keep this secret from John? Why pretend? John had never asked where she came from. Her English was flawless, she'd made sure of that, so why would he suspect? She couldn't bring herself to say, *I was there. I am German. Ich bin Deutsche.* She was as guilty as her father.

She broke away from her thoughts, looked up at him, smiled.

'No. Nothing. I was in town. In St Albans, as it happened,' she said, adding, 'It's not far away from Hatfield.'

'I know where St Albans is,' he said. 'What were you doing there?'

'Sitting down,' she said. 'In the marketplace. With our CND banners.' And her badge, now ground to dust in the garden.

'You're lucky you weren't arrested.'

'In St Albans? I think the police were bemused, that's all. Everyone was so young. School children, really. I was by far the oldest.'

'Well,' he said. 'I know how you feel. I'll tell you about that later. Come, this is our stop.'

She knew he lived in Bloomsbury, but had no idea it was so close to the British Museum. She followed him into Bury Place, through a narrow door next to a café. The hall was dark and she had to adjust her eyes. A man's bike was propped against the wall, ahead of them a flight of stairs with chipped brown paint, covered in torn green linoleum. It was dingy and shabby, and she thought of her father. He'd paint it all pale blue, rip out the old lino, put down Marley tiles.

'One more flight,' John said. 'Watch the step.' There was a grimy skylight that lit the last of the stairs and a small landing. John pulled out his key and opened the door.

'Won't you come into my parlour.' *Said the spider to the fly.* Betty felt a small knot of excitement. She'd never been alone with him. They'd always met in public places. Would he have suggested they come here if she hadn't mentioned it? Or was he, in his own way, luring her inside?

She brushed him as she stepped past into the sitting room, an inch too close but she couldn't stop herself. He touched her hand, let it linger. Her skin fizzed. Ahead was the mantelpiece, bookshelves either side and on them, a clock. Her blood drained, made her giddy for a moment. She shivered.

'Cold?' he said.

'No. Nothing.' She smiled, added, 'Someone stepped on my grave.'

Her parents had had an identical clock, until Lieselotte had sold it. Of course, thousands of them were made. The factory churned them out for years. Still, it was odd that John would have one. Perhaps he'd picked it up in Germany at the end of the war.

Either side of the mantelpiece were two sagging armchairs covered in a brown moquette. His table was heavy and plain.

Utility, no doubt. Solid. Value for money. Too clumsy, her father had said. Where is the flair? He had got rid of theirs years ago, bought a new G-plan dining set. The floor was covered in brown linoleum, and in front of the fire was a black semicircle with a long, shaggy pile.

'I didn't know you…' She was about to say *had a dog* before she realised it was a hearthrug. What an idiot.

'I thought it was one of those black retrievers,' she said. She pulled a face, *silly me*, looking either side of the mantelpiece, at the shelves in the alcoves stacked with books, paperbacks, mainly, though she could see some hardbacks on the top shelves, Schiller and Goethe, Brecht and Mann written on the spines, and a fat *Oxford German Dictionary*.

'You're taking it in,' he said. 'Does it meet with your approval?'

'This doesn't look too bad,' she said. 'I was expecting worse when you said it was a battlefield.' Could she ask him about the clock?

'It wasn't too bad in here,' he said. 'Though the bulb's gone in the reading lamp, which is a nuisance. Come through.'

He opened the door to the kitchen. There were blood smears across the window and down the walls, on the table and the cupboard doors, thin rusty blood, the kind you get from an insect or a reptile. She shut her eyes for a moment, squeezing out the memory of blood along the pavement, splattered on walls. Of Otto, pale against the cobbled street.

He'd called it a battle zone, but he'd obviously never seen one. Betty knew about blood, knew how to steel herself against it. 'Do you have a bucket? Disinfectant?'

'I think so,' he said. 'My charlady…' He bent down to the space below the sink and pulled out a small can of Jeyes from the back.

'Rubber gloves?' Betty said. 'This stuff burns like mad. Stinks like hell.'

John rummaged some more, produced gloves, a floor cloth and a bucket.

'Come on, I'll do it,' he said. 'I can't let you clean up for me. Why don't you put the kettle on?'

'I thought you were squeamish,' she said.

'Well, it doesn't look so dreadful now. It was the shock, I think.'

Sitting opposite each other, cradling their cups, Betty could smell the disinfectant on John's hands even from a distance. He was right, the place was tidy, and clean. She liked that, in a man. She'd have to ask him to wash his hands, get rid of the stench of the Jeyes, though she wasn't sure where the bathroom was. She looked again at the clock. The chrome had worn round the edge and on the stand, as it had on theirs, but the smoky glass and the Roman numbers telling the hours were clear and bright apart from the II.

'I like your clock,' she said.

'Do you?' he said. 'I think it's Bauhaus.'

'Well,' she said, 'it's art deco for sure. The designer was a man called Heinrich Möller and the clocks were made by Kienzle.'

'Good Lord,' he said. 'You know a lot about it. Nobody's ever told me that.'

'I'm full of odd snippets of information,' she said.

'Your pronunciation is excellent, too.'

'Thanks,' she said. *Keep to the subject. Don't let him ask.* 'My father had a similar one. He got it in Germany.' That was no lie. 'Where did you find that one?' She was heading into dangerous territory, towards Germany, to Berlin.

'In Germany too,' John said. 'At the end of the war. Possibly your father got it the same way as me. For cigarettes.' He reached over to the mantelpiece for a packet of Weights, his hand trembling.

'Possibly,' Betty said. 'Are you all right?'

'Fine.' He fumbled at the packet and it fell to the floor. Betty leaned forward and picked it up, tossing it to him.

'Butterfingers.'

He opened the flap, took out a cigarette, tossed the packet back. 'Help yourself,' he said. 'Where was he?'

'I don't know,' Betty said. She was practised in this lie. 'He won't talk about the war.'

She took a cigarette, waited while John struggled with the matches, striking one against the coarse surface, again, again, his hand shaking, his face twisted in anguish.

'Here,' she said, standing up and taking the matches. 'Let me do it. Perhaps you should see a doctor?'

She lit his cigarette and her own, blew out the match, threw it in the empty grate.

'It passes,' he said. 'It's nothing. A trapped nerve. Listen.' He leaned forward, picked up the ashtray from the hearth, balanced it on his quaking knee. 'Why don't we go for a drink? What time do you have to get back? Have you eaten?'

'Questions, questions. Yes to a drink. No, I haven't eaten. And my last train goes just after ten.'

'It's half seven now.' He stubbed out the cigarette, waited a moment, steadying himself. 'Let's go.' He stood up, placing the ashtray on the mantelpiece. 'If you want to use the, you know, lavatory…' He turned red. Why were men so squeamish about those things? 'The bathroom's down the stairs, on the landing below. I share it with my neighbour, Bob.'

She put out her cigarette as he grabbed his jacket and keys and opened the door for her.

She had a lemonade shandy. The pub didn't serve food in the evening, but they rustled up a Scotch egg and a couple of packets of crisps. She was hungrier than she realised and devoured the egg, wiping her mouth free of crumbs, fishing in the crisps for the twist of salt, washing it all down with the shandy, listening to John as he told her about this coffee house he'd found, about his vigil last weekend, about the boys in the school who'd carved the CND symbol on their desks.

'What did you do?'

'I turned a blind eye.' He nodded at her glass. 'Another?'

The pub was round the corner from where he lived, old-fashioned with dark mahogany panels below the dado, the walls ochred with tobacco tar. She watched while John bought the drinks. She'd known him now for five months. Long enough to fall in love, to dream. He was chatting to the barman. He was obviously a regular here. If they went back to the flat, what would happen? They'd never been alone before. She curled her hands, her toes, pulled in her stomach, smiled.

'You look happy,' he said. 'Happier than earlier. Here.' He handed her the glass.

'John...' She leaned forward, pushing her shandy towards his drink. She was tipsy, light-headed. 'For all we know, a bomb could be flying our way as we speak. It would only take a few seconds. We'd know nothing about it.'

'Just as well,' John said. 'I can't think of anyone nicer to be vaporised with. Besides, who'd want to live in a post-nuclear world?' He drained his glass. 'Drink up. Let's go back to my rooms.'

She swallowed. She'd never done it with anyone. Her father had left it to Mrs H to spell out the moral code. *No man likes second-hand goods.* Sex could be brutal, she knew that. She'd overheard Mutti once, in those night-time mutterings when her mother and sister thought she was asleep.

'The marriage act is not like this, Lieselotte. It is a beautiful thing.'

She left her drink on the table. He took her hand again as they crossed the road. It was dark, a clear night. Venus was glowing and other stars were beginning to appear.

'I used to think I could count the stars,' she said. 'When I was little.' Leaning out of her bedroom window with Lieselotte, *You see the Plough? The Bear, Bettechen?*

They climbed the stairs to his rooms at the top, the hot air rising with them. The flat smelled of disinfectant and they laughed as they came in.

'I'll open the windows,' John said. 'All of them.' She watched as he struggled with the sashes. 'Most of the cords have gone.' He took some books from his shelves, wedged them underneath the frames to keep them open. Turned and looked at her and it was a tender look of longing and desire, and when he held out his hand to her, she took it and leaned against him, no need for words.

'Are you sure?' he said.

'Yes.' She nodded. The hell with convention, with prissy primness, *nice girls don't*. 'You're the first, John.'

'I shall be gentle.'

He took her hand and led her into the bedroom as the book slipped from the window frame and the sash tumbled down.

CHAPTER TWELVE

London: July 1958

A hazy London dawn filtered through the bedroom window, the sun casting a faint filigree on her face. She lay still and serene, one arm across his chest, her head tucked in the crook of his shoulder. Her breathing was slow and shallow, feather puffs across his skin, her body limp. He edged out of the embrace, dozy and warm, his shoulder stiff, his hand dead. He caught the scent of her. He would remember this night, this first night with her.

London was quiet on a Sunday, but the early-morning silence was the quietest of all. He guessed it was about six o'clock. He crept out of the bed, wincing as it creaked. Her mouth twitched but she didn't wake, not even as the rusty bed frame brayed and the mattress bounced. She was sleeping deeply, and he was glad. He tiptoed to the door, pulled on his dressing gown and padded down to the half landing below, and the bathroom he shared with Bob. It was on a rear extension, damp and cold, mildew on the tiles and walls. They took it in turns to buy the soap and paper. He had to remember to add Bronco and Imperial Leather to his list this month, remind Bob it was his turn to complain to the landlord.

Back in his flat, the open windows had cooled the rooms, and the smell of the disinfectant had dispersed. He poured himself a glass of water and wandered into the sitting room, slipped off his gown and stood by the open window, letting the air breeze over his naked body. If he looked to the right he could see the portals of the British Museum, the Portland stone of its facade black with soot. He shut his eyes, imagining how it would have looked when first built, the cream edifice glistening as brightly as the Parthenon. A hundred years of London smog had made its mark. He ran his finger along the windowsill. Even now, in the summer, even after the Clean Air Act, fine grit layered the buildings, clouded the air.

A man cycled by and a lone taxi drove past, London's early birds. Or late birds. Worshippers off to matins at St George's. Revellers home from a night on the town. A man rounded the corner of Great Russell Street, sauntered into Bury Place. He wore a cap so his face was in the shade, but the walk was unmistakable. He stopped opposite, looked up. John stepped back from the window, heart racing. His hands grew clammy and the tumbler slipped from his grasp, hitting the lino with a thud, water spilling. John glanced down at the glass, then up and out of the window. The man had gone. John squeezed the curtain back, leaned to one side to see better. The man was nowhere to be seen. Neither right nor left nor straight ahead. How could he vanish into thin air?

He picked up the tumbler, fetched the floor cloth. He hadn't slept well. That's all it was. This time, he *was* imagining it. Besides, he hadn't seen the man's face. It could have been anyone. He imagined too much. Hallucinated. Flashbacks, the doctor called them. He threw the cloth onto the spill, watched as the heavy cotton absorbed the water, changing tone, texture. The man could have crossed the road. Of course. That would explain why he couldn't be seen. He hadn't disappeared at all. John couldn't see anyone on his side of the street unless he hung out of the window.

Footsteps. The laboured thud as someone climbed the stairs. He froze. Had he closed the door? Or was it still on the latch, as he'd left it when he went to the lavatory? He ran towards it. It was shut, but he pulled the bolt across, just to be sure. Ear against the wood. Bob must have left the street door open again. The footsteps had stopped. Were they on his landing? Was the man outside? Was he listening, waiting, ready to break in? Surprise gave the greatest advantage. Ambush at dawn. John's stomach griped. He looked towards the kitchen. Four strides, he'd be there, grab a knife, ready.

The lavatory chain, the rush of water, the tread of a foot on the steps, fainter and fainter, Bob's door shutting. Of course. He breathed in hard, let his shoulders droop. His mind was overactive. It always was when he was tired. He startled too easily. He should sleep some more. That's what the doctor said. Don't overtax yourself. Make sure you get your rest.

He went back to the puddle on the floor, picked up the floor cloth and wrung it out. Coincidence. That man was just coincidence. Who would be up this early in the morning? Anatoly had no business with him. He put the cloth in the bucket under the sink and tiptoed back to bed. Betty had turned over in his absence. He felt at ease, her presence an unexpected comfort. He crept in beside her, cradling her like a spoon, nuzzling his face into her hair. She must have washed it yesterday. It smelled clean, perfumed.

He'd never felt like this before. Not even for *her*. He could never let anything happen to Betty. He would protect her, care for her. Cherish her. His feelings for her had a depth and roundness, a certainty, despite their difference in age. He'd been six when she was born, twelve when the war started. He was just into long trousers, a young man, his father had said.

'Let's hope the war's over before you reach eighteen.'

The war was in its death throes when he was conscripted, but it had still had a final kick in it.

Was that why he felt protective of her? Was it love? Or fear? Was he frightened for her? For what could saunter round the corner and slash her life forever? He propped himself on his elbow, gazing at her sleeping form, the slenderness of her neck and the contours of her body, the grace of her hand on his pillow. He smelled her skin, the lingering of yesterday's soap, the sweet snap of her sweat. It was the smell of happiness. He couldn't bear to hurt her. It wasn't Anatoly snooping at dawn. How could it be? Most likely a market porter coming home from a night on the razzle. Silly that something innocent could still pluck at John's guilt and needle his grief.

He lay back down and shut his eyes, letting his body relax, soothed by her warmth, the softness of her skin, lulled by the rhythms of her breath, the quiet *putt-putt* of contentment. He woke when she stirred, lifting her arm behind her, fingering his head. She turned, buried her face in his neck, her hair tickling his chin. She was wriggling down, kissing him, her hands reaching out and stroking him.

He lifted her hand to his mouth, kissed her palm. He couldn't bear to hurt her. *No.*

'Do you know what time it is, sleepyhead?' He reached over to his alarm clock. 'Nine o'clock.' He had fallen asleep again. She sat up, swung her legs over the side.

'Oh my God,' she said. 'I should get back.'

He couldn't bear to let her go, let her out of his sight. He wanted her scent to trail his, their two shadows as one. 'Half an hour's not going to make any difference. Let me get you breakfast.'

'I shouldn't really,' she said. 'But I am hungry. That Scotch egg didn't do much yesterday.'

'You're in luck.' He ran his finger down her spine, pulled her towards him, nuzzling her back. 'I always treat myself to bacon and eggs on a Sunday. I don't go to church anymore, but Sunday wouldn't be Sunday without a fried breakfast. Do you want a bath?'

'That would be nice. I can't go home smelling of you, after all.' She laughed, pressed her finger against his nose.

He pushed himself off the bed and pulled out a towel from his cupboard.

'It's a bit old, I'm afraid,' he said, passing it to her. 'You can borrow my dressing gown.'

He lifted it off the hook and draped it over her. It trailed on the floor. She rolled up the sleeves. 'Back in a mo.' She unbolted the door. 'Leave it on the latch.'

'Here,' he said. 'Take the key.'

'It's perfectly safe, isn't it?' she said.

He shrugged. 'Sometimes Bob forgets to lock the street door. You never know.'

'Then shouldn't you come and stand guard?'

'You're fine.' He pressed his lips to hers. 'There's a lock on the bathroom door and you have a bird's eye view of the hallway when you come out.' He smiled. 'If there's a strange man there, scream your head off.'

She laughed, but it wasn't funny and he wished he hadn't said that because now, he thought, the street door could be open and the man hiding under the stairs, biding his time. He waited until she was in the bathroom, then ran down to the ground floor. The street door was shut. This, he thought, is ridiculous. His grand-mother kept checking locks, the first sign of her dementia.

He returned to the flat and pulled out the bacon from the back of the food safe. At least the crow hadn't pecked at the foods. He unwrapped the wax paper, took the eggs out of their box, spooned out some dripping. The frying pan was heavy and old, black with age. He lit the gas, watched the fat melt and sizzle, laid out the rashers, poked them with a spoon. Breakfast for two. They could cook while he laid the table, put the kettle on, sliced some bread. He'd fry that up, too. He wondered if she liked pickled onions, or whether it was only him who ate them with his bacon and eggs. Her key turned in the lock.

'Smells good. I'll be back in a second.' She shut the bedroom door. He wanted to watch her dress. How strange to be modest, now. She emerged a few minutes later. She'd rolled her hair into a

French twist, and her skin glowed. She was, he thought, even more beautiful than he dared imagine.

And even more fragile.

'Do you like pickled onions?' he said.

'At breakfast? No thanks.'

He served the food in the kitchen, carried it through to the sitting room.

'I only have tea, I'm afraid,' he said. 'I don't even own a coffee percolator, and I can't stand the instant stuff.' He wondered whether that's what they served in the Partisan.

'Tea's fine.'

She cut a slice of bacon, dipped it in the yolk, swallowed it down. He knew so little about her. How could he love someone he knew nothing about?

'You're not eating?' she said. 'This is delicious.'

He smiled. He was yearning for her already, missing her with a pain too sharp to bear.

'You're very quiet,' she said. 'Eat up. It's getting cold.'

He lifted the bacon onto the bread, placed the egg on top, the way he always ate his breakfast, had done since he was a child. He stared at his plate, at the fat congealing round the edge, at the rind he'd left on the bacon by mistake.

'Penny for them.'

If it was Anatoly he'd seen, then he had to protect her.

'Miles away,' he said. 'Sorry.' He cut into his breakfast, forked it into his mouth, dribbling egg yolk. He reached over to the drawer of the sideboard and fished out two napkins, giving one to Betty, wiping his mouth with the other.

'Forgot the refinements,' he said, adding, 'Must you go?'

'My father will be worried,' she said. 'We didn't leave on the best of terms yesterday, so he probably thinks I've stomped off in a huff.'

'Ah,' he said. 'Now you tell me. London wasn't so spur-of-the-moment after all.'

'I wanted to see you.'

He reached over and squeezed her hand. 'I'm glad you did. What was the row about?'

She avoided his eyes, looked down at her plate.

'Nothing, really,' she said. 'Father-daughter stuff.'

He'd have to tread carefully with him, he realised. Some fathers could be very protective.

'You're looking worried, though.'

'Am I?' he said. 'Sorry again.' He thought fast. 'It's just that I'm a bit behind with my marking. I was thinking how I'll have to work twice as hard today.'

'It's July. Hasn't term ended?'

'Not quite,' he said. 'There were some resits. Plus the "S" level boys. I'll be tutoring them through the holidays. Oxbridge entrance and all that.'

'Ah.' She smiled, wiped her mouth on the napkin and stood up.

'I'll take you to the station,' he said. 'If you've time, we can walk. Have a proper coffee, in Clerkenwell. Leave the dishes,' he added. 'I'll do them later.'

He took her hand as they meandered through the side streets.

'A long way round to St Pancras, I know,' he said. 'But it's one of my favourite parts of London.' He wanted to share this with her, linger with her longer. So many corners of London, so many memories and possibilities.

'Scuola Guida,' she said, reading the signs. 'Portelli Ltd. Organ builders.'

'Little Italy.' He pointed to a delicatessen. 'Come. Proper coffee, not the ersatz stuff they serve in these so-called coffee bars in Soho.'

He took her into the shop, watched as she marvelled at the cut meats and fancy cheeses, the cannoli and bombolone. He ordered two espressos, and they stood at the counter, pouring in the sugar from the paper packets, stirring.

'I had no idea about the Italians,' she said. 'Were they refugees?'

'Some of the new ones maybe,' John said. 'But most have been here for decades. They were rounded up in the war. Enemy aliens. Even though half of them were born here.'

Her face became serious and her voice when she spoke was soft. 'Yes.'

She stirred her coffee with an extravagant intensity.

'My turn to ask now,' he said. 'Are you all right? You've gone very quiet.'

'Sorry,' she said.

'Penny for them.'

'I was just thinking how awful it must have been. Did you ever see *Stromboli?*'

'The film?' he said. 'That was a few years ago.'

'I know. They showed it again when I was at college. That poor woman, the Ingrid Bergman one. What she must have been through. Those DP camps were dreadful.'

He smiled. He loved her tenderness, her understanding, as if she'd been there too. He leaned towards her, took her hand, turning it over, tracing the lines in her palm. A man behind him was ordering a coffee. The timbre of his voice made John turn. The man had taken off his cap, tucked it in his pocket.

'Let's go,' John said. He placed his cup crooked on its saucer so it rattled and tipped to one side. 'You'll miss your train.'

'But I haven't finished—'

He grabbed her hand, leading the way, out of the shop, walking fast. It had been Anatoly, loitering, spying. He had followed them.

'Slow down a bit,' she said. 'I'm getting a stitch.' He gripped her hand. *Never let her go.* 'It doesn't matter what train I get. What's the hurry? You look like you've seen a ghost.'

He had to let her fly, to safety, to freedom. He couldn't keep her, didn't deserve her. And Anatoly would not have her. He'd destroyed once before. It wouldn't happen again. Whatever Anatoly wanted of him now, he'd make sure he kept Betty out of it. He strode on, mulling over the words. She'd think him a cad, and she'd be right. One day, perhaps, they might meet again, and he could explain. *I had to let you go, and this is why.* He could feel his teeth grind against each other, the muscles in his jaw flexing and tightening.

'John, what's the matter?'

He didn't answer, turned into King's Cross Road. Looked behind him. They hadn't been followed, not here.

'Nothing,' he said. 'Nothing at all. Except…' He shut his eyes. He hadn't rehearsed this moment, didn't have the words, the easy patter of the bounder. 'Look, Betty…' He bit his lip, felt the perspiration on his neck. He loosened his tie, undid the button on his shirt. 'The thing is, it won't work.'

'What are you talking about?' He could see the hurt in her eyes. She wasn't making this easy. Did she need him to spell it out?

'You and me. We can't. It…' He wiped his forehead. 'I can't see you again. I'm sorry. This has to end.'

Her mouth made a zero and the tears sprang to her eyes. Her lips began to quiver and he thought she was going to cry. *Please, Betty, no.*

'Is it me?' she said, her voice breaking. 'Is it something I did?'

'No.' He wanted to pull her towards him, hold her tight, wipe her eyes, *it'll be all right.*

'Tell me. I'm really sorry. I won't do it again. I—' She broke off and he saw her struggling for words, her face furrowing. 'I don't understand.'

'It's just me. I'm not a very good person.' He put his hands in his pockets so she wouldn't see them shake, so he wouldn't give in and touch her. 'It's difficult for me. Maybe it's because of the war or something. I can't.'

'Do you want to talk?' she said. 'If it's the war, I understand. Honestly. What people went through, it affected them.'

He shook his head, looking away. He couldn't hold her gaze.

'You can trust me, John. I'll understand, really.' He knew she was searching his face for clues. '*Please*, John. Please, talk to me.'

He couldn't tell her even though her pain sliced through him and left him lame and crippled.

'I don't want it to end.' Desperation caught her voice, choking it. 'I can't bear it.'

He wanted to say, *Nor can I*, to pull back his words, but they were already out, reverberating like bullets in a firing range.

'I love you, John. Please.'

He was shaking his head. He couldn't bear this. He'd never wanted to do this, never planned it, never wanted to make her plead or beg. He looked up, but she was staring at him, her eyes narrowing with fury.

'I thought you loved me,' she said. 'I thought we had a future, you know? That's why I let you—'

He hoped his eyes were saying, *Forgive me, this won't be forever*, didn't see her arm swing up, her hand flatten, but he felt its sting as she slapped his face with such force he fell backwards.

'You bastard,' she said, words whistling through her teeth. 'You utter bloody bastard.'

She kicked him hard in the thigh, turned and ran. Round the corner, out of sight. He rubbed his hand against his cheek, feeling the welts bubble up. There was dust on his trousers where her sandal had landed. He pressed his fingers into his eyes, wanting his world to go away.

CHAPTER THIRTEEN

Berlin: May 1945

'Those stairs,' Frau Weber said, rushing into the apartment, fanning herself with her hand. 'They'll be the death of me.' She paused, taking in a lungful of air, turning to Mutti. 'The thing is. Turns out he killed himself.' She shaped her hand into a pistol and held it against her temple. 'The Führer. Did himself in. Pow! Bang! *Peng!*'

Greta and Waltraud followed her into the apartment. Bette stood in the entrance to the sitting room, one hand on the edge of the door.

'He wouldn't do that,' she said. 'I don't believe you.'

'And the Goebbels. All those beautiful children. Poison. The whole lot of them.' Frau Weber sniffed, pulled out a rag from her sleeve, blew her nose, rolled her eyes.

'*For all of this we thank the Führer*,' Mutti said, but there was something about her voice that mocked the familiar mantra.

'You're lying,' Bette said. 'That wouldn't happen.'

She stomped into the sitting room, slamming the door behind her. It caught the draught from the empty window sockets, shut with a force that made the handles shake. She rushed to the sofa, hid behind it. She hadn't meant to bang the door, nor to be rude to Frau Weber. She'd be in trouble now. She'd say sorry the moment

Mutti came in. The Führer could not have killed himself. He died a hero.

Chairs were dragged in the kitchen and muffled voices filtered into the room. She could hear her mother cough. The door handle clicked, and Greta sidled through.

'Bette?'

'Behind the sofa,' Bette said softly, as Greta crawled towards her. 'Is Mutti cross with me?'

'How should I know?' Greta said.

'What are they talking about?'

'I've been sent to find you and stay with you,' Greta said. 'But I know what it's about. It's about...' She leaned forward, cupped her hand over Bette's ear, whispered, 'Poison.'

'Poison?'

'My mother got some poison, because of Waltraud, you know? She says we'll all be slaves now. That's what it said in *Der Panzerbär*. Under the Russians. And the Americans. They're as bad. She'd rather die.'

'What about you and Waltraud?'

'We'd go with her.'

'What?' Bette said. 'Do you know what you're talking about?'

'Sure,' Greta said. 'It's cyanide. She has a little ampoule of it round her neck.'

'Do you want to die?' Bette said.

She lifted her knees towards her chest and hugged them close. Lots of people were dead, not just the Führer. Others too, people she knew. Herr and Frau Baumann. Tante Winkler. The Müllers. Otto. There were all the extra bodies buried in pits in Friedrichshain Park, as well as corpses she saw in the street. She didn't want to blow up like one of those, have her guts gnawed by maggots, eyes pecked by crows. She didn't know if Oma and Großvater were still alive.

'What would I do without you?'

The door opened and Frau Weber came in. 'Greta, come,' she said.

'Can't she stay?' Bette said. Her mother wouldn't be so cross with her in front of Greta.

'No,' Frau Weber said.

'Are you going to give her poison?' Bette said.

Frau Weber narrowed her eyes. 'What have you been saying, Greta?'

'Nothing,' Greta said. 'We were just talking about the Goebbels family.'

Bette had never heard an outright lie. She wouldn't dare be untruthful to her mother, not even a fib. Perhaps Mutti was right. They were common, after all. Greta scrambled to her feet, walked out of the door, waved her fingers at Bette. She watched as they left, Frau Weber, Greta, and Waltraud, her head low, her feet shuffling. She had lost weight.

She heard her mother shut the front door, her footsteps as she walked across the hall, into the sitting room. Bette stood behind the sofa, staring at her feet.

'I'm sorry,' she said. 'I didn't mean to slam the door like that. The wind caught it.'

'I know,' her mother said, but her voice was weak and she began to cough, a deep, phlegmy rumble. Bette looked up. Her mother was holding onto the door frame with one hand, the other clamped over her mouth. She looked paler than usual. 'I'm going to lie down.'

Bette rushed out, towards her.

'You haven't taken poison, have you?' she said.

'Don't be so silly,' her mother said. 'Go and wake Lieselotte. She has to take care of you today.'

'Why?' Bette said.

'I don't feel well.'

'What's the matter with you?' Mutti was never ill. 'Is it the Führer?'

'I have a nasty cold,' her mother said. 'That's all. A summer cold. They're the worst.' She gave a small, lopsided smile and coughed again, pulling out a rag, spitting into it. 'Go on. Wake your sister.'

Bette stood for a moment, then knocked on Lieselotte's door. She'd never had to do that in the old days, before the Ivans came. It had been her room too, and she could come and go as she pleased.

§

There were chores to do, the apartment to clean, even though there seemed little point, but Mutti insisted it was done every day and Lieselotte said they had to do it as Mutti was ill and otherwise she'd be cross. They used the last of the water to wash through their threadbare towels, then went out to refill the buckets.

A notice had been posted onto the wall.

'What does it say?'

'Just *bla*,' Lieselotte said. 'Looted goods to be returned. Weapons to be handed in, *bla bla*. Execution for anyone harming a Russian soldier, *bla, bla, bla.*' She looked round to make sure no one could hear. 'Chance would be a fine thing.'

'Boris?' Bette said. 'I thought you liked him.'

'I don't like him. But I pretend I do, and that protects us.' She smiled, turned to her sister. 'He keeps the others at bay.'

'But what if he goes away?' She didn't want Lieselotte to end up like Waltraud, because Greta said that it happened again and again, not just that first night, and there was nothing Frau Weber could do. 'What will happen?'

'I don't know,' she said, shrugging, but the pull of her mouth showed worry.

'No, I mean what will happen now? Now we have no Führer and Berlin has surrendered. Is the war over?'

'I don't know,' Lieselotte said. They'd reached the standpipe and Lieselotte filled one bucket, reached for the second. The spring breeze feathered her skin, soft as a bird. Bette turned her face towards the sun to catch its warmth.

'Here,' Lieselotte said. 'Let's go back.' She lifted up her pail, hooked it over her arm. 'Boris said that we Germans did some dreadful things.'

'What sort of things?'

'Destroyed villages,' she said. 'Murdered thousands. Rounded them up and starved them and killed them in cold blood. Jews and Gypsies and all sorts. Thousands and thousands and thousands.'

'Do you believe him?'

Lieselotte looked ahead, taking in the carcass of the street, as if the devastation were new.

'Yes,' she said, her voice soft and fretful. 'Yes. He saw it. Horrific things, beyond imagining. Except we did them, Bette, we Germans. Some of the things he told me, I couldn't repeat to you. They're too hideous, too evil. He says we will be punished. Germany will be punished.'

'So Frau Weber was right? We shall be slaves.'

'Frau Weber is a malicious gossip and a Party member,' Lieselotte said. 'Why else do you think Waltraud was so fat?'

'We could run away,' Bette said. 'Go to Dahlem, find Oma. Is it far?'

'Miles away.'

'Is she all right?'

'I'm sure she's fine,' Lieselotte said. 'We'll go and find her when the war's over.'

They rounded the corner. Boris was waiting for them outside their building. He was holding a bicycle, brushing the back of his hand over the handlebars as if it were a prize mare. He grinned as they drew close, the gap between his teeth dark and moist. The bicycle was large, a man's bike. It must have been kept under lock and key, for the paint was shiny, the chrome gleamed, the tyres were new.

'*Gut,*' he said in his German, pointing at the bike then at Lieselotte. 'You, me. We go.'

Lieselotte shook her head, nodded at Bette. 'Him, and me.' She made cycling movements with her finger.

'*Net,*' Boris said, shaking his head. '*Net.* Dangerous. Thief. Bad man.'

'Please,' Lieselotte said. '*Bitte.* Half an hour. *Bitte.*' She pointed to Boris's watch, painted a semicircle with her finger. 'For my brother.' She pointed at Bette. 'For the boy.' She made a pedalling motion with her legs. 'He needs fresh air. To get out.'

Bette hadn't even thought about a ride, but now Lieselotte had raised the possibility, she wanted to go too. The sun was high and she felt its heat and light, the brazenness of the afternoon. She stepped close to the bike, pointing to herself.

'There.' Lieselotte nodded at Bette. 'My brother will look after me.'

A Russian came out of their building, leaving a puddle of urine in the entrance hallway. He buttoned his flies and saluted Boris. Bette was staring at him, didn't see Vasily come up behind her, hook one arm round her chest and the other between her legs, squeezing. He hoisted her onto the crossbar, holding the handlebars to steady the bike. He was grinning, his face close to hers, pimples bloated with pus. He knows, Bette thought. *He knows.* He pointed to her, to himself and, straddling the bike, took the handlebars from Boris.

'*Nein.*' Bette jumped down, catching him off balance. He put his foot down to stop the bike from smashing on the ground.

Boris shouted at him in Russian, and Vasily shouted back. She couldn't understand what he said, but she sensed the menace, watched as Boris wavered. Please God, she thought, no. She had no doubt what Vasily intended for her, was mapping in her head how to get away when Boris grabbed the bike and, hoisting it over his shoulder, walked into their building and up the main staircase. They usually came up the service stairs, barging through their back door as if they owned the place. Vasily took Lieselotte's bucket and Bette followed behind, watched as Vasily climbed to the apartment, avoiding the broken bits, as if he knew each step and crack by heart, as if he had lived here all his life.

'Where's Mutti?' Bette asked as they entered. She ran into the bedroom. Mutti was sleeping, her breath rumbling, echoing in her chest. Best not to wake her. She heard the door to Lieselotte's bedroom click shut.

She didn't want to be alone with Vasily. His spots made her queasy and she was uncomfortable with him, especially now, now he knew. *He want good girl. Clean girl. You know?* He'd have no qualms about taking her, she was sure, raping her in front of her mother's nose. She slunk towards the front door and opened it without making a sound. Greta. She'd find Greta, sit with her, perhaps play a game of Ludo. Or they could tell stories. Greta knew what was going on. Mutti forbade her to go out alone, but she'd only be a minute. She sidled down the broken staircase, listening, holding her nose. The place smelled like a public lavatory. She stopped. Not a sound. She peered over the broken bannister. Not an Ivan in sight doing their business, or worse.

The back door had long since been removed, so she ran across the courtyard to the Webers' apartment, knuckles poised to rap on their door. She paused. What if Frau Weber had poisoned everyone? What if they were lying there dead and she, Bette, found them? Mutti was asleep and Lieselotte busy, so who could she tell? She thought for a moment. She'd knock, and if there was no reply, tell Mutti. She'd know what to do, wouldn't be cross with her for disobeying as this would be an *emergency*.

No, she told herself. Frau Weber would never dare kill them all. She might have fallen to pieces, like Mutti said, but she wasn't mad. She knocked hard, and called out. There was a screech as Frau Weber dragged the heavy chest of drawers away from the door and opened it a crack.

'It's you,' she said. 'Come in, come in.'

Greta was standing behind her.

'Guess where I've been,' Bette said. 'Just guess.'

Greta raised her eyebrows, and Bette circled her fingers as Lieselotte had done, then leaned on pretend handlebars, lifting her legs and pushing down.

'Dummy,' Bette said. 'I've been on a bicycle.' It wasn't quite a fib, but two could play at that.

It was almost dark when Bette came back to the apartment. Boris and Vasily had left, taking the bicycle with them. There was no sign of Lieselotte, or her mother. She guessed they were both in bed. Bette listened to make sure no one had come up the back stairs when they saw Boris and Vasily leave. She went into the kitchen. There was a slab of fresh butter on the table, some herring and bread. She cut a slice, slapped the pickled fish on top.

She couldn't waste a candle so tiptoed into the bedroom, changed into her nightdress and crept into bed. Her mother's breathing was silent now, but she was hot, hotter than Bette had ever known a person. Hotter, even, than she'd been when she'd had the measles four years ago.

She rushed out of the bedroom to Lieselotte's room, didn't bother knocking.

'Mutti,' Bette said, grabbing her arm and dragging her towards the bedroom. 'She has a fever. Come quickly.'

Lieselotte ran then into the room, felt her mother's forehead.

'Frau Weber,' she said. 'Fetch Frau Weber. She was a nurse. She'll know what to do.' It was dark now, not quite curfew but too late to be out. Bette pulled on her trousers and shirt and ran to the door. She felt her way to the staircase. It was dangerous at the best of times, but in the dark, who knew what could happen? She tapped the broken steps with her toe, listening. A step, a rustle. A stone fell. Bette jumped. Something ran across her foot. She choked back a scream, feeling for the wall. A scuttling. Her heart was hammering hard and she froze. Nothing. The building was silent, the street noises muffled. A rat. It was probably a rat. Or a ghost. Greta said that there were ghosts in the building. Bette felt dizzy, her breath thin and light. She wanted to climb back up, find her sister. *No.* Step by step. What if an Ivan was hiding in the shadows, grabbed her from behind, hand over her mouth, hand between her legs, like Vasily? *Clean girl.* She breathed in, tensed, counted the steps one by one, silent feet, no sound, no loose stones, hands on the wall walking her along until she knew she was on the ground floor. She ran through the opening, across the yard, hammered on Frau Weber's door.

'Frau Weber. *Kommt. Kommt. Schnell.*' She tried the handle, but the heavy furniture was blocking it from inside.

'*Frau Weber? Wo sind Sie?*' She could see that the apartment was in darkness. What if— She screamed, hammering on the door. 'Frau Weber, Frau Weber.'

She heard the furniture dragged back and the door opened a crack. Frau Weber peered through.

'What are you making this racket for?' she said. 'What's the matter?'

Bette began to sob. 'It's Mutti,' she said. 'Mutti.' She could say no more.

'A moment.' Frau Weber yanked Bette through the half-opened door, pushed her along the hall and into her room. Greta and Waltraud were in bed and the old grandmother was on a chair, her feet propped on a stool. Frau Weber pulled off her nightdress and stood, naked, while she grabbed her frock and tugged it down over her body. Bette stared. Mutti never did that sort of thing. She opened the door a fraction, sidling out, grabbing Bette with one hand, and they ran across the courtyard, stumbling up the steps, into the apartment. Lieselotte had lit one of the candles Boris had brought and had placed it on the table next to her mother's bed. Mutti was asleep, her breath cracked and strangled. Her lips looked blue in the flickering light.

Frau Weber went across, felt the forehead.

'Aye, yeh,' she said, shaking her hand. 'How long has she been like this?'

'We just noticed,' Lieselotte said. 'She seemed all right before.'

'She wasn't that ill,' Bette said. 'She just said she had a cold.'

'Water,' Frau Weber said. 'And a cloth.'

Lieselotte and Bette rushed to the kitchen. Bette grabbed a towel and the bucket, as Lieselotte filled a jug and lifted down a glass from the shelf.

'Will she be all right?' Bette said. 'What's wrong with her?'

'How do I know?' Lieselotte snapped. They came back into the bedroom. Even though the day had been warm, the night air was cold.

'Should we get a doctor?' Lieselotte said.

'It's curfew,' Frau Weber said. 'You'll get shot. Besides, what can a doctor do? We have no medicines.'

She dipped the cloth in the water, wrung it out, clamped it onto Mutti's brow. She pulled back the bedcovers, but Mutti arched, her mouth frothing, her arms flailing. Lieselotte screamed.

'Be quiet,' Frau Weber said, rolling Mutti onto her side, dipping the cloth in the water again, wiping it round Mutti's face and neck. 'Do you have an aspirin?'

Lieselotte shook her head.

'Fetch another cloth. Sponge her down.' Lieselotte ran out, returned with another towel.

'Is she going to die?' Bette said.

Frau Weber clamped her mouth in concentration. She grabbed the towel from Lieselotte, soaked it in the water and covered Mutti's body, dabbing as her mother grasped for air, her throat rattling and growling at the same time.

'She has pneumonia,' Frau Weber said. She looked up from her task, at Lieselotte, at Bette. 'She's very ill.'

Bette felt the tears prick her eyes, heard herself whimper. Lieselotte came over and put her arm round her, pulling her close.

'What can we do?' Lieselotte said.

Frau Weber shook her head. 'Have you heard from your father?'

'No,' Lieselotte said.

'We don't even know where he is,' Bette said. 'That's what Mutti told us. Top secret.'

'Top secret, eh?' Frau Weber smirked. 'She may pull through,' she said. She lifted the cloth from Mutti, dipped it in the water. 'I have to go. I can't leave my girls.' She handed it to Lieselotte. 'Keep sponging her. I'll come back in the morning.'

She walked around the side of the bed.

'Lock the door after me,' she said.

The candle burned out and Lieselotte fetched another.

'This is our last,' she said, lighting it from the embers of the old. It flickered in the breeze from the empty window, but stayed alight.

'We're running low on water,' Bette said, wringing out a cloth, wiping her mother's face. 'I wish Frau Weber had stayed with us.'

'Well, she didn't,' Lieselotte said.

Bette felt as if her blood had turned to oil, was flooding through her veins, heavier than grief.

CHAPTER FOURTEEN

Berlin: July 1945

The springs were soft and the mattress hard, but at least the old police barracks were undamaged and John had the room to himself, small though it was. There was a cupboard for his clothes, shelves in one half, hanging space down the rest. The previous occupant had left his roster on the inside of the door. Three nights on, two days off. Night shifts. Not for the faint-hearted. He'd had to work through the night more than once, took time winkling out the details in the Walterwerke and everywhere else he'd been sent in the last few weeks. Physicists, John thought, are not the most garrulous of men.

A small table and hard-backed chair nestled under a tall casement. The room was stuffy, needed some air. John opened the window. The thin yellow curtain blew inwards, tangled itself around the edge of the frame, caught on the latch, but the breeze was welcome in the July heat. He could hear a bird singing. There was a shrub not far away, and there in its thickets John could see the outline of a nest. A blackbird was entering the tangle of leaves and branches, a worm in its mouth. *Fledglings.* He liked that idea. In a landscape of soot, a baby blackbird was learning to sing.

He put his kitbag on the bed, pulled out his service dress and hung it in the cupboard, sorting the rest of his clothes and placing them on the shelves. At least here they'd have their laundry done, have cooks and a proper mess, running water and lavatories. Luxury after the sessions on the roads and bivouacs and billets along the way from Normandy to Berlin and all stops in between. He'd been run off his feet in Kiel. They all had. Navy. Air Force. Rockets, torpedoes. *Blimey.* The Germans might not have the A-bomb, but they could *deliver*, at speed, long-distance, on target.

He should write to his parents. They'd be worried sick about him, and he couldn't put it off any longer. He pulled out a notepad and pen from his bag and sat at the table.

So sorry I haven't written for a while. I've been a bit busy. What he did was top secret, so he couldn't say anything about that.

'Nothing goes beyond these four walls, is that understood, Lieutenant? Your job is to translate, and to forget.'

'Yes, sir.'

Gravity, friction, velocity. Equations churned and concepts swirled like rapids in a flood. Exhaust, propellant, combustion. No wonder his head reeled at night. *And I'm rather tired.* He paused, not sure what else he could write. *Germany is finished. Difficult to see how it can recover from this.* He hoped that would pass the censor. *Everywhere you go are defeated people, and displaced people and refugees.* His parents wouldn't have any sympathy for the Germans. If truth be told, nor did he or any of his men, not after Belsen. Or Celle. Finding all that evidence, those terrible experiments, and now they were in Spandau, where it had begun. G-agents. Tabun, sarin. Odourless. Tasteless. Deadly. He couldn't write that, either. *We're glad the war is finally over, though there's still a risk of hotheads who won't give up, taking potshots — so-called Werewolves carrying on behind our lines. I lost one of my corporals that way, but the rest of us escaped. No need to worry, though. That's all in the past.* He paused, chewed the end of his pen. Better not say that at all. His mother would go frantic. He screwed up the paper and began again.

It's a bit of a doddle now. Even a bit boring. Can't tell you how much I'm missing home, and Sunday lunch. Roast lamb with all the trimmings. Apple crumble. Promise me you'll make me that when I'm next on leave, even if it isn't a Sunday. He looked at his watch, checked the time. *In Berlin now. I have a day's leave tomorrow so plan to see a bit of the sights with my sergeant, an amiable Londoner called Arthur. We'll be here some time so it will be nice not to be on the move. Need to go now. Your loving son, John.*

An hour to kill before dinner. He'd welcome a bath, or even a shower, but there was a rota and his turn wasn't yet. He took his towel and walked along the corridor to the bathrooms, turned on the tap in the basin and watched as it spluttered and spat until a steady brown drizzle came out. He splashed water over his face, under his arms, across his chest, behind his neck. Cat's lick, that's what his mother would call it. Still, it was better than nothing.

He dried and dressed and wandered out into the grounds. If there had ever been gardens here, it would be hard to know. What might have been beds filled with marigolds or snapdragons were now buried beneath contours of dirt and neglect. The single shrub in which the blackbirds had made their nest was standing, but that was all, apart from buddleia pushing its way through the rubble. The lime trees had survived, though, their leaves in the flush of early summer, unfurled and brilliant. They were in full bloom too, their scent overwhelming with sweetness and promise. He breathed in, letting the fragrance fill his lungs, blowing out the fetid decay that wafted from the Spree, filling his nostrils with its cloying, suffocating stench. He understood now why they'd carried posies before their noses in the Middle Ages. It couldn't stem death, but it could hide it. He'd hoped that here, in Spandau, the smell wouldn't be so bad. He knew the town had taken its toll of bombing and killings and guessed the river had swallowed more than its fair share of corpses.

He leaned against the corner of the barracks building, one boot up against the wall, pulled out a cigarette and lit it, sucking the smoke deep inside and letting it snake out through his nostrils. A silent, solitary moment. Precious few of those in the army.

§

John and Arthur sat in the rear seats, another lieutenant, a new conscript like John, in the front with the driver. They bumped their way east on the pitted roads. Remnants of pillowcases and sheets, ripped and grey, still hung from windows or were strung on balconies. *Surrender.* One or two buildings had makeshift American flags sewn together from scraps of cloth. They were coming into Charlottenburg. There were still potholes. Some had been filled by the sappers, but it was a thankless task. The armoured vehicles churned them up again sooner than you could say Jack Robinson. A couple of Humbers passed by, bigwigs, John guessed, on their way to Spandau. Either side of the boulevard were large turn-of-the-century apartment blocks. Tree-lined avenues led away from the main street. It was random, John thought, what had been flattened, what survived, as if the war had been a tornado scooping up streets, sparing others. He spotted a crude cross. *Grave no 21.* A little further along there was a small earth patch with garish red markers, topped with a white star.

'Russians,' Arthur said.

John grabbed the sides as the driver swung round the corner into a landscape of brick stumps and stone hillocks. Women were in a line, digging at the scree, passing it along, one pail at a time.

'They get fourpence ha'penny a day,' Arthur said. 'To clear it.'

Arthur kept his ear to the ground, picked up intelligence that would float past others. It was one of the many things John admired about his sergeant. He looked at the straggling line of women balancing on rocks and stones, handing down the buckets of rubble, one hand to the next. Their dresses were faded and frayed, the hems uneven, their headscarves tied tightly. Some wore socks inside their shoes but many, John could see, had bare legs smeared in dust. He thought of the temporary graves, of the bloated bodies in the rivers, of houses resting in their ashes. He could see no hope. Where did these people live? So much was destroyed.

The women made no sound as they worked. Pedestrians walked without a word. It was as if defeat had swallowed language. An American jeep drove past them, its engine jarring in the mortuary quiet. Their vehicle veered left again, crossed a canal, barbed wire marshalled on its banks. All John could hear was the throb of their engine, the crash of gears. Not a birdsong, or the buzz of an angry wasp, no rustle of leaves or the bark of a dog. The great city was mute.

Ahead of them was a large space.

'Tiergarten, sir,' Arthur said. 'More like Teargarden.'

At the end was the Brandenburg Gate. The Baedeker guide in the school library was dated 1923. It showed imposing classical buildings embracing Pariser Platz, the French and American embassies forming one arm, the Academy of Arts and the Adlon hotel in the other. Through the archway, the finest avenue in Berlin. *Unter den Linden.* John knew the guidebook patter off by heart, knew the place as sure as if he had been a native of the city.

'They built big in Berlin, sir,' Arthur said. 'Fuck-off massive, if you'll excuse the French.'

Their jeep drew close and John peered through the arches. The corpse of a lorry sat where it had died in Pariser Platz, cushioned in the rubble. The buildings either side were headless, gaping holes where their features should have been. Wire and bricks had been pushed to the side and more women were shovelling and clearing. The British victory parade was in three weeks. He swallowed hard. Difficult not to think that the Germans had brought all this on themselves.

They turned to the right, drove on past stumps of trees, what had once been a great forest, John recalled, pictures from the school

Baedeker clear in his mind. Now the landscape was flat and bleak, broken by vegetable plots, and beyond that the ghostly silhouette of the Reichstag, the ribs of its glass dome buckled against the sky.

'Breaks my heart, that does,' Arthur said, turning away from the Reichstag and pointing to a battered sign pocked by artillery fire. *Zoologische Garten.* 'I take it that means zoo.'

John furrowed his eyebrows. 'Don't get me wrong, sir.' Arthur spoke quickly. 'It's not on a par with Belsen and all that. I'm not even comparing it. But, you know, it used to be a great zoo, one of the best…' He dried up, sat in silence.

'I'd always wanted to see it, that's all, sir, since I was a nipper,' Arthur said, his voice soft. 'To think they built a flak tower here. That the Nazis held out here.' He swallowed. '*Here*, of all places.'

They were moving left again, the spindles of a church tower before them, its nave caved in, buttresses bare against the void. They turned down another wide street, and the jeep stopped.

'Where are we?'

'Kurfürstendamm, I guess,' Arthur said. They clambered out, the buildings here little more than bare knuckles on the ground. Music was coming from one of the cellars. John recognised it. 'Rum and Coca-Cola'. The harmonies of the Andrews Sisters. Exotic. American. A group of Yankee soldiers with cropped hair and khaki uniforms came towards them, six abreast, arms on shoulders, veering left, right, swinging, singing. 'Rum and Coca-Cola'. There were some British soldiers standing on the opposite side of the road in their battledress, champagne bottles in their hands. They cheered as the Americans passed, held out their bottles, whistled 'Colonel Bogey', sang.

> *Hitler has only got one ball.*
> *Göring has two, but very small.*
> *Himmler has something sim'lar,*
> *But Goebbels has no balls at all.*

After the silence of the journey the Kurfürstendamm was brazen in its noise. An RAF sergeant appeared, his blue battledress dusty. He stood, arms akimbo, puffing his pipe. They were all, John noted, lower ranks. Triumphalist. He felt uncomfortable, but Arthur was grinning.

'After what this lot have been through, sir, they're entitled to let their hair down. Don't judge them. They're brave lads.'

There was something about the Yanks, though. They had a swagger that singled them out. Bigger, too. We look stunted, John thought, skinny runts. He felt a tug on his sleeve and looked down. A young boy stared at him, eyes sunken and round, face pasty and gaunt. His mouth was pinched tight with broken lips and snot ran from his nose. He was holding out a small, grubby hand. His shirt was too big for him, his trousers too short, his knees too bony. His shoes had no laces.

'How old are you?' John said. He spoke in German, and the boy smiled.

'*Zehn.*' Ten.

He looked much younger. The army said no fraternisation, but this was a child. John fished in his pockets, gave him two cigarettes.

'Take them to your mother,' he said, patting him on the head. The boy tucked them into his shirt pocket, grinned at John and ran off. John watched as he skipped and jumped over the holes and stones. An older boy approached the lad. John hadn't noticed him, saw him hold out his hand and the younger one take out the cigarettes and place them in his palm. An older brother. How sensible.

'Street Arabs,' Arthur said, standing beside him and watching the scene. 'I bet that big lad's running a right racket. Send out the pathetic ones to pull at the heartstrings. He'll be coining it in.'

'I thought it was his sibling,' John said.

Arthur laughed. 'Oh my, sir, you're still not versed in the ways of the world, are you?'

John's CO had said Arthur was too familiar with him, had instructed John to reprimand him for talking to a superior without due respect. John was damned if he was going to bawl Arthur out for impertinence.

'That's why I need you,' he said, instead. They turned their backs on the boys, walked along the street.

'Now,' Arthur said. 'First rule.' He kicked a stone out of the way, held up his hand. 'Basic exchange. One cigarette is worth five marks. Tobacco costs us nothing in the NAAFI. So if you have, say, two hundred cigarettes…' He paused and smiled. 'You can do the arithmetic. Result? We live like kings.'

'But there's a sign,' John said, pointing to a notice posted on a ventilation shaft. 'Says no goods from NAAFI or PX to be traded. It's written in German too.'

'Well I never,' Arthur said, eyes wide and innocent. 'Perhaps that's just a suggestion, sir.'

An old man was coming towards them, a child's bicycle tucked under his arm. His clothes were shabby, but John could see they had once been good. Perhaps he'd been a professional man, a teacher or a doctor. Arthur stepped forward, pointing to the bike. The man held up his open hand and balled it into a fist, again and again.

'*Fünfundzwanzig Mark.*'

'What's he say, sir?'

'Twenty-five marks.' John smiled, added, 'Current exchange rate, five cigarettes.'

'My little lad would love this,' Arthur said. He looked around him and John followed his gaze. Milling among the soldiers were men and women carrying bulging cloth bags, or cradling goods wrapped in paper. One had a queue in front of him, a battered suitcase on the floor, was lifting out candlesticks, a coffee-pot. Barter and exchange. It was, John thought, like the Forum.

'What d'you think, sir? Is it right?'

'Don't ask me, sergeant,' John said. 'Ethics go to the wind at times like this.'

Arthur put his finger on his lip, frowned.

'*Zwanzig*,' the old man said, closing and opening his hand four times.

'Twenty,' John said. 'He thinks you're haggling.'

'I wouldn't do that,' Arthur said. 'I'll pay a fair price. I don't want loot.' He breathed in. 'I've never seen my son, but I can imagine his face at this. I expect his own boy's grown out of it, got a bigger bike. How d'you say that in German?'

The man looked up at Arthur, then John, his eyes rheumy and grey. He hadn't shaved for some days and his chin bristled with sharp white hairs.

'Here.' He fished out his cigarettes and handed five to the man, lifted the bicycle and hoisted it onto his shoulder.

'*Danke.*' The old man held out his hand, and Arthur shook it.

'The market decides,' Arthur said. He laughed, nodded towards the man with the suitcase.

'But that lad over there...' He pointed to the bigger boy that John had spotted earlier. 'Capitalist accumulation. He hasn't lifted a finger. I rest my case. Here we are.' He tucked the small bicycle under his arm and dived down some steps into a cellar. Above him, a painted blue sign had been nailed to the ruins. The Blue Angel.

'I'm told it's the best of the dives.'

Der Blaue Engel. He'd watched it in the sixth form, in love with Marlene Dietrich, and now here he was, in Berlin. He hummed as he followed Arthur down the steps into the cavern below. *Falling in love again...*

CHAPTER FIFTEEN

Berlin: July 1945

Bette wrapped Mutti's dressing gown round her when she went to sleep at night, buried her face in her mother's smell, let it seep through her blood and course around her heart and lungs. The scent was fading now after so many weeks, but if she sniffed hard, Bette could catch its echo. Lieselotte had cut up a black slip and made armbands for them. Not that it mattered. Everyone in Berlin had lost someone and no one took notice anymore.

The day after Mutti died, Lieselotte had had to report to the Rathaus, along with Waltraud and Frau Weber and all the other women in their building. She said that the Russians were taking everything they could lay their hands on, not just watches. Machinery and cars, rail tracks and cables, engines and presses, and the women had to scavenge for the scraps left behind so they could be loaded up and carried away too. Convoys of trucks stalling under the weight, teetering with the height.

She came home that day, sat on the stool staring at the service door with the broken lock and the kitchen chair wedged against it. Her clothes were dusty, the seam of her shirt ripped, her eyes puffy and grey. The days were long but the evenings were balmy. The gas had even come on for an hour, and there was a rumour that the S-Bahn would be working. Perhaps the water, electricity.

'Do we have food, Bettechen?' she said. 'Can you prepare it tonight? I'm exhausted.'

'What were you doing?' Bette said.

'Rubble. We have to clear the rubble now.' She leaned forward, her head in her hands. 'Stood in a line passing stones from the front to the back. All. Day. Long.' She looked up, half smiled. 'Why is it always the women who have to pick up the pieces?'

She stretched her arm across the table, squeezed Bette's hand. They looked at each other. Nothing said, nothing needed. Lieselotte's fingers were chafed and raw and Bette wished they had some Vaseline to rub into them. The sound of an accordion wafted through the open window.

'What's that?' Lieselotte said.

'A squeeze box,' Bette said, shrugging.

'No, listen. What's *that?*'

Tread upon tread, echoing through the well of the service staircase. First flight. Second. Lieselotte groaned.

'Oh no,' she said, shutting her eyes. 'Please God, no. Not again.'

'Hide,' Bette said. 'I'll say you're out.'

'He'll find me. Then he'll be angry.'

Boris walked in through the service door. He was clean and freshly shaven, his uniform pressed, his cap brushed, its visor gleaming. His boots were blacked and shined, and he wore a pair of leather gloves. The sounds of the accordion drifted up through the opening. Vasily had been left outside. Boris removed his cap when he saw their armbands, held it against his chest, his head bowed.

'Sorry,' he said in his accented German. He pulled out a chair and sat at the kitchen table. He hadn't visited since the bicycle episode, the night Mutti died, and that was nearly four weeks ago.

'Perhaps he's gone for good,' Lieselotte had said.

'Will you get another wolf?' Bette said.

Lieselotte had shrugged. 'If necessary,' she said, adding, 'It wasn't easy.'

'What did you have to do?' Bette said.

Lieselotte had ground her teeth, nostrils flaring. 'What do you think? Let him rape me. Again and again and again.'

She gave a queer smile. 'I told him at the beginning he was the only one, made him feel important, told him to keep me for himself.' She'd wiped her nose with the back of her finger. 'Deep down, he's a halfway decent man, Bette. He kept us alive.'

Bette hadn't told Lieselotte that Vasily *knew*, that she lived in fear of him returning. There was too much else to worry about, too much sadness to bear. Grief hung over them like a vapour and they breathed it in with every lungful.

Boris carried a rucksack. He put it on the kitchen table and lifted out pickled fish and bacon, sausages, butter, cheese, a freshly baked loaf. They'd had little to eat since Mutti had died, rye bread, groats, rotten potatoes, a broth that Lieselotte had made from nettles and dandelions and a rib from a dead horse they'd found, its meat long since scavenged. Lieselotte had had to give the man at Friedrichshain Park the rest of Boris's sausage and herring for space in the communal grave, before they could lower Mutti into it. They'd wrapped her body in blackout paper.

Bette tore at the bread, broke off some cheese, gave it to Lieselotte, did the same for herself. She didn't care where it came from. Boris sat, nodding, waiting. Then he beckoned Bette over and put his arm round her shoulder.

'Man of house,' he said, pulling her towards him. For a moment she thought he was going to kiss her, that Vasily had told him. He delved into the bag again, took out a revolver and placed it in her hand. The gun was cold and heavy and Bette shrank away, shaking her head. She wanted nothing to do with it.

Lieselotte stepped forward. 'He's too young,' she said, taking the pistol from her and placing it on the table.

Boris shrugged. 'Bad men,' he said, ignoring Lieselotte, nodding at Bette, holding his arm out straight and pointing two fingers. He smiled, added, 'Luger. German gun. *Gut, ja?*'

All weapons had to be handed in, that's what the notices said. Boris was giving them one. Did that make it all right? Or did he want them caught? Everyone in the building would be punished if it was found, not just Bette.

'Your sister,' Boris said. 'You protect her. Bad men. Sometime Russian bad man.' He gave a crooked smile, pushing the gun towards her. 'For you.'

Bette picked it up. It was heavy, cold to the touch, its barrel cloudy with greasy fingerprints. She held it with two hands, lifted it to her nose, sniffing sulphur and the empty smell of steel. She'd never been that close to a gun before, able to lift it, breathe it. She rubbed her finger along the barrel, down the smooth wood of the grip, studying the trigger and the springs and toggles of its mechanism. She laid it down again, eyeing it while Boris rummaged in the bag once more, fishing out two heavy bolts and a screwdriver. He took off his jacket and walked over to the service door, pulled a pencil from his pocket, lined up the bolts and marked out the holes. He made a line of screws which he held between his teeth, took them out one by one, fixing them in place.

When the bolts were secured, he pushed them to, straightened up, bowed. He threaded his arms through his jacket, fastened the newly polished buttons, buckled the belt and stood to attention. Bette wondered why he was doing this. He'd never paid so much attention to his dress. He picked up his gloves, slapped them on the back of his hand. One was dark brown, the other a lighter tan, and the cuff of his shirt was frayed. She wanted to laugh, the *victor* trying to be all proper when his gloves didn't even match and his shirt was tattered.

'I leave now,' he said. '*Danke, Fräulein.* I will not forget you.' He picked up his cap and put it on. 'You marry me, yes?'

He walked out into the hall, paused by the door.

'My friend, Vasily,' he said. 'Very clever man. He lieutenant now. Big man.' The front door clicked shut behind him.

§

The steps leading to the attic were not as broken as the ones lower down, though the wooden bannisters and handrail had been ripped out over the winter and the plaster had fallen off the wall in places when the bombs had shaken the building. The stench wasn't as bad up here as nearer the ground.

Lieselotte opened the attic door and unlocked their storage space. The light cast a dim beam along the floor. Bette let her eyes adjust. They hadn't been here since Mutti had packed away their precious things, wrapped them in newspaper, sealed them in suitcases and hidden them under the broken chaise longue. She half expected them to have gone, the space to have been broken into, splinters and rubbish spewed across the floor. But it was as they'd left it. Dusty now from the ash that filled the city air, dull and unloved.

Lieselotte pointed to a shape at the back. 'That's it,' she said. 'Careful how you step.' She walked over and pulled away the dust sheet which Mutti had wrapped around it. 'Help me. It's too heavy to carry by myself.'

She lifted one side and Bette stepped forward and took the other. They sidled out of the space, and through the attic door.

'Sideways down the stairs,' Lieselotte said. 'One at a time.'

Step by step, to their landing.

'You stand guard,' Bette said. 'I'll fetch the records and lock up.'

She left Lieselotte on the landing, ran up the stairs to the attic. The records were in a box with a handle. Mutti used to dust them each week, taking out the black shellac discs and wiping them with a damp cloth. The holder was heavy and Bette knew the records would break if she dropped it. She flipped it open. Mutti had organised the music into sections. Ballet, dance, folk. Lieder, opera, orchestral. Each in alphabetical order, artist or composer, concerto or symphony. She lifted out the ballet and opera, the orchestral and lieder, and stacked them against the wall. The container was lighter now, and she could lift it. She locked the attic and heaved the box, a step at a time, to her landing, into their hallway, and the sitting room, two hands on the handle, *careful with your back, Bettelein, use your thighs*. Then she and Lieselotte carried the gramophone and placed it on the table between the window frames, where it always used to sit.

'Now what?' Bette said.

'Now we see if it works. You can choose the music.'

Lieselotte took out the handle and wound it up, checked the needle and blew on it, like Mutti did, *for the dust*. Neither she nor Lieselotte had been allowed to use the gramophone in case they scratched the records or put them back in the wrong place. Bette bit her lip. Everything they did spoke of Mutti. She lived in them still, filling her dressing gown with her smell, their bed with her shape. Sometimes Bette saw her in the cracked mirror in the bathroom or glimpsed her in the street. She had found Mutti's mother-of-pearl hairbrush which she'd hidden from the Russians, and used it every day, her hair rising with her mother's static. She wiped her nose with the back of her hand.

She plucked out a disc. 'Bimbambulla'. It had been a favourite. A foxtrot. Mutti said that after their performance, the corps de ballet would go to a cabaret, or to the Theater des Westens, watch Josephine Baker. *Can you imagine, Bette? A negro? In Berlin? Ach, damals...!* Sometimes the principal ballerinas came too. That was before, she always said, before That Man. Bette wiped her sleeve around the record, lifted the arm, placed the disc on the turntable, lowered the needle and waited. There was a moment of crackle before the music started.

'Now,' Lieselotte said. 'Stand so, feet together, then on your toes. I'll tell you what to do.'

'How can you dance?' Bette stood stiff and lumpen as a stone. 'How can you be happy?'

Lieselotte lifted the needle off the turntable and waited until it stopped spinning. She swallowed hard.

'I'm not happy, Bette,' she said. 'I'm not dancing because I'm happy. You don't understand.'

'Then what's this all about? Are you going to sell it?'

'Sell it?'

'It's Mutti's,' Bette said. 'We can't sell it.' Her voice choked. She almost said, *She'll want it when she comes back.*

'No,' Lieselotte said. 'Dancing classes.'

'Dancing? Classes? You?'

'Mutti taught us how to dance.' Lieselotte tried to sound superior. 'Waltz, foxtrot, quickstep. Tango.' She lifted herself onto her toes and turned a pointed foot to the right. 'Polka.'

'And who wants to learn to dance?'

'Actually,' Lieselotte said, 'this was Mutti's idea. She said to get people's minds off the war, the bombing. She said it was up to the women to make a new life.'

'Who will pay you?'

'We won't charge much,' Lieselotte said. 'We'll take food and cigarettes, marks, even those Russian marks. Anything.'

She started the record again, moved forward. 'Slow, slow, quick, quick, slow.' She grabbed Bette's arm, kicked her knee so she moved backwards. 'Slow, quick, quick.'

'Ouch,' Bette said. 'Do it on your own.' She walked out of the door, stomped into the kitchen.

'I didn't mean to hurt you.' Lieselotte was standing in the doorway.

'People will know we have a gramophone,' Bette said. 'And then what? They'll find a way in, steal it. Besides, my tummy aches.' Hunger hurt, gripped her guts in sharp talons, twisted them into tight skeins.

'Mine too,' Lieselotte said.

Boris had kept them alive these last weeks, bringing them food, supplementing their rations. *I'll fight my way.* Bette understood now what Lieselotte had done.

'I've another idea,' Bette said.

§

They struggled down the steep stairs from the attic, back to the apartment, laid the suitcases in the sitting room, opened them.

'Be careful,' Lieselotte said. 'It's Mutti's Meissen.'

Bette unwrapped a figurine, a small bird. 'I always loved this one,' she said. 'Mutti wouldn't let me touch it. She said it was too valuable.'

'It costs a fortune,' Lieselotte said, revealing a cake dish with a porcelain lace surround, purple and yellow pansies and butterflies painted in the centre. 'I know Mutti loved this. She always used it, do you remember? When Oma came to visit. She'd make an apple cake. Somewhere here...' She felt the packages in the suitcase. 'Somewhere there are the silver pastry forks.'

'Where shall we put it all?' Bette said. 'In the cabinets again?'

Lieselotte stared into the suitcase as if her look could reveal the contents, but Bette saw her sniff.

'We can sell it.'

'No.' Bette grabbed the paper again, shawled it round the figurine. 'No. This is Mutti's.'

'We have to,' Lieselotte said, her voice calm. 'We have no money.'

'No.' She clutched the package close to her. 'You can't.'

'It's only porcelain. They're only things.'

'No,' she whimpered in that grizzly tone that Mutti never tolerated. *Tears get you nowhere.* She stopped, paused. '*My* idea was to sell the clocks.'

'But they're Vati's.'

'Vati's not here,' Bette said. 'He's probably dead.'

Lieselotte rocked back on her heels and looked up at Bette. Dusk was approaching and the room was dim. Bette couldn't see her sister's face, not clearly, but she heard her take a breath as if she was about to speak.

'The clocks,' she said. 'I didn't think about Vati's clocks. They can't be hard to find in all this.'

'You see,' Bette said. 'I do have some good ideas.'

They both reached towards the remaining suitcase, each took out a package.

'I wonder why he collected clocks,' Bette said, unwrapping a small mantel clock. He had taped their details to the backs of them. 'He used to have this on his desk.'

'Perhaps it wasn't the most valuable,' Lieselotte said. 'Because he kept the others under lock and key in the cabinet.' She paused, smiled, ripped off another wrapping. 'Do you remember this? *Kienzle. Designer: Heinrich Möller. 1933.*'

'I never liked that one,' Lieselotte said. 'Just too modern.'

'Nor me,' Bette said. 'Its face is cold and empty.' She lifted a small brass carriage clock. 'I preferred this. And wasn't there one that showed the phases of the moon?'

They both leaned forwards into the suitcase and for a moment Bette felt light-headed, as if the sorrow from Mutti was flowing away and the anguish which had sat in her bones was leaching out. They could sell the clocks. She hated every one of them. If her father came back, she'd ask him, *Where were you?* They'd start with the Kienzle clock.

'Tomorrow,' Lieselotte said. 'I'll take it tomorrow.'

They bumped their heads as they rummaged and laughed, the first time since Mutti had died. Stopped. Hammering on the back door, shouting. Bette froze. They hadn't heard them climb the stairs. Soldiers. Russian soldiers.

Lieselotte began to shake, her face crumpling, her blood filtering away. Bette had never seen her sister so frightened.

'Where's the gun?' Bette whispered.

Lieselotte pointed to Mutti's bureau, her hand quivering. 'Secret drawer.' She clamped her hand over her mouth, shaking her head, eyes wide in terror.

Bette crept to the bureau. They used to play with the secret drawer all the time. She knew the crannies where the latches were hidden, the sequence to be pressed and pulled, but her fingertips were damp and the latches slipped. She could hear Lieselotte whimpering behind her, the soldiers yelling and hammering outside. She wiped her fingers on her trousers, played through the sequence again, *please, please work*, and the drawer swung open. Bette pulled out the gun, turned round. Lieselotte was not there.

She looked behind her. Lieselotte stood on the window frame, filling the empty space.

'No,' Bette said, her voice quavering with fear. 'Come away.'

The soldiers were kicking the door, their voices loud, coarse. Bette guessed they were drunk.

'I'll shoot them,' she said. 'I will. Don't jump. Don't go.'

She wanted to cry, *Don't leave me*, but her heart was pounding too hard to say a word, to think at all. She crept into the kitchen, holding the pistol in front of her, two hands, finger on the trigger as Boris had mimed.

The soldiers were shouting. *Fräulein.* Vulgar guffaws and belches. *Hure.* Whore. Bette was standing in front of the door. If they broke in, she'd shoot. Point-blank. Grab Lieselotte, run.

There was a sound of laughter, of water running. A trickle of urine seeped under the door. They hammered again. Bette heard them talk, heard their tread as they went back down the steps, their banging on the service door of the apartment below them. She didn't know who lived there now. So many people were bombed out, strangers moved in anywhere, like hermit crabs into empty shells.

The bolts had held. Bette ran back into the sitting room. Lieselotte was crouched on the floor, vomiting over Mutti's Meissen. Bette went over to her, knelt down next to her, laid her head against her sister, fear and grief punching like a fist from the earth. And hunger. Such hollow, angry hunger.

CHAPTER SIXTEEN

Berlin: July 1945

Life was routine, humdrum even, and John was glad for that. It had been tough on the road but now he was collected each morning and taken to Spandau prison, delivered back in the evening. The interrogations tested his vocabulary, but he had a good dictionary and was able to correct the transcripts afterwards, writing in the margins, reproduced *in triplicate*. Admiralty orders. Bloody bureaucracy. He wasn't sure how Arthur was deployed, but their paths hadn't crossed so often in recent days and the sergeants' mess was a ten-minute distance from his own. He missed his company.

It was early evening, the summer air hot and sticky, thick with flying ants. Sure sign of a storm. His brain buzzed with formulas and impacts. Walking helped clear his head, even if it was just around the barrack grounds.

'Well, sir, good to see you, sir.' Arthur stopped, saluted.

'What are you doing out, sergeant?'

'Thought I'd stretch my legs,' he said, smiling. 'As a matter of fact, sir, I've got a bit of news.'

'Oh?' John batted an ant, caught it on the back of his hand, slapped it hard.

Arthur pulled out his cigarettes, offered the pack to John, took one for himself and lit it, dragging hard before he looked up and smiled.

'My demob papers have come,' he said, cupping his cigarette in his hand, holding it behind him. Smoke furled through his fingers. John was silent for a moment, gathered his wits.

'That's wonderful news, sergeant,' he said. 'When do you leave?'

'Not long after the Victory Parade. Just under two weeks. I'm counting down the days.' He smiled, added, 'You won't see me for dust.'

'I think this calls for a celebration,' John said. He should be smiling, sharing the joy, but he felt as if his guts were drawing tight, grabbing him hard. Arthur was the only friend he had here, even though he was an NCO.

'I'd like that, sir,' Arthur said. 'We could go back to the Blue Angel, if you like.'

'The Blue Angel it is, sergeant. This time the drinks are on me. Tomorrow?'

His liver wouldn't survive another night drinking with Arthur, but he'd make the effort. He owed much to his sergeant. In the distance, he heard the rumble of thunder and the first few gobs of rain splattered on the ground.

§

They sat at a wooden table, a magnum of champagne on the side. Arthur's chair was tilted on its back legs and he was grinning, his thumbs in his waistband. His lighted cigarette lay on the ashtray, a thin column of smoke winding its way to the ceiling.

'I'm not under any illusions,' Arthur said, blowing through his lips. 'It's not going to be easy, back home. Never met my son. Haven't seen my wife for years. Don't know my own home. They moved. Couldn't take the bombing. He lifted the cigarette and tapped the ash. 'I know the address well enough, but I couldn't tell you the way to my own lavatory.'

He laughed. He was slurring his words. John felt his own slip too.

'But I heard today, sir.' He swung his chair forward, landed with a jolt, poured another glass of champagne. 'I've matriculated. Six subjects.' He drew his cigarette to his mouth again, sucking the smoke deep into his lungs, added, 'Distinction in the whole bloody lot of them.'

'You did *what*, sergeant?'

'Ma-tric-u-la-ted,' Arthur said, pronouncing each syllable with fervour.

'That's what I thought you said.' John stretched out his hand and Arthur grabbed it in a clinch, shaking it hard. 'That's fantastic. Well done. How did you do it? When?'

'Correspondence courses, sir. University of London. Couldn't believe my luck. Never thought I'd have a second chance. Kept it quiet, just in case, you know?'

'You've every right to brag now,' John said. 'You must be very proud.' He lifted his drink. 'Here's to you, sergeant.'

'And all who sail in her.' He clinked his glass against John's. 'Hello?' he said. 'Who've we got here?'

John turned. A young woman was approaching their table. Her hair was tucked inside a scarf tied in a turban, her face was soft, with clear, even features, her body lithe and petite, like a ballet dancer. She was, John thought, the prettiest girl he had ever seen.

Arthur was beckoning John to lean forward, elbows on the table.

'Bit of fatherly advice, sir. Don't even think about her. Or any of them. They're riddled with it.'

'Riddled?'

'Syphilis. VD. You name it, they've got it.'

The young woman approached their table, stopped, smiled, nodded. '*Guten Abend*.'

Arthur flicked his hand without looking at her. '*Nein*. Not interested.'

She looked puzzled, turned to John, lifting a string bag and placing it on the table. She pulled out a package wrapped in newspaper and laid it down carefully, opening it up. A clock. Modern, simple, elegant, an unfussy face with Roman letters and a chrome base.

'*Das ist sehr schön,*' he said. 'Beautiful. Don't you think, sergeant?'

Arthur had leaned back in his chair again, rolling his eyes.

'*Sie sprechen gut Deutsch,*' she said.

'*Danke.* Thank you,' John said, continuing, 'But it's very formal, very old-fashioned. My everyday German is non-existent.'

She shrugged. 'You need to practise, that's all.' She pointed at the clock. 'Would you like to buy it?'

The slender clock hands stemmed from a simple disc in the centre of the face. John turned the clock round to reveal the mechanism at the back.

'*Eine Acht-Tage-Uhr,*' she said.

John whistled. 'Eight days, eh? Does it work?'

She pointed to the hands, and John checked his watch.

'It keeps perfect time,' she added.

'Is it Bauhaus?'

Arthur was scowling, shaking his head. John ignored him. Anyone could see they were talking about a *clock*.

'You know about the Bauhaus?' She seemed surprised.

'Not much,' he said, thinking fast in his stilted, formal German. 'Form follows function and all that. Seems like that clock embodies it all.'

'I agree,' she said. 'It is for sale, if you'd like it.'

'Really?' It was, John thought, perfect in its simplicity and honesty, with its smoked glass front and silvered surround, its neat, discreet mechanism. 'How much?'

'One hundred marks.' Everything in this city was bought and sold for a hundred marks. It was, John thought, *nothing.*

'I could give you five cigarettes,' he said.

'Haggle,' Arthur whispered. 'It's a bloody awful clock. Not worth it.'

John pulled out his cigarettes and, counting out five, gave them to the young woman.

'*Danke,*' she said. 'Thank you.' She handed him the newspaper she'd wrapped it in, took the string bag and stuffed it into the pocket of her skirt. She turned to go but he found her presence alluring, magnetic even.

'Sit for a minute,' John said. 'Have a glass of champagne.'

'*Nein, danke, kein Champagner,*' she said, shaking her head as she pulled out a stool from beneath the table and perched herself on the edge, holding her knees together, tugging her skirt down and tucking it under her thighs.

'What is your name?'

'Lieselotte,' she said.

'Lieselotte who?'

'Just Lieselotte. And yours?'

'John.' He stretched out his hand. 'Lieutenant John Harris, and this is Sergeant Arthur Gambol.' She turned and nodded at Arthur, who shook his head, mouthed, *No fraternisation.* She was thin, her arms lean, her neck frail. He could see the jut of her collarbone beneath her blouse, the frame of her hand beneath its skin. Her fingernails were broken, the cuticles torn and black. He wanted to ask if she picked stones with the other women. She seemed too fragile for such work.

'Can I offer you a sandwich?' John said. 'A ham roll?'

She hesitated.

'*Nein, danke,*' she said. 'I must get back.'

'And where are you from?'

'Berlin.'

He wasn't sure she wanted to talk, and yet she had taken a seat. She didn't have the air of a streetwalker, though John wasn't sure he'd recognise one anyway. She was, he guessed, about his age, a little younger perhaps. There was a serenity about her that he couldn't fathom. Was it a calmness? Or numbness? Was she sad, or solemn? She needed food, a good square meal. He had an overwhelming urge to find out about her, how she came to be here, selling her clock, sitting on the stool beside him with her skirt wrapped around her thighs. He wanted to know all about her, to know *her*.

'Why don't you teach me German?' he said, words crashing out before he'd had time to think them through.

'You speak German.'

'Conversational German. I'll pay you. A hundred marks an hour.' She breathed in sharp, her dirty hand across her mouth, eyes wide. She neither smiled nor scowled. Arthur drummed his nails on the tabletop, coughed.

'I have no classroom,' she said.

'Who needs a classroom? The summer is here. We can walk and talk.'

'Just walk and talk?'

'Yes.' He put his hand across his heart. 'Yes. Promise.'

She frowned, thinking. He wondered if she always did that, frowned when she thought. She didn't answer. Please, he thought. *Please*. He didn't want to push her. *Say yes*. She seemed brittle, as if a decision would crack her in two. He had to see her again, even if it meant buying every clock she sold.

'Where shall we meet?' she said at last.

'Here,' he said. 'Tomorrow. Sunday. We could talk all day.'

She smiled. 'Not here. Not on the Kurfürstendamm. In front of the Brandenburger Tor. I will be there at six o'clock in the evening.' She pushed herself up. 'For one hour. *Auf Wiedersehen, mein Leutnant*. Until tomorrow.'

She walked out of the cellar, her skirt loose on her hips, the slender bones of her ankles swallowed in the heels of her shoes.

'Don't say I haven't warned you, sir,' Arthur said. 'She's trouble.'

'No, sergeant.' John shook his head, rubbed his hand round the circular rim of the clock. Arthur snorted, tapped the side of his nose.

'Watch yourself.'

§

Russian soldiers patrolled the Brandenburg Gate, squinting into the late sun, with dusty boots, forage caps, rifles under their arms. These soldiers were dark, squat, looked Asian, from Turkmenistan or somewhere like that, but then, John reasoned, the USSR was a big place. It was just before six, and the evening was hot even in the late afternoon sun.

Arthur had grumbled at first. 'I'm not going to be your bloody chaperone,' he said, 'while the pair of you jabber in German. Nor a bloody wallflower if you take her behind the bushes.'

'It'll only be an hour,' John said. 'Promise. I'll buy you a beer. You know the regs as well as me. A soldier alone is fair game.'

John didn't want to walk too close to the Russians, though he had his papers secure just in case. Arthur stood near enough to make it clear John wasn't alone, far enough to give him space. He wasn't sure which direction she'd be coming from or where she'd be waiting for him, so he positioned himself some yards from the tower. It was badly damaged, he could see, bullet holes and cracks. The statue of Nike was toppled, her horses hobbled, broken stumps on the pediment. More like the apocalypse, John thought, *conquest, death, pestilence, famine.* A suitable metaphor.

He could see through the arches to Pariser Platz and, beyond, Unter den Linden. He craned his neck but there was no sign of her. Most of the rubble had been cleared and a small band of women were sweeping the loose debris. To the right were the ruins of the Adlon Hotel. Buddleia were already poking through, profiteering from the dust like flies from a corpse.

For as long as he lived, John thought, he'd never see buddleia as anything other than the opportunists of nature. A creature jumped and disappeared beneath the broken bricks and mortar. A rabbit? More likely a rat. Of course, she probably wouldn't come, was stringing him along. Arthur would be happy. He'd give her ten minutes.

A young woman emerged, balancing on the mounds of scree. She was carrying a jug. He watched as she stepped onto the even ground of the square, heading towards the gate. It was a while before he recognised her. The scarf had been removed and her hair hung loose in chestnut swags. She wore the same skirt and blouse as yesterday, was pulling out the string bag from her pocket, pushing the jug inside it.

She walked through the side arches and saw him. He waved and walked towards her as she began to run.

'*Guten Abend*,' he said. 'No need to rush.' He reached out for her bag but she clutched it tight, her face colouring in a blush. John felt awkward, unsure what to say. Such an odd thing, to *have* a conversation. She didn't look pleased to meet him.

'I'm so glad you came,' he began. 'Where shall we walk?'

She pointed towards the Tiergarten.

'What should we talk about?' John said. The obvious topic was the war, but that was the last thing that could be mentioned. The central boulevard was closed, so they skirted to the left. Out of the corner of his eye he saw Arthur follow.

'Whatever you want,' he said. 'Anything.'

They walked on in silence. This, he thought, was not a good idea. He heard her take in breath, as if she was to give a speech.

'When I was a child,' she said, 'I used to come here with my parents. My grandmother lived in Dahlem and she'd take the U-Bahn to Tiergarten. I could run around while the grown-ups sat in in the café with their coffee and cake.'

She stopped and pointed at the landscape.

'It used to be a beautiful park.' She sighed, as if to apologise, pointing to the crops that had been planted and the trees that had been felled. 'But we have to eat, we have to cook and keep warm. Beauty is a luxury we can't afford.' He wondered what she thought now, about Hitler and his dream. So many of the scientists he talked to said politicians came and went, what did it matter to them? It was science they valued.

'Where are your parents now?' John said.

She looked away. Her shoulder blades were sharp against her blouse, the vertebrae on her neck neat jacks stones in a row. When she looked back, there were tears in her eyes.

'It doesn't matter,' she said. 'I cannot talk about myself, please. *Bitte.*'

John wondered what they could talk about if not themselves. Apart from the weather, there was nothing that seemed neutral.

'How old are you?'

'Eighteen.' She paused. 'And a half. And you?'

'Eighteen. And a half.'

They laughed. Her teeth were uneven and her lips cracked but her smile made creases in her cheeks, the hint of a dimple.

'When is your birthday?' she said.

'February. The nineteenth.'

'Mine too.'

He laughed as she gave a grimace of recognition and he reached for her spare hand, shaking it.

'What are the chances of that? Sharing a birthday.' This was, he thought, fate. He was excited, relieved too. Now they had something to talk about. 'Tell me how people celebrate birthdays in Germany. Do you sing *Happy Birthday?*'

'We have a birthday song,' she said. She opened her mouth. '"*Hoch soll er leben.*"' Her voice was light and clear, supple as a fiddle. She sang the words. The tune was catchy and he tried to sing with her, a word behind, a beat too late.

'Perhaps,' he said, 'there are songs we have the same, could sing together?' He liked the idea of singing with her. 'Ah. I know.' He opened his mouth, hummed first, then sang. 'Silent Night'. It took five bars, and she was singing with him, walking round the outer path, in harmony, in step.

'I have another Christmas song,' she said. 'I can teach you all my songs. It's a good way to learn language. A new way.' She opened her mouth. He knew this tune too. 'Twinkle, Twinkle, Little Star' by any other name.

She turned, her eyes glistening, as if the music had lifted a weight, breathed life and energy into her. 'This is fun,' she said. 'Let's sing.'

He wondered what else to sing. The school had had a good choir, but the repertory was classical. Even the folk songs were *composed*. He wasn't sure he wanted to start on the Messiah, or the *St Matthew Passion*. Seemed a bit sombre for a first encounter. He turned, checked. Arthur was a discreet distance behind them.

'I have a song,' she said. 'We would sing it as children.' He'd seen film of the Hitler Youth on the Pathé newsreel at the cinema before the war. He could hear the commentator: *These happy boys and girls are marching to the* 'Horst-Wessel Lied'. *Raise the flag, they sing, the ranks tightly closed! They certainly put our Boy Scouts to shame...* Had she been a member of the Hitler Youth, or whatever the girls' equivalent was? Perhaps this was not such a good idea.

'*Muss i denn...*' she began. '*Muss i denn...*' Hand on her heart. He wanted to reach out, to catch her crystal voice and let it echo in his memory, to hold her hands and draw her close. She was wonderful, this young woman, swathed in sadness and enigma. Perhaps love felt like this.

'*Tanz mit mir, Johann?*' She stopped singing, put down her bag with the jug. She curtsied, held her skirt wide and pointed her foot. He could see how she arched it, even inside the shabby lace-up shoes with the flapping sole. Her eyes were glassy, her cheeks flushed.

'Pom-pom, *polka*,' she said. '*Eins, zwei, drei. Eins, zwei, drei.*' She held her arms in front as if she were embraced by a partner, dipping, whirling, her skirt mushrooming round her legs, her hair flying behind her like a peacock's train, tripping off the path out of sight into the shrubby bushes at the edge of the park, the skeletons of the spindly trees behind silhouetted against the pinking sky. She was entrancing, mesmerising. He couldn't see her, she had gone.

'Lieselotte,' he called, searching, trying to glimpse her. 'Lieselotte.'

He turned to Arthur but he stood with his back to John, hunched as he lit a cigarette. She rounded a corner, came closer to him, breathless, her breasts rising and falling as she gasped the air.

'Dance with me, *Johann*. Dance. *Tanz*.' She grabbed his hands and swung his arms, her eyes shiny and wild. Her fingers were moist, electric, delicate. He wondered if she wasn't touched in the head, if Arthur had seen this when he hadn't, her moods swinging so fast from sombre to exuberant. She twisted away from him and he caught the odour of her perspiration, the must of her dusty hair as she pirouetted round and round, fast as a dervish, arms outstretched, eyes focused, round and round, her feet in their clumsy shoes rising and falling and turning in time to the deep rhythms in her head.

She stumbled, fell panting to the earth.

'I'm a little giddy,' she said. 'But I was an angel, was I not, *Johann*? A hummingbird? A butterfly?'

She was sweating, beads of moisture on her forehead and nose running down her neck, her thick hair tangled and matted. He thought she might be ill. It wasn't normal to sweat so much.

'Perhaps,' he said, 'I should take you home?'

She pushed herself up on her elbows.

'That won't be necessary,' she said. John held out his hand and she pulled herself up, brushing down her skirt, picking up her string bag with the jug and clutching it close.

'I found it,' she said, pointing. 'A little chipped, but useful.'

She shuffled on her feet. 'Shall I give you another lesson?'

'Is it over for today?' He looked at his watch. It had been an hour. She had her eye on the time and he was wounded.

'*Johann*, are you all right?'

He nodded. 'Yes,' he said. 'I'm fine. A little bewildered. But yes, another lesson would be good.'

'I let myself go,' she said, wiping her hands across her cheeks. 'For one hour, I let myself go.'

'That's all right.' He shrugged.

'When shall we meet then?'

'Next Sunday,' he said. 'Same time? Same place?'

She shook her head. 'No. Not here.'

She thought, puckering her brow.

'They blew up Lichtensteinbrücke,' she said. 'But I've heard the razor wire has gone, and perhaps we can walk along the banks of the canal. It's quiet.' She nodded, sombre once more, and pointed with her finger. 'It's just down there, down that street that leads from the gardens.'

'Let me walk you to the Tor.'

'No,' she said. 'It's all right.' She stood for a moment, added, 'You have to pay me.'

'Sorry,' he said. 'I forgot.' He felt the hot grasp of a blush as he fumbled for the cigarettes. *How stupid of him.* She put them in her pocket, turned, swinging her bag with the chipped jug, walked away. He watched as she grew smaller and smaller.

Arthur stepped forward, took his elbow.

'Let's find a bar,' he said. 'Before a redcap sees us.'

Round a corner, out of view. She hadn't looked back, not once.

CHAPTER SEVENTEEN

London: July 1958

There was an empty bench outside the station and Betty crumpled onto it, her toes still throbbing from the kicking she'd given John, her lungs tight from running. She shut her eyes, memories shifting through her mind, montage after montage. Had he grabbed her as he fell, or when she ran past him? He had been alive, hopscotch over the body, terror thundering through, fast as a train, driving her on. A trolley bus trundled past, its engine silent, its poles sparking on the overhead wires. She stared at it, batting away the angry ghosts scrambling from the wastes of her past.

She lifted her knees up against her chest, held them tight, sobbing. Anger began to billow, and with it a burning rage. She unravelled her arms, pushed them straight out, hands close together, two fingers stretched and pointing. Blood was on the floor, splattered on her shoes, a bloody handprint on her calf where he'd grabbed her.

'Bets.' A woman's voice. 'Betty. Is that you?' Someone was shaking her shoulder and Betty looked up. 'Bets, it is you. Are you all right?'

Betty blinked, stared. 'Dee?' Behind the woman were two small boys in short grey trousers and white shirts, holding hands. 'Dee?' She shook her head, memories falling and reshaping like pick-up sticks. She put her feet back onto the ground, sniffed a dribble from her nose. This was London, summer 1958, not Berlin 1945. *Pull yourself together.*

'What are you doing here?'

'More to the point,' Dee said, 'what are *you*?' She sat down next to her. 'It's been years, Bets.'

'I was thinking only yesterday that I'd give your dad a ring, get your new address.'

Dee brushed the hair from Betty's face. 'What's happened? You look terrible.'

A small, tender gesture. Betty leaned forward, tucked her head against Deirdre's shoulder, felt Dee's arms circle her and rock her gently. She pulled away, wiped her cheek with the back of her hand. What could she say?

'I've just been jilted,' she said.

'Thought you wanted to kill someone just now,' Dee said. 'From the look on your face, and the way you were pointing your fingers.'

'I did,' Betty said. 'I really did.' A Luger. He'd played dead, like a snake. 'I kicked him so hard, my foot hurt.'

Dee laughed. 'Well, good for you, Bets. I hope you got him where it matters.' She clamped her hand over her mouth, looking at the small boys standing in front of them, staring. 'Whoops.' She pulled a face. 'Young ears flapping. What are you doing here?'

The memories were slinking away, leaving footprints, debris. She sat, still, *collecting* herself. Picking up the broken bits, fitting them together, putting them in place. A jigsaw of her life. She'd just knocked her boyfriend for six. Half an hour ago, not half a lifetime. She was sitting outside King's Cross station with trolley buses passing by and her oldest friend beside her.

'I was on my way home,' Betty said, breathing out, turning to Dee, smiling. 'Where are you going?' She hadn't seen her for years but it was as if they had never parted. Fate, that's what it was, Dee being here.

'Taking the kids to see my dad,' she said. 'Duty visit. Are you still living in Hatfield?'

Betty nodded. 'Unfortunately, yes. You?'

'No,' Dee said. 'Me and Kevin are buying a little house in Willesden. It's only a semi, three bed, but it's ours.'

'Buy?' Betty said. 'You've done well for yourself.'

'Everyone wrote us off, me and Kevin,' she said. 'But he's a qualified electrician now. Earns good money, and once the kids went off to school, I trained as a nurse. You haven't met my boys, have you? Here.' She tugged at the biggest one's sleeve. 'Say hello. This is Auntie Betty. This is Graham, and this little tiger is Martin.'

Betty smiled at them. 'They're lovely boys,' she said. 'You must be proud.' Dee was the only friend she knew with children. Hearing herself being called 'auntie' was a shock.

'Mmm,' Dee said, her face stern for a moment, before she smiled and winked. 'Sometimes. What train are you catching?'

'I don't know,' Betty said. 'It doesn't matter.'

'Well, we're heading for the 12:10,' she said. 'So why don't we go together?'

Dee was a proper adult, with a job and family and mortgage. She was taking charge and Betty knew that Dee would always take charge, that when the chips were down, Dee would know what to do. The nuns, her father, everyone, they'd all been so wrong about her at school. Dee was a stalwart, shoulders like Atlas.

They had the carriage to themselves. The boys grabbed the window seats and Dee produced two comics, a bag of crisps and a bottle of Tizer.

'Now I want you two to sit quietly while I talk to Auntie Betty,' she said. 'Because I haven't seen her for years.'

Betty and Dee sat on the corridor seats, side by side, thighs pressed against each other.

'Tell me about the bastard.'

Betty swallowed, memories close to the surface once more. Her eyes filled with tears and her hand trembled. She hadn't thought about that *other* moment, not since she'd been in England. Locked away in the dungeon of her mind. She couldn't tell that to Dee. Perhaps she had more in common with her father than she wished to acknowledge.

'You don't have to, of course,' Dee went on. 'But you know, a problem shared and all that.' She groped for Betty's hand, squeezed it again.

'Did you sleep with him?' she said. 'Give yourself to him, as Sister Monica would have said?' She took a breath, pinched her mouth, fumbled with an imaginary crucifix. '*Well, girls, if a man tries it on, think of St Maria Goretti. Pray to her...*'

Betty laughed.

'You were always brilliant at taking her off,' she said.

'That's why she loathed me,' Dee said. She grew serious. 'And the pig got what he wanted and now he's dumped you?'

Betty groped in her bag and pulled out a handkerchief. She blew her nose, dabbed at her eyes. Kev had married Dee, done the decent thing, stuck by her.

'It didn't feel like that, Dee,' Betty said. 'It really didn't. Something suddenly happened and he—' She broke off, added, 'He went all funny, turned. Said it wouldn't work.'

'Is he married?'

'No.'

'Sure?'

'No.' Added, 'I'm pretty confident he isn't.' She shifted, looked at Dee, eye to eye. 'And now I've got to face my father and I'm not sure I've got the stomach.'

'Don't tell him,' Dee said.

'I don't plan to tell him,' Betty said. 'It's not that.' She fiddled with the handkerchief, twisting the corner, spinning it between her thumb and finger. 'We had a row and I stomped off. He'll expect me to grovel but I'm damned if I will.'

'What was it about?'

'Oh, Dee.' She sniffed hard, stifling tears. 'I wish I could tell you.' Her voice quavered. 'I can't. I...' She leaned and grabbed Dee's hands, turning them over, looking at the palms. 'I don't have the words.' How would Dee understand? She'd only ever known Hatfield.

She let go of Dee's hands, fingered the hem of her skirt. 'To be honest, I can't take much more of him. We've never got on, but what can I do? I can't move out. I can't afford it on my wages. They wouldn't even cover some sordid bedsit in Westbourne Grove.'

Dee was silent for a moment. 'Are you serious?' she said.

'About what?'

'Moving out? Only we were thinking about taking in a lodger but Kev said the room was too small. It's only a little box room, really, above the hall. The estate agents called it a bedroom.' She pulled a face. 'But they would, wouldn't they? There's just about room for a single bed and a cupboard. A small chest of drawers. It's not great, but if you're interested...' Her voice trailed off.

'Interested? Of course I am. Are you sure Kevin wouldn't mind?'

'Positive. He always liked you, Bets. I mean...' Dee paused, pulled a face. 'Honestly, the room's no bigger than a cell. Couldn't swing a cat. We wouldn't charge much because it's, well, it's not really commercial, is it, between friends? Or being so small? Perhaps you could babysit for us instead, pay your bit of the bills, rates, that sort of thing. Perhaps a token rent. We'd have to share the kitchen, obviously, and the bathroom, if that's all right.'

'All right?' Betty said. 'It sounds perfect. When can I move in?'

'As soon as you like. Why don't you pack your things and I'll meet you at the station? I'm getting the 5:20 back.'

The train was slowing down, the fields giving way to suburban gardens, to red-brick buildings, to the station. Hatfield.

'Right, boys,' Dee said, 'up you get.' She turned to Betty. 'I'm serious.'

'I don't know if I'll be ready by then, Dee,' Betty said. 'I'll try, but you know, if my father kicks up a fuss, it might take some time.'

'Then just leave.' She smiled. 'Here.' She delved into her bag, pulled out a diary and a pencil tucked in its spine, tore out a leaf and wrote something down. 'My address. We don't have a phone but my neighbour has, so if you ring this number...' She pointed at the paper. 'She'll pass on a message. If you're not here this afternoon, come whenever you can. Give me notice so I've time to make the bed.'

'I'll bring my own sheets,' Betty said. 'Towels. I won't be any bother. Do my own washing.'

'I should bloody hope so, Betty Fisher,' Dee said. 'I don't have a housekeeper, I'll have you know.'

Dee used to tease Betty that she was rich, with a housekeeper and a garden and her father's pre-war Daimler. They'd both lost their mothers, but Dee's father mothered her, and Betty envied that.

'No hanky-panky, either,' she added, grabbing the boys by their hands. 'There's our bus. See you later.'

Yesterday was so very long ago.

§

The house was quiet, stuffy in the summer heat, as if it had been closed all day. She walked into the kitchen, spotted a note on the table. *Dear Betty. How dare you behave like that to me?* She breathed in sharply. *Until I receive an apology, I neither want to speak to you nor see you. I have never experienced such ingratitude...* Breathed out. The effrontery of the man, the insensitivity, the sheer, bloody stuffed-up Prussian arrogance of the man. She screwed the note up, hurled it across the room, where it bounced against the side of the sink and tumbled to the floor. Well, he needn't see her. The feeling was mutual.

She stomped upstairs, yanked a couple of suitcases from the top of the cupboard in the box room and dragged them into her bedroom. She pulled the sheets off her bed, folded them roughly, placed them in a pile. She didn't have many clothes, but she was damned if she was leaving them here. Shoes, nylons, underwear. Skirts, blouses, jumpers. Dresses, swimsuit, towels. Books. Her books. She laid them on top, shoving them in, wrenching the suitcases shut. She left the tutu with the sequined straps. He could have that, serve him right. Her lips twitched. The press of his thumb as he wiped the lipstick away.

They were too heavy to carry so she bumped them down the stairs, chipping the wainscoting. Tough. Luck. She'd have to get a taxi. Her father kept a cash box in the kitchen cupboard. The bastard could pay. She took out a ten-shilling note, went into the hall, rang the taxi number. Eight minutes. Perfect.

She supposed she should leave her father a message but not tell him where she was. The crumpled note was on the floor so she picked it up, smoothed it out. *Mrs H has very kindly asked me over for dinner*, he'd written, *and to go on an outing with her tomorrow (Sunday). If you wish to say sorry, you know where I am.* No, she wanted to write, I do not wish to say sorry. She grabbed the pen that he'd left on the table. *I have moved out, so you never need to see or speak to me ever again until you apologise to me.* He knew where she worked, so he could send *his* apology there. She underlined *you* and *me* so there was no mistake. The taxi sounded its horn. She should have added, *I hope you and Mrs H are happy. You deserve each other*, but there wasn't time and she wasn't sure her father would understand the irony.

§

Even with the pair of them dragging the cases, it had been a struggle to get up and down the stairs in the station, then the Underground, changing platforms and what have you.

'Where are the porters when you need them?' Dee had said. Graham and Martin tried to help but really, Betty thought, they made it worse. They piled into a taxi at Willesden Junction, the boys wide-eyed at the extravagance of it all.

'I'm frightfully rich,' Betty said, winking at them.

'You'll rue the day you said that,' Dee said.

Kevin was waiting for them, bear-hugged the boys, pecked Dee on the cheek, shook Betty's hand then took her suitcases and carried them upstairs. The room was tiny, the cupboard too large, the chest of drawers old-fashioned.

'You can paint it if you want,' he said. 'Make it your own.' He put the cases on the floor, shook his hands. 'What on earth do you have in them? They weigh a ton.'

'Books,' Betty said. 'Sorry.'

'Well, tea's all ready,' he said. 'I've made enough for you too.'

She wasn't hungry but she was drained, relief rinsing over her in waves.

'If you'll excuse me,' she said, 'I'll unpack and call it a night.' She crept up to her room, made her bed, tumbled into it. She'd need to buy hangers, lining paper for the drawers, odds and bobs. She'd forgotten her toothbrush. Little things.

They'd agreed a rent and ground rules on the way home.

'That way,' Dee said, 'we know where we are.'

When had Dee become so wise and sensible?

§

Betty took after her father, built for sport, not ballet. She'd played netball at school, hockey at college. She had time now she lived closer to work. Perhaps she should join a team, take up a hobby, go to talks and lectures. Dance. Sing.

'Plenty more fish in the sea,' Dee said. 'You could try the Hammersmith Palais.'

'Give me a break,' Betty said. 'Let me get over John first.' Trying to fathom what had happened, that was the hardest. If they'd not being getting along she could have understood it, even though seducing her and then abandoning her was unforgivable. But out of the blue? From heaven to hell in five seconds? Hadn't even stopped and written her a letter.

Both Dee and Kevin were members of the Labour Party, so Betty babysat on those nights, reading *Tribune* and *Peace News*, checking out the meetings close to work or close to home. There was a women's campaign that made the front pages. Diane Collins, asking 'What can women do?' Join the campaign, wear a badge, write to MPs, make one new contact a week…

Why is it always the women who have to pick up the pieces? Lieselotte had been fading from her memory but sometimes she sprang from nowhere, vibrant and vivid with her little dancer's feet like Mutti and her thick chestnut hair that Betty loved to brush and plait, when Lieselotte let her.

There was an advertisement for a journal called the *Universities and Left Review* and Betty bought a copy in Dillon's, reading it on the Tube back to Willesden. Their offices were in Carlisle Street and she thought she could try her hand at writing for them. She could start with a letter, since they said that's what they wanted. Discussion. She had time now, and one or two ideas, though they probably weren't good enough as everyone who wrote for them seemed awfully clever. They were all men, too. But they were young and even though she hadn't gone to Oxford, she did have a degree and she was a woman and, well, she wanted to write about that, about the women's side of things, as no one considered that. Not about peace, not about how they'd just been left to pick up the pieces, like Lieselotte had said.

Nobody answered the phone when she rang, so she thought she'd pay them a visit. It was a coffee bar. She checked the address. This was 7 Carlisle Street. She was in the right place, but this was the Partisan Coffee House. Perhaps they'd moved. The new people might be able to tell her where. She pushed open the door. There were young men and women sitting around tables, chatting or reading. Someone had a portable typewriter and was working on it. It had the air of a club, though there'd been no bouncers at the door. The place was packed, the rumble of conversation punctuated by laughs and in the distance the sounds of a skiffle band rehearsing. It was nothing like the espresso bars around them, reminded her of the cafés in Berlin that she remembered from before the war, the ones Mutti had dragged her to when she went to meet her friends. It had the same buzz, the same hum of people spending time, and although the decorations were nothing like the ones there, Betty could see they were well designed, and tasteful and probably rather expensive. Nor, Betty thought, were the clientele remotely similar. This was as far from the Berlin bourgeoisie as it was possible to get. This lot were bohemian. Probably believed in free love and all that. In fact, on reflection, it was nothing like the Kranzler Café or the Bauer.

She walked over to the counter. 'Excuse me.' The server was a young woman with a smiley face. 'Do you know where the *Universities and Left Review* have moved to?'

'*U & LR*? They haven't moved,' she said. 'They're on the top floor. But they're all at a meeting now.'

'When will it be over?'

'Oh, you can go up,' she said. 'It's the Direct Action Committee. All are welcome.'

'Direct action?'

'Ban the bomb and all that.'

'I'd be interested,' Betty said. 'Where do I go?'

The waitress pointed to the staircase and Betty threaded her way through the tables and up the wooden stairs to a large room on the floor above. Like the café, it was full of young men and women, the air thick with smoke, the table littered with coffee cups and papers, and there in the middle of the table was a model made from papier mâché of a homeosaurus, painted grass-green, the same colour as the front door her father had redecorated.

CHAPTER EIGHTEEN

London: July 1958

She packed a punch, he'd give her that. He deserved it, but even so he hadn't expected *that*. He'd let her go. Hooked a fish and thrown her back in the sea. It was the stupidest thing he'd ever done. Anatoly had blindsided him, made him see the world through trick lenses. He should have explained, told her who Anatoly was. Coded it in some way.

She was a fast runner, long out of sight. She'd be heading for King's Cross. He had to talk to her. It wasn't too late. He'd hail a cab. With a bit of luck he'd get there before she caught her train. He pushed himself up but his leg buckled and he fell back. He sat on the pavement, rubbing his thigh.

'Quite some hiding she gave you, my friend.' Anatoly was looming over him, blocking the sun, extending a hand. 'Knock spots off a boxer, I can tell you. Let me help you up.'

'No,' John said. He spat the words. It was Anatoly's bloody fault. 'Get lost.'

'That's not very friendly.'

'I'm not your friend.' He rested on one hand, pushed himself up. His leg couldn't take the weight so he hopped on his good one.

Anatoly grabbed his elbow. 'Lean on me.'

John shook himself free, began to limp away, but Anatoly was by his side.

'We need to talk,' he said, taking John's elbow and gripping it tight as he steered him towards Argyle Square, and an empty bench. John's gut knotted and he began to sweat, moisture wetting his shirt and collar, palms tacky. He wanted to cry out, to call for help. He began to twist, yanked his arm, elbowed Anatoly.

'Keep still, my friend,' Anatoly said. 'If you value Bette.' He pronounced it Bette, the German way, and her name was as sharp and sinister as if he'd punctured him with a poison dart.

§

John had the address but no phone number. They sent each other Christmas cards, but John wasn't one for saying much. What can you write in a card? There was so little space and he had no news. *Still teaching at same school. Still living at this address. Still single.* Arthur didn't share stuff either. Just signed his *Arthur.* He hadn't seen him for years. It had been unfair to embroil him, John recognised now. He wouldn't want to be involved again, and John had to respect that. Still, he needed reassurance.

He opened the carriage window to let in more breeze and lit a cigarette. There were two other people with him, a middle-aged man in shirtsleeves and paint-splattered trousers, a tool bag at his feet. He was reading the *Daily Sketch*, and opposite him was an elderly woman who had got on at London Bridge and sat knitting, needles clacking faster than a loom. She looked up, smiled, as if she knew him.

'Sorry,' she said. 'You're not related to Jimmy Braithwaite, are you? You look just like him. You could be his brother.'

'No,' John said. He didn't want to talk. He wanted silence, space to think what he was going to say to Arthur.

'Only he died in the war,' she went on. 'Tobruk. Shocking thing that. Only twenty-one. He was my neighbour's nephew.' She paused, counted her stitches, and John hoped that was the end of it.

He nodded in sympathy. 'She said her sister never got over it. Well, you wouldn't, would you? Were you in the war, son?'

John looked out of the window. He shouldn't be rude, and the woman needed to talk.

'No,' he said, matter-of-fact, hoping it would put her off. 'My call-up papers came after the war.'

'Well, you were lucky,' she said. 'Lots weren't. My husband fought in the last war. Well, the war before the last war, so he wasn't needed again. He would have gone, but they said he was too old. We only had daughters, so that was all right, though one of them was a WRN. She did look lovely in her uniform. The WRNs' uniform was lovely, don't you think? Such a pretty blue, and so flattering. Where are we?'

'Coming into Eltham,' John said.

'Goodness me, I get off here.' She stuck the needles in the ball of wool, wrapped the half-knitted garment around them and shoved it all in her bag.

'Nice to meet you,' she said. 'I could have sworn you were Jimmy's brother.'

The middle-aged man got up too, folding his paper, pulling out his pipe from his pocket as he stepped down. The carriage was empty. John leaned back in his seat, staring at the advertisements opposite. *Magical Margate. Finest Sands in England. Frequent Fast Trains.* He stood up and checked his appearance in the mirror. The welts on his face where she'd slapped him had faded now, but he'd nicked himself shaving this morning and there was a small scab on his chin. The bruise on his thigh wasn't so tender, and had turned a lurid yellow. At least he wasn't limping now. Arthur would see him as he'd last seen him, a little older, with lines around his mouth, faint creases on his forehead and one or two premature flecks of grey in his hair. He wondered how Arthur would look, what he was doing with his life now. He'd never said. He dropped the cigarette on the floor, stubbed it out with his heel.

The train drew into Bexleyheath. There was a map at the station and John memorised the way. He reckoned it was about a mile. A good stroll. He checked on his watch. Quarter past two. He'd be there about half past, just after. A decent time to arrive. He hoped Arthur was there, wasn't on his summer holiday, or at work, even though it was a Saturday. This conversation had to be done man to man. He couldn't write. Nor did he want it in writing. You never knew who might get hold of it.

He stepped out of the station, past a small parade of shops, stopping at a newsagent's and buying some more cigarettes and a box of matches. The day was warm, that dusty heat of midsummer. The gardens looked dry and the trees had lost the freshness of spring, their leaves flat and dark. They weren't yet showing the exhaustion of August, but it wouldn't be long. Interwar houses lined the streets, rows of 1930s semis or bungalows, pebble-dashed in sandy stone, woodwork painted brown or green. Bay windows lined with net curtains. He shouldn't be so sniffy, John thought. On a teacher's salary, he'd be lucky to afford one of these. There weren't many cars parked, and they were all pre-war, he noted, an old black Austin Seven, a deep red Morris Eight.

Only twenty years ago, this had been countryside, farms and lanes and woodland. Now there were hedges, saplings, lawns. Everyone must have arrived a stranger. Where had these people come from? Men like Arthur, home from war?

What if he had moved, and not given John his new address? Never got John's cards, but sent his anyway? Gipsy Road. John counted out the numbers, odd one side, even the other. He could see the house now, like all the others, bay window and green paintwork, a privet hedge that needed cutting, a garden gate swinging on its hinges. The path was crazy-paved and moss grew in the cracks. Somehow, he'd imagined Arthur would be more house-proud. There was a small lawn in the front garden, but the grass was long. Perhaps they were away. He knocked anyway.

A dog barked inside and a woman's voice could be heard. A door shut. The barking became muffled. Footsteps, then the front door opened. The woman had a crease in the centre of her forehead that made her look cross, worried. She wore an apron and was wiping her hands dry on it. The door behind her creaked. She turned.

'Don't let the dog out,' she said. A black and white terrier rushed towards him, stumpy tail wagging. The woman grabbed his collar, turned to a young girl behind her.

'Take him back in the kitchen.'

'But who is it?'

'Do as you're told,' the woman said. 'Go inside. With the dog.' It was a harsh voice and John remembered that she was an infant teacher, used to scolding and playground duty.

'Sorry,' she said. 'How can I help?'

'No need to apologise.' John smiled, hoping to reassure her. 'I'm looking for Arthur Gambol. Does he still live here?'

'Who's enquiring?'

The kitchen door opened a crack. John liked that little girl, not afraid to disobey. He saw the dog trying to push his way out and wanted to smile. He liked the dog, too.

'My name's John Harris,' he said. 'I was in Germany with Arthur, at the end of the war.'

She leaned her head back, squinted at him. 'Yes,' she said. 'He talked about you.' Her voice was flat, disapproving even. She wasn't going to give anything away.

He wondered what Arthur had said, sensed that his visit could be a waste of time. He should leave now, before Arthur saw him.

'Come in,' she said. 'He's in the garden.'

The kitchen door was opened and the dog bounded out, jumping up at John.

'Whisky, down.'

'It's all right,' John said. 'I like dogs. Here, boy.'

'He's called Whisky,' the girl said. 'Because he's black and white.'

'Black and white?' John said, before he recognised the connection. 'Very good.'

'It was Daddy's idea,' she said. John laughed. Yes, it would be.

'Go and tell your father there's a man to see him,' Arthur's wife said, adding, 'An old friend.'

She smiled then. She could be gracious. 'Come on through.'

She led him into the back room. French windows opened to the garden and John spotted Arthur at the end, putting up a green-house with the help of a young lad. His daughter was running across the lawn towards him. He couldn't hear the conversation but saw him nod, say something to the boy as his daughter took hold of his hand and ran back, pulling him across the lawn. John stepped through the door.

'Good Lord, sir,' Arthur said. 'Good heavens.' He wiped his hand down his trousers and held it out. 'It's a bit rough, I'm afraid. But what an unexpected pleasure.'

John grasped his hand, looking at his old friend. His auburn hair had lost some of its vibrancy, but his eyebrows were a rich ginger, his blue eyes unchanged.

'Well,' he was saying. 'Well. I can't believe this.' He turned to his daughter. 'Go and tell Bobby to come here. Can I get you a cup of tea, sir? Or maybe this warrants something stronger?'

'Please.' John felt a weight lift away. 'None of this "sir" business now. We're not in the army. It's John.'

The boy came into the room.

'Shoes off,' his mother said.

'This is John Harris,' Arthur said. 'Bravest man I ever met. I told you the story of how he took that grenade and ran with it half a mile? Saved all our lives. Do you remember?'

John shook his head, laughing. 'Your father's exaggerating,' he said. 'Who are all of you?'

'I'm sorry,' Arthur said. 'I'm too taken aback. Introductions, of course. This is my wife, Gladys.'

John smiled, took her hand. 'So pleased to meet you.'

'This is Robert.' He pointed to the boy, as tall as his father but without his father's colouring. 'And this is Christine.' She had her father's complexion, his red hair and freckles and she grinned back at him, grown-up teeth too large for her child's face.

'Please,' Arthur said. 'Please, come and sit down. Make yourself at home.'

He pointed to two chairs by the fireplace, shielded by an embroidered screen.

'I'll put the kettle on,' Gladys said. 'Christine, come and help me. Robert, finish outside. And take the dog with you.'

'I still can't believe it,' Arthur said. 'You finding me, you sitting here.'

'Nice place you've got,' John said, taking in the sideboard and the table, the Vernon Ward picture above the mantelpiece.

'My wife moved here,' Arthur said. 'And now we're buying it. A miracle.'

'What line are you in now?' John said.

'Well.' Arthur leaned back in his chair, grinning. 'I trained to be a teacher. Never thought that would happen, eh? A boy like me, leaving school at fourteen. But they were short of them, and turned out I had the makings – ex-serviceman, full matriculation. I'm the geography master, Welling Secondary Modern.' Arthur laughed. 'Tickled pink, you coming here.'

Arthur insisted John stayed for tea, and it wasn't until early evening that John was able to suggest – if Gladys didn't mind – that he and Arthur went out for a pint. The Red Lion was on the way to the station and the landlord let them take their drinks into the garden at the back.

Arthur sat down at the table, took a sip of beer, froth sticking to his upper lip. 'I've a feeling this isn't just a social call,' he said. 'Otherwise you'd have done it years ago.' His voice had a bitter edge and his mouth was firm.

John put his glass down on the table. 'I had a visitor,' he said. His hand had begun to shake and he slipped it into his lap. Hoped Arthur hadn't noticed. 'You remember that Russian?'

'Which one?'

'The spotty one.'

'Yes,' Arthur said. 'I do.'

'His name is Anatoly, so he tells me, works at the Soviet Embassy, though when I rang them they said no one of that name works there,' John said. 'That they would admit, at least.'

'I hope you rang from a call box,' Arthur said. It wouldn't make any difference wherever he rang from, John thought. They had his number anyway.

He took a long drag of his beer, placed the glass carefully back in place. He felt better with a bit of alcohol inside him, though his hands were gummy and his stomach churned and his leg tremored out of control.

'The thing is, Arthur,' John said, 'there's been a new complication.'

'Forget it, John,' Arthur said. 'I want nothing to do with this.' He stood up, turning to go.

'No,' John said. 'I don't need your advice. I know what to do.'

Arthur raised his eyebrows.

'I just had to talk to someone, get it off my chest,' John said. 'You're the only person who knows. Please...' He took a deep breath. 'Just listen.'

John saw Arthur's face, that look of disdain and mockery and tolerance that he remembered so well. He thought of all the kindnesses Arthur had shown him, when Private Nash died, when he went against orders with the morphine, when he'd sought him out in Berlin. That's what camaraderie was, being a comrade. Doing, not saying. John was an idiot, but he'd earned his spurs with Arthur. He watched as Arthur sat down again, lifted up his glass, gulped the beer so his Adam's apple quivered.

'Go on,' he said.

CHAPTER NINETEEN

London: August 1958

This was not what she wanted to do for the rest of her life, typing out patents and partners' correspondence. *Dear Sirs, Further to my communication of the 5th, inst.* Her eyes had been opened, dazzled, as if her past life had been a chrysalis and now she was free to fly. The typing pool was a stupid use of her talents. She would like to write. Forget her dreams of travel, living among the aborigines. She could be a journalist. A serious writer. The *U & LR* had encouraged her, but she had nothing new to say that they'd be interested in. The bomb would blow them all up. There was nothing distinctive to write about that, not as a woman, except to point out that it was men who were the bellicose ones and women who picked up the pieces, and if women wanted to ban the bomb they should back up principles with action. What was original in that?

She wanted to write about Lieselotte, what had happened to her, what happened to women in war. Most of her new friends in the Partisan Coffee House had left the Communist Party after Hungary, but they still had a soft spot for Russia. *No Soviet soldier would do that, comrade. Communism respects women as equals.* Well, that wasn't true, but they'd never believe her. Besides, she wanted to know if those husband-comrades helped around the house or whether the women went home from work and did the laundry and the cleaning and the mending. She doubted there was equality in revolution. Women were invisible.

She wanted to say more, that rape wasn't just in Germany. It had happened to Russian women by German soldiers. Chinese women by Japanese. Rape had no borders, no ideology. Rape was a weapon, every bit as vicious as a bayonet or a pistol. But who would agree with her? They wanted to read about imperialism and the Third World, Stalinism and Communism. They wanted to read about the Cold War and proxy war, NATO and disarmament, culture and consumption, and even though they said to draw on personal experience, she wasn't sure it meant *her* experience. Well, if they didn't want it, then *Peace News* might be interested.

Still, she liked going to the Partisan, even if she was a bit in awe of everyone. There was always something happening, the New Left Club and the Direct Action Committee, music, talks, films, theatre. You name it. It was – she reached for the word – affirming. No, exciting. Banning the bomb wasn't just about being *against* things. It was *for* things, for life, for living, for fun and gaiety, health and happiness. Being young and active, having a cause. It was a new kind of politics, of being together. It was exhilarating. Joyous. Life sparkled. It was for the day, for light, for the sun. It smothered the nightmares that plagued her, the firestorms, the peeling skin, the charred flesh. Berlin. Dresden. *Hiroshima.*

She used to wonder if John ever went there, and if she met him, what she'd do. She thought of him night and day, crowding into her dreaming time at night, her thinking time on the Tube, the slack moments at work. But she was bone-tired and her breasts were tender. She wanted to cry all the time. And always the swirling hurricane of a question. Why? What had she done wrong? She thought there'd been such good omens at first with the way they met, and what they had in common. She'd let herself go into free-fall, her mind in chaos, her body tender at the thought of him. And then, *rupture*, as if she had been flayed alive, skin on that side, flesh on the other. Raw and bloody, like those poor souls in Hiroshima. She put a brave face on it at work, and at home, playing with the boys, reading them stories, helping with the washing-up since her cooking wasn't up to it, as Dee had said. She'd never paid attention in Domestic Science.

§

She sidled through the door and into the meeting, where a young man was holding up the model of the homeosaurus, exposing its underbelly.

'Each scale,' he was saying, 'points in the wrong direction, but if you look here' – he unhinged a section, pointed to a yoke made from matchsticks – 'there's a wooden yoke that fits over each person's shoulders.' He hooked it back together. 'Altogether it will be about thirty feet long. I reckon the body will need about twenty grown-ups to carry it, and then the children can carry the tail.'

'Children?' Betty said.

'In ever diminishing sizes. Why not? They'd love it, and we could really get the message across. Take it everywhere. Schools. Parks.'

'What's it made of?' Betty asked, thinking of Graham and Martin.

'Well, the head will be of papier mâché. The frame, balsa. And the scales tarpaulin. Painted. Varnished. It goes stiff then, so won't flap. And we'll strap it taut, anyway.' He smiled at her. 'It won't be heavy, if that's what you're thinking. A woman could lift it.'

Betty nodded, but she wasn't sure she liked him after that comment, even if his idea was exciting.

'But, comrade, how long will it take to make?' Betty turned and looked at an intense young man with black hair and a deep voice, an oboe of a voice, she thought.

'A few months,' the young man replied. 'Section by section. But we need a workshop...' He looked around at his audience. 'Anyone have a garage, a shed?'

Betty followed his eyes. They were all young. None of them would have that kind of space.

'I know,' the man with the oboe voice said. 'The Theatre Royal, Stratford. They'll have room. I can ask Joan...'

The young man smiled. 'That's brilliant, Ralph,' he said. 'They'll have a proper workshop. Props. Of course.' He slapped his forehead. 'Why didn't I think of that?'

He lifted the homeosaurus and put it in a shoebox. 'I'll need help, though.'

She longed to do something practical with her hands. It would take her mind off things.

'I'll volunteer,' Betty said. And then it came to her. 'Why don't we make its head look like Macmillan? Could we do that, in papier mâché?'

She could hear others laugh, but they were nodding.

'Genius,' the young man said. 'What's your name?'

'Betty.' She smiled, at home, here in the Partisan.

§

Perhaps she was just late. She'd had a few shocks lately. That could have an effect. She looked at herself in Dee's bathroom mirror. She didn't look any different, not on the outside, at any rate. Lieselotte had looked the same too, standing in the window of their bedroom, her flimsy frame silhouetted against the sun.

'I'm pregnant, Bettelein,' she'd said, just like that, matter-of-fact. She was wearing her faded cotton skirt, and a clean blouse, her hair pinned back from her face with Mutti's tortoiseshell comb. 'I've heard of a doctor who'll help.'

Betty had no doctor to help her. Or anyone. None of her friends were *fast*, had ever needed those kinds of services. Or if they had, they'd never admitted it. Perhaps she should approach one of those call girls in Soho. They'd know who to go to. But how would they know she wasn't a policeman on the sly? They wouldn't talk to her, and in any case Betty wasn't sure she could go to some backstreet abortionist. There were terrible stories about them.

'Hurry up, Betty.' Dee was banging on the door. 'I need to clean my teeth.'

'Sorry,' Betty said. 'You can come in. I'm just putting my face on.' She reached over and opened the door.

'Dee,' she said, dabbing on lipstick, 'I've got to talk to you.'

'Fire away.' Kevin was downstairs making tea. A door slammed and Martin burst into the bathroom.

'Mu-um,' he said. 'Graham said I was a selfish, fishy-faced idiot.'

Dee rolled her eyes. 'How many times have I told you to knock before you come into the bathroom?'

'Well, he did.' He glared at Dee. 'Do something.'

'Go down and help your father.'

'Aren't you going to tell him off?'

'I'll deal with this in a minute. I need to talk to Auntie Betty.'

He glared at Betty now, and Betty smiled back, winking. She waited until he'd left the room. Dee shut the door.

'Well?'

'Later,' Betty said. 'After the children have gone to bed.' She put the lipstick back in its holder and lifted her comb from her cosmetic bag.

'You're pregnant, aren't you?'

Betty turned her head fast, her neck cricking. She felt dizzy, nauseous.

'No, nothing like that.' Sniffed, peered into the mirror at a spot on her chin, combed her hair behind her ear. 'Well, yes. Maybe. How did you know?'

'Tone of voice,' Dee said. 'It was either that. Or nits. I took a guess.'

'Graham.' Kevin had bounded up the stairs, crossed the landing, hammered on the boys' door. 'Come down *now*.'

'What are you going to do?'

'I don't know,' Betty said. 'Can we talk later? Please?'

'You'll have to have it adopted,' Dee said. 'Won't you?'

'Please, Dee.' Her voice was quavering and her eyes were tearful. 'This evening?'

Dee blew through her mouth. 'God, Bets, what a mess. I mean, this changes everything.' She looked at her watch. 'Got to dash.'

She ran out of the bathroom, down the stairs. Betty could hear her in the kitchen. *Bye, kids, be good. Bye, Kev. Must rush. Auntie Betty's taking you to school.*

She'd forgotten it was her day.

§

Kevin was in the sitting room listening to the wireless, Dee and Betty in the kitchen. Betty had made some tea and they sat at Dee's new Formica-topped table, hands round blue-striped mugs.

'How far gone are you?' Dee said.

'How should I know?' She'd never been pregnant before. When had Lieselotte known?

'Well, how long since your last period?'

'About two weeks,' Betty said. 'Perhaps three. I'm not always so regular.'

Dee thought a moment.

'So you're due April sometime,' she said, adding, 'It's John's?'

Betty nodded. 'I didn't think you got pregnant the first time.' She looked out of the window, at the garden beyond, the swing on the cherry tree, the lilac bushes.

Dee laughed. 'Crumbs, Betty, where have you been? Why didn't he use something?'

Betty shrugged, turned to her friend. 'We weren't planning to do anything.'

'He could have withdrawn,' Dee said, raising her eyebrow, adding, 'Oh, never mind. That never worked. What are you going to do? Only...' She paused, rubbed her nail against the rim of the mug. 'I don't think you could stay here. We don't have room, and I don't think Kev would approve. Bad example to the kids, and the neighbours, you know, gossip.'

'Kevin? He's a fine one to talk. He got you in the family way.'

'But he married me, before I showed,' Dee said. 'You'll have to marry John.'

Betty screwed her eyes tight, shook her head. 'I don't want him to marry me if he doesn't love me. I can't think of anything worse.'

She'd rather live in purgatory than with a man who felt trapped by her.

Betty stared into her mug, at the tea leaf floating on the top. 'What shall I do?'

'I don't know,' Dee said. 'Does John know?'

Betty shook her head.

'Are you going to tell him?'

She looked up at Dee. 'No.'

'Don't you think he has a right to know?'

She raised her shoulders. 'Why? He doesn't care. *Obviously*. He wouldn't have ditched me otherwise.'

'Bets.' Dee put her mug aside and reached over for Betty's hands. 'He might change his mind when he knows.'

'And what difference would that make? If he doesn't love me, he doesn't love me.'

'So what are you going to do?'

'I don't know,' Betty said, pulling her hand free. 'I don't want his baby.'

Dee sipped her tea, both hands cradling the mug, elbows on the table. 'Have you thought about adoption?'

Betty nodded. 'I can't be pregnant. I'd lose my job. Then what would I do? And where would I go if I can't stay here?' She shook her head. 'I'm not going to some mother and baby home run by a bunch of sadistic nuns.' She took a gulp of tea. It was lukewarm.

'I don't think you have any choice, Bets.'

'Perhaps I could get rid of it,' she said. 'Can you help?' She had no alternative but to say it.

Dee's forehead furrowed. She was cross. Or shocked. Betty had forgotten. Dee still went to church, dragged the boys there every Sunday. Graham even served at Mass. She should never have asked her.

'How do you think I can possibly help?'

Betty hesitated for a moment. She knew what she was about to say would be hurtful. 'You're a nurse,' she said. 'Don't nurses know these things?'

'That's a shocking thing to say,' Dee said. 'Who do you think we are?'

'I'm sorry,' Betty said. 'I didn't mean to upset you. I just thought, you know, midwives, I mean, they must know things?'

'It's illegal,' Betty said. 'You do know that, don't you? Not just immoral. *Illegal.* No one I know would risk it.'

'Please, Dee, can you just ask around? It wouldn't get you into trouble, would it?'

Dee pulled her hands back, lifted the teapot.

'There's a drop more,' she said. 'Would you like it?'

'No thanks,' Betty said. Dee poured the stewed dregs into her mug, spooned in a teaspoon of sugar.

'How can you drink it like that?' Betty thought of Mutti's Meissen tea set, the golden liquid she drank and savoured, a treat to live for. She'd died before she knew what happened to Lieselotte, to herself. Perhaps it was just as well.

'I can't promise anything,' Dee said. 'You need to make your own enquiries too.'

'Thanks,' Betty said. 'Thanks so much.'

§

The model-maker was called Nick.

'Can you sew?'

'No,' Betty said. 'But I can glue. Or paint.'

He rolled his eyes. He wanted a man. Too bad, Betty thought. Beggars can't be choosers.

'Come back when the frames are made,' he said. 'And we can put you to work on the scales.'

She left them, the men, *boys* really, sawing bits of balsa and tapping them in place with tacks. She caught the train home, sat in the carriage, knots in her gut twisting and tightening. Was it hot baths and gin? Difficult to do in Dee's house. She'd have to book a hotel room. Could she *will* this thing out? Could her body absorb it, get rid of it? Like a giant panda. She'd read that. If she wanted it enough, could it happen? But an abortion. She should never have asked Dee. It went against everything Dee believed in. And what if something went wrong? She'd heard stories about women bleeding to death, or getting blood poisoning, or going batty. What if she was caught? She'd end up in prison, her reputation, her *life*, ruined. She couldn't go through with the pregnancy either. How would she survive without a job, or somewhere to live? She couldn't go home, even if she wanted to. Her father would throw her out for sure. She was trapped. Whichever way she turned, there was no exit point. Ruined. An old-fashioned word, but it hit the nail on the head. It was all right for John. He got off scot-free. Lieselotte's words came back. *Why is it always the women who have to pick up the pieces?* Why did women always pay the price?

§

Dee took her into the kitchen when she arrived home.

'We've kept your tea warm,' she said, taking it out of the oven and placing it on a mat on the table. 'Toad in the hole.'

'Thanks.' Betty poured herself a glass of water and sat down. The batter looked heavy and the gravy thick and lumpy.

'Ah, Bisto,' she said, sniffing.

'Well, the kids like it.' Dee shut the kitchen door, pulled out a chair and sat next to her.

'Don't ever ask me to do this again,' she said, pulling out a piece of paper from her pocket, her mouth set in a hard, straight line. 'Seems you have two options.'

Betty felt as if the weight had dissolved, her shoulders freed from their burden. 'You're an angel,' she said.

'I don't approve,' Dee said. 'I hope you know that. You put me in a very difficult position.'

Betty nodded. 'I know that, Dee,' she said. 'I wouldn't have asked you if I hadn't been desperate.'

'This is a mortal sin. I mean, I believe in the sanctity of life and all that,' Dee said. Her mouth was tight and she shifted in her seat, adding, 'But I know what it is to be up the duff too.' She paused, nodded at the food. 'Start before it gets cold.'

Betty cut into the sausage, shoved a piece into her mouth. She wasn't hungry.

'Right,' Dee went on. 'If you can get two doctors to say you'd be reduced to a mental wreck, you can get it done legally.' She smiled. 'That's the good news.'

'And the bad?'

'It would cost about a hundred guineas, plus you'd need to pay the psychiatrists. God knows what they charge.'

Betty coughed hard, her stomach tightening. 'A hundred? Where could I get that kind of money? That's four months' wages.' She pushed the plate away. The batter was cold anyway. 'You said there were two options?'

Dee opened the piece of paper, pushed it across the table. Betty pulled it towards her. A name, a telephone number. And written below it, *£30 or £40? Depending.* She shut her eyes. If she did it after payday, and lived on next to nothing for a month or two, she could rustle up perhaps a tenner. She had just over five pounds in savings. She fingered the gold chain round her neck. Her father had given it to her for her twenty-first. She could sell that. But even so. She twisted the ring on her finger. Mutti's ring. She could pawn it. She'd never been into one of those shops, but then she'd never been in this position before. What did Dee call it? Up the duff?

'Promise me one thing,' Dee said. 'That you'll think very hard about what you decide to do.' She stood up, added, 'The woman used to be a nurse.'

Betty nodded. She looked at the debris on her dinner plate, the empty surface of the tabletop, the bare walls of Dee's kitchen, and beyond, the garden with its patch of worn earth below the swing. She folded the paper and put it in her pocket.

CHAPTER TWENTY

London: September 1958

It was over four weeks now.

'Hide away,' Arthur had suggested. 'Lie low. Think about your options.'

'And Betty?' John said.

'Nothing's going to happen to Betty unless you're around.'

A damp cottage in mid-Wales miles from anywhere, outdoor privy, spring water, Rayburn cooker. Just the job. There was a wireless, but nothing else. The beds were old, the furniture shabby. The previous owner had died and his children rented the house out.

'Born in it,' they'd said as they handed him the key. 'It was his father's before him. Goes right back, it does. Great-grandfather and all. Was a wooden house once, you know? Our father bricked it in. That's why it's called Larch Cottage.'

'Nothing to do with the forest then?'

'Oh no. These were put up for the navvies working on the railway. Jerry-built, the lot of them.'

It was by chance he'd found it, really, stuck a pin in a map. Pantydwr. A bit of a palaver to get there, especially with his bicycle and rucksack, but now he was settled in, it couldn't be better. The land sloped down to the Marteg.

'It's illegal to fish, though.' All he saw were tiddlers anyway, and keen-eyed kingfishers. He woke in the morning with the chatter of the house martins, went to bed with the screech of the barn owl. There was a farm up the road which sold eggs, and it was a short bike ride to the village for the basics and a newspaper.

He was used to living by himself. Once he had a routine, it wasn't so bad. Out by day, cycling or walking, packing a sandwich and a thermos of tea, rain or shine. A pint after supper in the pub. The landlord was called Berwyn, spoke Welsh to the locals, English to him.

'From London, eh? I expect it's a bit quiet for you round here.'

'That's what I want,' John said. Anatoly wouldn't find him here.

'You're not married then?'

John shook his head, sipped his beer.

There was an old man in the corner with grey whiskers and unkempt hair. His brown trousers were tied up with binder twine and his baggy tweed jacket was ripped at the shoulder seams. A Welsh collie with matted fur curled at his feet.

The barman beckoned John close, eyeing the man in the corner.

'If it's peace and quiet you want,' he said, 'avoid Dai. He may be the richest farmer round these parts but he talks the hind legs off a donkey.' He smiled. 'I'd go outside if I were you.' Added, 'Before he spots you.'

John sat on the bench, leaning against the wall, soaking in the evening sun. Perhaps he could jack in his job, get another one round here? Teach in the village school? Live in the cottage, get a dog for company. Who would ever find him?

Anatoly.

Though *how* Anatoly had traced him was a mystery.

§

He stepped off the train at Paddington, wheeled his bike along the platform. The train had been crowded and he'd retreated into the guards' van with his luggage, sitting on the floor for hours. Now the noise and bluster of the city bombarded him. He took a moment to get his bearings, to take in the traffic, the double-decker buses and the taxis, the people scurrying like uncovered woodlice. He had been used to solitude, the gentle sounds of sheep and the wind rustling through the birch and larch trees round the cottage.

His flat smelled stale, airless, his mail was piled on the hall table. He'd thought it best not to get it redirected in case, somehow, Anatoly discovered where he was. He opened the windows, let in the noises and the fumes, looked around him, at his books ordered alphabetically, his saucepans tucked inside each other, the clock on the shelf that had stopped at twenty past five. Perhaps he should move. Get somewhere bigger, with fresh air and a garden. In the country. He heaved his rucksack into the bedroom, pulled out his dirty clothes. He'd have to go to the launderette at the weekend, perhaps pay a visit to the Partisan, see what was happening in the world.

§

The first week of term was always a gentle re-entry into the year. He cycled home the first day. Lincoln's Inn Fields. Old habits, he thought. He wanted to see her, to explain, beg forgiveness. Start again. The gardens were busy with visitors in the last of the summer warmth. He passed her offices, stopped a small distance away, bike propped on the kerb. He leaned against the railings, clips on his trousers, tie tucked in his shirt front, jacket folded in the basket. He pulled out his cigarettes from the pocket and lit one. He could see the office door and a steady stream of workers coming out. Women first, from the typing pool, he guessed, and the tea ladies. He craned his neck. There was no sign of her. He waited, watching. One by one the men in suits and bowlers emerged. He checked his watch. Six o'clock. The café was shutting and people were drifting from the gardens, heading for the Tube or Southampton Row. He'd missed her. Perhaps she'd left work early, or was off sick. Perhaps she'd quit her job, worked somewhere else now. If he hadn't spotted her by the end of the week, he'd write to the company and ask after her.

§

The Sunday afternoon meeting was packed. John squeezed through the door. Standing room only. The room was hot and smoky. He could see the speaker through the haze but he mumbled into his notes, was hard to make out.

'Speak up,' the man next to him called out. 'We can't hear at the back.' The speaker pulled his shoulders up, lifted his chin. Some of the audience had turned to see who was calling out. A fleeting glance before she twisted back and faced the front. Her chestnut hair was flicked up at the ends and secured from her face with an Alice band. She wore the same skirt and blouse as the last time he'd seen her, fidgeted in her seat like the first time they'd met. He focused on her, the slender neck, the contours of her shoulder blades. If she'd spotted him she didn't show it, didn't turn round to check if it had been him she'd glimpsed.

The talk was of a week of activism, to end the tests, of the midnight procession to London Airport at Hallowe'en to support the women flying off to lobby the Conference in Geneva. He could go on that, walk side by side with Betty, with the flares and torches. Would he hold her hand? He yearned for her touch, the feel of her flesh, the taste of her mouth. The last four weeks in Wales had left him with a craving he couldn't satisfy. Now she was here. He had to have her. They'd fly away to Wales, rent that cold, damp cottage and hunker down all winter, safe under the blankets while the hare changed its coat and the snow fell on the Cambrians.

'...the homeosaurus. Even Betty could lift it.'

He heard her voice. 'Oh shut up, Nick. A child could lift it.' He had no idea what they were talking about. 'The homeosaurus is for the schools and parks. Not parliament, not the vigil. I've said that so many times.'

Could he reach over to her, sidle down the aisles and beckon her out? There was an argument going on. Homeosaurus. That was madness. What had palaeontology to do with CND? He should listen, note it down, the week of action, the vigil, the midnight procession. There was an announcement, an emergency meeting of the New Left Club, to talk about the riots in Notting Hill. Tuesday, six o'clock. The meeting began to break up, men and women sauntering down the aisle, some standing in small groups, chatting, others pushing forward, anxious to leave. John moved to the door. Betty was talking to two men, her face animated, angry. She looked as if she was going to cry. She turned, pushed past the chairs, walked fast towards the exit. He stepped forward.

She stopped, raised her hands at him. 'What are you doing here?'

'I want to talk,' he said.

'I don't,' she said. 'And certainly not now.'

'Later?'

'Never.'

She pushed past him and ran down the stairs, stopping at the bottom, turning round. 'Don't follow me.'

He reached forward, hand on her arm. 'Betty, please,' he said. 'Please. Hear me out.' He hadn't expected to see her here, had no idea how to explain, even though he'd spent the summer talking to her in his head. *It was like this, Betty...*

She shook him off but he saw her hesitate, face him. 'Not here. Outside.' She rushed for the door and he followed her. She sprinted, round the corner, towards Soho Square. It was hard to keep up with her. She went into the square and stopped, bending over like an athlete, catching her breath.

Betty stood up straight and stared him in the face, eyes hard, mouth set. 'You used me,' she said. 'You used and abused me.' She was swallowing, trying not to cry.

'Betty,' he said. 'No, listen, it wasn't like that.'

'Then what was it like?' She pursed her lips, hissed. 'Seems to me if someone says "This has to end," there's no mistaking.' She sniffed. 'I gave myself to you. You were the first. I thought we had a future. Then you just...' She swallowed back the tears. 'Chucked me away. Soiled goods.'

He held his face in his hands. This wasn't how he'd imagined the conversation would go.

'And now,' she said. 'I'm—' She broke off her sentence, shook her head, pulled down her Alice band, pushed it back up, catching her hair away from her face, turned and walked towards the market cross in the centre of the square. This was his last chance. He ran up, grabbed her, spinning her round. She glowered, pushed his hand away from her arm.

'You're what? What were you going to say?'

'Nothing. Doesn't matter.' She stepped out again.

'You looked upset.'

'Of course I'm upset.' She faced him, voice raised in fury. 'I'm devastated. I've never been so hurt, so...' Her lips moved as she groped for a word. 'So *debased.*'

'Betty,' he said. 'It just wasn't like that. I thought your life could be in danger if you were with me.'

She stared at him. 'Are you mad?' She twisted her forefinger on her temple. 'Paranoid?'

He shook his head. 'Nothing like that, Betty. It's a long story.' He took a breath. 'You need to know, be aware.'

She stood, arms akimbo. He should never have panicked, never have parted. He could have told her, explained. Between them, they would have worked something out. She would keep a secret, he was sure.

'Make me aware.'

'Let's sit.' He pointed to a bench. His legs ached, his stomach was knotted. He led the way, one step, two, as if each stride were a mile, the path mountain scree. His feet splayed forward, out of control. He grabbed the arm of the bench, lowered himself onto it. She sat at the far end, sideways, facing him. He leaned forward, elbows on his knees, fingers threaded in a cat's cradle.

'I told you I was in Germany at the end of the war.' She raised an eyebrow, *yes*. 'Well, something happened that came back to haunt me.'

'We're all haunted by the war,' she said. Her words could have soothed, but her voice had a challenge in it. 'So what was so dreadful you couldn't get over it?'

What did she know about getting over things? She was casual, callous almost, as if she had no understanding of the suffering of war, the choices made in the heat of the moment, no way of imagining what it could be like. She'd been a child. Evacuated, most likely. Spent years in the countryside collecting chickens' eggs and running free.

'I was in Berlin,' he said. His voice had an edge, and he was glad. 'I can't tell you what we were doing.' He looked up at her. 'I'm sorry, even now. Official secrets and all that. It's not important. All I can say is that I was a translator. Very lowly on the scale of things.'

'Well,' she said. 'You teach German. Makes sense.'

She was staring at the statue of Charles II, at the gravel path, at the grass, threadbare after the summer.

'My German was formal, pedantic.'

He wasn't sure, but he thought there was a half-smile.

'I'm a perfectionist,' he said. 'I like to do things well. I wanted to improve it, my everyday German, to become fluent.' He leaned against the armrest. 'To be light-hearted, conversational. To banter. The sort of thing that native speakers take for granted.'

Betty shrugged, eyes focused on the grass. She tucked her hands under her thighs, the fabric of her skirt taut across her legs.

She had done that, tucked her skirt beneath *her* thighs, stretched it tight. He gulped, swallowing his saliva the wrong way, coughing, his eyes streaming. Betty didn't look up at him, not once, hostility high as a cliff, hard as rock.

'I found a teacher,' he went on. He was trembling, jellied with nerves. 'Who would be prepared to help with my German, for a hundred marks an hour.' He smiled. 'Or five cigarettes. That was the currency in Berlin at the time. Cigarettes. Did you know that?'

The muscles in her jaw tightened and her eyes filled with tears. She sniffed, wiped them with the back of her hand. He couldn't understand why she should be upset. Very few people here worried about the Germans.

'So you told me,' she said, adding, 'Where is this leading?'

'This is what I'm trying to tell you.' How would she understand? He couldn't tell her the truth. 'A man was involved.'

'You're not making sense.'

He swallowed. 'No,' he said. 'I'm not. Let me start again.'

A pigeon came towards them, pecking at the ground. John flicked his hand, watched it fly off, lazy wings barely lifting it. It landed a few yards away.

'It was a young woman who gave me lessons.'

'A young woman?'

'Yes.'

It sounded so corny now, a young soldier, a young woman.

'What was her name?' She stared ahead, without looking at him. 'Was that the person you bought the clock from? For five cigarettes?' Her voice was bitter.

'The clock?' he said. 'Does it matter?'

She nodded, brushing her skirt for imaginary crumbs, pleating the hem so it draped in folds.

'I don't want to hear any more,' she said. She was close to tears. Was she jealous? *Jealous*.

'Betty, I didn't love her, not like I love you,' he blurted out. 'If that's what you're thinking.'

'You have no idea what I'm thinking. What was her name?'

'Hear me out.'

'Tell me her name.'

'Will you listen if I tell you her name?'

'Don't bargain with me,' she said. Her nostrils fanned with fury. She let go of her skirt and gripped the handle of her bag, knuckles white and bare.

'Her name was Lieselotte.'

She stared at him, mouthing, *Lieselotte*.

CHAPTER TWENTY-ONE

Berlin: July 1945

'Why can't I come?' Bette pivoted on the kitchen stool as Lieselotte placed the bowls in the sink. 'Why do I have to be here alone?'

'You'll be in the way.' Lieselotte with her *I know better, I'm in charge now* voice. 'See if Greta's free. Perhaps she'll stay with you.'

'Where are you going that I can't come?'

'Nowhere secret.' She flicked a tea towel at Bette. 'Kurfürstendamm again.'

'I won't get in your way.'

'Bette, will you leave it, please? The Americans haggle and you'd only be a distraction.'

'But the British?'

'They're not so bad. Afterwards I'm meeting that soldier.'

'The one who wants to learn German?'

'Yes, Bette.' Lieselotte smiled. 'His German is very old-fashioned. Like Großvater's.'

'And where are you meeting him this time?'

'At the Lichtensteinbrücke.'

'Why there?'

'It's quiet.'

Bette swung herself off the stool, padded after her sister into the sitting room. 'It's a long way,' she said. 'How do you get there?'

'Walking, obviously,' Lieselotte said. 'It's not so far.' She bit her lip, added, 'If you're not hungry.'

'What's his name?'

Lieselotte stood and stared at Bette. 'I can't remember. It's not important.'

It made her nervous, not knowing what went on. Lieselotte had been catapulted into the world of grown-ups, leaving her behind.

'What will we do with the money?'

'Oh, Bette,' Lieselotte said, her voice sharp and cross. 'It's not a lot of money and we need to buy food. This is all we have.'

'I still don't see why I can't join you.' Bette flounced on a chair, crossed her arms, watching as Lieselotte lifted a suitcase from behind the sofa. 'I won't be a nuisance. I won't interrupt.'

'Stop it,' Lieselotte said. 'You're getting on my nerves. The answer is no, no and no. Understood?'

Bette huffed, scowled. 'When is Vati coming home?'

'I don't know.' Lieselotte bit her lip. 'Perhaps he's a prisoner somewhere.' She smiled. 'Come, help me pick which piece to sell this time.'

They chose the Bavarian clock, with its incessant chimes that they had both wanted to suffocate. Bette lifted it out of its wrappings as if it were a hot coal.

'Are you all right?' Lieselotte said. 'Sorry, I didn't mean to get cross.'

Bette shrugged. 'Are you sure I can't come with you? I don't want to be here by myself.'

'Don't be silly,' Lieselotte said. 'You'll be fine. Besides, *man of house.*' She laughed, mimicking Boris's Russian accent. 'You've got the gun to protect you.'

'That's not a joke,' Bette said. 'It's probably not even loaded. Please let me come.'

'Go to Frau Weber,' Lieselotte said. 'I'm sick of arguing.'

'But what if something happens to you?'

'What's going to happen to me?'

Bette shrugged. 'I don't know,' she said, adding, 'You're going to marry this soldier and leave me alone.'

'Marry him?' Lieselotte spat the word. 'Oh, Bettechen.' She squatted on the floor next to her, pulled her close and cradled her head. 'Of course not. He's just a soldier. I've no idea who he is.' She kissed Bette on the forehead. 'I would never, ever leave you.' Bette felt her sister's hands on her cheeks as she pushed her face away. 'Look at me.' Lieselotte's eyes were gold in the sunlight, flecked with bronze and emerald, far richer than her own dull, grey ones. 'I will never leave you,' she said again. 'Do you understand?'

Bette nodded. 'It's just that…' She paused, looking at her sister, fears curdling. 'Mutti died and left me, and Vati has gone, and if you went…' She felt a tear, wiped it away fast. 'What would happen to me?'

'For a start, nothing will happen, and even if it does, you go and find Oma in Dahlem. Now, I need to get ready. So move.'

Bette sat cross-legged on the bed, watching her sister pulling on the faded skirt and blouse, her socks and shoes. She used to envy boys their shorts and shirts, but now she had to wear them all the time she'd give her eye teeth to dress in a skirt again. She was sick of pretending. Lieselotte sat at the dressing table, brushing her hair, pinning it back with tortoiseshell combs.

'Those are Mutti's,' Bette said. 'Did she give them to you?'

Lieselotte took a moment before she turned. 'No, but Mutti wouldn't want her things in a museum, would she? Be practical, Bette. We can't be sentimental.'

She leaned forward, dusting her cheeks with powder.

'That's Mutti's make-up. You aren't allowed to use it.'

'Bette,' Lieselotte's voice snapped. 'Will you *shut up*?' She stood up, frail and beautiful, silhouetted against the light through the window. She took a breath and Bette thought she sucked the air as though it were the last she would ever take. She opened her mouth as if to speak. Shut it. Bette saw her chest rise as she swallowed the air again. Let it out. *Whoosh.*

'I'm pregnant, Bettelein,' she said, just like that, adding, 'I've heard of someone who'll help. A doctor.'

'How?'

'There are lots of women like me,' Lieselotte went on. 'After the Russians...' She paused. 'She helps us get rid of them.'

So matter-of-fact, the way she said it. Bette opened her eyes wide. Greta had said something like that about Waltraud but Bette hadn't paid her much notice, didn't understand how you *undo* a baby.

'But I need money,' Lieselotte said. 'She doesn't charge much, only what I can afford. Do you understand now?' She felt the comb with her hand, made sure it was secure. 'I want to look respectable, Bette. So no one thinks I'm, you know...'

Bette nodded, not quite sure what Lieselotte meant.

'And also.' She pulled her skirt straight, stood on tiptoe to look in the dressing-table mirror. 'The German lessons.' She spun round. 'Do I look like a professor?' She laughed, came over, kissed Bette on the cheek. 'I won't be late,' she said. 'Finish the soup if you like.'

She placed the clock inside her bag, hung the front door key around her neck and tucked it into her blouse, and for a moment, before she slipped out through the door, she looked happy.

Bette watched from the window as her sister turned the corner. There were a few hours to kill before she returned, and although Greta's prattling was getting on her nerves, her company was better than nothing and she *knew* things, like how you get rid of a baby. Bette took the spare front door key from the hook and left the apartment. The steps were still damaged and the plaster not repaired, but she had got used to that, and the people who lived in the Müllers' old apartment swept the staircase once a day so the loose stones had gone. She'd slipped on them more than once. She crossed the courtyard, knocked on the Webers' door. There was laughter inside, a man's voice. Footsteps, the door opened. Frau Weber blinked at Bette, as if she'd been expecting someone else. Her hair was dishevelled, her face flushed.

'Not now, Bette,' she said. 'You can't play with Greta now.' She looked behind her. 'Greta's vati has come back.'

Greta never talked about her father.

'Oh,' she said, not sure what to say. 'When can she play?'

'I don't know.' Frau Weber shut the door with force and Bette wondered what she had said that was so wrong or rude.

Bette climbed back up the stairs to their apartment, and into Mutti's room. The soft ghost of her mother was there, breathing in the silk coverlet on her bed, smiling at the colours on the wall, lounging on her bedroom chair. Her perfumes were lined in order of size on one side of her dressing table, her vanity set on the other. Bette had taken her mother's brush, so the mirror and comb were all that was left. She liked Mutti's bedroom, its calm and comfort. It had been a haven when the Ivans hung around, their unwashed stink and foul smoke clinging to the walls in the rest of the apartment and woven into the fabrics. She sat on the stool. The dressing table was dusty, needed a wipe. She wrote *Mutti* in the motes, rubbed her sleeve across the top, wiped it away.

They'd taken off her wedding ring when she died, and rolled it in a handkerchief. Bette slipped it onto her finger. It fitted, more or less. Mutti had always been petite. Lieselotte took after her. Bette had her father's build, *big bones*, Mutti used to say, palm against palm. *We're the same size now.* She opened the drawer. Nail polish. Lipsticks. Mutti's embroidered handkerchiefs, her suspender belts, an unopened pair of silk stockings. She reached further back, pulled out a small brown casket with *Mensinga Membran* written on the top. It must, she thought, be something secret for Mutti to hide it so far back, something forbidden. There was a small rush of excitement as she opened it, stared at the round rubber cap, at the sprays next to it. A flush crept up her neck, burning her cheeks. She had no idea what this was but knew it was private, *womanly*. Mutti would be angry. She shut the box, pushed it back, picked up a lipstick. It was almost finished, but she dabbed some on her lips, smacked them together as she'd seen Mutti do, sat back to look at herself, smelling its faint perfume.

Her hair was growing but it was still boyish. She went into her bedroom and took out a summer dress, pulling off Otto's trousers and shirt, tugging the dress over her. Her breasts had grown even in the last few weeks, and she was taller than last summer. She tried to tug the bodice down but the seam tore. Even if she wanted to wear girls' clothes, she had none. They were all too small. She ripped it off and flung it on the bed, opened Lieselotte's side of the cupboard where her clothes hung on their hangers. She had been raiding Mutti's wardrobe, not just her tortoiseshell hair combs, but her summer blouses and dresses.

Well.

Bette walked back to her mother's bedroom. If Lieselotte could do this, so could she. The wardrobe smelled of Mutti, of her skin and perfume and the musty odour of worn, unaired clothes. At the far end were her evening outfits, ball gowns and cocktail dresses. Where had she gone in them? She sifted through the hangers, lifted down a midnight-blue frock, chiffon silk with a satin lining. Bette could remember her mother wearing it. Where had she been going? Somewhere grand. Bette had made her a necklace from buttons, which she gave her mother before she left. She'd draped it round her neck, thanked Bette, said it was the most beautiful jewellery she'd ever owned and swept out of the door, trailing her fox fur stole, Vati by her side in a dicky bow and dinner suit. Had they met the Führer that night? Had he admired it? She couldn't remember, and Mutti had never said. The necklace was laid out on the dressing table the next morning.

She held the gown against her, then slipped it on. It fitted, once she had hooked it up, though it was a little long. She rummaged in the back of the wardrobe, pulling out a pair of high heels and slipping them on her bare feet. She lifted the dress up above her ankles, balanced her way towards Mutti's cheval mirror, and let go of the folds so the dress flowed to the floor. It had a halter neck, but no back. She turned sideways. The dress draped so she could see the dents on her bottom. Lieselotte said they were called the dimples of Venus, and Bette liked the name. Still, she wasn't sure they should be on show, but if she didn't turn, the dress was perfect. She bowed towards her reflection, smiled, threw her head back, laughing at an imaginary companion, holding a pretend cigarette, taking a drag. She could wear this if they started a dancing school, or when she met her husband.

Nail polish. She teetered towards the dressing table, fished out a crimson varnish. The top was stuck tight, and she didn't have the grip to open it. She tried the others. All the same. Ah well. She could pretend. She dabbed at the lipstick again, tucked her hair behind her ear, imagined when it would be long, when she would be a grown-up, go to a ball. She would insist to Lieselotte that this dress was hers. Lieselotte could have the everyday outfits. Bette the dreamtime ones.

She opened the wardrobe again, fingering through the rest of the evening clothes, a short black dress, a long red frock with a fantail, an emerald-green silk suit. Mutti hadn't worn them in the last few years, not since Vati had left to join the war. If Greta's father was home, Vati could not be far away.

Unless Lieselotte was right and he was a prisoner somewhere. What if they had shot him? What if he had died in the last battles of the war and nobody had been left to count the bodies? Mutti kept a picture of their wedding day in a silver frame by her bed.

She'd hidden it when the Russians came but Lieselotte had put it back in place, now that it was safe.

The photo had been coloured. Her mother's dress was cream and she carried a posy full of pansies, deep purple flowers that tumbled from her hands. Her father wore a suit and bow tie, had a clipped moustache and hair slicked to his temples. He wore it with a side parting. Herr Hitler had the same. It had been fashionable then, as she remembered. She'd recognise him, she was sure, even though she hadn't seen him for years. People didn't forget their parents. Did parents forget their children? She'd grown since he last saw her, her face had lost its chubbiness, her body had changed. Her hair was cut like a boy's. What if he didn't recognise her? What if she met him again and he said no, she wasn't his daughter? She hadn't thought about that. She squeezed her eyes shut. He'd never taken much notice of her, even before the war. Vati worked hard, that's what Mutti always said. He came home for dinner and wouldn't let them chatter at the table. She had been afraid of him. *You mustn't disturb him*, Mutti said, all the time. *Bette, don't pester your father. He's a busy man.* What if he said *Get out of my home? You're not mine.*

She'd ask Lieselotte when she came home.

She took off Mutti's gown and hung it back in the wardrobe, putting on her trousers and shirt. They had placed their favourite clock on one of the tables in the sitting room. Lieselotte had been gone for two hours. She'd said to eat the soup. Nettles and dandelions. The gas had come back on so Bette warmed it up, sat at the kitchen table, spooning it in, mopping her plate with a roll. There was one left. She should save it for breakfast. Perhaps the baker would have delivered fresh supplies by morning. Perhaps Lieselotte wouldn't notice. She'd have a little bit, that was all. She grabbed the second roll, tore it apart, soaked a quarter in the remains of the soup and gobbled it down. She eyed another quarter. She was too hungry to care. She wiped it round her plate, savoured the last of the moisture. There was only a half left and that would be stale by morning. It was wrong to waste it. Lieselotte shouldn't have gone out, shouldn't have left her. The bowl was dry now so she ate the bread as it was, savouring the rye, holding it in her mouth until it was soft and mushy.

She took her bowl and spoon over to the sink, turned on the tap, waiting while it spat and lurched before enough of a stream of water flowed and she could rinse the dishes from lunch and supper, put them to drain.

It was still light. Bette looked out of the window in the sitting room. Perhaps Lieselotte was coming round the corner. *Now.* She counted. In ten, she would come. *In forty, watch, she'll arrive.* Once more. *In fifty.* She shut her eyes, counting, *achtundvierzig, neunundvierzig, fünfzig.* The game didn't work. She sauntered over to the gramophone, took a record from its sleeve and placed it on the turntable. Tchaikovsky. *Swan Lake.* She pranced around the sitting room. It wasn't fair that Lieselotte was the only one they said could dance. She could, if she wanted. She flapped her arms, pirouetted to the window. No sign of her sister.

The music finished. She pulled out *The Nutcracker.* Mutti had danced them all, though she'd never become the principal ballerina.

'I married your father,' she'd said once. 'And that was that. You couldn't dance if you were married.'

'Did you miss it?'

Mutti had tilted her head to one side, fixed her eyes in the distance.

'Oh yes, Bette,' she said. 'I missed it all the time.'

Bette took the photograph albums from the bookcase and pored over them, turning each leaf and the delicate tissue paper that protected the pictures, staring at her mother as a young woman, so like Lieselotte it could have been her. Her beautiful, glamorous mother. Was Lieselotte as glamorous? Bette could only see her sister. How could she see her as others did?

She looked out of the window again. The light was fading, the long, slow sleep of the sun. It would be curfew soon. Lieselotte would be back by then. Perhaps she should go to Frau Weber before night fell. Tell her Lieselotte hadn't come home and could she please stay. Greta's father wouldn't mind, surely?

Frau Weber had been unfriendly this morning, and it was already gloomy in the stairwell, with no natural light coming in. What if she turned her away again? She couldn't be sure, but she thought Frau Weber had been drinking alcohol. People did funny things then.

It was hard to make out anything in the dark. Movements were silent shadows, no clacking heels, no rattling bicycles, no talking. She stood by the open window. Ivans were singing in the far distance, their voices waxing and waning in the summer breeze. Were those footsteps too? She leaned out, watched as a blurred figure turned the corner and walked towards their building. The candlelight from the Müllers' old apartment flickered on his face as he walked past.

Lieselotte would be home by morning. She'd promised. Bette changed into her nightgown, crawled into bed, picked up *Emil and the Detectives*. She'd read the story so many times, but its certainty was a comfort now. She snuggled down on her stomach, pulled the eiderdown over her, lit the candle, and began.

CHAPTER TWENTY-TWO

Berlin: July 1945

It had taken a pounding, John could see, become a furnace hot enough to melt the iron and twist it. The trusses of the bridge lay mangled, sharp diagonals gnarled and bent. The floor had collapsed, the base posts deformed.

'I don't like it,' Arthur said. 'It's too lonely. Why did she suggest you meet here?'

Some of the razor wire along the banks had been removed. Lieselotte was right. It might be possible to walk along parts of the canal. A single willow had survived the bombing. Its singed branches hung over the canal in a graceful arc, their tips stroking the surface of the water, new pale green fronds rustling in the summer breeze.

'To saunter, sergeant.'

'I suggest we leave, now.'

John checked his watch. Six o'clock. On time. She had been punctual last week. She was probably that kind of a person, thought it selfish to keep people waiting. He had thought about little else but her for a week, talking to her in his head, walking with her in his dreams, kissing her in the dark recesses of his sleep. It wasn't unusual, he reasoned, for a pupil to have a crush on their teacher. Fall in love.

The workers in the Tiergarten had gone home, leaving their plots and crops. He wasn't sure which direction to look for her, down Lichtensteinallee or Tiergartenstrasse. Both were empty. Arthur raised an eyebrow. He was wrong to make Arthur hang around with him. He was pulling rank and he knew it, and that was unfair.

'How long will you give her, sir?'

'What time is it now?'

'Ten past.'

He'd wait here all night if necessary, but Arthur would never put up with that.

'Till half past,' he said. He crossed his fingers, willing her to come. She must live at home. He wondered what she told her parents. Perhaps they didn't care, so long as the money came in. He didn't understand why Arthur was suspicious, although he could understand his fear now. The place was deserted. The war was over, but soldiers were sitting ducks for the trigger-happy in an occupied country.

Lieselotte. Cradling her blue enamel jug as if it was as precious as her clock, dancing, prancing around him, peek-a-boo in the dusty shrubs. Singing in her clear, soft voice. In all the destruction of this city, she was life. She was the single, singed salix along the bank, the baby blackbird in the bush. Perhaps, when he had time, he'd write her a poem in German, give it to her so she would remember him. Perhaps, when this was over, he'd come back to see her. Would it be the same?

Arthur was wandering close to the bridge.

'Be careful,' John said. 'There could still be mines.'

Arthur turned, walked back to John. 'She's not coming, sir.'

'Give her a few more minutes.'

Twenty past. He swallowed. He had no way of knowing where she lived, of contacting her. He'd had a German penfriend when he was at school, before the war. Her name was Gisela and she lived in Mannheim. They wrote stiff, stilted letters to each other, exchanged photos, had nothing in common. Lieselotte would be different. He'd take her address this time. She was passionate, he could see. She loved to dance, to sing. Did she love music? Art, literature? She was cultured, not rough and ready like some of the women he saw on the Kurfürstendamm or loitering by the barrack gates. Their letters would be full of life and joy.

Two soldiers were walking towards them along the Tiergartenufer. He recognised the uniforms and caps of the Soviet army. They looked different from the Red Army guards around the Brandenburg Gate. Officers, most likely. One was a squat man with a rolling gait, the other taller and more slender. The Russians stayed for the most part in their sector now the Allies had arrived. John wondered what they were doing this side of the Tiergarten. They drew close. Arthur had his hand on his pistol, but they seemed harmless, talking. As they passed, the squat one stepped forward.

'*Guten Abend*,' he said, removing his cap, nodding politely.

'*Guten Abend*,' John said. '*Es ist ein schöner Abend, nicht wahr?*'

'*Ja, ja.*'

'*Genießen Sie Ihren Spaziergang?* Are you enjoying your walk?' the squat Russian asked. His German was thickly accented but plain enough. He smiled, added, 'Or are you waiting for someone?'

The question was direct and John jolted. He tasted metal, began to sweat. Two British soldiers, alone by the empty canal. They should leave, not wait for Lieselotte. Arthur was right. The Russian raised an eyebrow.

'Perhaps we can help?' he said. 'And take you to the young lady?'

John's breath was shallow, perspiration on his lip. 'What do you mean? How did you know?' He wanted to drag the words back. He'd fallen for the oldest trick in the book. They had their confirmation.

'Follow me,' the Russian said.

John looked back at Arthur. 'Keep your distance,' he said. 'But cover me.'

'Where are you going?'

'The Russian wants me to follow him.'

'It's a trap, sir.'

'It's about Lieselotte,' John said.

'Don't go.' Arthur stepped in front of him, added, 'Sir.'

Arthur was right, but Lieselotte was drawing him like a magnet.

'Move aside, sergeant.'

Arthur stepped back, hand still on his pistol. John nodded at the Russian who, he now saw, wore the insignia of a major, and walked after him towards the ruins of the bridge. The other Russian had disappeared. The officer stopped, beckoned John closer, pointing beneath the bridge and the contorted posts that had once supported it. John stood on the shore and peered into the hollowed space beyond.

Lieselotte.

Knees twisted to one side, torso to the other. Her skirt was ruched around her thighs and there was blood on her legs. Her hair was fanned around her, a rich, dark halo against the thin ivory of her skin. He rushed to her, knelt down, cradling her bloodless face, wiping ash and leaf mould from her cheek. There was bruising on her throat, scratches on her arms. He ran his fingers down her neck, feeling for her pulse. Her dead pulse. Her blouse was torn and a shoe was missing.

'Who did this to you?' he said, his words thick with grief. 'Who did it, Lieselotte?'

A clock tolled the half hour, deep, solemn, *dong, dong*. John saw it a few feet away, lying in its walnut case in Lieselotte's string bag, cast away in the frenzy of her life.

'Who did this?' He tried to lift her, cradle her.

'You did.' The words were sharp in his ear. He turned. The officer's dusty boots were close to his chest. John hadn't heard him approach.

He laid her head back gently and stood up. The other soldier was walking towards him. He was thin, young, gangly, his skin punctured with weeping spots. John saw the chevrons on his sleeve, the stripes on his collar. He, too, had the ranking of an officer, a lieutenant perhaps, like himself. He stopped close to John. The two Russians, crowding either side of him. He wanted to stretch his arms, push them back.

'You murdered her,' the major said.

John looked from one to the other. His stomach lurched, his throat choked. He vomited into the charred earth, his frame heaving. He wiped his mouth on his sleeve.

'That's nonsense,' he said. His voice quavered but he willed it firm. He stood straight, jutted his chin, added, 'And you know it.' He leaned forward as another wave of nausea swelled inside.

The major smirked. The younger officer was nodding. The Russians stood their ground, John caught between them. Lobster claws, large and small, lethal. John wiped his forehead. He was sweating hard, his knees trembling as if detaching from his legs. He was dizzy.

'You have no evidence.' John groped for the words, pointed towards Arthur standing a few yards away. 'I have a witness.'

The younger officer produced a camera which he'd been holding behind his back.

'We have what we need,' he said in slow, minted English. John stepped back, arms flailing for balance, brushing the Russians as he fell. Had they taken pictures as he crouched over Lieselotte's body, held her face, hands on her neck, feeling her pulse?

John pushed himself up. 'No.'

He elbowed the lieutenant aside, stalked past the major, who grabbed his arm, spun him round, face up close so that John could see the bristles on his cheeks, the blackheads on his nose, smell his breath when he opened his mouth.

'We know who you are. We know what you do.' He jerked his head towards Lieselotte's body. 'We can help each other. Come to an agreement.' He reached over and picked up Lieselotte's bag with the clock, handed it to John, grabbing John's hand to make sure he grasped the handles.

'A memento.'

Evidence. John shook his head, let go of the bag so it dropped to the ground. The clock struck once, coils singing, fell silent.

'Come,' the thin lieutenant said. 'Walk with me.' He paused, added, 'Just you.' He nodded at his colleague. Arthur held up his arms as the major pointed his pistol at him.

The lieutenant clasped his hands behind his back, strolled as if this was a pleasure outing. John got the sense that he was the one in charge, even though he was the junior officer. John's mouth tasted sour, and his empty stomach rolled in painful spasms. His legs had no feeling, no gristle. They went through the motions of walking. One foot, another. The officer was silent. They drew close to the willow tree. He stopped, turned to John.

'My proposition is simple,' he said, his accent thick as a noose. 'You have military secrets that are, rightly, ours. Certain scientists you have interviewed, certain formula you privy to.'

'No,' John said. 'You're wrong. I haven't interviewed them. I know nothing.'

'I apologise,' the officer said. 'I exaggerate. You are translator. Am I correct?'

His English was faulty, but the meaning was clear. John nodded.

'As translator, you learn many thing.'

John shook his head.

'No,' he said. 'You're wrong again. I reproduce a sentence, but I work without meaning.'

The officer pursed his lips. 'I forget. You are new to this in the West, translating as someone speaks. We are doing it many years in Soviet Union. It is rare skill. And you are young. Inexperienced. Doing it for first time.' He paused, eyeing John, scrutinising him. John stood, fighting the trembling, the urge to run. Keep your wits, he thought, be agile. 'You correct transcripts, do you not?'

The officer knew too much about their practices. John said nothing.

'Let me explain your situation,' he went on, articulating each syllable. 'The British do not allow their men to fraternise, any more than we allow ours. Disobedience is an offence, is it not?' He peered closely at John, studying his insignia, added, 'Lieutenant. Same as me.' He patted his chevrons, grinned. 'Before, soldier. Now, lieutenant. Very clever.'

John's sinews tightened, tendons cramped. Paralysed.

'And murder,' he said. 'Cold-bloodied murder. That is capital offence, no? I believe penalty is death. Hung by neck until dead. Or perhaps, in army, you would be shot.' The officer picked off a willow leaf, rubbed it between his finger and thumb. 'Such an elegant tree,' he said. 'Good for hide-and-seek.'

John breathed hard. Arthur was a distance away, standing by the major, back to the bridge, his arms hovering over his head.

'My offer is as follows,' the lieutenant began. 'You pass us information we require. We have interest in particular scientists, particular subjects. If you accept our offer, we give you our shopping list. In return, we keep this murder to ourselves. Your commanding office, Major Buchanan—' he looked at John, he knew a great deal '— may never know you rape and murder innocent young woman.'

John's mind was frozen, hard and cold as a glacier. 'That's preposterous,' he said, his voice thin, reedy. 'You have no evidence.'

'We have all evidence we need to prove case.'

'You wouldn't be believed,' John said.

'You wouldn't want to put that to test, would you?' He clicked his heels, saluted, walked away, stopped. 'I almost forgot. I meet you here next week. Same time.'

John watched until he was out of sight, then turned and walked back to Arthur. The major put his pistol away as John approached, went behind the broken bridge, hidden from view. Arthur lowered his arms, rubbed his aching muscles. He looked angry, said nothing as he joined John. John's reckless, foolish passion had put Arthur in danger, implicated him in a crime, an accessory.

The evening was silent, save for the pigeons' breathy calls and the grating screech of a grey hooded crow. There was a loud splash, as if a crescent wave had broken, or a body fallen into the canal. The surface of the water rippled, lapped against the shore.

The major came out from behind the bridge, wiping his hands down his trousers.

There is no way out, John thought.

Arthur's silence was as loud as the plash of Lieselotte's body as she was rolled into the canal. He couldn't have known what the Soviet officer had said, but the way he held himself, the set of his cheek muscle, the veins in his temple told John that he understood its gist.

'I owe you an apology,' John said.

Arthur carried on walking, black army boots heavy on the broken pavement.

'Sorry won't get you out of this mess, sir,' he said. 'Not to me, not to anyone. Least of all that young woman.'

John swallowed. He should have said no, the bridge was too isolated, they'd meet by the Brandenburg Gate. He'd allowed his infatuation to colour his judgement. Her body had still been warm, though her skin had palled. He had smelled the damp soil in her hair, the blood caked on her hands and legs, the cloying scent of death. Her eyes had been open, bronze coins that had lost their lustre. He hadn't closed them. Why not? It was the least he could have done.

'If I report this,' Arthur said, 'you'll be court-martialled.'

He was right, but John was in no position to plead with him, *Keep quiet, please.*

They had entered the Kurfürstendamm. The barman from the Blaue Engel was serving tables on the street.

'We have transport back, sir,' Arthur said. 'In a while.'

John heard the words, nodded. Arthur beckoned the barman over as they came close.

'Two brandies.' He was walking and pointing to an empty table in the farthermost reach of the forecourt. John followed him over, sat down.

'I should have listened to you,' John said.

Arthur pulled out his cigarettes, took one and lit it, putting the pack away without offering it to John.

'You're on your own, sir,' Arthur said.

The barman brought two large bulbous glasses filled to the brim, and a carafe of water and tumblers. He put them on the table, waited, his hand outstretched.

John reached for his wallet, pulled out the money, gave it to him. 'Keep the change.'

Keep the change. A pittance.

John stared at the glasses, at the brandy refracting the light from the setting sun into a rainbow. How could he have been so idiotic? Mixed up Arthur in the whole business. He was about to be demobbed, to go back to civilian life, to his wife and little boy whom he'd never seen. He'd been fighting for five years. That was enough for any man. And he, John, had put that at risk.

'I'm not asking for your help, sergeant,' John said. 'I'm thinking how I can extricate you from my mistakes.'

Lieselotte. Had he loved her? It had felt real. Had his feelings for her been reciprocated? Had she, too, wanted a quiet spot where they could be together? Even so, he should have kept her safe, been a man. She'd died as if by his own hand.

They knew a lot about him, those Russians. Who he was, what he did. They knew where to stick their stiletto in, where to turn it. How did they know that?

He took a long sip of the brandy, its warmth gliding across his tongue and down his throat, his brain coming alive as the alcohol hit. Too much would leave him with a thick head and a thundering pain, and he might welcome that later, but for now it lifted him, made his senses more alert, acute. Arthur's face was in sharp focus, his ginger hair and freckles like a halo shedding gold dust. He hadn't noticed how his hair was wavy, how his eyes were a deep, Atlantic blue.

'Captain Thornton,' Arthur was saying, 'GSO3 in the Berlin Garrison. Perhaps best to make a clean breast of it.' Adding, 'Sir.'

John heard the name, leaned back in the chair, fingering his brandy, avoiding Arthur's eye.

'See what he can advise.' Added, 'Tell him I sent you.'

T-Force was the invisible wasp of the army, gobbling prey then dying away. Top secret. The bigwigs on the ground didn't know. John couldn't blow that cover, even with Arthur's recommendation. He'd be in worse trouble than he already was.

He stared into the distance, willing her to appear, sauntering between the tables, sitting with her skirt tucked tight around her thighs. Not ruched around her waist. Not raped. Murdered. Lieselotte. Who was she? He knew nothing about her. She had been expendable. No more than an object, like her clock, or this glass. He picked it up, swirling the drink around so it rose and fell, coating the sides with an amber sheen. He stared at it, at her eyes reflected there. He gulped it down, her image dissolving.

John stood up and threw the glass onto the ground, where it shattered into a thousand shards.

CHAPTER TWENTY-THREE

Berlin: July 1945

She woke up, startled by the birdsong, by an unease, as if there'd been an explosion, or a door banging. Lieselotte's side of the bed was empty. Bette flung back the cover but the sheet was smooth, the pillow plumped up. Lieselotte had not returned.

Bette swung her legs over the side of the bed and stood up, going to the window, leaning out. The bedroom faced the back courtyard and the place was deserted. Lieselotte had said she'd never leave her. But she had. She'd run off. That's why she hadn't let Bette go with her yesterday, because she was eloping. With her soldier.

Or Boris. *Boris.* She was carrying his baby, after all, and he'd said he would marry her.

She fingered her nightdress, scrunching it between her fingers, staring into the early-morning silence. What should she do? Who could help her? Frau Weber? Frau Weber had changed. She was drunken, coarse, played up to Greta's father, told Bette she wasn't wanted.

Bette sat down on the side of the bed. Lieselotte wouldn't leave her to marry Boris, or anyone. She just wouldn't. She'd said she knew a doctor who would fix the baby. Perhaps that's where she was going yesterday. Something had happened to her. She'd had an accident. Or died. How would Bette know? Who would tell her? Her sister was missing, but there were so many in the same boat, there was no point in adding Lieselotte to a list, even if she knew where to report her. Perhaps she'd joined the refugees, the people finding a way home or running to safety. She'd heard about them, though they hadn't seen so many in Mitte, not coming into the heart of Berlin. Only leaving. Would the Americans know? Or the British? She wouldn't do that without Bette. Unless she'd gone ahead to pave the way, would send for her later.

Yes. She was in a camp somewhere, where they put those kinds of people.

She padded out of the bedroom. The clock in the sitting room showed half past five. She had slept for hours. Bette dressed, pulling on the trousers, the dirty shirt, Otto's socks and shoes. Fear gnawed inside her, chomping at her gut, chewing on its gristle. Lieselotte wasn't in a camp. That wasn't what had happened. Something else had cropped up. She had been right to have been anxious. A premonition. She went to the bureau, pressed the buttons and pulled the levers in sequence, fingered the pistol Boris had left them. Bette brought it out of its secret place, took it with her into the kitchen, laid it on the table. She wasn't sure how to use it, except to point and squeeze the trigger, but it felt all right, sitting there, shielding her.

She should eat. Perhaps she'd feel better, settle her stomach, but there were no more rolls left. Perhaps Lieselotte had been out after curfew, taken shelter somewhere. She'd be hungry when she came home. Would Herr Grossman have more bread today?

The heft of a boot on the broken stone echoed round the empty stairwell. Another. Strangers had moved into the Baumanns' apartment but Bette never heard them coming and going. This step was laboured, deliberate. Lieselotte's was light, nimble. This was a man's tread. It was early in the morning. He was coming closer, louder. She heard him pause, heard the hiss of water as he pissed against a wall. Treads again. Up, up. Stopped. He was on the landing outside, his breathing laboured, wheezy. Who would be out at this hour? Perhaps he'd come to visit her new neighbours.

The key stabbed at their door, and she moved her fingers close to the gun. This was not Lieselotte. Those were not her steps. Who had a key to their apartment? Lieselotte knew how to jig the key, just so. She didn't need to stab at it, rattle it. Vati. Perhaps Vati had come home. Had forgotten the knack with the lock. She should open the door, let him in.

A man shouted, in Russian. Bette grabbed the gun, held it like Boris had shown her, arms out straight, two hands, squinting along the sights, pointing at the door. Her body was tense, firm, but inside it trembled. She couldn't shoot. What if it didn't go off? What if it wasn't loaded? She held the gun steady as the door gave way. Vasily stumbled in.

She smelled the alcohol, even from the end of the hall, the stale sweat. He staggered towards her, opening his mouth in a leer.

'Bert.'

Lurched forward. Three metres away. The gun was heavy. She held it tighter, to steady it as it shook in her hand. Two metres. She must shoot. Her stomach griped, iron in her mouth. His arms were reaching out as he pitched to the side. *Now.* She must do it now. Bette pointed, eyes blurred, the sights out of focus. Fired. The sound exploded in her head, the recoil pushed her off balance, but Vasily had slumped to the floor. Bette stood, trembling, taking in what she'd done, the noise drumming in her skull, echoing in her ears, the smell of sulphur filling her nose and mouth. Blood oozed through his trousers, puddling on the rug. He was groaning, holding his leg. Bette stared, unsure what to do. She had shot someone. Her heart was hammering, and she was sweating, hands sticky on the gun. He shouted at her. He was alive, could kill her. *Run, run.* She had to get by him, get over him. She breathed fast, jumped towards the door. He leaned out as she passed, grabbing her shin so she tumbled forward, hitting her nose on the edge of the door.

His fingers gripped as she fell, and the gun tumbled from her hand. She lay on her back as he snaked around. Her mind was spinning fast, her breath shallow. *Think. Now.* She pushed the gun beyond his reach, lifting her leg sharply so he lost his hold, brought her heel down on his hand, kicked out at his face, pushed herself into a sitting position, legs flailing, heels flying. The strength was sudden, came from nowhere, out of control. He was trying to stand, hovering over her. She cowered, waiting for his blows, but his leg gave way and he crumpled. She jumped up without thinking, kicked his wounded leg hard, and hard again as he curled in pain, still as a sleeping snake, leaping over his body, through the door, slamming it behind her, two steps at a time down the broken stairwell and into the street.

Round the corner. Don't stop. Don't look back. He could be following. He had a gun. Lieselotte. She must find her. She'd been in the Kurfürstendamm. That's where she was. Bette knew the way to the Tiergarten at least. Run and run. On. Run on. Her lungs hurt, her muscles were soft. No gristle, no strength. *Run.* She had a stitch. She needed to stop. She turned around but the street was empty behind her. She leaned against the wall of a building, doubled over, pressing her gut, chest heaving, her breath in short, shallow gasps.

A gang of women had started work clearing rubble opposite her. Was this where Lieselotte worked? She ran over.

'Excuse me, excuse me.' A Russian soldier moved towards her. Of course, he was in charge. She hadn't seen him. She froze. Did he know? He flipped his wrist, *move on, move on.* She backed away, looking carefully. Lieselotte was not there. The women had formed a chain. The last woman stood on the street close to her. The Russian had turned his back and Lieselotte went over.

'Have you seen my sister? Lieselotte?'

The woman shrugged, turned, stretched out her arms to take the next bucket, empty it out. She didn't care.

Bette sniffed. Her nose hurt. She touched it with her fingertips. Blood. On her hands, on her shirt. Her face, damp and sticky. Of course. She'd smashed it against the edge of the door. It hadn't hurt at the time, but now it throbbed.

She must go on. Apart from the women and their Russian gangmaster, the street was empty. She turned around, trying to find her bearings. She used to know the way to Unter den Linden, to the Kranzler Café, but the streets bore no resemblance to the boulevards she had known. The handsome buildings which had flanked them were mounds of rubble, the elegant cafés and shops no more than memories, their signage burned and buried in the ruins. Without the tall apartment blocks, the landmark signs, the streets merged into one desolate landscape, a topography of death, of destruction.

Bette turned. Spotted the cathedral. She knew where she was. Its spire was gone, its dome scarred, open sores where the windows had been. Behind it, the museums, their buildings black and battered with gaping windows and crumbled porticos, their walls gnawed and chewed. The Neues Museum had lost its cupola, its corners skewed, piles of broken bricks. She blinked. Mutti used to take them here once a month. They knew the Pergamon like an old friend, had stood in awe, she and Lieselotte. How had they got them here? That ancient altar? Those biblical gates?

She could not stop. On and on. Over the bridge. Past the Zeughaus, past the Neue Wache, its walls blasted out. The Friedrich Wilhelm University. She was out of breath, had to rest. She paused, gasping hard. Had Vati worked there once? What had he done there? She could not see Vasily, no soldiers were chasing her. Perhaps they had lost her, or she'd shaken them off. The penalty for injuring an Ivan was death. Would they know it was her? She'd been stupid enough to boast to Greta that she had a gun, and she wasn't sure Frau Weber wouldn't tell. Tears were filling her head, her mind. She looked around. Who could help her? Who could tell her, *You're all right, you're safe?*

Opposite, there were more rubble gangs at work, but the street was clear. They'd had the victory parade here, the road made passable so that the British could drive along. She hadn't gone to see it. Lieselotte had said there was no point. A couple of jeeps drove past her, Russian, but no one walked along the deadly boulevard, no one she could stop. *You look kind, can you help?* She didn't want a Russian. It couldn't be a Russian. She ran on, her breath coming in sharp, painful gusts. The Americans, or the British. They were in the Tiergarten, that's what Lieselotte had said, and Frau Weber had said they were in the western part of the city. Ahead of her she could see the crippled silhouette of the Brandenburger Tor. Her city. What had happened to her city?

The Führer had only ever spoken of Germany as powerful, as great and good. Reborn. Righteous. Germany would defend itself, he'd said, fend off the Russians and the others. Germany would be victorious. All she saw were ruins and death. She'd lived through the bombing, the pounding and blasting that went on for days and weeks and months, the dust and stench of cordite, the buried corpses and the scavenging homeless. She hadn't seen how wide the bombing was, how the heart had been wrenched from the body. Germany had been killed. Why did people hate Germany so much? What had her country *done?* To deserve this? There had been rumours, of murders, of Jews and Gypsies and others, of feeble children, of old people. Russians. Poles. Thousands. *Millions.* Bette couldn't imagine. It didn't match what the Führer told them, what she'd learned in school. She could see *this.* She couldn't see his words. She didn't know anymore. She didn't *understand.*

She was close to the gates. Soldiers were strutting up and down, cockerels in the coop checking who passed through, who passed out. Bette looked down at her shoes, the blood smears on her leg that Vasily had left. Her face was bloody, filth on her hands. She hoped they would see a dirty urchin and let her through. She walked towards the side gates close to the grand hotel where she and Oma had had tea on her tenth birthday. Through the ruined Tor she could see the Reichstag, its dome burned out, its walls charred and scarred.

A soldier was walking towards her. They had found Vasily, were searching for a boy who matched her description. This soldier would stop her, shoot her on the spot. This is the criminal who did it. String her up. Let this be a lesson to you all. She hesitated. She could run away, back the way she came, find another route through. Hide in the ruins of the buildings until the coast was clear. At night. The soldier drew level with her.

'*Papiere.*'

Bette shrugged, pretended not to understand, pointed to the Tiergarten. Bluff.

'*Meine Schwester,*' she said. My sister. He raised an eyebrow, tilted his gun so it pointed up, nodded his head. *Go on. Skedaddle.*

She guessed from the sun that it must be about ten o'clock. She crossed the road and walked into the Tiergarten. There were more women, bending, weeding, picking. That wasn't work that Lieselotte had done, so there was no point asking them if they'd seen her. She wasn't sure where the Kurfürstendamm was from here, whether it was far. Her legs were tired, her muscles quaking, as if she'd just run a race. She was faint, hungry, thirsty. She couldn't go back home. She had no home. What if Lieselotte had gone back, found Vasily there? Was he dead? He'd been alive when she left him. Would he shoot her?

'*Ja?*' A man had come up behind her. 'Can I help?'

Bette blinked. 'Where is the Kurfürstendamm?'

He pointed. 'That way. It's a bit of a stretch, mind.'

She nodded. She'd come so far. Just a little further. To the Kurfürstendamm. Then she could stop, ask around. Beg for water. Ask the way to Dahlem. To Oma. Lieselotte could find her there. Oma would understand. She half walked, half ran. The Tiergarten was huge, unfamiliar now in its nakedness. At last the zoo was on her right, but it looked abandoned, empty. There were two soldiers walking. British, she thought. She asked again.

They pointed. *That direction.* It all looked so different, as if she were walking in a moonscape, something she'd seen in the far crevices of her memory but which close up was no longer what she knew.

The single spire of the old Kaiser Wilhelm Church rose from the dead, hollowed out like a bad tooth, the nave flattened. Wind whistled through its empty windows, a ghostly melody.

Bette crossed the square and entered the Kurfürstendamm. She had expected it to be thronging with soldiers, but the street was empty save for a few women loitering by the cellars of the bombed-out shops and apartments. She saw a sign outside one. Der Blaue Engel. The door was open and she stepped down inside. An elderly man in an apron was wiping a table. He looked up.

'Out,' he said. 'Get out. We don't want the likes of you in here.'

'Please,' Bette said. 'I'm looking for my sister, Liese—'

'Clear out.' He didn't let her finish. 'Ask the women outside.'

'Please,' she said. 'Could I have some—'

'Out.' He shouted. She wanted water. That was all.

'*Bitte, Wasser.*'

He threw his cloth on the table, stomped to the bar, came back with a glass.

'Then clear off.'

She gulped it down. Her throat was dusty and dry and the cool water washed it smooth. She'd have liked some more but knew she shouldn't press her luck. What if he called someone, and they took her away?

'*Danke,*' she said, handing him the glass. He scowled.

She went outside. Opposite her, two women were sharing a cigarette. Bette went up to them.

'Sorry, sonny,' the younger of the two said. She had a gold tooth and brash lipstick. 'I only go with the big boys.'

'And the Yanks,' the other, an older woman with a sagging stomach, added.

Bette looked from one to the other, unsure what they were talking about. Her hand went to her face and she felt the crust of blood on her nose.

'Have you seen my sister?' she said. 'Lieselotte?'

'Does she work round here?'

'Work?'

'Yeah, you heard me.'

'No,' Bette said. 'She was selling a clock.'

The younger woman flung her head back and laughed, a coarse, common *ha-ha-ha.*

'That's what she called it, eh?'

Bette looked, one to the other. She didn't like that woman. Didn't *trust* her.

'What did you do to your face, sonny?' the older woman asked.

'I bumped into a door,' she said. 'And my nose bled.' This woman's voice had softened and Bette warmed to her. 'I know I look a mess but, please, I must find my sister.' She looked at the older woman's face, saw kindness there, enough to reassure her. 'She didn't come home last night,' Bette went on. 'She went out to sell one of Vati's clocks, and to meet a soldier, to teach him German.' Blurted it out. The older woman looked at her, pulled out a rag from her pocket, spat on it and gave it to Bette.

'Here. Wipe your face with that.'

Bette took the rag, wiped her face, handed it back.

'Don't give it back. I don't want it.' The older woman smiled. She was missing two front teeth. 'There's lots of folks come down here selling stuff,' she said. 'What did your sister look like?'

Bette breathed easier. This lady would help.

'She was a little taller than me,' Bette began. 'Brown hair, gold eyes. Thin.' Added, 'Dainty.'

'Dainty? That could be anyone,' she said. 'Why don't you go home and wait for her?'

'I can't,' Bette said. 'I can't go home.' She could hold it in no more. 'There's a Russian there. And Mutti died. I don't know where my father is. Lieselotte said if anything should happen to go to Oma in Dahlem but I don't know how to get there.'

The older woman looked at the younger, nodded.

'Listen, sonny—' she said.

'I'm not a sonny,' Bette said. 'I'm a girl. Lieselotte said it was safer this way, to dress as a boy.'

'Then what's your name?' Her voice had lost its vulgarity.

'Bette,' she said. 'My name is Bette Fischer.'

'Well, Bette,' she said. 'I'm going to take you to someone who can help.' She smiled. 'Follow me.'

§

The man who translated was Dutch but the officer in charge was American. They had given her water and some hard, dry biscuits and a nurse had wiped her face and cleaned her nose, gesturing, *it's not broken.* She'd given Bette a mirror. There were still traces of dried blood and speckles of dark dust. Two black eyes were emerging. Her face didn't look her own.

She spoke, a sentence at a time, so the Dutchman could put her words into English. The American nodded, raising an eyebrow, writing in his notes. She didn't tell them that she had shot the Russian. She told them she couldn't go home. She didn't know the address. She told them that her mother was dead, her sister was missing, and her father hadn't come back from the war. She had nowhere to go. Her grandmother was very old and she didn't know if she was alive, or how to get there. Could they please give her a lift? She didn't have the street or the number, but she'd recognise it when she got there.

'Listen, Bette,' the American said.

'*Hör mal, Bette,*' the Dutchman said.

'I don't know how we can help you,' the American went on. 'You're not a Displaced Person, you're not a Jew, or a Pole, or Ukrainian. You're a German. Maybe you're an orphan.' He leaned back in his seat. 'Maybe not. Maybe this is a trick, maybe not.'

'A trick?' Bette said.

'Yeah. They send the kid out first to get sympathy, then pile in behind.'

'I don't understand,' Bette said. 'I want my sister. I want my Oma.'

'But you don't know where she lives. You don't know your own address.'

She couldn't give them that. What if they went and found Vasily? Or made her return and wait for Lieselotte? Her hands were quivering and she was shaking her head, tears of frustration welling up.

'Please.' Her voice was soft, fretful. 'Please help me.' She looked at the American, at the nurse. 'I don't know what to do. Where to go.' *I'm frightened.*

The American leaned forward, nodded at the Dutchman.

'How about I say you're running away from the Russians?' he said, as the Dutchman put it into German. 'We can put you in temporary care for the time being, with other orphans, get you transferred somewhere else later. Maybe get you adopted if no one comes to fetch you?'

Bette nodded.

It was a house in Eisenacher Strasse, in the south of the city, a long way from Dahlem. But his voice was tender, and the place sounded safe.

He picked up the telephone. Another soldier came in, a woman, stout, with UNRRA on her armband. She smiled, held out her hand, and Bette took it. Didn't matter she was nearly thirteen.

CHAPTER TWENTY-FOUR

Berlin: August – October 1945

'How did they know? Informed guesswork,' the major said. 'We don't have a mole in our outfit. The Soviets work the same way as us. Only less efficiently.'

He picked up a paper knife, tapped it against his forefinger, nodding at the officers either side of him. As it happened, Major Buchanan had called in Captain Thornton from the army garrison, and another officer John had never seen before. Major Somebody-or-other. He'd forgotten his name already. JIC. Joint Intelligence Committee. John was waiting for the bollocking, but his CO and the army officers were all smiles, as if John had excelled himself.

'Some of the scientists they had their eye on slipped through their net. We got there first, evacuated them before they could.'

Major Buchanan put the knife on his desk, tilting the blade so the handle lifted up, rocking it like a see-saw. The JIC major leaned forward.

'This young woman...' He paused, looking hard at John. 'There's plenty of starry-eyed radicals and fellow travellers who are only too happy to ease the Russkies' way in here.' He nodded. 'Our guess is that she was one of them. Used by the Soviets, dispensed with when she was of no further service. Pretty clumsy attempt to blackmail. Typical, mind you.'

He spoke sense, and yet, John thought, what he said was nonsense too. Lieselotte was young. He couldn't see her as an agent. And even if she had been, why would they have murdered her if she could help them? Perhaps someone else had killed her, and the Reds were exploiting it? His thoughts hurtled round, ricocheting from front to back.

Unless she knew the bandy-legged Soviet officer and his skinny, spotty sidekick, had been instructed to seek John out and lure him to the bridge? It had been her idea to meet there. She knew it would be deserted. Had the Russians put her up to it? Had something gone wrong and they had eliminated her? Had she been about to blow her cover? Perhaps she wasn't as innocent as she had seemed. The major was right. He'd know this sort of thing.

'Wouldn't waste tears over her,' the major said. 'Not worth it, women like that.'

John remembered their first meeting. There had been nothing contrived about it. A chance encounter. He found it hard to accept that he had been targeted, or that she had dangled herself as bait.

Lieselotte murdered, the imprint of the ligature fresh on her neck.

'If you want to sacrifice your career, your reputation, perhaps, even, your life for her, that's a choice you alone can make.' He sniffed, twisted his mouth. *You're on your own, sir.*

John stared at his hands, at the vein in his thumb. Strange how sometimes it was hidden deep beneath his skin, at other times pulsed on the surface.

'But if you come on board,' the JIC major was saying, 'then SIS have a use for you. Sprinkles of brilliance there, among a bunch of amateur duds.'

An offer he couldn't refuse, as good as an order.

'Yes, sir,' he said.

'I'll inform the funnies,' the major went on, adding, 'MI6 to you.' He ran his finger inside his collar. 'They'll take it from there. Any questions?'

'What do I do?'

'Do? You *do* as we say.' He leaned back, twisting his mouth into a smile. John wasn't sure whether it was meant to reassure, or to mock. 'When their shopping list arrives, Second Lieutenant, we get a rough idea of the gaps in their cupboard. So we help fill it. We give them solid information to start with. Nothing that damages us. To establish your credentials. Good God—' He stood up and walked to the window. 'Did you see that? A European roller, if I'm not mistaken. Bright blue plumage.' He leaned out of the window, head craned to his left. 'Gone now. Rare round these parts.' He returned to the table, sat down. 'Cheers my heart up no end to see a rare bird like that,' he said. 'Almost as good as a pretty girl. Are you into birds, Lieutenant?' He raised an eyebrow. 'Or women?'

'You were saying, sir,' John said.

'Yes.' He sighed, pulled his chair closer. 'Well then,' he went on. 'As time goes on, the information becomes not so much solid as supple. We see it as a spectrum, Second Lieutenant. Verifiable truths at one end. Downright lies at the other. But clever lies. Plausible lies.'

'And my job is to feed this to them?'

'Do you have qualms?'

'But if they think I'm giving them the truth' – that made him a *double* agent – 'and then they discover it's not, what happens then?'

'What happens then?' The major looked at his colleagues, eyes left, right. 'If you're rumbled, we'll deny everything, that's what will happen.'

John could feel his knees quiver. He was on his own now, no protection, not from anyone, not even his own side.

'They'll interrogate you,' the major went on. 'Try to squeeze out all the information you have. I don't suppose they're too scrupulous with their methods, Second Lieutenant, so you need to brace yourself. It won't be a cosy chat, not like this.' He took a deep breath. 'Then I expect they'll shoot you, that's what will happen.'

I don't want to do this, John wanted to say. *I can't do it.* He was no hero. He wasn't made for spying, wasn't duplicitous enough. Wasn't *sure* enough.

The major smiled. 'On the other hand, if we think they're getting suspicious, we'll try and pull you out in time. Don't worry.' The major waved his hand, dismissing him. 'Your handler will take you through it. Operation Birdcage. That's its name from now on. Rather good, isn't it? What with the sighting of that roller...' He checked his watch. 'If you'll excuse me.'

John pushed his chair back, saluted.

'Good chap, that officer,' Major Buchanan said, once the major had gone.

'I'm sorry,' John said. 'What was his name again?'

'Goodfellow,' Major Buchanan said. 'Appropriate, eh? Major James Goodfellow.'

'Sir.' John tipped his forehead, turned on his heel and left. He'd have liked to have had a drink with Arthur, but Arthur was already back home, and this new task was top secret. Arthur hadn't given him advice, not in so many words. Just a name that in the end Major Buchanan called in. But the implication had been clear. Face up to it, and take the consequences.

John went into the mess, bought himself a beer, retreated to a corner. His stomach gurgled, juices and adrenalin storming inside him, while his mind saw her body, sacrificed for him.

He wasn't cut out for the murky world of intelligence. He couldn't lie to save his life. It wasn't right. He gulped his beer, swallowed too hard so it clogged his gizzard. This pain was how he felt, choked and angry. He'd been pushed into a corner by the

Russians, he knew that. His idiocy had led to Lieselotte's death, and now his damned *weakness* had been manipulated by his own side. He slammed his fist on the table, making the glass tilt. He grabbed it before it toppled, ignored the scowls of the bartender. He didn't want to do this. He should have accepted demotion, imprisonment, or any other punishments the army meted out to those who broke the rules. Risked the wrath of his father, sullied the family reputation. Could he run away? Go AWOL? Desert? Join the French Foreign Legion? Did he have the courage? No. He was a coward, drifting flotsam swallowed by any strong-armed current. He couldn't even say *no*. Perhaps he could pretend he was a refugee and hide out in some DP camp. They'd shoot him if they found out. He'd prefer that.

He swallowed his beer, went up to his room, lay face down on the bed, pulling the pillow over his head. Screwed up his eyes and wept.

§

The lieutenant said his name was Anatoly.

'One Minox camera. Two cartridge. Our list.' He handed John a slim package. 'There is kiosk by the Kochstrasse U-Bahn. Every Friday at 5 p.m. *on time* you pick up copy of the *Deutsche Volkszeitung*. You slip cartridge inside, hand seller money, he give you paper. New instruction. New film.'

He wasn't much older than John, but he was confident, assured. He handed over the slim package and John slipped it inside his pocket. Anatoly nodded. The evidence was out of sight.

'No talk. No questions. You pay man at kiosk, you go. Understand?'

John had been assigned a driver, Corporal Baxter, from Arbroath.

'My orders, sir,' he said, handing John a sheet of paper. *Fridays. 16:15 pick-up. 16:30 collect Birdcage as instructed. 17:00 transaction. 17:05 return barracks.* 'Until further notice.'

The meetings with the handler came later. John never knew where or when. A shadow from a portico, an unexpected companion at the bar, a *do you have a moment?* at the end of the day. Certainty. Uncertainty. It blanked his mind so only memories remained, piled high in the rubble of his life.

Lieselotte. Had she been recovered from the canal? Buried with a name? Or was she fished from the water and dropped in a communal grave? Not knowing chewed at him, grieving drowned him, tear by tear. And all the time. This *mission*. His official job hadn't changed, appearances were being kept up, except there was probably a handwritten note of it in some War Office file and a duplicate in MI6. At what point would the Russians realise he was spinning them along? That he was passing them duds? How long before the garrotte tightened round his neck too? How long before his body was tossed into the slurry of the Landwehr canal?

Fear was a gale that blew his breath away. Fridays it was a tornado, spinning him round, John caught in its eye, not knowing where he'd land.

The film was in its envelope, the checklist marked up. He had no idea what it contained, what messages were sent. It was in his breast pocket, ready to be whipped out and inserted in the newspaper. He could feel that final rush of adrenalin as he prepared to step out of the car. Corporal Baxter slowed down. The kiosk was shut.

'Don't stop,' John said. 'Drive past.'

'Round the block, sir?'

5 p.m. *on time.*

'No,' John said. 'Return to barracks.' Baxter did a U-turn, and they passed behind the back of the kiosk. Anatoly was leaning against it, lighting a cigarette, hands cupped over the match, eyes focused down. He looked up as John drove past, shook the match dead and threw it into the gutter.

§

Orders were orders. Major Buchanan didn't waste time.

'Your translation duties are terminated with T-Force,' he said. 'You've been reassigned. International Military Tribunal. Nuremberg. Start Monday. Leave tomorrow. Thank you, Second Lieutenant.' He held out his hand, and John took it. 'It's been a pleasure working with you. Good luck.' He saluted, turned, walked away.

Not a word more, or less. Terminated. *Boom.* Nuremberg must be three hundred miles away at least. A good day's travelling, straight into the fray. The trials were scheduled to start in November. He wasn't sure he had the guts for it. But he wasn't sure how long he could have lasted doing what he was doing. It would have taken very little to flip him over. Perhaps they saw that.

CHAPTER TWENTY-FIVE

London: September 1958

'Lieselotte?' Her breath bubbled, had no depth, no strength. She leaned towards him, spine frail, spindly. 'Lieselotte?'

Two query lines creased his forehead. 'Yes.'

She studied his face, as if she could see her sister etched between his brows. She had to be sure.

'What was she like, this Lieselotte?'

John raised his shoulders. 'She was lovely,' he said. 'But I didn't really know her well.'

'No,' Betty said. 'What did she *look* like?'

'Oh.' He rubbed his chin with the palm of his hand and she heard the scritch of his whiskers. 'It's been a while. I need to think.' He paused, looking at her, his upper lids half closed. 'She was about your height, I'd guess. Maybe a little shorter. Brown hair, brown eyes. Slim…' He paused, added, 'I think you'd call it *petite*. She reminded me of a ballet dancer. And she could dance.'

'You went dancing?'

While she'd sat by herself, alone, frightened? The resentments, the *anger* against her sister rose to the surface. Of course Lieselotte hadn't wanted her clumsy, two-left-footed sister there. *How dare she.*

'No,' John said, waving his hand as if to bat away her thoughts. 'We didn't go dancing. That wasn't possible. But she danced. And sang, too.' He sighed. 'It was a way of connecting, that was all. Why are you asking?'

'Where were you?' Betty said, ignoring his question. 'Singing and dancing?'

'Does it matter?'

'Yes.'

'If you don't know the place, it's meaningless.'

'Tell me.'

'All right. We were in a huge park in the centre of Berlin, called the Tiergarten.'

'I know,' she said. 'I know where the Tiergarten is.'

'I'm sorry.' He rubbed his chin again. 'I didn't know you knew Berlin.'

'*Du hast nie gefragt.*' You've never asked. She used the familiar, '*du*'. She'd have to tell him now, anyway, and it seemed right to talk in her native tongue.

He cocked his head to one side, a curious pigeon. 'Of course, you speak German.' His voice was low, as if he was talking to himself, and Betty wondered if she'd heard him right.

'Why do you say that?' she said.

'I can't tell you how I know,' he said. 'Not now, at any rate. Not here.'

She was so close to him, her face tight against his, apprehension plunging inside her like an axe in a mineshaft.

'What do you know about me?'

Dee knew a bit about her, but not everything. Not the personal stuff, the woman stuff. Or about Vasily. She'd never shared her past with anybody. What did John know? How had he found out?

He looked around him, left, right. 'Let's go somewhere quiet,' he said. 'We have to talk.'

'Nobody can hear us.'

'We could be seen.' He paused. 'Could we go to my rooms? Everywhere else will be shut. Could you bear it?'

She picked up on his fear now, this lurking unseen presence in the peace of Soho Square on a late summer's afternoon where the insects buzzed and the pigeons wooed and the sparrows flitted from tree to tree. There was her own fear now, that tumbril of anxiety that she'd had the night Lieselotte had left and not returned. This man linked the two. Because although his description of Lieselotte could match anyone in Berlin, and goodness knows Lieselotte was a common enough name, Betty had no doubt that he was talking about her sister.

Did he know that?

Lieselotte had been pregnant. Did he know that, too? She clasped her hands over her stomach. She should tell him she was expecting his baby. She needed help, and it wasn't fair that she should shoulder this alone. But he'd rejected her once. She wasn't sure she could take it twice.

'All right,' she said. She followed him out of the square and walked beside him in silence, the ten minutes it took to reach Bury Place and his rooms.

He made a pot of tea, pulled out some malt bread from the pantry, slathered it with butter which had turned a little rancid. Betty scraped it off. They sat at his table, on opposite sides. Behind him was the clock, marking time, soundless. An eight-day clock with its neat, modern mechanism tucked away at the back, its smoked glass face and elegant numerals.

'Who are you?' she said.

'You know who I am,' he said.

'I'm not sure I do,' she said. 'How did you know I was German?' She wondered if he was some kind of spy, except that would be too absurd. What on earth would he want to spy on her for? Besides, he was a teacher, for heaven's sake.

He lifted his cup, put it back crooked on his saucer so it rocked. He settled it, long fingers round its rim. He's playing for time, she thought.

'I can't tell you that now,' he said. 'It involves someone I met in Berlin, from those days.'

'You've just lured me here,' she said. 'You're not going to give me anything, are you?'

'I'll give you what I can.'

She pushed her chair back, walked over to the shelf, picked up the clock and put it down on the table. 'Start by telling me how you got this clock. And how you met this Lieselotte.'

He looked up, searching her face. You're so transparent, she thought. You'll make up anything. He was a fantasist, unbalanced.

'Don't lie,' she said.

He reached for his cigarettes, offered the pack to her.

'No thanks.' Who needed cigarettes now? Buying time again. She wouldn't make it easy for him.

'Not long after I arrived in Berlin,' he said. 'My sergeant got his demob papers. We went to celebrate, in the Kurfürstendamm. Some of the bars had re-opened in the cellars and Arthur and I went to one, the Blaue Engel.'

She could feel her teeth grinding, jaws clammed tight.

'We drank champagne.' He looked at her, as if to apologise. 'It was so cheap. A criminal luxury, really, when all around us was shattered and people starved.' He took a drag on his cigarette. 'Let alone those poor so-and-sos in the camps. And all those murdered.' He shuddered, paused. 'I don't think there'd ever been a war like this one. Looking back, I don't know how we could have drunk it, but the likes of Arthur had been fighting for years. I guess they thought they deserved it.'

'Spare me your sensibilities,' she said. 'Your justifications.'

He stubbed out his cigarette, took another from the pack. *He's nervous.*

'Perhaps we'd had too much, I don't know. But all of a sudden a young woman appeared. My sergeant thought she might be on the game, you know? He told her to go away.' John batted his hand, as if he was reliving the scene. 'But she sat down and pulled out this clock from her bag.' He reached over, ran his hand around its circular rim. 'I was taken with it.' He looked up at Betty. 'I was taken with her, too. She was so pretty, sitting there. So neat. Innocent, or so I thought.'

'Why do you say that?'

He fidgeted in his chair. 'No reason,' he said. 'I shouldn't have said it.'

'But you did.'

'I'm sorry.' He paused. 'I'll come to that. Will you hear me out?'

'Go on.'

'I bought it. Five cigarettes. Simple as that.'

'Simple?' she said. 'Everything has a story. Every*one* has a story. Did you ask her?'

John picked up the teapot, took it into the kitchen. 'Would you like a top-up?'

She didn't answer, waited while he poured on more hot water, came back.

'Did you?'

'I planned to,' he said. 'I planned to ask her. I wanted to see her again, so suggested she gave me German lessons. She agreed, and we met at the Brandenburg Gate, walked in the Tiergarten.' He stirred the tea, poured himself another cup. 'But our conversation was awkward, until we started singing. Sounds silly, but there's German songs and English songs that are the same. We shared a birthday and—'

'Wait,' Betty said, holding up a hand. 'Tell me. When was her birthday?'

'February nineteenth,' he said. 'Same as mine. Same birthday. Same year. That's what broke the ice. And then she danced.' He looked up. 'A polka. Can you believe that? It was a joyous moment.'

Lieselotte had looked happy, for one second, that last night, before she went to see him again. Betty had no doubt that John was the soldier she had planned to meet.

'We forgot where we were, who we were. Why both of us were there.'

'And then?'

'Then we agreed to see each other again, and she suggested the Lichtensteinbrücke. She said it would be quiet, and we might be able to walk along the Landwehr canal.'

He was cradling his cup, but his hand trembled. She let him steady himself.

'Only she didn't come. Instead, two Russians were there, and they took me to her.' He put his hand over his eyes, dragged it over his face. 'She'd been murdered.' His voice grew soft, quavered. 'Raped, murdered.'

Betty stood up and walked over to the window, staring into the chasm of the street below, the blackened buildings, the sombre porticos of the British Museum. She wanted to howl like an animal, rip out her heart and every ounce of feeling she possessed, rid herself of the agony of knowing.

'You see,' John was saying, 'it may have been an ambush. It was an odd place to meet. It was isolated, out of bounds, almost. Perhaps I had been lured there—'

A dam broke within her. She spun round, flew at him, hammering her fists into his shoulders, his body.

'She was my sister.' Her voice was loud, choked with sobs. 'She was my sister.'

He sat back in his chair, hands up to protect his face. 'What? Your *sister*?'

'This was no ambush. She'd never lure you there. That's not who she was. She hated the Russians, after what they did to her.'

'I didn't know that, Betty,' he said. His voice had a catch in it and she watched as he struggled with his words, small beads of sweat glistening on his forehead. He looked at her, examining her face, her eyes and nose and mouth. 'How is that possible?' He breathed out, pulled his handkerchief from his pocket, wiped his forehead. 'I'm so sorry. If I'd known she was your sister I'd have broken the news more gently.' He stiffened in his chair, holding out a hand towards her. She looked at his hand, at his frame sunken in misery. She felt a sudden rush of tenderness towards him, an urge to touch his hand, hold it, squeeze out all this sorrow. His fingers flexed. She waited until he withdrew it.

'I couldn't be sure, at the time,' he was saying. 'That it wasn't a set-up.'

Her lips tensed up and she bit down hard, trying not to cry. 'She was happy to meet you. She went out to sell another clock, then was going to join you after.' Her hair loose, and Mutti's comb holding it in place. 'We needed the money, from the clock. From your lessons.' Betty hadn't told a soul this, not to her father, not to Dee. 'You see, she was pregnant.'

And so am I.

His eyes were moist when he turned to her. 'Oh my God.' He raised his hands, palms facing out. 'The baby wasn't mine. I swear.'

Of course it wasn't his, she knew that. She didn't want to hear his denials, his excuses.

'And then what?' she said. 'What happened then?'

'I can't tell you what happened after.'

'Why not?'

He took a deep breath. She knew he wasn't going to answer. This was her *sister*. Did he enjoy this mystery? This cloak-and-dagger war? Was he doing it to hurt her?

'It's all top secret, that's why, to do with my job, in the war. I said that earlier. They wanted information, that's all I can say.'

'Who's "they"?'

'The Russians.'

'What information?'

'I can't tell you that either.'

'You can't tell me anything,' she said, fury and exasperation bubbling. Her head tensed and she felt dizzy. 'You could be making this up. For all I know, you could have killed her and blamed it on the Russians. How convenient.'

'Please, Betty,' he said. 'You must believe me.'

'And now?' she said. 'What's this got to do with *now*?'

'One of the Russians I met that day is in London, and has made contact with me.'

'Why?'

He wet his lip, fiddled with the packet of cigarettes in front of him. He took one out, lit it. The ashtray was brimming over with butts.

'They think I owe them. Can help them again.'

'Do you? What with?'

'Nothing,' he said. 'But I have to play them along.'

'Who says?'

'Please, Betty. I didn't want to get you involved. I can't tell you anything.' Betty could hear the clang of a fire engine in the distance, and below in the street, the distinctive chug of a London cab. A cool breeze crept in through the half-open window, made her shudder. 'Except that they have you in their sights.'

'Me?' She laughed. 'You're out of your mind. Why on earth would they want me?' She watched as he sat down again, his mouth playing with silent words. '*I can't tell you*,' she said, mimicking his reply before he said it. He breathed in, and she saw the veins on his neck swell and pulse.

'What I can tell you,' he said, 'is that you are their route to your father. What I can't tell you is why.'

She could feel her guts tighten.

'My father? What for?' The Nazis. It had to be that. He said he never knew. But she saw how terror drove people into silence, fearful for their families. There were plenty who believed, too.

Waltraud. The Baumanns. Perhaps her father. 'War crimes,' she said. 'Is he a war criminal?' On Sark? Perhaps he committed some crime before he went there.

'No,' John said. 'Not that.'

He stared ahead. She sat down on the edge of the chair, the clock in front of her, John's face distorted through its glass. She went cold, as the truth rose like the sun on the horizon.

'Are you in with the Russians?' she said. 'Did you befriend me so they could get to me? Seduce me on their orders?'

He sat, unmoving, expressionless save for a muscle twitching in his cheek. He opened his lips as if to speak, clammed them shut as he lifted his hands to cover his face. She leaped up, pulling out her cigarettes, throwing five on the floor.

'Take your filthy money back.' She grabbed the clock, chucking the rest of the packet at him. 'Keep the rest, too, give it to the Russians. Settle the debt, you cynical bastard.'

She ran out of the door, down the stairs, onto the street, John's voice echoing after her. *Stop. Betty, please.*

Round the corner, into Bloomsbury Way. John had manipulated her in cold blood. What debt did John owe the Russians? What terror had they injected in him that he would sacrifice her to save his own skin? Or was he just a scheming reptile without a qualm? Or deranged? She should have recognised that the first time they met, with his bouts of frenzied tremors. This Russian could be a figment of his imagination.

Lieselotte. Her beloved sister, murdered. Why? *Why?* It happened often enough at the end, she knew that. But every murdered woman was someone's sister, mother, daughter. Not another body. Had she struggled before she was plunged into darkness? There had always been a sliver of hope that perhaps somehow she had survived, would turn up, *Hallo, meine Bettelein*, although that hope had grown smaller with every day and year that passed until it was no more than a pinprick on the horizon.

Betty stopped. She was tired of running. Tired of running from him. She looked at the clock, at its familiar shape, the worn chrome, the chipped II on the Roman numerals of its face. Her sweaty fingers had left greasy prints. Her father had never asked about his clock collection, any more than he'd asked about what happened to his family, or to Germany.

She was about to set off again when she spotted him.

Vasily. Walking in the opposite direction, on the other side of the street. There was no mistaking him. She froze, ice sliding down the follicles of her skin. He'd bulked up since she last saw him, his weeping sores now pitted scars. He limped, a stiffness in his leg, as if a muscle or a tendon had been severed, or a bone chipped, once. He passed by, not noticing her. He turned into Bury Place.

If he suspected she was there, he didn't show it, his eyes focused forward. She stood on the corner, checking her watch, peering along the street as if waiting for someone. She saw him stop at the door to John's rooms. Ring the bell. He pulled out something from his jacket and for a moment she thought it could be a gun before he disappeared into the building and she saw it was a bottle.

She could hear in her mind the thud of his tread as he stumbled up the broken stairwell in Mitte, the scratch of the key in the door. Of course. Strange how memory plays tricks, how it buries a detail so deep that only the right trigger releases it, like the secret compartment in Mutti's bureau, levers pressed in sequence before the big reveal.

He'd had the key to their apartment. He and Boris always entered from the service door. But he'd come through the front door. The key could only have been taken from Lieselotte. She kept it on a chain around her neck. Had he taken it from her after she was dead, or before? Or had John taken it, and given it to him? She stared down the street to John's doorway. Nothing made sense except the terror of those memories, a frozen axe that stilled her nerves. She saw him as he lurched towards her, felt his hands grab her crotch as he lifted her onto the bike.

He had come for her that morning. Not Lieselotte. *Her.*

The Russian was real. It was Vasily, and John was in cahoots with him. John claimed he was protecting her. How could she trust him? He could be playing for time, ready to deliver her. She couldn't imagine what business they would want with her father. But she could see what business Vasily might want with her.

Betty was breathless, her heart heavy in her chest, its hefty drum thumping the beat. She swallowed, shut her eyes for a second, organising her thoughts. Dee had made her promise to think very hard about her decision. The embryo inside her was no larger than her little fingernail, a tumbling mass of cells and glands and fluids. She couldn't forgive John. Ever.

There was a telephone box in Southampton Row. She opened the door, waited while the stench of piss and cigarettes billowed out, took out the four pennies that she kept for emergency phone calls, and the number from Dee which she'd slipped into her wallet for safekeeping.

CHAPTER TWENTY-SIX

London: September 1958

Of all the young women he could have met in Berlin, and London, for them to have been *sisters* beat all odds. Did Anatoly know they were sisters? If he did, that made it more urgent than ever. He couldn't see now how he could win her trust. She'd rushed away so fast, he hadn't time to think. He had lost her forever.

The cigarettes were on the floor. Not quite Judas money, but tainted nonetheless. One had snapped as she'd pulled it out of the packet and lay with its tobacco in flecks around it, golden pollen on his shabby brown linoleum. He scooped it up with his hand, threw it in the fireplace.

Was there a likeness between the two, something that had drawn him to both? They didn't look like sisters – different builds, different complexions. Beyond that? He hadn't had time to know Lieselotte but he'd thought of her as light-headed, a dreamer, a fantasist, perhaps. Betty was serious, committed, ambitious. He knew so little about her, too. Why hadn't she told him who she was? Why hadn't she said at the outset, *I am German*? But then, even now, so many years after the war, emotions ran high. People took a long time to forget, or to forgive. Krauts. Nazis. Hun. Bosche. If he had been in her place, he'd have probably kept quiet too so no one could point a finger, would have done his utmost to speak English without an accent. Not easy for a German to do that, though she'd been a child when she learned. That helped. Besides, who was open at the end of the war, or honest? Whose voices were muffled because there was no vocabulary for horror, whose muted out of guilt or self-protection? All of history was masked, a mass lying. Lying in wait. Hoist up the biggest guns in Nuremberg and let them swing for their sins, but leave the everyday man with no accounting.

He had nothing to report. Anatoly could whistle in the wind. But John's job had got a whole lot harder.

The doorbell clanged, echoing through the hall and stairwell. Perhaps Betty had changed her mind, come back for more information. Bob usually got the outside door, but he must be out. The bell rang again. John went down the stairs, strode across the hall, pulled the lock.

Anatoly whipped out a bottle of vodka from his inside pocket as John opened the door. He strode past without invitation and began to climb the stairs to John's flat. He'd never been before, but he knew where he was going.

John wasn't used to spirits. He couldn't read the Cyrillic lettering on the label, but Anatoly said it didn't matter. This was courtesy of the Soviet embassy. He'd never be able to buy it here. Not this quality. Only in the Soviet Union. Pride of the diplomatic corps. Wheat and rye. Bay and caraway. It made him happy, relaxed.

'You went away in the summer,' Anatoly said. His English had improved since Berlin and although his accent was thick, his grammar and syntax were correct. 'Were you on holiday? We couldn't find you. Were you somewhere nice?'

John wasn't sure whether he was bluffing or not. *Give them the benefit of the doubt.* They hadn't traced him, he had been safe.

'Yes,' John said.

'Would you recommend it?'

'That depends on what sort of holiday you like,' John said. He'd lie if necessary.. Claim he walked the pilgrims' route from Oslo to Trondheim. Four hundred miles. He'd give him a daily account if he wanted. Bore the pants off him. 'Why are you here?'

Anatoly shifted in his seat, looked at the bookcase. 'You have a gap in your shelves,' he said. 'As if something has been removed.'

'I had some pottery,' John said, thinking fast. 'Leach. But I broke it.' He shrugged, added, 'Irreparably.'

'A shame. Always a shame if one loses something precious,' Anatoly said. He raised his glass, a sherry glass, the smallest John could muster. '*Za vstrechu,*' he said. 'To our meeting.' He swallowed it in one go, reached for the bottle. 'To refresh,' he said, topping up his and John's glass. 'Tell me, how long has it been since we renewed our acquaintance?'

'You know as well as I,' John said.

'And where have we got to?'

'I cannot do this.'

'You helped us before,' Anatoly said, lifting his glass again and eyeing the vodka. He rubbed his finger round the rim of the glass until it squealed. 'Did your handlers know?' He leaned back, smiled.

They knew so much and no more. Operation Birdcage. SIS took the photos. John delivered them. Until the day he was given two instructions, one for MI6 and one for himself, and he knew that they knew he was a double agent. He'd panicked. After all, Major Goodfellow had spelled out what would happen to him if the Russians rumbled him. Best to keep them on side, so he gave them the information they wanted, slid his carbon copies between the pages of the *Deutsche Volkszeitung* alongside the false information from MI6. The Russians returned the copies the following week, and he filed them away in their proper folder in the proper drawer of the proper filing cabinet with no one the wiser. He wasn't proud of what he'd done, and he'd only done it the once. He wished he could say it was for a higher motive, a cause he believed in. It wasn't important information, he knew. The Russians had been testing him. He'd done it out of fear, and that was no defence.

Espionage. Was that a capital offence? Did MI6 know? Possibly. They'd pulled him out sharpish after all, packed him off to Nuremberg. They must have had people in Russian intelligence, monitoring what John was sending. What if MI6 didn't know he'd double-crossed his own side? That was the sort of insider information the GRU would know. And use. The Soviets kept close tabs on them all, sometimes even the ones who'd turned, held at arm's length, ready to be reined in or reused when the time came. Or left to the wolves. The British did the same. Only in his case, John knew, his father's name had protected him then. For God's sake, he hadn't even come of age, was still a minor in the eyes of the law. He was on his own now, in a place he never wished to revisit. This was a subterranean world of bottom feeders and if he rose to the surface, he'd be fed to the sharks. MI6 wouldn't come to his rescue, not this time. He thought he had escaped it all, pursuing the quiet life of a nondescript schoolmaster, albeit one with war damage. Nothing that tilted at mental illness, though, just enough to garner sympathy and not the sack.

'We were a little unsubtle before,' Anatoly said. 'We didn't win you to our cause.'

Murder and blackmail. Not good arguments.

'I take it you have not double-crossed me this time?' he said. 'Because if you have, that would be a very foolish move.'

John shook his head, eyes fixed on his glass.

'We are impressed with your commitment to peace,' Anatoly went on. 'Your activities with CND, for instance. The Direct Action Committee.'

John swallowed hard so his Adam's apple grated against his collar. He coughed, wiped his nose with the back of his hand.

'Drink up,' Anatoly said. 'Clear the throat.' John raised his glass, sipped. 'If you sip it,' Anatoly said, 'you will get drunk. Did you know that? Alcohol is absorbed quicker through the tongue than the gut. That is why we Russians gulp it. Straight down the hatch, as you British say.' He lifted the glass, swallowed it in one go, nodded to John to do the same.

John had always been wary of vodka, a rough spirit of doubtful provenance, but this was an altogether different drink, mellow and refined. He looked at the bottle. There was nothing to indicate its strength, but it packed a punch at least as heavy as whisky or brandy. He liked it, its dry, aromatic taste. John smiled, waited as Anatoly topped the glass again.

'We are a peaceful people,' Anatoly said. 'We Soviets. A socialist democracy. A true democracy.' He leaned back in his chair, pulling out his cigarettes, nodding. 'There is no such thing as an aggressive democracy.'

'What about Hungary?' John said. 'Wasn't that an act of aggression?'

Anatoly laughed, dragging on his cigarette, picking tobacco off his lip. 'What information have you been fed? That was no aggression. We intervened to save our comrades, like a father pulls a child from a burning fire. Who do you think is the greatest threat to peace?'

Anatoly's cigarette had burned down, giving off a foul acrid smell with an arc of ash which fell, dusting Anatoly's trousers. Anatoly brushed it off as John grabbed the ashtray from the mantelpiece, placed it on the arm of Anatoly's chair.

'Well?' Anatoly went on. 'I'll tell you. The greatest threat to peace comes from the capitalist powers in the West and their ruthless pursuit of cheap labour and ready markets. Of profit. What is imperialism if not capitalism with pomp? What is NATO if not a war machine for the bankers?'

He stubbed out his cigarette but a strand remained alive, glowing red in the deepening gloom of the room.

'Who has caused more wars since 1917? The socialist states, or the imperialist states?'

John had no ready answer.

'Let me list a few,' Anatoly went on, holding up his hand. 'The Irish War of Independence.' He bent down his little finger. 'The Italian invasion of Abyssinia.' Ring finger. 'The wars against fascism in Spain, Europe, the world.' Middle finger. 'The Korean war.' Forefinger. 'Kenya, Malaya, Egypt. The struggle for independence against the imperial invaders.'

John nodded. He had no sympathy with the British Empire and every sympathy with the underdog, an unfashionable view, he knew, and one he kept to himself at school, especially on Empire Day with all its jingoism and Cadet Corps lads strutting round the playground reliving the Zulu wars.

'Is it any wonder that the Soviet Union sought to defend itself? To surround itself with allies? That is all the Warsaw Pact is, a buffer against the innate aggression of NATO. What is it you say, one for all and all for one?' Anatoly paused and smiled, swallowing down another glass of vodka, refilling his glass. John stayed still.

'So when the Hungarians wanted to leave the Warsaw Pact, we had a duty to protect them from themselves.' He paused. 'What would happen if Britain, say, withdrew from NATO? Do you not think the Americans would object?'

'They wouldn't invade,' John said.

'No?' Anatoly said, holding up his hand again. 'Look at history, my friend. Past and present. Puerto Rico. Nicaragua. Costa Rica. Guatemala. Paraguay. Shall I go on?'

'They didn't invade,' John said.

'True,' Anatoly said. 'They used their money to pull strings behind the scenes, to topple any government that was not in their interests. Even in the British Empire.' He paused. John was out of his depth. 'British Guiana. Jamaica. The British are supposed to be their allies.'

John held up his hands. 'I take your point,' he said, his words slurring. Another vodka would settle his nerves. He reached forward, lifted the glass. 'Down the hatch.'

'The only way peace can be secured is to match strength with strength,' Anatoly said, pulling out another foul cigarette from its packet and lighting it. John could smell the lighter fuel, as if his senses were on fire.

'We don't like nuclear weapons,' Anatoly added. 'No sane person does. But we have to defend ourselves. It's a war of nerves, a game of chicken, but if the West don't believe us, then what is the point?' He smiled. 'You are very quiet, my friend. I think it is because you have no answer.'

John looked over Anatoly's shoulder, at the empty space on the shelf. It was almost dark, though he resisted turning on the light. He wanted the anonymity of gloom. 'Go on,' he said.

'It is simple, comrade.' John felt his gut twitch. Anatoly was including him in his world. 'We have the Nuclear Test Ban Treaty. Perhaps the Americans signed because they are in the weaker position. We can fire a nuclear missile at Washington. Sputnik made that clear. Of course, give them a few months, and they'll catch up. We could destroy each other. Stalemate. But we would like to develop other missiles, shorter-range, that threaten the United States forces in Europe or Asia, before they attack us...' He pulled out another cigarette, pointing it at John. 'You can fire missiles at our cities, and we would like to fire at yours.' He dragged in the smoke, exhaled. John watched as it unfurled and drifted into the night air.

He sensed Anatoly lean forward, could tell his position by the light of his cigarette, circling in the gloom.

'We need your expertise to boost our own.'

'This is ridiculous,' John said. 'I'm a schoolteacher. Not a physicist.'

'But you have the ear of a physicist's daughter, and she is sympathetic to our cause.'

'You seem very sure,' John said. 'How do you know that?'

Anatoly nodded, that same foxy nod he'd given the Russian major at the bridge in Berlin.

'You're bluffing,' John said. 'You know nothing about her except that she wants to rid the world of nuclear weapons.' He caught Anatoly's eye, fixed his gaze. 'And that includes the Soviet Union. If you think she's a route to her father, you must be mad. She won't even talk to him.'

The cigarette tar hissed as Anatoly stubbed it out, and John heard him swallow the last of his vodka.

'She is your conduit. Your only route.' He stood up, walked over to the window and looked out, before sidling back into his seat.

'Her father was on our wanted list at the end of the war. He should, by rights, have come to us.' John heard him sniff. 'We found out too late that Lieselotte was his daughter. We had no idea who she was at the time. Didn't care who any of them were. If they had a pussy, we fucked them. Sweet revenge. What is it you say? Revenge is a dish best served cold.' He laughed. 'Cold revenge.'

You bastard.

'Did you rape her?' John said, fury rising so fast, so hard he had to hold his chair in case he threw himself at Anatoly, hands on his throat, squeezing out his breath. 'Did you kill her?'

Anatoly smirked, puffed through his lips. 'Does it matter now? Does it make a difference?'

'Yes.' John grabbed his glass, smashed it on the floor where it snapped in two, sharp shards for the grabbing.

'Then no,' Anatoly said. 'But I know who did.' He leaned forward, picked up the broken glass, placed it on the arm of his chair, out of John's reach.

'Piece by piece, a puzzle fell into place,' Anatoly went on. 'We kicked ourselves about losing Lieselotte, but once we knew who she was, I knew she had a sister, dressed as a boy, called Bert.'

He sniffed again, and John saw the glint of his cufflinks as he wiped his nose with the back of his hand.

'Bette. Bert. Betty. I knew Bert, did you know that? I knew she wasn't a boy, too. But Bert disappeared.' He tapped his leg. 'Not before she did me serious harm.' He shrugged. 'I don't blame her, really. But she must pay for her behaviour. Everyone must face up to the wrongs they have done in the past, don't you agree? Take the punishment like a man.' He laughed. 'Bette. You.'

John heard the quiet pull of the stopper on the bottle, the glug as Anatoly poured himself another drink.

'If we'd have known,' Anatoly went on, 'we'd have kidnapped his daughters and he'd have come running. We'd have saved you all this bother. It's strange, isn't it, how history turns on blunders?' His lips glistened from the vodka, were thin, could twist like a wire. 'It's always the little things that trip you up. Of course, we knew you'd be a double agent. We weren't naïve. You'd report to your Major Buchanan like a schoolboy sneak, and they'd use you to give us disinformation.'

Anatoly was becoming talkative, as if the drink had relaxed his mouth. Don't be fooled, John told himself. His wits are sharp.

'We didn't expect you to be withdrawn so soon, that was our miscalculation. But we kept tabs on you, just in case. Once an agent, always an agent. I expect your side does the same. Have you thought of that?' Anatoly hiccupped, lifted his glass once more, drained it. 'So now you know. We told you everything about your new lover. Her patrimony as a German, her lineage as the daughter of a physicist.'

He stood up, his tall frame looming in the dark.

'You have four weeks before we let it be known that you double-crossed your own side, that you were a double, *double* agent.'

He turned at the door.

'Don't get too upset about Lieselotte. It was a long time ago, and all's fair in love and war.'

He sniggered and walked out of the door, his limping steps echoing down the stairwell, *heavy, light, heavy, light*. John reached over and switched on the standard lamp.

Anatoly had left the remains of the bottle.

CHAPTER TWENTY-SEVEN

London: September – October 1958

Her name was Miss Joan Scott. She stressed the *Miss*. One rumour had it that she'd been a WRN and lost her fiancé in the war. The other said she was a lesbian. She had her own office, a small cubbyhole next to one of the senior partners, looking out over the fire escapes and roofs at the back of the building. She supervised the typing pool, enforced discipline with a sharp tongue and a strict adherence to the rules.

'Only this is very short notice,' Miss Scott said. 'And we're very busy.'

'You can take it off my holiday entitlement.' Betty wished now she'd just called in sick on Monday. 'It's important,' she added. 'Urgent.'

Miss Scott crossed her hands on her desk. 'Are you in trouble?' she said.

'Oh no,' Betty said. 'Nothing like that. It's a family matter. Crisis, really.'

'Crisis?' Miss Scott gave a lopsided smile, pushed herself up from her chair and walked over to the window, her back to Betty. She folded her arms, her fingers tapping her back. She wore no rings. 'What about?'

'I'd rather not say, if you don't mind,' Betty said. She'd have to make up a lie if Miss Scott pressed her. She should never have asked for time off. Just taken it. She was entitled to sick pay, not a holiday at short notice.

'I'd like you to be straight with me. This family crisis, is it of a personal nature?'

Betty swallowed. 'Sort of,' she said. 'Yes.'

'Mmm.' She lifted up the sash window, leaned out and shooed away a pigeon. Betty watched it fly off. It'll be back, she thought.

'I knew a young woman once, before the war,' Miss Scott was saying, peering out of the window. 'Madly in love with her boss, a married man. He promised he was going to leave his wife.' She paused and Betty saw her shoulders rise and fall with her breathing. 'The young woman got pregnant and when she told him, he didn't want to know. He fired her, instead. She was destitute. No job. No money. No family to speak of. It's the loneliest place in the world, to have no means and be expecting a child, don't you agree, Miss Fisher?'

Betty stared at her lap, not daring to look up. 'Yes. It must be.'

'It was the loneliest decision that young woman ever made,' Miss Scott went on. 'To go on a short holiday like that. Will you be alone, Miss Fisher, on your little trip?'

Betty hoped Miss Scott would not notice her eyes welling up. 'Yes,' she said.

'And which hotel did you say you were staying in?'

'I didn't,' Betty said, sniffing hard. How did Miss Scott know? The nurse had said she shouldn't be on her own, not that first night. They'd be blood, she'd been warned. She couldn't be at Dee's. It wasn't fair on her, or right for the children. Kevin would suspect something. There was only one lavatory. There'd be people in a hotel, so she could get help if needs be. There were some cheap B & Bs near Paddington. She could stay in one, just for the night. She could just about afford it.

Miss Scott had returned to her desk, had put on her reading glasses, was staring into a drawer, tilting her head so she could see at the back. She stopped, peered over the tops of her spectacles.

'I know you girls think I'm an ogre,' she said, and smiled with those strange, twisted lips. Betty hadn't expected her to react like this. It was possible that Miss Scott would turn her over to the police, but then, Betty thought, she hadn't actually admitted anything, or incriminated herself.

'You mustn't be alone,' Miss Scott went on. 'If something went wrong, it could prove fatal without medical help.' She pulled a key from the drawer. 'There. I knew I had it somewhere.' She smiled and this time there was a warmth there, sympathy. 'Where are you having it done?'

'Herne Hill.' Betty swallowed.

'That's convenient. As it happens, I live in Streatham High Street, in one of those mansion flats above the shops, opposite the ice rink.' She pulled a compliment slip from a stash on her desk, wrote on it and pushed it over to Betty, along with the key. 'This is my address, this is my key. You can stay with me.'

Relief flooded through Betty, a rush of safety and warmth.

'Get a cab.'

'I don't know how to thank you,' Betty said. 'I truly don't. You've been so kind, so considerate. How did you know?'

'I have a nose for these things,' she said.

'Do you help everyone like this?'

Miss Scott waved her hand. 'There's something about you, Miss Fisher,' she said. 'I can see you're no flibbertigibbet. I don't suppose you'll stay in the typing pool for long. You'll go far. Now, get back to your work.'

Betty stood up, extending her hand. 'I can't thank you enough, Miss Scott.'

'Not a word to the others. Or,' Miss Scott added, 'to anyone.'

Betty could hear the clacking of the typewriters on the floor below. She didn't have many strokes of luck, she thought, but this was one for sure.

§

The typing pool looked out over Lincoln's Inn Fields. She used to see him waiting there, would rush to meet him, holding his arm with two hands and leaning close as they sauntered in the gardens, or up to King's Cross before she caught her train back to Hatfield. Now as she glanced out of the window she felt the bite of panic. It was three weeks since she'd last seen him, two weeks since the abortion. She'd been pushing the whole encounter with him — there was no other word for it — to the back of her mind, shuffling it into place with other unpleasant encounters. Encounter, she thought, was a good word. Something difficult, and unexpected. Like the pregnancy, the abortion.

She hadn't thought it would hurt so much, or bleed so heavily. She'd felt as if she were on the rack, her bones torn from their tendons, tendons from muscles, hour after hour. Miss Scott came back after work, took her temperature. Betty screwed her eyes tight, screamed as the catheter tube the woman had inserted slipped out and with it the little slug covered in blood, which she flushed down the lavatory. She hadn't thought it would leave such a hole of longing, of what might have been.

She'd had no choice. But she hated John with a bloodied, visceral contempt, as powerful as a fist.

She looked out again. She'd have to get past him. There was a fire escape, but that led nowhere. If she left with the others, she could hide behind them, safety in numbers. Or ask one of the partners if she could leave with him. John wouldn't dare approach her if she was with another man.

'Hurry up, Miss Fisher,' Miss Scott said. 'I need to lock the room.'

Betty pulled her bag from the desk drawer, and the cardigan off the back of her chair. She'd used her lunch hour to type out two articles, one for the *U & LR*, one for *Peace News*, and the folder sat on her desk. She picked it up as Miss Scott raised an eyebrow.

'When I gave you permission to use the company typewriter on personal business, Miss Fisher,' she said, 'I rather imagined it to be a short letter or something similar.'

Betty smiled. 'I used my own paper,' she said. She walked past her, into the Ladies, locking the door behind her. She'd wait here. John would see the other women leave and think he'd missed her, and with luck he'd go on his way.

'Miss Fisher.' There was a knock on the door and Miss Scott called out, 'I just need a brief word with you, when you're ready.'

Apart from using the company typewriter, in her own time, with her own paper, Betty knew her work was exemplary. Still, she felt nervous. Miss Scott had made it clear when Betty was staying with her that friendship was off limits, and she'd maintained a professional distance ever since. Betty pulled the lavatory chain, waited a moment, unlocked the door.

'Sorry to rush you,' Miss Scott said. 'Or intrude. I forgot to tell you that a gentleman rang.'

'Oh?'

'You know we don't permit personal calls. Fortunately, he didn't want to talk to you. Just to confirm that you still worked here.' She pointed with her hand, *walk along*.

'Did he give a name?'

'I didn't catch it,' she said. 'Some foreign name.'

They reached the staircase. Betty grabbed the bannister. 'What did you tell him?'

'I referred him to one of the partners. I said I wasn't authorised to give that kind of information.'

'Thank you,' Betty said. Miss Scott opened the street door. John was leaning against the railings.

'Would you like me to accompany you to the Tube?' She looked at Betty through the side of her eye, a glance that said, *I've been there too.*

'Yes please,' Betty said. Hesitated. She had to have it out with him sometime, understand why he was seeing Vasily, find out the connection with Lieselotte. Whether it was he who had rung inquiring, or someone else. Now was as good a moment as any. 'Actually, no thank you. I'll be all right.'

Miss Scott smiled, that lopsided twist which made her look tart and cynical but which, Betty now knew, was neither of the kind. 'He looks respectable enough,' she said. 'But then looks can be deceiving. By the way, you left a carbon copy on the typewriter.' Added. 'It read very well.'

She waited until Miss Scott had turned the corner before she faced John. He hadn't moved, stood at the entrance to the forecourt, one fist on the handlebars of his bike.

'Betty,' he said, 'please. I must talk to you.'

She shook her head. 'You expect me to talk to you? Did you ring me today? Or was it Vasily?'

'Vasily?'

'Don't play the innocent.' She narrowed her eyes, temper rising like magma in a volcano. 'Don't lie. The Russian.'

He stopped, pulled breath.

'Who is he?' she said.

She saw him hesitate, as if weighing up whether to tell her or not.

'The Russian I met is called Anatoly.'

'No,' Betty said. 'His name is Vasily. I saw him go into your building.'

'It's possible he goes by several names,' John said, pulling off his cycle clips. 'Given his line of business.'

'And what is his line of business?'

'He's a spy,' John said. 'His official role is cultural attaché, but that's a cover.'

'And how would you know that?'

'This is what I've been trying to tell you,' John said. 'Please, let's go and sit somewhere quiet.' He pointed to the gardens.

She waited while he chained his bicycle to the lamp post. They walked through the square until they found an empty bench. It was chilly in the shade, a first cut of autumn, but the bench basked in the last of the September sun.

'How do you know this man?' John said. 'This Vasily man. Anatoly, as I know him. One and the same. He'll use several names.'

'No.' Betty shook her head. 'Oh no. You tell me how *you* know him.'

It must have been Vasily who'd told John she was German.

'Betty, I can't tell you everything. Not because I don't want to.' He turned to her. 'I want to more than anything, to be able to make up again. I can't bear that we are apart, that I've lost you.'

'So what's stopping you?'

'I can't even tell you that. Perhaps, one day, you'll find out. Let me go on.'

She shrugged.

'I told you already that there were two Russians when I went to meet Lieselotte.'

Russian and British soldiers never met, not to converse, not at ordinary level, soldier to soldier, not then. He was making it up.

'She hadn't turned up but they knew I had arranged to meet her, because they said they'd take me to her.' He breathed in deeply and she saw his leg begin to shake, the tremors return.

'How did they know that?'

He shrugged. 'I don't know. They knew a lot about me.'

She looked at his face in profile, the bridge of his nose, the creases in his cheeks, his five o'clock shadow. Features once familiar and now strange. She'd been in love with this man, and even now there was desire that cut sharp as a scythe. It surprised her, shocked her even, nestling there as powerful and urgent as the need to injure him.

'I didn't know she was dead.' His voice was soft as he went on. 'I followed them, underneath the Lichtensteinbrücke. She was in the mud.'

He lurched forward, his head in his hands, shuddering. He paused a while before he spoke, his voice soft and cracked.

'I cradled her. There were bruises on her neck where she'd been strangled.'

'Was there a chain around her neck?'

'A chain? No. Just bruises, ugly blue bruises. Whatever she'd been strangled with had broken the skin at one point.' He paused. 'Perhaps it was from a chain. Why?'

He stared into the distance. Betty followed his gaze, at the leaves in their autumn retreat, at the last of the summer's dahlias. Perhaps John had told the truth.

'She was wearing a chain,' she said. She'd mention the key later. 'What did you do?'

'Nothing,' John said. His eyes clouded over, and he wiped them on the back of his hand. His lips began to quiver. 'I'm so sorry, Betty.' He shook his head 'I didn't even shut her eyes.' He held his head again, sobbing as if his body would break. 'I couldn't.'

'You left her there?'

'These two Russians,' he said, 'one was Anatoly and the other was an older man.'

She watched as his face twisted and contorted, as if he was squeezing out the memory, or squeezing it away. But the memory was already hers, had landed like an eagle on its prey, plucking at her heart, her guts, clawing at her flesh. She could see Vasily as clearly now as she had then. Boris too. Had he been the older man? Did it matter now, did it make a difference? Someone had grabbed Lieselotte, choked her to death. She must have struggled, tried to fight him off, eyes popping and lungs straining. She was small, weak. They were all weak. She hadn't stood a chance. Lieselotte had been murdered.

'The younger of the two, Anatoly, took me aside,' John was saying, his voice so soft Betty didn't hear him speak at first. 'They wanted information that I had access to. They were going to blackmail me with Lieselotte's murder.' He ran his hand over his face, through his hair. His eyes were heavy with tears and his knee was shaking in a violent spasm. She understood the cost of his pain.

He sat up straight then, shoulders back, and she saw him as a soldier looking brave. Or an actor squaring up to his audience.

'And?'

'I've already told you more than I should. I'm sorry. I can't tell you more.'

'You spied for them?'

He shook his head. 'No, it's not as simple as that. Please, Betty, trust me.' He looked at her and she found herself shaking her head. 'I can't answer that.' He was telling her a barefaced lie, she was sure. He had been an eighteen-year-old conscript. What could he possibly know that was of interest to the Russians? He was an English Walter Mitty, living on fantasy and lies.

If the older man had been Boris, could he have killed her? It seemed unlikely. In his way, he had been fond of her sister.

'And Lieselotte? What happened then?'

He fidgeted on the seat, crossing, uncrossing his leg.

'The older man rolled her into the Landwehr canal.'

Betty cried, hand over mouth, trying to take it in. Her beloved sister, tossed into the water, carrion for the pike and eels.

'No,' she said. 'No.' She'd seen them dredging the corpses from the canals and lakes. Was Lieselotte buried in some mass grave, or was she still in the water, her bones stripped and her skull gaping?

Had Vasily murdered her? Ripped the chain from her neck and strangled the life from her? A pointless, needless murder. Had he wanted her for himself? *He want good girl. Clean girl.* And then he had come for her. Or could it have been Boris, after all? Questions moiled in her head, churned into waves, smashing against the walls of her mind. Perhaps Boris had wanted to marry Lieselotte, like he said? Had she spurned him? People murdered for less. Or had she told him she was expecting his child? That she was on her way to see a doctor? Had he flown at her in a rage, choked her life away? She had no doubt that Boris was capable of murder.

But it was Vasily who had made contact with John. Was he looking for her, Betty, after all these years? Was her father just a ruse to hoodwink John? Nothing made sense.

'How could you?' she said, her voice icy. She stood up, walked away fast, down the path, across the gardens. She heard him run after her, grab her elbow.

'Betty, please, listen.'

'Get away from me.' She was half shouting, half sobbing, shaking him off. 'You let that happen to Lieselotte. Will you roll me in the canal too?' He was a weak man, she saw that now. Weak and cowardly.

'Betty, please, *please*. This is serious.'

'You're lying. A *liar*. That wouldn't have happened, you and your Russian. I was there, remember, in Berlin? I know it. I just know it.' She faced him, her thoughts careering round her head. 'Nothing makes sense.' He was taking her for a fool. A rage began to forage, to feast on her pain and she had a sudden, unstoppable urge to hurt him.

'I was pregnant too,' she said. She hadn't meant to tell him. 'Your baby. I got rid of it.'

He let go of her arm, his mouth open, his eyes skimming her face. 'Tell me that's not true.'

'Why?' she said. 'It's as true as I'm standing here.'

'But why did you do it?' She saw him clench and unclench his fist. 'I don't understand.' He reached out, fingers poised.

'Don't touch me.'

His arm fell to his side, a dead weight.

'Are you all right?' He slapped his hand to his forehead. 'Tell me it wasn't some backstreet abortionist. You could have died. Was it safe? Who did it? Why didn't you tell me?'

'Why do you think? You made it clear you wanted nothing more to do with me.' Her breath was coming in sharp, angry bursts, barbs into her lungs. 'I never want to see you again. Ever.'

She ran towards Great Turnstile, away, out of reach, glad that she had tried to hurt him as lethally as he had hurt her.

She'd always felt that Lieselotte was dead, and in some ways it was a relief to know. But the murder haunted her, needled at the memory of her sister, what had happened that evening. Had Vasily followed her to the bridge? Or had she planned to meet him there too? Before John? For what purpose? Had he promised her food, like Boris in the old days? John had said there were two Russians. Could the other one have been Boris? Now she'd seen Vasily in the flesh, she felt as if a boa constrictor had lashed itself around her body, was crushing the life out of her.

She'd have to see John again, though now she doubted he'd want anything more to do with her.

§

They were due to take the homeosaurus on its maiden journey the first Saturday in October, and Betty had promised the boys they could help.

'You can't let them down,' Dee said. 'It might do you good and all. Bit of fun. Take you out of yourself. And Ally Pally. They'll like that.'

Nick had insisted they went to Alexandra Palace. 'Iconic,' he'd said. 'The People's Palace and all that.'

But since the whole homeosaurus had been Nick's idea, she let him take it there, even if it had been a struggle to fit it into the van.

Ally Pally was a trek from Willesden, but the boys sat on the Tube with their *Beano* and *Hotspur*. Dee had packed them some fish paste sandwiches and a bottle of Tizer which they consumed on the grass in the park before being strapped up inside the husk of the great model. *Ban the Bomb* had been written on the sides, a letter on each scale, and it was topped with a papier mâché head of Harold Macmillan. Betty had been sceptical, but she had to admit it was eye-catching. Thirty feet long, each segment hooked into the one adjacent. It took some practice to put on and link up, and then to manoeuvre, walking in syncopation. She could hear Martin and Graham laughing behind her, along with the other children in the tail.

Nick had booked a jazz band which played alongside them, saxophones and trombones, banjos and guitars, and the human homeosaurus stomped in time, swaying in rhythm. She could hear clapping, laughter. They had attention, were making a point. This was sure to make the papers. Perhaps the front page, or the main item in the evening news on the Home Service. Nick planned to take it on the next Aldermaston march, though, given the rains that had descended last time, she wasn't sure how waterproof the paint would be even if the tarpaulin held out.

But it was hot, airless beneath the canopy, with the autumn sun bearing down. The smell reminded her of the inside of tents, damp canvas and wet grass. She'd never taken to camping, not even as a child in the Jungmädelbund, with the smelly latrines and tin mugs. It brought it back, those fearful days, made her cringe with guilt. She wanted to slip out, take off her jacket, find a water fountain and drink. The boys could probably do with a drink too. Nick was in the lead, handing out leaflets as he went. She'd promised the boys an ice cream and a ride on the roller coaster and there was no shortage of volunteers to work the beast. She passed a message up the front and the monster stopped.

'Sorry, Nick,' she said. 'I need to take the boys now. I promised them an ice cream and a bit of fun in the playground.'

'No problem,' he said. 'It works, doesn't it?'

'If I'm honest,' she said, 'it looks more like a giant centipede than a homeosaurus, but it does pull the crowds.'

'Thanks for your help,' he said. He shuffled his feet, flicked through the leaflets he was holding. 'I don't suppose you fancy a drink sometime?'

She smiled. 'That's kind, Nick. Sometime.'

She grabbed the boys by the hand. If she wasn't mistaken, John was applauding the homeosaurus.

§

He was there, three days later, at the meeting of the Direct Action Committee in the Partisan. The vigil in Downing Street had garnered attention, along with the homeosaurus, and they were doing the final planning of the week-long campaign, and the march to Heathrow airport at the end of the month. John was there, taking notes. He sat a few rows in front of her, didn't see her behind him. His shoulders shifted beneath his jumper as he wrote, his neck creasing when he looked up. He had looked hurt, bewildered when she'd told him about the abortion. Perhaps he did care about her, perhaps there was some truth in what he was trying to tell her, fantastical as it sounded.

She waited for him after the meeting.

'John—'

He looked at his watch. 'I can't really stop now.'

'I'll walk with you,' she said. 'I rushed away too soon.'

'I'm on my bike,' he said, walking towards his cycle propped up against the kerb. She had to trot to keep up with him. 'You need to know about Vasily.' She reached out for his arm, tugged at his sleeve. 'Please slow down.'

'Tell me,' he said. 'Quickly.' He had grabbed the handlebars, lifted the bike to free the pedal.

'I knew him. His superior…' She swallowed. 'His superior, a man called Boris' – she paused again, she'd never used the word before – '*raped* Lieselotte. Again and again. Vasily stood guard while he did it.'

John was studying her face. She had to speak fast, make sure she kept his attention.

'He'd leer at Lieselotte,' she went on. 'He wanted a girl, he wanted *her*. We thought they'd left, been posted elsewhere, back to Russia. But now…' She looked at John. He was frowning, as if he was layering this information onto what he knew. 'Now I know he didn't, because Lieselotte kept the key to the apartment on a chain round her neck and the morning after she went missing, Vasily used it to come into our flat.' She stopped, catching her breath. 'I shot him. That's why he limps. It gave me time to run away. I haven't seen him since. He's not looking for my father, is he? That's just nonsense. He's looking for me. For revenge. Is that what he's doing here?'

John carried on staring at her, his face blank, expressionless.

'I think he may have murdered Lieselotte,' she said. 'How else would he have come by the key?'

'I'm sorry, Betty,' he said. 'I can't explain now. I have to go. I have an appointment.'

'With Vasily?'

He shook his head. 'No.'

Anxiety washed over her, a sudden, unexpected surge of fear, and jealousy. He was meeting a woman.

She watched him push off, pedal away, was tempted for a moment to run after him, find out where he was going, who he was meeting. But he'd turned a corner, was out of sight.

CHAPTER TWENTY-EIGHT

London: October 1958

He switched on his front and rear lights and set off, hoisting his right leg over the crossbar, settling into the saddle, the steady rhythm of pedalling. He didn't want to go to this rendezvous. He wanted to stay with Betty. She'd begun to talk for the first time, and like an idiot he'd let the moment slip. The hell with this meeting. Betty was more important. He pulled over, one foot on the kerb, looking past his shoulder, hoping to see if she'd run after him. She wasn't there. He turned, pedalled back through Soho Square, into Carlisle Street.

She'd gone. He jumped off his bike, throwing it on the kerb, running into the Partisan, searching. He couldn't see her. Nick was there.

'Have you seen her?' John said. 'Have you seen Betty?'

'Sorry, comrade,' Nick said. 'She left after the meeting. Said she was in a rush.'

John backed out, picked up his bike, his heart hammering against his sternum. It felt bruised, painful, his bones shattered into shards pinching and pricking his flesh. He'd been trapped. He wished he could chew off a limb, free himself, like a fox or a hare. He envied them their bravery, their determination, their will to live. Their freedom.

He had lost her. She and his baby. He would have married her, cherished her. They'd have lived together, raised a family, like Arthur, like so many men and women after the war, putting the past behind them, looking to the future. They had been separated, as if the twisted metal and sordid secrets of war still raged, as if its aftermath had the power to haunt and live on through them all.

John swung his leg over the crossbar, settled on the saddle without thinking, pressing down on the pedals. He had to push her from his mind, understand that he had lost her, know there was no return. His mouth tasted sour, his limbs felt limp. He'd better keep this meeting, but it would be the last. He checked with one hand that his notebook was in the inside pocket of his jacket, and turned out of Soho Square, cycling down Charing Cross Road, passing the theatres, quiet now the plays had started, boisterous when the performances were over, trying to keep his mind off Betty. Trafalgar, the Strand, Waterloo Bridge, left into Stamford Street. It had been bombed in the war, ignored by the Festival of Britain. Large parts of it were still derelict and the street lighting was haphazard and low. It was eerie at night. No houses, nothing *homely*, just industrial buildings and bomb sites barricaded with corrugated iron fences. A rat ran across the road, skittered through the railings down to an empty area. This route was the quickest way to Borough but it always made him uneasy, as if the shadows themselves were made of evil and the wind through the empty ruins screamed of betrayal.

He propped his bike against the railings and walked to The George. A man was loitering outside, leaning against a lamp post, reading the *London Evening Standard* under the light. John knew who he was, knew to ignore him. The lookout, making sure John wasn't being followed, that the GRU weren't on his tail. The street may have been empty but the pub was crowded, its courtyard full of drinkers, most of them, John guessed, porters from the market, or railway workers from London Bridge. He made his way to the taproom. Norman was sitting in the far corner, gabardine raincoat unbuttoned, trilby on the table next to a half-drunk pint of bitter. If you wanted to look like a copper, John thought, you couldn't try harder. Special Branch. A cigarette rested on the edge of an ashtray, smoke unfurling into the haze. He was doing the crossword, the paper folded into four, while he chewed on a stub of a pencil. John watched for a moment as he filled in a clue and stuck the pencil behind his ear.

'Sorry I'm late,' John said. 'I got waylaid.'

'I've kept myself busy,' Norman said, squeezing himself free of his chair. 'What can I get you? A pint of the best?'

'Thank you.' Norman was the price John had to pay. He was a pleasant enough man, lived in Sidcup, so he said, with his wife and two children, the youngest of whom had passed the eleven-plus and had just started at the grammar school.

'Pity you don't live our way,' Norman had said. 'Could keep an eye on him.'

'He'll be fine, Norman.'

'Well, you know, I'm chuffed, of course I am.' He'd puffed out his chest to prove it. 'I only had an elementary education myself.'

'A good enough education, in its way,' John said, thinking of Arthur. Norman had done well too. His size gave him one entry point into the police force, a service record the other. Graft and intelligence had had him promoted to detective, then Special Branch. He had the edge on John in years and experience, but John sensed an old class deference lurked close to the surface, an awe of John.

'You being a university graduate,' he'd said when he first made contact. 'From *Oxford*, no less.'

Norman returned with two pints of bitter, placed them on the table and squeezed himself back into the seat. Too long catching criminals or tracing subversives made Norman furtive and self-effacing. Like the rat in Stamford Street, squeezing his body beneath a door frame or through the grille of a drain. The man outside approached their table, nodded at Norman and John, sat himself down and reached forward for the beer. Fred. His name was Fred. The lookout, giving the all-clear. John knew they weren't their real names, any more than his was Birdcage.

'Cheers,' John said, raising his glass.

'So what do you have for us?'

'Not much more to report,' John said, pulling out his notebook and tearing off the pages of notes. He slipped them over the table to Norman. 'The activities remain the same. The activists too. You have the names already.'

'No incitement to break the law?'

'Minor inconveniences,' John said. 'Trespass, blocking the highway. Look, Norman...' John leaned forward. 'These people are pacifists. They're not throwing Molotov cocktails or fermenting a violent overthrow of the state. It's peaceful protest they do. Civil disobedience.' He paused.

'We'll be the judge of that,' Norman said. 'Any new names? What about that young woman?'

John crossed his legs, loosened his tie. 'It all just got a whole lot more complicated,' he said, adding, 'I never wanted to do this, and I want out. Now.' He stood up, felt someone tug at his sleeve. Fred tilted his head towards the seat. *Sit down.*

'I know you have a soft spot for her,' Norman went on. 'And I can see why. She's a lovely-looking girl. But you need to keep your distance, is my advice. Don't want lovey-dovey stuff to get in your way.'

Too late for that, John thought. I loved her before you came on the scene.

'I was tasked by MI6 with befriending her,' John said, teeth tight, hoping he sounded braver than he felt. 'They bullied me into it. They still had that hold over me, after Berlin. Once an agent, and all that.' He winced. Anatoly's words had been the same. 'They used me to keep the Russians on side, find out what they were up to.' He pulled himself up in his chair. 'I was too weak to say no, to stand up for myself.'

There was a commotion from the corner of the taproom. John turned as a man swayed, tipping the table as he fell. A barman was coming over, talking to him, taking charge, lifting him to his feet. *Come on, Sid, now, time to go home.* John looked away, back to Norman.

'That would have been fine. I could cope with that,' he said. 'Then MI5 and you lot muscled in, for your own reasons.' He picked up his glass, gulped the beer. 'Monitor the movement. Monitor the girl. I can't straddle these horses, Norman. I really can't. I won't spy on the woman I love.'

He put down his glass and stood up.

'Or on a cause I believe in.'

His knees felt frail, as if he'd cycled from John O'Groats, muscles without juice. *The woman I love. The woman I've lost.*

He'd blown it with Betty. They all knew, of course they did, but they kept the pressure on him all the same.

The October night had turned cold, the first nip of frost. He hadn't brought his gloves, or a warmer jacket. He pedalled back along Stamford Street, his heart racing, expecting Anatoly to step out from the area where the rat had disappeared, or from behind the corrugated hoardings.

He was not a spy. He was not an informer. He knew what Anatoly was after, but he'd lost Betty in the process, the conduit that Anatoly relied on. And the funnies. And then this new twist. Vasily. Anatoly. One and the same. She'd been right to think he'd used her. If the boot had been on the other foot he'd be angry, hurt beyond measure. Could they ever rekindle what they had, put all of this far behind them?

Waterloo Bridge. He skirted up Aldwych and into Southampton Row. The leaves were falling from the trees, crisp from the autumn, from the emerging frost. One caught in his rear wheel, crackled as he rode along.

Anatoly was ruthless and John had no doubt that he would use the most brutal weapons he could to secure his goal. Of course, she had her own reasons to fear him. He should have told her tonight, but it was too long a conversation and he needed her to be calm, receptive. He owed it to her, at the very least. This would shatter her. He still had no idea where she was living, or if she had a telephone. He couldn't ring her at work. He'd have to meet her after hours, hope it wasn't too late. Drop her a line at the office.

He turned into Bury Place, eyes darting, scouting. There was no one there. He opened his door, wheeled his bike into the hall, propped it up against the wall and, pulling off his bicycle clips, went up to his rooms.

§

He was in the habit of buying the *Times Educational Supplement*. From time to time there were interesting articles, on selective versus comprehensive education, or language teaching, and he kept an eye on job vacancies, although it would need to be something like a head of department job to tempt him to move school. He tried to act as if nothing was wrong, but his sinews screamed at the strain, his limbs in free-fall. He couldn't eat and his mind raced. He'd caught Jarvis in the third form imitating him more than once, walking down the corridor like a victim of St Vitus's Dance, all palsied steps and jerking hands and head.

'Listen, old boy,' his father had said at their regular dinner at the Rag. 'Far be it from me to pry, but you're not yourself.' He tapped the side of his head. 'Take some time off. Come back to your senses.'

This new terror lay on the old one like strata in a volcano and John could see no way of stopping the final eruption, squeezed between pressure from Anatoly to betray his country and the security service to protect it, and in between, like a lava neck suppressing it all, was Betty. *Bette.* He yearned the loss of her, grief as wide and deep as a canyon.

He flipped the *TES* to the back section, turned to secondary schools. *Rhayader Grammar School, established in 1793, is looking for a dynamic new head of its modern language department to replace Goronwy Davies, who is retiring after 39 years' service. The department offers French as a first language, and German as a second...*

He'd felt easy over the summer, at peace, in that tumbledown cottage in Pantydwr. Of course, a rural grammar school wouldn't be a patch on Camden Boys, and he wouldn't get London weighting, but the classes would be smaller and the rent cheaper. Perhaps he could even buy a little house, that little cottage, for instance. Anatoly could go to hell with his threats. The security boys knew all about the accusations, and he reckoned he'd more than discharged his debts to them by feeding them details of what went on at the Partisan Coffee House. He was damned if he was going to hand Betty up on a plate to them, and he'd said as much to Norman.

He heard the letter box open and shut. He knew what it would be. Judas money. *Thanks. Here's the quid I owe you. Norman.*

He could live like a hermit with the kites and owls for company, waking in the morning with the silhouette of a hare on the brow of the hill, counting chickens and collecting the eggs, rich and tasty from the grubs and worms they'd eaten. He checked the time. It wasn't too late to ring Arthur, though he'd do it from the public phone on Southampton Row. Couldn't risk his own being bugged.

His daughter answered. 'I'll just fetch him,' she said. He heard the phone placed down on the table, her shout, *Dad, Dad. Phone.* There was a pause. Arthur picked up the receiver and John could hear his muffled voice.

'I said, go to bed. You were supposed to have gone up half an hour ago.' There was a pause. 'Yes, I'll come up and kiss you goodnight.'

Arthur spoke into the receiver, voice clear. 'Sorry about that, John,' he said. 'Kids. Drive you to Bedlam.'

John laughed. He'd give his eye teeth to have Arthur's life. 'Sorry to ring you so late, Arthur,' he said. 'But there's been another complication.'

'You do pick them, if you don't mind me saying so. What is it this time?'

'The young lady I told you about. Remember?'

'Betty?' Arthur said. 'Don't tell me, she's married.'

'No. It turns out she's Lieselotte's sister. Not only that, she knew Anatoly in Berlin.'

Arthur whistled, soft as a bird.

'Thing is, Arthur. We've had an almighty falling-out. She thinks I'm using her.'

Arthur laughed. 'So I'm your agony uncle now, am I? As well as your confessor.'

'Yes,' John said. 'The only way I can see to win her back is to tell her everything, and to hell with the consequences.'

'That's about as sensible as shooting yourself in the foot to get out of the army, if you ask me,' Arthur said.

'I can't carry on like this, Arthur.'

'Tell them to bugger off, if you'll excuse my language,' Arthur said. 'Say you can't do it anymore. Just walk off the bloody job and take the consequences. I doubt anything will happen. Have a change. Good as a rest and all that.'

John looked out of the windows of the booth, at the buses passing by.

'I have told them,' he said. 'I'm waiting for the repercussions.'

'What can they do?' Arthur said. 'Move on.'

'Actually,' John said, 'this is why I'm ringing. There's a job come up.' He wound the telephone cord round his hand. 'Head of Department, Rhayader Grammar School.'

'That'd do it,' Arthur said. 'Throw them off the scent. Settle your nerves. What have you got to lose? When's the deadline?'

'End of the week,' John said. 'They want a January start, so they need to get a move on with the appointment.'

'And Betty?'

'It's over,' John said. This was the first time he'd admitted it, and the words stuck in his throat.

'Well, there'll be a Gwyneth or an Angharad in Wales,' Arthur said. 'Plenty more fish in the sea. Or sheep on the hills.' John could hear him chuckle.

John shook his head. He had waited a lifetime for Betty, lost her in a moment.

'Apply anyway,' Arthur said. 'See what happens.'

'Do you think I stand a chance?'

'You won't know till you try,' Arthur said. 'But if I were a governor, I'd snap you up. Listen, I have to go now. Let me know how you get on.'

John sauntered back to his rooms. He'd write his application tonight, post it first thing. Goronwy Davies – he already saw him as his predecessor – had been at the same school for nearly forty years. That was a good recommendation, though the department was probably stuck in its ways. It wouldn't be easy, bringing in modern teaching practices, but it would get his mind off things, be a challenge in its way.

CHAPTER TWENTY-NINE

Berlin: August – December 1945

The jeep stopped at a tall house, one of a short row that had survived the bombing. The sergeant left the engine running as the UNRRA nurse rang the bell. She turned to Bette, smiled to reassure her.

'*Sie kommt*,' she said in her primitive German. '*Jetzt.*'

Bolts slid back and a woman opened the door. Another nurse, older, plumper.

'*Willkommen*,' she said without smiling. '*Ich heiße Fräulein Schneider.*'

The nurse handed over a file to the Fräulein and leaned close to Bette, her breath sweet with lipstick, the same that Mutti used, and for a moment Bette held the scent inside, willing it to stay in her nose, filter into her lungs and heart.

'Fräulein Schneider will look after you for now,' she said. 'Until we get you sorted. So goodbye. And be good. *Gut sein.*'

Bette watched as she turned and climbed into the jeep, waved as the sergeant put it into gear and drove away. Fräulein Schneider shut the door. The hallway was dark but silent except for a rhythmic *bom*, echoes like a kettledrum. Bette peered into the shadows. A small boy was rocking himself on the floor, his arms wrapped round bony knees which he clutched tight to his chest, banging his head against the large, hollow radiator, *bom, bom.* The Fräulein walked past him. *Stop*, Bette wanted to say, *what's wrong with him?* The boy stared ahead with ancient, empty eyes, an old man in a child's body. He didn't flinch.

'Follow me,' the Fräulein said, leading the way into her office. She sat at her desk and opened the folder.

'You are German?' She looked at Bette with critical eyes. 'Why are you dressed as a boy?'

Otto's trousers were filthy and itchy and the buttons had come off one of the braces. Bette knew how shameful she must look. She swallowed. 'My mother and sister thought it would protect me,' she said, adding, 'from the Ivans.'

The Fräulein looked up. 'And did it?'

It hadn't fooled Vasily. He'd come back for *her*. But she couldn't tell the Fräulein that, nor that she'd shot him.

'Yes,' she said. The Fräulein smiled.

'Well done. Some mothers said their daughters had typhus. That worked too. There is no end to the ingenuity of mothers, don't you agree?'

Bette nodded. She'd heard that said so many times in the Jungmädelbund, the cleverness of mothers, their resourcefulness.

'But it says here you are an orphan.' Her voice was sharp, as if she'd caught Bette in a lie.

'Mutti died.'

The Fräulein nodded, turning back to the notes. 'And your father?'

'He never came back. But my sister is here,' Bette said. 'Somewhere.'

Fräulein Schneider leaned forward. 'We'll put a notice up,' she said, her tone softening. 'With your name. Ask if anyone knows you.'

Bette had seen them, pinned to boards, everywhere. *Has anyone seen my wife, Frau Gerda Wagner?* Some had photographs. *Do you recognise this person? Fräulein Hildegard Krüger, last seen on 26 April...?*

'Could I put one up about Lieselotte?' she said. She didn't have a photograph of her. She didn't have photographs of anyone, she realised. How long would she remember Lieselotte's face? Or Mutti's? She was losing them now in a vortex of forgetting, as if her past were dissolving. Smells brought Mutti back, dried perfume on her clothes, sweet lipstick wax on a stranger.

Fräulein Schneider was shaking her head, lost in her own thoughts. Bette had seen that often of late, the shaking of the head, the bewildered, angry faces.

'*Was ist mit uns?*' the Fräulein said under her breath. 'What about us?' She turned to Bette, her voice far away. 'What have we done to deserve this?'

Bette thought of Frau Weber. That was the kind of thing she'd say, no care for another. Just herself. Obsessed, as if this war had turned on her, was personal. The night Mutti died, she left her and Lieselotte. The night Lieselotte went missing, she told Bette to go away. 'We're starving too,' she'd said once to Bette, her upper lip twitching in fury. '*Was ist mit uns? Was ist mit uns?*' What about us?'

Bette had never *considered* Hitler. He was all she'd ever known. But she wondered now.

'Where did you get that ring?' the Fräulein asked, pointing to Bette's hand. 'Did you steal it?'

'No,' Bette said. 'It was my mother's.' It was the truth, though Bette understood how to lie to get by, for she'd cheated the Russians by dressing as a boy and told the Americans she couldn't remember her address, kept quiet about Vasily. In this world, she thought, this *new* world, you needed cunning to survive.

'Shall I look after it for you? It could get stolen. The children here…' She shrugged. *Thieves.*

Bette clutched her hand. She'd never take her mother's ring off. They'd have to kill her to remove it. She backed into her seat, pushing away from the Fräulein. '*Nein,*' she said. 'No. No.'

The Fräulein held up her hand in surrender, turning once more to the notes. 'It says you're a refugee, but I can tell you're a Berliner from your accent,' Fräulein Schneider went on. She looked cross, as if she'd finally caught Bette cheating her in some way, as if she was used to being lied to, disrespected. 'How much schooling have you had?'

Bette calculated. 'Five full years,' she said. 'But the last year...' Her voice trailed off. She added, 'I'd passed the test for the secondary school, and had started there.'

The Fräulein smiled for the first time. 'That,' she said, 'is excellent news. You can teach the younger ones. Come.' She beckoned her forward. 'Let's get you something to wear.'

She led Bette into a room where freshly laundered clothes hung on rails arranged according to size and gender.

'Thank the Red Cross,' the Fräulein said, running her finger along the rack, pulling out a dull brown dress, holding it up against Bette.

'That'll do.' The dress next to it had a net skirt, like a tutu.

'I prefer that one,' Bette said.

'Prefer? There is no choice, my dear.' She thrust the dress at Bette. 'Put it on.'

She selected a second dress, and a cardigan, a pair of shoes from a rack. She walked over to a shelf, pulled out two vests, two pairs of knickers, socks and a nightdress.

'You need to mark these with your name.' She pointed to a worktable and a reel of tape. 'I take it you can embroider?' There was no mistaking the disapproval in her voice, *dressed as a boy.*

'Now?' Bette said.

'Yes. Now,' the Fräulein said. 'And have you come on yet?' It sounded strange, put like that. Mutti had called them monthlies. Bette shook her head. 'Well, that's one blessing.'

The dress had a pleated skirt and a Peter Pan collar in cream. It was baggy and long and old-fashioned. Her legs were naked without the thick flannel of trousers, and the swish and whirl of the skirt let in the draughts. Was it only yesterday that she'd tried on Mutti's evening gowns, had longed to wear a dress? Now that she had to, it felt strange and wrong. She sat embroidering her name on pieces of tape, sewing the tags inside her new wardrobe, eyeing the dress with the tutu which, she now saw, had sequins on the straps.

The house in Eisenacher Strasse was full of old, heavy furniture. The woodwork was dark, the glass in the windows murky. Still, Bette thought, at least there *was* glass. The Fräulein allocated her to the girls' dormitory, a large room at the top of the house with twenty beds. It smelled of stale clothes and pee.

'You will sleep with the younger ones. Keep them in order.' She looked at her watch. 'Put your things away, and come down.'

Supper. Apart from the hard biscuits the Americans had given her, Bette hadn't eaten all day. Hadn't eaten properly for days. Weeks. She folded her clothes, made her way down the stairs. The noise of children grew louder the deeper she went. Below ground, in the basement. She opened a door. Approximately forty children sat at tables. The Fräulein directed her to one where some younger ones fidgeted on stools, as if they were unsure what to do with them. The boy she'd seen upstairs sat by himself on the floor, eyes cast down, twitching. There was a basket of rolls on the table, bowls of steaming soup, glasses of water. Bette reached over to grab one as the Fräulein rang a bell.

'The eyes of all look to You, O Lord, and You give them their food. You—' She stopped, rang the bell again, caught Bette's eye and glared. Bette pulled back her arm. 'Manners. Maketh. Man,' she shouted, breathed in, added, 'You open Your hand and satisfy the desires of every living thing.' She looked up. 'Amen.'

The children lunged at the rolls, shoving them in their mouths, sinews charged like feral dogs over a carcass, eyes wild and murderous. Bette knew that look, could have killed for food herself once, cut off another's arm for the sake of a mouthful. There was a bowl of broth in front of her with chunks of fat and vegetables. Bette hadn't seen real food for months, not hot food, not like this.

She wrapped her arm around the bowl, shovelling the stew with her spoon, licking her lips as it dribbled out and down her chin, watching that the other children didn't snatch at it. She wouldn't share this. She mopped the sides with her roll, stuffing the bread in her mouth, Waltraud *bla-bla*-ing in her ear about better to die of hunger than let a soldier starve. Waltraud might have been one of the BDM leaders, but she had grown fat on it too. Who'd die for hunger? The Jungmädelbund was so long ago now. She'd liked the sports, mind, had been good at running, *swift as a greyhound*. She shut her eyes. She'd run enough today. She was very tired.

§

Most of the children couldn't read, nor knew how to sit still, nor keep in order, but there was a blackboard on an easel, and chalk. Someone had drawn a crude picture of a head with zigzag lines around it, eyes wide, mouth open. Bette knew that fear, the kind that exploded, the thunder of terror. A small child got up from her desk and slipped her hand into Bette's. Bette looked down at her and the child smiled. She'd lost her front teeth.

'*Bitte*,' she said, her voice light and breathy. 'Are you my sister?' Bette swallowed. She knew that neediness, too. Fräulein Schneider shooed the child away.

'You mustn't encourage them,' she said. 'They must forget. That's the only way. Put it behind them, forge a new life.' She looked at Bette. 'That's how we civilise them again.' The child was no more than five or six. 'We must all forget. Don't talk about the past.'

Bette wondered what had made the Fräulein so harsh. Perhaps she'd been an orphan once too, for Bette could see how that would build a brittle wall from thorns and fear. Had these children been cherished once? How long had they lived unloved and alone, fending for themselves like wild creatures, attached to none but the pack and the instinct to live? Wolf children with cowed, snarling faces.

§

The chestnut trees went first, tired, dusty green leaves turning to gold and bronze as the first frosts curled and severed them from the branches. And then the trees were felled for heating, fed into the boiler in the house on Eisenacher Strasse that still smelled of coal by a man who came to help them. The children came, and the children went. The house was always temporary, a transit station, Bette learned, to other children's centres, where the lucky ones were plucked by family or sent to America or even Palestine. The little boy with the nervous tic, the girl who wanted a sister, and all the time Bette thought it should be her who was going and every time the UNRRA nurse shook her head, *not now*. Bette wondered if Fräulein Schneider wasn't keeping her here on purpose as a helpmate. Still, Bette thought, at least it would be easier for Lieselotte to find her, or Oma and Großvater. Perhaps even her father, should he ever come back. If she was sent goodness knows where, like Bavaria, who would know?

At the end of October Fräulein Schneider gave her a pair of lisle stockings and a cloth coat shrunken and misshapen from washing. At the end of November she gave her a comb to tie her hair back, and summoned Bette to her office. Even with her stockings and her coat, the office was cold. The heating could only come on for a few hours in the evening. An army man sat there in khaki uniform, and the UNRRA nurse who had delivered her earlier.

'This is Major Buchanan,' the Fräulein said. 'From the British army.'

The nurse leaned forward, said in faltering German, 'We need to ask you a few questions.'

Bette looked at her, at the major, at the Fräulein, who shrugged her shoulders. *I don't know.* Bette swallowed. Perhaps they'd found

Lieselotte. She said she preferred the British, they didn't haggle and the Tiergarten was in the British zone.

'Please confirm your full name,' the UNRRA nurse said.

'Bette Ingeborg Fischer.'

'Address?'

Bette paused. They weren't going to trick her. She'd told them she didn't know where she lived. 'In Mitte,' she said. 'I can't remember the street.'

The nurse translated and the major raised an eyebrow.

'Your father's name?' the nurse said. 'Date of birth? Place of birth?' Question after question. Mutti, Lieselotte, Oma, Großvater, aunts, uncles, godparents, intimate details about her family, where they went on holiday, what they did, Father's interests, Mother's, on and on and on. Bette sat on her chair, tucking her skirt tight under her thighs, wrapping her coat around her, crossing her feet, uncrossing, cradling her hands, uncradling. She fiddled with the ring on her middle finger.

'Where did you get the ring?' the major said.

'It was my mother's,' Bette said. A memory flashed past. 'It has writing, inside. Mutti said my father's ring has the same, only the opposite.'

'May I see?' the major said.

Bette pulled the ring off and handed it to him. He took it to the light, peering at the inscription. '*25.12.23. Hermann Fischer. 3.5.25,*' he said. 'What does that mean?'

'It's the dates of their engagement and wedding,' the nurse said.

'May I borrow this?' the major said.

Bette shook her head, held out her hand. 'No,' she said. 'I will never let this out of my sight. Please give it back to me.' She said it as politely as she could. The major nodded, passed it over to her. She slipped it back on her finger.

'Thank you,' he said. 'I think we have all we need for the moment. We'll be in touch again in a few days.'

'Why did you ask me all those questions?'

The major smiled and the nurse translated. 'I don't want to get your hopes up, but we might be able to reunite you with a family member.'

'Lieselotte?'

'I can't say for the moment.'

He stood up, collecting his cap, shaking the Fräulein's hand. The UNRRA nurse smiled at her. Even the Fräulein was smiling. Bette's heart was pounding and she knew her face was flushed, could feel the heat pumping around her body even though she could see her breath in the cold air.

§

The major returned a week later. It had snowed in the night, and a hard frost gave it a crust that crunched under foot. Bette heard him on the pavement, watched from the upstairs window, saw him step into the house. She skipped down the stairs, two at a time, knocked at the office door before the Fräulein had summoned her, stood in the lintel, her lisle stockings concertinaing round her ankles, the buttons on her coat open, revealing the dull brown dress beneath.

The nurse beckoned her. '*Komm herein.*' Bette looked at the Fräulein. This was her domain but she nodded, smiled, as if she knew. 'We have located your father,' she said in German. 'And you are to join him.'

'In England,' the major added. It needed no translation.

Her thoughts bounced and raced, dodgem cars in a circus ring, no reason to their journey, no destination.

'Aren't you happy?' the nurse said.

Bette nodded, could stand no more, collapsed onto the floor, knees up to her chest, head banging the side of the desk as she sobbed.

Vati. She had no memory of his face, just the photograph of him and Mutti on their wedding day. Would he know her?

'So you need to collect your things,' the Fräulein was saying. 'The major has your papers and you're flying to England today.'

'Flying?' The words bounced off her forehead. 'England?'

'Lucky you.' The Fräulein beamed. 'An aeroplane.'

'My father? Vati? And Lieselotte?'

The UNRRA nurse looked at the major, back to her. 'I'm sorry,' she said. 'We have no news of your sister. But come...' She held out her hand and Bette took it. 'Let's go and pack your things. Where do you keep them?'

'They're in the laundry room,' the Fräulein said.

'Then lead the way, Bette.'

A rush of excitement, a *thrill*, a topsy-turvy ferment, froth on a wild, raging sea. Bette ran to the laundry room, sorted out her underwear, her nightdress, her spare dress, checked the name tags, all in order. The Fräulein had followed them in, and Bette could tell she didn't trust the UNRRA nurse.

The dress with the net tutu was still on the rack, unclaimed.

'And that one,' Bette said, pointing, turning to the Fräulein, asserting herself with a new confidence. 'I will wear that one.'

The UNRRA nurse nodded. 'How pretty.'

She lifted it off the rack and gave it to Bette. The Fräulein scowled but said nothing. Bette unbuttoned the brown dress, pulling it over her head, discarding it on the floor and slipping on the tutu. No matter her vest showed through the straps and the cardigan covered the sequins.

'Here,' the nurse said, delving into her pocket, pulling out her lipstick. 'Open your mouth.' She dabbed on the lipstick. 'Now smack your lips together. Like this.' *Like Mutti*, Bette wanted to say. *I know how to do this.*

'Don't you look a treat. Your father will be so proud to see you.'

She could dance, too. She would be a dancer like Mutti and Lieselotte. For her father, smelling of Mutti's lipstick.

CHAPTER THIRTY

Nuremberg: November 1945 – January 1946

He became that defendant smoking cigarettes, one after the other, holding them between languorous fingers, eyelids half closed. *We were under attack, we had to dispose of the Jews. I did a good job and nobody thanked me.* There in that booth, searching for the word, John *was* that man. And the others. Flick left, right. Life. Death. He was *that* Nazi, too, corralling the skeletal slaves, dropping gas into the chamber, shifting the dead like ballast.

His German wasn't up to it, he'd told them. He needed time and a dictionary. Subsequent, yes. But *simultaneous*. That wasn't possible, not for him. Not with these words, groping for their meaning, their accuracy.

They came in his dreams, memories storming the walls of oblivion. Words polka-stepping between the corpses, *Dance with me, John,* women with withered dugs, *give me a smoke*. Lieselotte sliding from a pack of cards, and the cards were bodies, stacked and shuffled. She smiled as she came towards him, became Anatoly with worms bursting from his pustules, and the boy with the mangled foot cried out that he was under orders, he had his orders. *Don't go near him.* Otto Ohlendorf nodded, said we had to understand, *I did a good job, don't you agree?*

John jerked awake, his leg stiff with cramp. He'd drunk too much last night. They all had. Drowned their sorrows in whisky and beer. Each to his own. A silent club of proxy victims, soaking up the pain of the survivors, the witnesses. The excuses of the henchmen, the quibbles of the murderers. The dry, forensic questions of the lawyers.

He pushed himself out of bed, washed himself and shaved. He'd only just started shaving when he'd been conscripted. Twice a week to start with, then every other day. Now he had to do it every morning, lather his face and *scritch* with the razor. He used to watch his father shave. These days his chin made the same noise, his lips twisted the same way, fingers pulled his cheeks like his father before him, *scritch, scratch.*

Did that make him a man? His father had never cracked, not even under enemy fire with shrapnel searing his leg.

'Mustn't mollycoddle the boy,' he used to say. 'Needs to toughen up. Too soft for his own good.'

Was he soft? A coward? He loved words over fists, languages over bayonets. He'd won an exhibition at Merton, Modern Languages, deferred it. He'd prove to his father he had the stomach for war too.

He made his way towards the Palace of Justice. The old town was in ruins and the air thick with dust. He coughed. They all coughed, the Nuremberg Cough, *ha ha.* A cough like no other, from the ashes and stench of death. John thought it was nerves, too, day in, day out cramped in the booth, twenty minutes on, twenty minutes off, tense as he struggled, lungs tight, tendons taut. Léon Dostert had given them all training in the new technique, in the microphones and headsets. He was an American, an army man, a lieutenant colonel, expected discipline.

'My German isn't good enough,' John had said. 'I'm not a native speaker.' Not like the other men and women. He found it hard groping for the word when he didn't want to say what he had to say.

'Your superiors think otherwise,' Lieutenant Colonel Dostert said. 'You come with excellent reports. Give it a go. We can move you on to translation if necessary.'

John walked through the doors as the soldiers standing guard saluted him, and up the main staircase ahead. His legs dragged, as if he were ploughing through a quagmire of bloated forms with stippled fingers pulling him down. The dry, forensic posts planted to guide the way were beyond his reach.

He slipped in next to Sieg, almost as young as himself, sitting with the other translators in the side room as the lawyers opened the day's proceedings, coffee and cigarettes for the taking. They listened on a loudspeaker to the deliberations, waiting for their shift. Russian speakers, German, French and English. John's cup clattered back on its saucer and he righted it, fingers shaking. Sieg looked up, placed a hand over John's to steady it, raised an eyebrow, smiled. They'd been drinking together last night.

'You cannot feel *and* do your job,' he said, voice hushed so the others didn't hear. 'Remember what we said? You must not feel.'

How can you do this? John had asked him last night. *How can you listen?*

John swallowed now, nodded, his mind stewed in misery, his muscles pulsing out of control. He could no sooner detach himself from the task than sever his own head.

'It does not make you a monster,' Sieg said. He'd escaped on the Kindertransport, had lost most of his family. Sieg spoke English with a Scottish lilt. 'Or a sadist,' he went on. 'It doesn't make you amoral. Any more than a ventriloquist becomes his dummy.'

Like Archie in the *Navy Mixture* on the wireless, John thought, except it wasn't. He envied Sieg his calm, his detachment. The other translators too, with bruised, chequered histories. He dreaded making a mistake, dreaded his job. Why did it affect him so badly?

'Five minutes to switchover,' the monitor said. He was American, a lieutenant like himself. John began to sweat, coffee moiling in his gut. He wanted to vomit. He clasped a hand over his mouth and stood up abruptly, knocking his cup as the window spun to the side and the walls crashed towards him. He felt the furniture as he fell between it, the sharp wooden arm of the chair piercing and wrenching his side as he lost consciousness.

He came to in the first-aid room, an army nurse feeling his pulse.

'The doctor will be here soon,' she said. 'You fainted. Nothing to worry about, though you have a nasty bump on your head and the makings of a fine bruise on your left side.' She poured him some water. 'Sit up.' She hooked an arm behind his back, pushed him forward and stuffed pillows behind him.

'I'm on duty,' John said. 'I have to go—'

'You're going nowhere,' she said. She smiled. 'Where are you from?'

He lifted the glass to his lips, dribbling the water down his chin as his side throbbed with pain.

'Here.' She took the glass, held it while he sipped.

'Thank you.' He leaned back on the pillows. 'Surrey. And you?'

'Northumberland,' she said. 'Can't you tell?' She laughed, a tinker bell of a sound.

'It's supposed to be beautiful,' he said. 'The North.'

'Have you never been?'

He shook his head.

'Aw, pet,' she said. 'You have a canny treat ahead then.'

He tried to laugh, but the pain in his side was vicious as a shark's bite.

The doctor suspected a ruptured spleen. He was in his late fifties, John guessed, might even have served in the Great War, an old-fashioned doctor with a moustache and wire-rimmed glasses.

'There's no way of knowing for sure except to confine you to bed and monitor you,' he said. 'Wait and watch. And while we're at it,' he added, 'we'll find out why you fainted in the first place.'

John leaned back on the pillows and shut his eyes. He hadn't slept properly for weeks. He'd drunk too much. He hadn't eaten breakfast, tanked up on black coffee. It was obvious why he had fainted.

'Though of equal concern,' the doctor added, 'is this palsy. Hold out your arms straight.'

John stuck his arms out, watched as they quivered.

'How long has this been going on?'

John wanted to say, *Since Private Nash's death, since Lieselotte's murder, since Anatoly. Since Nuremberg. Since now.*

'Doctor,' John said, 'I have to get back. I'm one of the translators, at the trial.'

'They'll have to get a replacement,' the doctor said. 'For the time being.' He took John's pulse. 'I'm not a neurologist or a psychiatrist,' he went on. 'And don't have much truck with them either. Dizziness. Tremors. How are you sleeping?'

'I'm not,' John said.

'Chest pains?'

John nodded.

'Could be some kind of war neurosis,' the doctor said, sniffing and wiping his nostrils with the back of his hand. 'Insufficient training, I'd wager. Though you're too young to have seen much active service, if any.' He pulled out a handkerchief, blew his nose, inspecting it for ash and soot. He shook his head, added, 'The PIE system works well.'

'War neurosis?' John said. 'PIE?'

'Proximity. Immediacy. Expectation of recovery. Sends you back fighting fit. Can't have square pegs in round holes, not in the army. But you'll have a good rest anyway with this suspected rupture. That'll probably do it.' He nodded to the nurse, turned at the door and pointed at John. 'Don't think nervous exhaustion is an honourable escape route,' he said. 'I've always thought it a sign of social and emotional immaturity.'

John pushed his head back into the pillows, as if it was too weighty for his neck, misery pressing its savage palm across his face. He didn't hear the nurse come back into the room.

'Don't mind him,' she said. He opened his eyes. 'And his so-called bedside manner.' She leaned over, adjusted his pillows. 'Get some rest. The ambulance will be here in due course.'

'Where are they taking me?'

'To the American army hospital in Munich,' she said. 'Then one of our field hospitals.' Adding with a soft, low voice, 'I've seen this before. Push for a rehabilitation hospital, like the one at Mill Hill. And a job back at base. Aw, pet. You're awfully young. And what's going on here...' She tilted her head towards the door and the courtroom beyond it. 'That's too much for a lad. Too much for anyone.'

He pushed himself up on his elbow, fell back, yelping with pain.

§

Effort syndrome. That's what the doctor diagnosed. Soldier's Heart. War Neurosis. The Mill Hill Emergency Hospital had closed, so it had to be the Maudsley. It was his old CO, Major Buchanan, who stepped in.

'Just had a chat with your father,' he said. 'Brigadier Harris, DCO.' As if John needed to be reminded who his father was. He could imagine the conversation. *Can't let the boy have that stigma. Mental instability. Dog him all his life.*

'And the War Office,' the major added. He pulled a chair close to John's and leaned towards him.

'You could spend the rest of your time in the army weaving baskets in the Maudsley,' he said. 'Or twiddling your thumbs in

Düsseldorf. Either way, it's a waste of your talents.' He pulled out a packet of Senior Service and offered them to John.

'Thank you, sir,' John said, leaning forward to take the cigarette, wincing as his bruised flesh stretched. He took a deep breath, savouring the nicotine inside his lungs, filtering into his blood, coursing around his body. It was the first cigarette of the day, made him light-headed. He exhaled.

Major Buchanan twisted his nostril to one side. 'Bally good interpreter, that's what I said. Damned clever at translation and what have you.'

'Thank you, sir,' John said, again.

'So I've asked for you,' he said.

John reached over for an ashtray, suppressing a yelp. 'Asked for me?'

'My man isn't a patch on you,' he said. 'I've put in a request for your transfer. Base duties, I'm afraid, but I don't suppose you'd mind that, eh?'

John smiled, though he was unsure what the major was suggesting.

'Translating.' He smiled, went on. 'You won't be counting the dead again, or staring at lampshades made from human skin.'

John coughed, the ash from the cigarette settling on his trousers. He brushed it away. 'You've lost me, sir,' he said. 'Translating what?'

'Physics, mainly. We're working our way through the detail from their top scientists. You're the only man I trust on this. Billets in Hounslow. Cavalry barracks. Welsh Guards. Handy.' The major stood up, pulled down his jacket, picked up his cap and tucked it under his arm. 'Start Monday,' he said. 'There's a RAF flight tonight. I'll be on it too. They're expecting you.'

'You flew over here for me?' John said.

'I have the highest regard for your father,' he said.

John watched as the major left the room. He wasn't sure if he was relieved, or humiliated. Old boys' networks and all that.

CHAPTER THIRTY-ONE

Hatfield: spring 1946

Betty put the empty milk bottle back in its crate, threw the straw into the bin, and walked out into the playground, pulling her school coat around her. It was cold for March, with a chill wind. Mrs H had come with her to buy the uniform, a size too large, *to allow for growth.* It was a dull navy-blue tunic, strapped at the waist with a blue and yellow girdle. Cream blouse, blue and yellow tie. She had to tuck the sleeves up, pull the sash tight and bunch the bodice over it.

'Tie?'

'You'll get used to it,' Mrs H had said, showing her how to knot it, long side over, and under, up and down through the top. 'Pull the short end and slide it up to your neck.'

Her father wore a tie these days, and a suit. A car had collected him at first and driven him to work, but now he'd bought his own, a 1937 Daimler. *Good as new. Pre-selected gearbox.* The seats were leather, the dashboard walnut. She could just about remember the car he'd driven before the war. That had been a Daimler, too. His new job at the aircraft factory came with a house and he'd employed Mrs H, a widow, to cook and clean for them. Ever polite round her, Betty noticed, always correct.

'Such a gentleman, your dad,' Mrs H said. 'I thought all Germans were bad. He must be the exception.'

'And me?' Betty said. 'Am I an exception?'

Mrs H had nodded, but her look said it all.

§

She'd had English lessons from a retired teacher with a ruddy face who picked the skin on the palm of his hand. His name was Mr Hopkins and he came to the house every day, sat opposite her in the dining room with his legs straddled wide and his belly over his belt. He reminded her of Boris. Betty was nervous around him, insisted that the door was open, that Mrs H was in earshot. Still, he did the job, explained to her that English had German roots as well as French, had her talking in no time, her accent flawless, though the spelling had taken longer.

'So now you and I, Betty,' her father said, 'we speak only English from now on. German we put behind us. Germany we put behind us. The war.'

'When it ended,' she said, 'I was glad.'

'Glad?' He thumped his fist on the table so the crockery jumped and the milk splashed from the jug. 'You have no idea, child.' He grabbed a napkin, dabbed at the spilt milk, curled his lip, huffed. '*Glad*.'

He has no idea, Betty thought. He doesn't want to know.

'But they talk about it at school,' Betty said. 'All the time. The trials, at Nuremberg.'

'Rotten apples,' he said. 'We're not guilty for what the hotheads did.' He wagged his finger. 'If it hadn't been for them…' His voice trailed to nothing before he added, 'Dönitz was right. We could be the bulwark against Communism, but who listens?'

He changed her name to Betty, his own to Arnold. *Dad, daddy*. That was too cuddly a word for the father who was the perfect gentleman, blind, deaf and cruel to the core.

§

She stood on the edge of the playground. Some of the girls in her class were skipping, two long washing lines twisting in opposite directions. A girl was jumping over two ropes, fast, *left, right, left, right* while the others chanted.

'Sweetheart, sweetheart, will you marry me?' It was hard to make out the words, but the rhythm was clear enough. 'Yes, love, yes, love, at half past three.'

Another girl jumped into the spiralling ropes.

'Ice skates, spice skates, all for tea.' Betty furrowed her brows. That made no sense. Spice skates?

'And we'll have a wedding at half past three.' The voice was close to her ear. Betty jumped, turned. Deirdre O'Cleary. Brown hair, green eyes, skin stippled with dark brown freckles. Betty had never seen a complexion like it. She'd been put to sit next to her in class, sharing the double desk in the front, under the teacher's nose. Deirdre would run off at break time, sit by herself with a book. None of the other girls spoke to her, any more than they spoke to Betty.

'Can you skip?' she said.

'Yes, of course.' Betty shrugged. 'Doesn't everybody?' She hoped she sounded casual, not surprised that someone was talking to her, even if it was Deirdre O'Cleary. 'Spice skates? What are they?'

Deirdre laughed. '*Cakes.* Iced cakes. Spiced cakes.'

Betty could feel a blush creeping up her neck. It was bad enough they called her a Kraut to her face, did Hitler salutes behind her back. Now they'd think her stupid as well. She'd never make friends. The school might be one of the best around, but she hated it. She hated the nuns who ran it, the teachers who policed it, the girls who peopled it. *Poisoned* it.

'I had to push to get you in there,' her father said. 'School is not a party. School is for study.'

'Why did you come to England?' Deirdre said.

'My father was a prisoner of war here,' Betty said. 'And volunteered to stay.' She shrugged. 'They're short of workers. In the factory.'

'Did he fight in the war?'

'I suppose so.'

'What about your mother?' Deirdre said. 'Is she here?'

Mutti, Berlin, Lieselotte. That seemed so very far away, such a very long time ago.

'My mother died,' Betty said, holding down the choke in her voice. 'At the end of the war.'

'Mine too,' Dee said. She kicked at an imaginary stone, scuffing the toe of her shoe. 'What did she die of?'

'We think it was pneumonia.'

'Think?'

'There was no doctor,' Betty said. 'We couldn't get one.' Dee stared at her feet, twisting them onto their sides.

'I'm sorry,' she said.

'What did your mother die of?'

'A tumour,' Dee said. 'About a year ago. Who looks after you?'

'Mrs H cooks and cleans,' Betty said. 'My father leaves early and comes back late.'

'From the factory?' Dee said. 'He must work two shifts then.'

Betty shrugged. She had no idea. 'Who looks after you?'

'My father. Me. My Auntie Bridey says I have an old head on young shoulders.'

Betty thought for a moment, translating its meaning. She smiled, a tight, cautious tweak. *We have much in common.*

'You can call me Dee,' Deirdre said. 'If you like.'

Betty tried not to smile, but they were the kindest words anyone had spoken in all the months she'd been in England.

§

Dee brought a piece of tarpaulin and two faded cushions, frayed round the piping, threadbare in the corners. They borrowed Mrs H's dustpan and brush and swept the floor as best they could, but the earth was dusty and damp where leaves had drifted in and settled. Betty held her breath as she swept them up, woodlice scuttling and an earthworm glistening. She couldn't tell Dee she was scared of worms. They rearranged the gardening tools in a stash in the corner, the spade and fork, the rake and the lawnmower, stacked the flowerpots inside each other, rolled the hose into a tight coil. Dee laid out the tarpaulin, threw the cushions onto the ground.

Betty pushed the door wider and let in a long sliver of light. 'Did people really shelter here in the war?'

Dee nodded. 'My father said they were a wing and a prayer. He said it made the government feel good and was cheaper than building deep shelters.' She paused. 'Did you have them in Germany?'

They'd never talked about the war in the months they'd been friends, not even when it was the VE anniversary. The nuns said she needn't go to Mass with the others for the celebrations, given that she was German. She hadn't told her father they'd done that.

'No,' Betty said. 'We had some deep shelters. And the buildings have cellars.' Sitting with Mutti and Lieselotte as the buildings shuddered above them and the stench and smoke closed in. 'It was terrifying.'

Dee nodded as if she understood, but Betty wondered. She knew there'd been a bit of bombing in Hatfield, because of the factory, but nothing really heavy. She shifted her cushion, adjusted it under her bottom and sat cross-legged. The wall was damp and the floor hard. She couldn't imagine having to spend a night here.

'What did your father do in the war?' she said. She'd been asked the question so many times, had never dared ask it herself.

'He was a Conscie,' Dee said.

'A Conscie?' This was a new word to Betty. 'What's that?'

'A conscientious objector,' Dee said, adding, 'He doesn't believe in war.'

Old Herr Baumann called them traitors. Bundled up in the Wehrkraftzersetzung. Subversives. Defeatists. Deserters.

'Wasn't he shot?'

'*Shot?*' Dee said. 'Not in this war. But he had to go away, worked in a forest. He said it was hard.' She uncurled one leg, rubbed her thigh. 'And people called him names. He went to prison once, too. My leg's gone dead. Here—' she reached into her satchel and pulled out a packet of five Woodbines and a box of matches. 'Would you like one?'

'I've never smoked,' Betty said, watching as Dee opened up the packet and held it towards her. Dee was daring. Betty took a cigarette, leaned forward as Dee struck a match.

'Put one end of the cigarette in your mouth,' Dee said. 'And the other end in the flame, and suck.'

Betty leaned forward, her hair singeing as it brushed the match. She sucked, eyes watering. 'That's disgusting,' she said, coughing hard.

'Gaspers,' Dee said. 'They're called gaspers.'

Betty thought she was going to choke.

'Don't suck so hard next time,' Dee said. 'You get used to it. But you have to make an effort, to like it, I mean.'

Betty tucked her hair behind her ear, took another drag, smaller than the first, felt the hot smoke burn her throat, tasted its acrid bitterness, watched as Dee recrossed her legs and held her fingers scissored and aloft, like the girl in the Craven 'A' advertisements. Betty took a small puff. Well, she thought, this wasn't so bad, but nothing to write home about, although Dee looked sophisticated and Betty envied her that.

'Why doesn't your father believe in war?' she said.

'Oh, well.' Dee flicked the ash onto the earth floor. 'He says it's not the way to settle a quarrel.'

'How else do you settle one?'

'You talk.' Dee shrugged. 'Or there's international policemen. Law. I don't know.'

'Like the United Nations?'

Dee shook her shoulders with an irritable flair. 'Who cares?'

'I'm just interested,' Betty said. 'I don't want another war. Especially with the bombs they dropped on Japan.'

'Well, you should talk to my dad sometime then,' Dee said.

Betty pulled out her cushion and leaned it up against the wall behind her, looking at her friend. 'Is that why they don't talk to you in school?'

Dee looked down at her school tunic, folded and unfolded the pleats. She straightened her legs, crossed them at the ankles. She didn't need to answer.

'That's awful,' Betty said.

'You can see their point,' Dee said, stubbing out her cigarette on the earth floor, throwing the stub in the corner. 'Their fathers risked their lives. Maggie Ascombe's father actually died in the war. And what did mine do? Gardening.'

And what did *mine* do? Betty thought. He was happy to carry out the Führer's will. Had he ever stopped to question it?

'What about now?' Betty said.

'He works for the council,' Dee said.

'No, I mean, about war? About stopping war?'

'I don't think he does anything except shout at the wireless,' Dee said. She looked up then, and smiled. 'He's the loveliest man, Betty. He just doesn't believe that violence is the way out of a crisis. Though he did say once that perhaps it had been necessary to get rid of Hitler. I don't know.' She pulled out the cigarettes again, offered one to Betty, who took it, holding back her hair as she leaned forward to light it. 'This can be our little house,' Dee said. 'Our secret place. Shall we go out this weekend? A cycle ride?'

'That'd be nice,' Betty said. 'We can pack some sandwiches.'

Dee stood up, brushed the skirt of her tunic, and pulled out a small lipstick which she dabbed on, smacking her lips. 'Does your father let you wear this?'

'No.' He'd taken his thumb and pressed it hard against her lips, wiping it off.

Dee was modern, the best friend anyone could have.

§

Mrs H told her father and he summoned Betty into the shelter. He made her sweep up the cigarette butts and burn the cushions and tarpaulin.

'I sent you to the convent so you would become a lady.' His eyes grey like her own, icy as a glacier. 'Not to mix with the Irish.'

He didn't say it, but Betty heard. *Untermenschen.*

CHAPTER THIRTY-TWO

London: November 1958

John suggested the British Museum. It was too wet for a walk, and the nights were closing in. The museum would be warm and quiet, with little chance of anyone recognising them.

He stood between the pillars at the top of the steps, the hood of his duffel coat pulled up, a scarf muffled at the neck. He'd bought a two-bar electric heater for his flat and it cosied up his sitting room, but his nerves stayed frozen and his flesh goose-pimpled and now the chilly, dank air made him shiver. He'd come early and she was late. He thrust his hands deep in the pockets of his coat, fiddling with the fluff at the bottom, stomping to stir his circulation. He could slip inside the building, but then he might miss her. And if she didn't come soon, there'd be no time before closing.

He peered across the courtyard, trying to make out the figures in the thick, mustard light. Someone tapped his shoulder. He turned.

'I've been waiting inside,' she said. 'Have you been here all the time?'

'This was where we agreed to meet. On the steps.' Her breeziness made him cross. He didn't care if he sounded irritable.

'I know. But it was cold and I thought you'd see me. No matter.' She turned, led the way through the revolving doors. 'Where to?'

'Coins,' he said. 'Korea. No one ever visits.'

They threaded their way up and into the empty gallery with its serried ranks of display cases in dark wooden frames.

'You have to be seriously interested in coins,' he said, 'to come here. It's all a bit forbidding, don't you think?'

She nodded, drifting over to a cabinet against the wall, her coat tucked over her arm. Her face gave nothing away.

'Let's get down to business,' she said. 'Shall we?' He'd hoped they'd talk their way into the matters at hand, pleasantries to make them feel better. He was still in love with her. All he needed was a signal, however slight, to suggest that all was not lost.

She stared at the coins in front of her, pretending to study them, one finger on the glass as if she was pointing at something.

'You begin,' she said.

He breathed in hard. He'd thought through what he had to say, but not how to start the conversation. He'd expected her to be less forthright, to coax him, tickle it out of him. He had no ready words.

'I had no idea—' He coughed, a nervy *ahem*, buying time. 'I had no idea that you and Lieselotte were sisters.' She was staring ahead at the coins. *Joseon Dynasty. 1752.* 'She didn't speak about her family.' He glanced at her sideways, added, 'Any more than you.'

'I learned to keep my counsel,' Betty said, her eyes fixed on the inscription. 'Nobody wants to hear from a German. Much less a self-pitying one.'

'Did you lose anyone else in the war?'

'Of course,' she said. 'But not like the Jews, or the Roma or Sinti. Or the labourers or the prisoners. Or the millions of others who died. We were the lucky ones.' She paused and he watched as her lips moved, as if she was about to say something more. 'My mother died. My grandparents too, shortly after. And my father.' She spoke into the display, as if describing what she saw, an alloy coin with a hole in its centre. 'In a manner of speaking.'

'How so?'

'I was six when he left. I never saw him again until the war was over. I was twelve, almost thirteen. I was sent to England.' She turned, faced him. 'I'd never been out of Germany and I had to meet him in England. Our enemy. Our conqueror. I travelled alone. Can you imagine? I was terrified. I had an envelope with my papers and was put on a RAF plane at Tempelhof. It was full of demobbed airmen.' She gave a half-smile, shook her head. 'My father met me at the airport. Croydon, I think it was. Walked across the tarmac. Of course, I'd grown, changed, but when he saw me…'

She sniffed deep and turned away, but he saw the tears welling in her eyes. 'He didn't hug me. Didn't say he'd missed me. Just dragged me by the hand out of sight.'

'Why did he do that?'

'I'd shamed him, apparently.' She swallowed. 'You see, I'd been allowed to pick an outfit for the journey. The Red Cross had these second-hand clothes, donations, I suppose. I'd been living dressed as a boy, but now was my chance.' He could see her smiling at the memory. 'There was a party dress, with sequins and a tutu. It looked so pretty. I put it on and the UNRRA nurse gave me some lipstick. I thought I looked like a queen.' She laughed a little. 'Now, of course, I see I looked an absolute fright.' She paused. 'But I did it for him.' Betty was facing the cabinet but he could see the tear trail down her cheek. 'And he turned me away.'

She rummaged in her bag, pulling out a handkerchief, blowing her nose.

'Sorry,' she said. 'I haven't ever told anyone that. Bottled it up, you know?' She blew again. 'I think he expected a nice wholesome child to emerge in a dirndl and plaits, the pride of Germany. Not an urchin in a cabaret dress.' She blew out, as if the telling had exhausted her breath. 'I wasn't the child he thought I should be. I don't know why I'm telling you this now. It's not important.'

But it is, he thought, it hurt. She was sharing this with him. Perhaps she still cared for him, enough to trust him with this?

'What was he doing in the war?'

'He was in the Wehrmacht, part of the occupying force in the Channel Islands.' She smiled again. 'He spent his war learning cricket in Sark. And English.'

John wondered if Anatoly had got it all wrong, that Betty Fisher was not Bette Fischer but some other namesake.

'What's his name?'

'Arnold Fisher,' she said. 'He changed his name too. Anglicised it. It was Hermann Fischer.'

John stood behind her, watching her reflection in the glass. Her hair had been twisted into a pleat and a wisp had come loose, resting on her collar. He wanted to lift it, tuck it back in place, brush her neck, smell her scent.

'There's a physicist called Hermann Fischer. Is that your father?'

'No. He's an engineer,' she said. 'He works on aeroplanes. On engines.'

'Where?'

'At the de Havilland factory, in Hatfield. I told you this ages ago.'

'Why did he leave Germany?' John said.

'He never went back,' Betty said. 'He was a POW. He fell in love with England, and England was crying out for workers at the end of the war. Europeans, ideally, like him.' She laughed. 'The people who came in the end were West Indians. But one or two of the POWs stayed, like my father.'

This was going nowhere. Anatoly had got the wrong man. Fischer was a common enough surname, and Hermann a popular first name. This whole business was shambolic, he thought, had cost him his love, his sanity.

'So who is Hermann Fischer the physicist?' Betty said, daring him to contradict her.

John took a deep breath. He looked at her, trying to lock her eyes with his, pumping up his courage.

'There's a man by that name who works for de Havilland,' he said. He spoke slowly, softly. 'In a secret division of the company. He was a German physicist during the war. Among other things, he helped develop the V1 and V2 rockets.'

She faced him, her colour fading from her cheeks. 'Go on.'

'After the war, he was invited to come to Britain.' His eyes steadied on her, monitoring her, drilling into her, willing her to respond. 'A number of Germany's top scientists left at that time. Some went to the Soviet Union. Some to the United States. Some here.'

'So?' she said, shrugging her shoulders, a tone of defiance. 'Why? What's that to do with my father? That's some other man.'

'They came,' he said, his voice level, authoritative, 'to work on the nuclear programme.'

Betty opened her mouth, hand to her lips. 'I didn't know this,' she said. 'Those scientists? Who worked for the Nazis? Came here?'

He nodded.

'You think my father was among them?' She shook her head, staring at the coins, at their inscriptions. 'Who knows this?'

'It's not a secret,' he said. 'Not with a capital "S". But it's not common knowledge, either.' His lips were dry and he moistened them with his tongue. 'They were vetted, of course, to make sure they weren't still active Nazis, and some of them were given alibis.' She was listening hard, her forehead creasing, taking in what he was telling her, making sense of it.

'Why?' she said.

'There was a race to develop the A-bomb.' She nodded. 'The big fear was that the Germans had already developed it, or were damn close to developing it.'

'I didn't know that,' she said.

'It turned out that the Allies were more advanced than the Germans on the A-bomb,' he said. 'Or the Americans, at least, as we learned in Hiroshima and Nagasaki. But the Germans were more advanced in their delivery systems. They didn't need bombers. They could send weapons on rockets. Ballistics. The Russians were way behind both.'

'And Hermann Fischer?'

'He came to work on ballistic missiles.' He paused. 'De Havilland was a cover. He commuted from Hatfield to a secret location in Buckinghamshire where he and a bunch of other German scientists used their expertise to work on rockets and guided missiles.' He shouldn't be telling her this, could be had under the Official Secrets Act, but she had to know.

'The Brits and Americans agreed that the Americans would develop the Intercontinental Ballistic Missiles,' he went on. 'And we would focus on the Intermediate Range Ballistic Missiles. All the more urgent now, after Sputnik.'

She stood nodding, silently.

'De Havilland are building the rocket,' John went on. 'And Hermann Fischer, Arnold Fisher, is the principal scientist responsible for its production.'

She said nothing, but he saw her swallowing, again and again.

'My father.' She walked out of the room and he followed her. There was a stone bench, and she sat down.

'How do you know this?' she said. 'Who are you? Some kind of spy?'

'When I was in Berlin my job was to translate,' he said. 'I was there when they interviewed the scientists.'

'Did you interview him?' She twisted on the bench, searching his face.

'I may have done,' he said. 'I can't remember. We interviewed so many.'

She breathed in deep. 'Are you sure?' she said. 'Are you sure it's the same person?'

'Yes.'

She turned to face him once more, her face flushed, lips twisted. 'He lied. He *lied*.' She stood up, slinging her bag over her shoulder. He held her arm, gripping it hard as she winced.

'Bette.' He used her German name. 'There is more. *Lass' mich bitte ausreden.* You must hear me out.'

He pulled her back down on to the bench, holding her firm. She must not run off again. He looked at her, the grey water of her eyes, the framing of her nose and cheeks.

'I'll go to prison for telling you this,' he said. 'But I'm prepared to do it if it saves you.'

'Saves me?'

'Anatoly. Vasily. Whatever his name is. He's a colonel in the GRU.'

'A spy?'

'They want the secrets of Blue Streak. And you are their means.'

'Me? How?' She shook his arm free and stood up. 'How do you know all this? Are you working for them?' She shook her head. 'Or someone else?' She flung her head back. 'What is going on?'

John swallowed. If there was any lingering affection from her to him, it would be blown forever now.

'They needed me to get close to him. I was their go-between, and you were mine. I've told you that already, but not why.'

Her eyes narrowed, and the tips of her ears blushed red. She shook her arm to free herself.

'No, Betty, no.' He held her hand, resisting her efforts to pull it free. 'I met you in good faith, and I fell in love with you in good faith. But Anatoly had followed us the morning I broke off with you. Do you remember? I pulled you out of that café?'

She nodded.

'He knows who you are. And he blackmailed me again, unless I complied.'

'I saw him. He didn't recognise me.'

'He probably didn't notice you,' John said. 'He knows everything about you. Where you live, where you work.'

She swallowed, searching his face. 'Somebody rang at work,' she said. 'Asking if I worked there.' Her eyes opened wide. 'Funnily enough, the night we met, there was a man in Lyons, sitting by the door. He was wearing a coat and a hat, a trilby or fedora, pulled down low. It was just a glimpse, as I passed him, but he reminded me of Vasily. It was too ridiculous a thought, so I put it out of my mind.' She looked up at him. 'Now I wonder.'

'You will know how ruthless they are,' John said. 'And you could be in danger.'

'You've said this before,' she said. 'How am I in danger?'

'It would be the simplest thing in the world for them to kidnap you,' he said. 'Use you to bargain with.'

She laughed out loud, too loud. He hadn't expected that.

'My father doesn't give a toss about me,' she said. 'I doubt he'd trade.'

'Then they'd kill you.'

Her face froze. She turned to him, twisting in slow motion, searching his eyes for an answer. She fumbled her lip with her teeth, rubbed her hand along her cheek. 'Chinese ceramics,' she said. 'Let's look at those.' Betty pushed up from the bench and stepped forward. She was unsteady and he walked behind her, arms at the ready, to catch her, in case she fell.

'More cabinets,' she said as they entered the gallery. 'More dreary cabinets.' She walked into the centre of the gallery. 'Plates and pitchers and cups and ewers.' She stared, pointing. 'Though that is very beautiful. Ming. I like it.' She pressed her nose against the glass, her voice muffled as she spoke.

'You seem to know a lot about my father,' she said. 'Have the Soviets told you this?' She pulled away and faced him. 'If you're working for the Soviets, why don't you just feed me to the wolves?'

'Because I love you,' he said.

She bit her lip, turned away again. 'Before,' she said, bending down to study a teacup at the bottom of the cabinet, 'you said they blackmailed you, in Berlin, but you wouldn't tell me if you'd given them secrets.' She stood up, level with him. 'Why are they blackmailing you now?'

He looked away, the fine ceramics merging into one blue and white porcelain blur.

'You fed the Russians what they wanted, didn't you? This was my sister they used. Murdered. You didn't give a damn, did you? Too busy saving your own skin.' Her voice had risen, and though the gallery was empty, he put a finger on his lips and a hand on her shoulder.

'No,' he said. 'I told my commanding officer. Came clean with him. Betty…' He blew through his mouth, lips vibrating. 'I was used as a double agent, feeding the Soviets misinformation.'

She narrowed her eyes, her mouth open, her head turned to one side. 'Why can they still blackmail you?'

'I also fed them real information. Just once. Something specific. Something not important, but by then they knew I had been double-crossing them. The British didn't know what I'd done but they knew I was in danger, so moved me to Nuremberg.'

She was taking it in, working through the levels of trickery and duplicity.

'And are you still a double agent?'

He nodded. 'I was. A quid pro quo,' he said. 'The government won't prosecute me for that one lapse if I monitor you.'

'Me?'

'As they see it, you're a weak link, a security risk, because of your political leanings.'

'My political leanings? What on earth do they mean?'

'CND and all that.'

'Good God, I thought this was a democracy. Why would I be a threat?'

'For the same reason the Russians see you as an asset. You could turn him.'

'Don't they understand? I am opposed to war. Especially nuclear war. Full stop. This is nothing to do with Left or Right, East or West. Nothing to do with ideology.' She paused and he could see her calculating it all. 'You've been spying on me, haven't you? Feeding me to the Soviets, and MI5 or 6 or whoever it is. I'm the piggy in the middle here.'

'No,' he said. 'Believe me, please. I've passed nothing on you, or anyone, anything, to Special Branch that they don't know already. But yes, I have been used by them. As much to sniff out the Soviets as to sniff out CND.'

'Special Branch?'

'They were collaborating with MI5,' he said. He could hear himself, knew what she must think of him, was powerless to claw it back. His stomach clammed tight and he could feel a tremor creep out and convulse his body. He clenched his hands. *Don't move.*

She wandered off, running her finger along the cabinets, leaving a trail of condensation. 'He lied to me,' she said. 'My father lied to me.' She looked at her feet, then up at him. 'I'm going to have it out with him. Tell him what I think of him. What it's like to have a bastard for a father. He betrayed me. All of us.' She threaded her arms through the sleeves of her coat in sharp, awkward gestures. 'And you lied to me.'

'No, Bette,' he said, using her German name again. 'I never lied to you.'

She fumbled with the belt, knotting it tight.

'Let me come with you,' he said.

'Haven't you caused enough pain and havoc?'

Yes, he wanted to say, *yes, you're right*. But he couldn't let her slip away, not again. Nor did she say no, not in so many words.

CHAPTER THIRTY-THREE

Hatfield: November 1958

John was the last person she wanted with her, but she was nervous about going alone. She knew her father's metal, the freeze-cold steel of his heart, but this felt like a deeper betrayal. Mutti used to say that his work in the war was top secret. Bette had thought it a mysterious, important job that put her a cut above Greta with a common foot soldier of a father. She had no idea how insidious it was, how evil. Had Mutti?

It was raining when they got off the train and the wind had picked up, gusting drops of icy water that stung her cheeks.

'We can get a bus,' she said. 'But it's quicker to walk. It's not far.' She set off with large strides, her hair limp and sticky from the wet. John walked beside her, hands in his pockets, silent. Her thoughts spun round, ribbons on the maypole, always the same. Why had he lied to her, over and over? Had he lied to himself, too? To Mutti? Lieselotte? It was such a slippery line between delusion and lies.

A police car drove past, seconds later, an ambulance, their bells bouncing off her roiling emotions like radar. What if he wasn't there, after all this? Mrs H would know where he was. She knew everything. Did *she* know who he was? Did she care?

'Not too far now,' she said, more to herself than to John. At least he had the gumption to keep his mouth shut on the journey here.

It was bad enough coping with thoughts about her father. She couldn't begin to think about John and his two-faced treachery. She felt as if she was at the centre of a world that was crushing her in the weight of its ambitions, like a walnut between nutcrackers, a disposable shell.

They turned the corner into her street, the rain silver sequins in the light of the street lamp. She slowed her pace, fearful of the confrontation with her father, her anger burning and erupting. What would she say to him? *You lied.* Lie was too small a word for the betrayal she felt. *Why didn't you love me?* That was as much a crime as anything. *Why didn't you take me in your arms at the end of the war, nuzzle me with your moustache, Bettechen, meine Bette.* Tell her she was safe, that everything would be all right, that he knew about Mutti, and Lieselotte, understood how lost she was, how frightened, how very young? He'd pressed his thumb on her lips, skidding it hard across them so the lipstick came off. She'd wanted to look so pretty. Her eyes began to blur and she stopped, wiped them with a gloved finger. She didn't want him to see her crying, to see how frail she was, how vulnerable. She would be strong. She *was* strong. He was nothing but a pigeon of a man strutting with a puffed neck, *Look at me. Look what I can do.*

Deliver a nuclear warhead. He made instruments to kill.

Betty opened the gate. 'Stay here,' she said. She walked up the garden path, knocked on the door. The hall light was off and the front room was in the dark, its curtains undrawn. Her father liked to keep the curtains open. *We have nothing to hide.* He was frugal with the electricity and the heating, never lit a room or warmed it unless he was using it. This was one thing she had agreed with him on. The English didn't know how to heat their homes.

The house was silent inside. She knocked again, expecting to hear his impatient voice, *Hold on, hold on, I'm coming.* She peered through the letter box. There was a light in the kitchen.

'No reply,' she called to John, standing by the gate blowing on his hands with the hood on his duffel coat up. 'I'm sure he's there. I'll try the back door.'

'Let me come with you,' he said, adding, 'I won't come in.'

She opened the gate, sidling past the dustbin. John was close behind her, breathing hard. She tried the handle on the door. It opened. She stepped inside, wiping her feet out of habit on the mat. The kitchen was empty, no traces of cooking, no cups on the draining board, bread on the dresser. That was how her father liked it, without the footprint of the living.

She held out her hand, reaching for John, as she walked into the hall, flicking on the light. The dining room was on her right, the door shut. She peered through the keyhole. The room was in darkness.

'Perhaps he just forgot to lock up,' John said.

'You don't know my father,' she said. 'He always checks and double-checks.'

'Not if he left in a hurry,' John said.

She twisted round. 'Why do you say that? Do you know something?'

John put up his hand, palm outwards. 'Of course not,' he said.

She breathed in. 'Vasily,' she said. 'Do you think—' She broke off, unsure what she thought. 'Kidnap?' she said. 'If the Russians want him, why don't they just take him?'

'That's ridiculous, Betty,' he said. 'Governments don't do that sort of thing.'

'But they did,' she said. 'At the end of the war. The British took my father.'

'They didn't kidnap him,' he said. 'He came of his own free will. You're letting your imagination run away with you. There'll be a simple explanation. Perhaps he's ill. Or asleep. Where's his bedroom?'

He was probably right. But her father's hearing was acute, as sharp as his eyesight or his sense of smell. He was a light sleeper, too, would have heard them. She led the way up the stairs to his bedroom in the front of the house, opened the door, turned on the light. His bed was made, the candlewick bedspread unruffled, a pair of shoes tucked beneath the bedroom chair, their polished heels just visible.

She looked at John. *He isn't here.* She backed out, opened the door to the small room above the hall. They used it as a box room to store her father's DIY tools. It had been cleared. A treadle sewing machine was under the window, a dressmaker's dummy in the corner.

Her old bedroom was in the back. She flicked on the light. Her bed behind the door had a new pink ruched eiderdown on top of the blankets. There was a kidney-shaped dressing table with chintz drapes under the window where her desk used to be, and on its glass top a vanity set and perfume bottle with a pink atomiser. The wardrobe hadn't changed, filled the alcove as it had before. Betty went over, flung it open. It was full of women's clothes, dresses and skirts and blouses smelling of cheap perfume and Daz and Mrs H.

The tutu dress had gone, the last memento of her, erased. The hurt burned, white hot.

She could hear John opening the bathroom door, the lavatory door, closing them, *click*.

'Let's go downstairs,' he said. 'I'm sure there's nothing to worry about.'

'She's moved in,' Betty said. 'Mrs H has moved in.' She didn't know why she was shocked. Anyone could see that's what the woman had angled for from the day she arrived. It was more than shock. It was a *slash*, a cut so deep it could never heal. Her father loved that woman more than her.

'Then they'll be out somewhere,' John said. She wanted to scream *Weren't you listening?* 'Let's just check the other rooms, and we'll go.' His step was lighter. He was uncomfortable here, she could tell.

The sitting room was as dark and empty as the other rooms. There was only one room left, the dining room at the back of the house with French windows leading to the garden. They always ate in the dining room, her father one end of the table, she the other, with her back to the outdoors. It was where she sat when he reprimanded her too. Had he ever praised her? Had he ever said, *You've done well, Betty, I'm proud of you?* John opened the door, felt for the switch, turned on the light. The room had a pungent smell she couldn't identify.

Her father sat in her chair, his back to the garden, facing the blank wall. His head had lolled to the side, his mouth twisted, a livid tongue protruding, like some grotesque gargoyle. His grey eyes were open, as hard and empty in death as in life. She could hear herself breathing, struggling to drag the heavy air in, out, her chest rising and falling. She stood, numb, dead to herself, thoughts and feelings moiling like debris in a storm.

She felt John's arm around her shoulder. 'I'm so sorry, Betty,' he said, pulling her towards him. She was limp, fell against him. 'So sorry.'

Betty tried to speak but a lump of anger and grief blocked her throat. He had left her, abandoned her, again. There was a bang. She jumped. One of the French windows had been pulled open by the gusty wind, slammed shut. That was strange. Why were they unlocked in this weather?

'Does your father have a telephone?'

She nodded, pointing to the hall. She watched as he walked away, listened as he dialled the emergency number.

'Ambulance. Police.' Called out, 'Betty, what's the address?'

'Oh,' she said. Why didn't he know that? 'Forty-seven...' She listened as he repeated it, gave his name again, gave hers. 'Yes, dead. His daughter.' He put the receiver down.

Her father had lost his power to terrorise her. She should go over and close his eyes, shut his mouth, but she didn't want to touch him. He repulsed her in his crude, brazen death. She had never loved him. Was that a terrible thing?

She waited for John's steps along the hall, for his hand to pull her away, but she heard him dial another number, the soft purr of the rotary. A moment. His voice was muffled as he spoke, but she could swear he said *birdcage*. It made no sense.

Her eyes were fixed on her father, his purpling, flaccid flesh, his hands on the table, the fingers stiff and white. There was a small brown glass phial next to him, a tiny cork beside it. Betty stood, transfixed. Frau Weber had had one the same, looped on a cord round her neck. The Baumanns too. Handed out like chocolates at the end of the war.

John stepped behind her. 'Come,' he said. 'Let me take you away.'

'Cyanide,' she said. 'He took cyanide.'

'How do you know?'

She pointed at the ampoule. 'Why? Why now? He'd had his chance in 1945.'

'I don't understand,' John said.

She was shaking her head. 'How would you?' Her voice was soft but vibrated with rage. 'After the war. So many people, one after the other. It was an epidemic.' Sitting with Greta behind the Biedermeier sofa, the Baumanns' chamber pots, memories shoved for space, overlapping like a montage, Berlin at the end, Germany at the end. 'They couldn't come to terms with their own idiocy.' She looked at John. 'Or their defeat. You see...' His face was searching hers and she knew he was listening hard. 'They'd swallowed Hitler and everything he promised. But it was a chimera.' Was she making sense? Could he comprehend how people coped with the criminal calamity that had been Germany? That they had been party to? 'He just took longer to grasp it than most.'

John placed his hand on her elbow, leading her away into the front room, helping her into an armchair as if she was an invalid. The room was cold, the fire unlit.

'Who were you talking to?' she said.

He didn't answer but reached over to the mantelpiece for the matches, struck one and lit the gas poker, nestling it in among the coals.

'That'll make it warmer,' he said. 'I'll make some tea.'

'You don't know where anything is,' she said.

'I'll find it.'

She rolled off her damp coat and sat back in the armchair, pulling out from beneath her a pleated cushion in synthetic silk. She looked at the familiar room. The wooden standard lamp with its fluted shade and tassels, the coffee table, the bureau. The grey carpet with the red diagonal slabs, parquet-patterned linoleum round the edges. There was a new clock on the mantelpiece, a brass carriage clock, and either side were two plaster Toby jugs. They looked cheap. The more Betty looked, the stranger the room became. A picture calendar had been tacked to the wall. The animal for November was a hedgehog, and two crocheted anti-macassars were draped over the back of the sofa.

She heard the bell of a police car, an ambulance, could hear John opening the door to them, the tread of boots to the dining room, hear him talking. She could see Mrs H through the window, standing outside, her voice shrill, her words indistinct. Betty waited. Listening. John came back with the everyday teapot and cups.

'I found some biscuits,' he said, placing a tray on the table. 'The police are here.'

'What's she doing?' Betty said. 'Mrs H?'

'She'd been out all day,' John said. 'Visiting her sister. Has just come back. A bit of a shock, I imagine.'

'I don't want her in here,' Betty said. 'I don't want to see her.'

'Let the police take care of it.'

He poured the tea and handed her a cup, checked his watch. He's going somewhere, she thought. He's going to leave me. She could hear another car draw up in the street outside, the door slam. Voices in the hall, *yes, sir*. John was nodding, as if he knew, as if he was expecting someone. The door opened and an older man entered, grey hair matching his suit.

'Detective Superintendent Fielding.' He held out his hand to her, his face sombre, like a pallbearer. 'I'd like to offer my condolences for your loss, Miss Fisher,' he said. 'It must be very hard for you. A dreadful shock.'

Betty nodded. Shock. That was the word. She fixed her eyes on the fire, the glowing red coals, the flicker of blue and orange flame drifting in and out of focus. She was cold, shivery.

'I'm so sorry to intrude,' he went on. 'But your father's death...' He paused. 'We have to investigate, you understand, to find out how he died.'

'Won't a post-mortem show that?'

'Yes, of course,' the DS said. 'It's just that your father was a rather' – he searched for the word – '*prominent* man.' He took a deep breath. 'There may be some official interest. I'm afraid this means asking you some awkward questions which you may find intrusive.'

She nodded. *I know.*

He smiled then. 'Do you mind if I sit?' He looked at the fire. 'I think this has caught now, don't you? Shall I turn the poker off?' He didn't wait for her answer, reached down and turned off the gas tap.

'Can you tell me more about him?' he said. 'What was he like?'

'I don't know what I can say,' she said. *I never really knew him*, she wanted to add. 'He was strict, liked his own way. He was a bit of a bully, to be honest, at least with me.'

'Well, sometimes fathers can be overprotective, you know, especially with daughters.' He smiled, *I know all about this*. 'Your father's fiancée—'

'Fiancée?' Betty said. 'You mean Mrs H? She's just the housekeeper.'

The detective shifted his position, raised an eyebrow. 'Mrs Henderson said you and your father were estranged.'

Betty shook her head. 'That's none of her business.'

'Were you? Estranged?'

'We had a disagreement, yes.'

'How long ago?'

'In the summer. July, I think.'

'May I ask what it was about?'

'Politics,' she said.

The detective nodded, scribbled in shorthand. 'Anything in particular?'

'I don't want to talk about it,' Betty said. 'It's not important, not now. It's too complicated.' It was about politics, but it was about denial, too, and how could she explain that to this detective?

'Why did you come back?'

Betty swallowed. 'He'd lied to me about something, and I wanted to—' She was about to say *confront him*, but checked herself. 'Find out what he had to say.' She looked at the policeman. 'Ask John. It was he who told me.'

John sat on the edge of the sofa, his teacup still in his hand. He was staring at it, as if reading the leaves. The room was silent save for the hum of their breathing, the faint rumble of a train in the distance, the muffled tones of people coming and going in the hallway. The fire needed more coal, but she didn't have the energy to shovel more on.

'I'm sorry,' she said. 'I'm not being any use.' She flapped her hand towards the window. She suspected Mrs H pulled the curtains to each night. *There, that's cosier, isn't it?*

'Is there anyone who would wish your father dead?'

'Do you think he was murdered?' she said. What secret operations had he been caught up in, this little man in big man politics? John would know.

'He committed suicide,' she said before he could answer. That was obvious.

'You seem sure,' the detective said, but his voice hinted at a question. 'Is there any reason why he would want to take his own life?'

She shook her head. 'I can't think of any.' Had he felt remorse? 'He swallowed cyanide, didn't he?'

'Only a post-mortem will tell us that,' DS Fielding said. 'What makes you think he took cyanide?'

'I recognised the phial on the desk.'

'Had you seen it before?'

She shook her head. 'Not that one. Not since we came to England.'

The detective flicked through some notes, took a glance at John. 'In 1945,' he said, looking up at her as if for confirmation. 'From Germany.'

It was supposed to be a secret, she thought. *We will not talk of it.* But the detective was aware of it, about her father. Highest security. Of course. Everyone knew about her father. She was the only one who didn't.

'Did you know your father had it?'

Betty shook her head. 'I had no idea,' she said.

'But you recognised it.'

She breathed in deep, gathering thoughts, words. 'We came here in 1945.' In all the years in England, she'd never gone against this injunction of her father's, *We do not talk of Germany*, but the detective knew this anyway. Arnold Fisher, aka Hermann Fischer. 'People talked about suicide, all the time. Anyone could put their hands on phials of potassium cyanide at the end of the war,' she went on. 'Just like that one. They were that easy to come by.' She wanted to shake her shoulders, feel the shackles of silence as they slid away. 'Cyanide was the weapon of choice, you must know that. Zyklon B. Mass murder. Individual suicide. It was no coincidence that Eva Braun took cyanide. Or the Goebbels. You'll have heard of them. But not the thousand others like them.'

DS Fielding took notes, squiggles of shorthand. 'Where did your father keep it?' he said.

'I don't know,' she said. 'I had no idea he had any.'

'Did he have a safe? Or somewhere under lock and key?' She thought of the secret compartment in Mutti's bureau in Berlin. Did her father have one?

'Not that I know,' she said.

'His passport? Documents? A will? Things like that? Where did he keep all those things?'

Betty shrugged. They'd never been abroad, had no need of a passport, but now, she thought, there must be *something* official, somewhere. 'Perhaps in the bureau,' she said, pointing. 'That was always locked.'

'Do you have the key?'

'No.' She sniffed. 'Sorry. You must think me hopeless.'

'Don't worry,' he said. 'We'll find it. Perhaps Mrs Henderson will know.'

'Perhaps,' Betty said. 'She seems to know everything.' She hoped the detective didn't hear the cut to her voice.

'May I just ask, what were you doing today?'

'Today? Before I came here, you mean?'

'Yes.'

'I met John at four, at the British Museum.'

'John? The gentleman here?' The detective looked across at John. 'Your boyfriend?'

'He's not my boyfriend,' Betty said, screwing up her eyes. She sounded petulant, she knew, but she didn't want to be associated with John.

'And you both came here then?'

'We left when the museum closed, about five, and came straight here.'

'Before you met John, what were you doing?'

The detective's tone was silky, like a spider, but she sensed a menace there. Did he think she'd come to Hatfield, poisoned her father?

'I was writing,' she said, adding, 'An article.'

'Where? Did anyone see you?'

She laughed. The absurdity of the question. 'I can't write at home,' she said. 'My room's too small and the house is too noisy. So I go to the public library, the reference part, Willesden Green.' She looked at him. 'Near where I live. Then I went to the Partisan—'

'The Partisan?'

'It's a coffee house, in Soho,' she said. 'And a sort of meeting place. I can use their typewriters, so I typed up my article. Then I walked to meet John.'

'And others can vouch for you?'

'Loads,' she said. 'I even walked with someone to meet John.'

'His name?'

'Nick. I don't know his surname.'

John reached forward to put his cup on the tray, glanced at her. Yes, she thought. His name's Nick.

'And you, sir?' the detective said. 'Where were you?'

'I was at home marking,' he said. 'And no, no one can vouch for me. I live alone.'

DS Fielding flicked his notebook shut. 'That'll be all for the moment,' he said. 'Miss Fisher. Thank you for your time. You'll be contacted later, I'm afraid. Others will need to talk to you.' He stood up, held out his hand. 'My constable will take your details.' He turned to John. 'If you don't mind, sir, may I have a word in private with you?' He led the way out of the room and John followed.

Betty turned to the fire, absorbed by the glowing coals and the warmth that was finally seeping into her body.

§

A Major Goodfellow rang her a few days later, wanted to meet her *for a quick chat*. He gave an address in Millbank, not far from the Tate. She took the morning off work, said it was to do with her father's arrangements. The building stood behind innocuous ivy-clad walls. There was a bell by the gate, but no indication of what the building was used for. No plaque, no sign. The windows were dark and she sensed that even if she pressed her nose against them, all she would see would be her own reflection.

The gate swung open, clicked shut behind her. She walked to the front door. Another bell, another silent entry. She stepped inside. If he hadn't been a major and therefore, in some way, official, she'd be worried, a young woman, alone, stepping into an empty building with no street number, no name.

'Follow me, miss.' A young soldier appeared and led the way up the main stairs, skirting round the landing, along a corridor. He knocked at a door, opened it. 'She's here, sir.' He indicated for Betty to enter.

'Miss Fisher.' A tall man stepped from behind a table, smiled at her, his hand outstretched. 'How very kind of you to come. I'm James Goodfellow. Let me take your coat.' He walked towards her, standing close as Betty slipped the coat off, handed it to him, watched as he hooked it onto a stand.

'Please sit.' He pointed to a chair in front of a table at which sat two other men. They were all, she guessed, about her father's age, with manicured nails and well-cut suits. James Goodfellow resumed his place between them, pointed left, and right.

'My colleagues, Frank Lloyd, Brian Cullis.' They smiled, backs straight, heads tilted in acknowledgement. Betty had no doubt who they were: military men, and this was a delegation from the Security Services.

'Please let us offer our condolences,' James Goodfellow said, and his colleagues nodded in agreement. 'And our apologies for bringing you in at this sensitive time.'

Betty sat, hands on her lap, threading and rethreading her fingers.

'There are just a few small things we need to clear up,' James Goodfellow said. He looked at his colleagues, as if waiting for their approval to proceed. 'We understand you are aware of the nature of your father's work.'

'I am now,' Betty said. 'But I had no idea. He never said a word. No, well…' These formal, formidable men in suits were in a strange way comforting, and for reasons she couldn't fathom she wanted to blurt out everything. 'He did. He said he worked for de Havilland. He gave the impression he was some kind of engineer, a factory worker.' She swallowed. 'That's what I thought. I trusted him. He was my father. He didn't talk about his work, except about the Comet. Its teething problems, metal fatigue and stress and turbojets and boring stuff like that.'

Should she have paid more attention? She had her own problems to cope with, settling into a new country, a new language, school. He hadn't given a toss about what she was going through, had never asked how her day had been.

'He lied.'

'A little white lie,' Brian Cullis said. 'I'm sure you forgive him for that.'

'Actually,' Betty said, inhaling, shoulders rising, head high, 'I don't.'

Cullis coughed, pulled a handkerchief from his breast pocket, wiped his mouth.

'Did your father ever talk about Germany with you?' Frank Lloyd said.

Betty shook her head. 'Hardly ever. He wouldn't even speak German.' He denied me language, she thought, the language that shaped me, my thoughts and feelings, loves and hates. Perhaps that's why he was so bitter too, the loss of his language had puckered his heart.

'Did he talk about politics?'

'We didn't really talk about very much at all,' Betty said, adding, 'He pontificated.'

Frank Lloyd smirked. 'About what?'

'Communism, mainly.' There was a silver cigarette box on the table. 'May I?' she said, leaning forward. James Goodfellow flipped open the lid and passed it across the table to her. 'Thank you,' she said. He scraped back his chair, walked round with his lighter, smiling as if she was a dinner guest, leaning over her as he lit her cigarette, close enough for Betty to see the hairs in his nostrils. 'Thank you again,' she said. She felt suddenly gripped by nerves. She sucked the smoke inside, feeling it swirl through her blood, tightening her thoughts.

'Such as?'

'He did once say that the Third Reich had been right to try to purge Europe of Communism.'

James Goodfellow leaned forward, his head on one side, nodding encouragement. 'Go on.'

'Well, he said that all that was needed was to rid the Party of its rotten apples, like Admiral Dönitz had suggested, and Germany could rise again, complete its destiny. He said the Nazis who were prosecuted in Nuremberg were evil, but not to throw the baby out with the bathwater.'

She watched as the men made notes.

'Did his views change?' Frank Lloyd said.

'A bit,' Betty said. 'Not much.'

'How?'

'He thought Germany wasn't to blame for the Nazis,' she said. Sitting at the end of the dining room table, knife and fork laid to rest, he waited until the dessert was served, lifting his spoon, waving it for emphasis. She wasn't allowed to start before he did, had to watch the custard go cold, congeal, a thick skin forming. He knew she hated the skin. 'He believed it could have happened to any country and said the Allies were happy to go along with Hitler when it suited them before the war. It just seemed unfair that Germany had to bear the brunt of it, he used to say, when it wasn't Germany's fault.'

Brian Cullis was nodding. 'Strong views. Controversial. Did you agree?'

Betty stared at him. 'Of course not. It *was* Germany's fault. He couldn't reconcile himself to that. It would mean confronting his past, coming to terms with it.'

'Adenauer's done a pretty good job. Bringing the country together, moving on. What do you say to that?'

This was not about her father's views. It was about her own. Betty shook her head. 'There needs to be a wider reckoning, don't you think? An acknowledgement of what Germany did, and why, a shared responsibility.'

'And how will that come about?'

'I don't know,' Betty said. 'But it will happen, I'm sure.'

James Goodfellow leaned back in his chair. His jacket fell open and Betty caught a glimpse of his waistcoat, the bulge of his paunch, the lie of his genitals beneath his trousers. She looked up, over his head, at the picture of the Queen on the wall behind him.

'Did he discuss his views with anyone else?' He tilted forward once more.

'Not that I know,' Betty said. 'But I was away at college for years, and before that, when I was at school, I didn't pay much attention to him. You could ask Mrs H. He seemed to be in her thrall. Perhaps he confided in her too.'

The men exchanged glances and Betty understood in that moment that Mrs H wasn't *just* the housekeeper Betty had always assumed, but something more sinister.

'Was she spying on us?'

James Goodfellow laughed, but it was a synthetic, patronising *ha-ha*. 'She kept us informed, that's all.'

Her life in England fell apart once more. And into place. The house in Hatfield, Mrs H, the school. Her father was an immigrant, but he had never struggled, not like the fathers of other immigrants in her class. He'd had it handed to him on a plate. Her father had never relinquished his goals, just swapped his paymaster. If the Third Reich wasn't allowed to rid Europe of the Communists, then he'd carry on its work.

Did he now realise Germany had been a lost cause, all of it? Was that why he had taken the cyanide?

'Miss Fisher' – James Goodfellow leaned forward, clasping his hands, elbows on the table – 'your father's work was top secret, you must appreciate, and we had to protect ourselves, be sure that nothing jeopardised our national defence, no moles passing information to extremists on either side.' He steadied his gaze on her. 'We had to protect him, too. And you.'

She stubbed out her cigarette.

'Vasily Kuznetsov,' he went on. 'You might know him as Anatoly Kuznetsov. What can you tell us about him?'

'Nothing,' she said. 'I knew a Vasily once but have no idea of his full name.'

'You are aware he is in London.'

She blew out, the questions coming closer, a steamroller out of control. She could feel her fingers quake, sat on her hands so no one could see. 'Yes.' Her voice was quiet.

'When did you first meet him?'

'In Berlin. He was with his superior, a major, Boris Somebody-or-other. He used to come to the apartment when Boris was...' Three men. What did they know? What could they know? She breathed in, gave the word its full airing. '*Raping* my sister.'

Cullis and the other man looked down, but Major Goodfellow kept her gaze, nodding, *continue.*

'Then they left. Only the morning after Lieselotte disappeared, Vasily came back to our apartment.'

'What did he want?'

'He wanted me. He wanted to rape me, but I shot him.'

'Is that why he limps?' Frank Lloyd asked.

'Yes,' Betty said.

'A good shot,' he said, and smiled at her.

'I didn't think that at the time,' Betty said. 'I was too terrified. I dropped the gun and ran.'

'He came back after your sister had been murdered,' Goodfellow said, looking at his notes. 'You're an intelligent young woman, as well as a pretty one.' He smirked, but Betty sat, her face blank. It didn't feel like a compliment, more like a threat. 'Do you think he had another purpose in returning to your apartment?'

Betty stared at him.

'Your father would have been quite a coup for the Soviets,' Goodfellow went on. 'Have you any idea how they could persuade him to come over to them?'

Betty shook her head. 'No.'

'Could they have argued their cause?'

'It wouldn't have made any difference,' Betty said. 'He was vehemently anti-Communist.'

'What about bribes? Do you think he would have succumbed to those? The promise of a good apartment, a lucrative salary with plenty of perks, the best laboratories and brains. What do you think?'

'I don't know,' Betty said. 'I doubt it. He always said he was a man of principle. He never did anything to excess.'

'Emotional levers?' the major went on. 'Kidnap of his surviving daughter would have been a strong incentive to persuade him to come over to them, whatever his principles.'

It had never occurred to her there could be more to this.

'Why is he here now?' Her voice was weak. She knew the answer. John had said as much. Kidnap.

'They wanted his secrets.'

She blinked, stared out of the window, at the plane trees beyond. Two-way mirrors. That's what they were. Two-way mirrors.

'Did my father know?'

The French windows had been open. Had he wandered into the garden first, talked to the pansies, said farewell to Mutti? Not bothered to lock the door behind him? Had he been thinking of Betty as he sat in her chair and tipped the powder into his mouth? Or had he had a visitor? Perhaps he hadn't been alone.

'We will never know,' James Goodfellow said. 'He left no note. But your liberty may well have been in danger. Or...' He looked at her, studying her face. They all were, monitoring every twitch and flutter, every turn of her body. Why had she thought they were sympathetic?

'What was your contact with Vasily?'

'I never made contact.'

'Not through CND?'

'Oh, for goodness' sake,' she said. 'This is nonsense. CND?' She edged forward in her chair, readying herself to leave.

'Do you have sympathies for the Russians?' the major said, leaning back again, chair tilting on two legs. 'I remember the butter-before-guns argument between the wars,' he went on before she could answer. He nodded at his colleagues either side of him and ran his tongue over his lips so they glistened with spit. He narrowed his eyes and looked at her, half leer, half sneer. 'Yellow-livered pacifists. If they'd been in charge, we'd all have been under the jackboot.' The chair slammed forward as the major propped his elbows on the desk, leaning towards her. 'If we disarmed, the Soviets would overrun us in a blink.' Spittle gathered in his mouth. She'd heard the argument before, was weary of it. 'Is that what you want? To be under a dictatorship hell-bent on supremacy?' He blew through his mouth, pulled out his handkerchief from his top pocket and wiped away the dribble. 'Against everything we hold dear. Christianity. Democracy. Freedom...' His voice trailed away.

'That's not the point,' she said.

'And what is the point?' Cullis said, his lip curling.

'The point is nuclear weapons. Do you know what they do? It would be the end of the world if they were unleashed.' She softened her voice. 'Don't you see that? No one would win. There'd be nothing left.'

'Well,' Goodfellow said, 'what *are* your sympathies for the Russians?'

They weren't listening. Fixed on their tracks like freight trains.

'None.'

Communism?'

She hesitated, marshalling her thoughts.

'I consider myself a socialist,' she said. 'I vote Labour. This is not a crime.' She reached over for a cigarette. She saw them note the move. *Chain-smoking. Nervous.* 'And I am passionately against war, especially nuclear war,' she said. She fiddled with the cigarette in her fingers. 'You'll know where I stand on that, since you seem to know everything about me.' She looked at James Goodfellow, staring him out. She would not be intimidated. 'May I trouble you for a light?'

He pushed the lighter towards her. Gloves off, she thought. He hadn't come round the table to light it for her.

'Pretty girl like you,' James Goodfellow said, his lips slick and rubbery, 'good Lord, in another time I'd have claimed the *droit de seigneur* over you.' He chuckled, and his colleagues smirked. He licked his lips again, the drool gathering in his mouth. 'You don't want to get involved in all of this left-wing ban-the-bomb nonsense.'

'Thank you,' she said, standing up. 'I have nothing more to say.' She turned, grabbed her coat off its hook, opened the door and left without looking back. The door clicked behind her.

She hurried from the building, over Vauxhall Bridge. *Bastard. Sleazy bastard. How* dare *he.* He hadn't been serious about her, hadn't a clue what troubled her, probably didn't care either. Just saw a pretty face to crush beneath him. Had her father had regrets about his former life? Remorse? Despaired of Germany? Or had he killed himself to save her? Perhaps Vasily had been at the door and he'd felt he had no choice.

What demons were in his head that drove him to do it? She would never know. It was a selfish act in a life that revolved round him, leaving behind an eternity of questions with no answers, a particular kind of earthly hell.

EPILOGUE

London: May 1959

Betty cradled her coffee, opened the French windows and stepped onto the balcony. It wasn't large enough for a chair, but it would take a window box and perhaps a couple of pots. She'd grow pansies for the spring, geraniums for the summer. She heard the click of the letter box, a gentle *plop-plop* on the mat. Letters, addressed to her, in her own home.

The coroner had taken his time but had returned an open verdict, which was odd given the cyanide, then she'd spotted a piece in the *Manchester Guardian* reporting the expulsion of a Soviet diplomat engaged in active espionage. It didn't mention Vasily by name, but the coroner's verdict made a kind of sense. The doors to the garden had been open after all, the handles wiped clean of fingerprints.

John had come to her father's funeral, stood at the back in a dark suit and black tie. She'd wanted to be angry, but his presence had touched her. He hadn't come to pay respects for her father. His respects were for her. He'd acknowledged her with the smallest nod and the hint of a smile, left at the end of the service, without a word.

Vanished from her life.

She'd sold her father's house, cleared out the furniture, every damn pleated cushion and Toby jug, and bought an apartment in West Hampstead. The hell with Mrs H. She had a fat pension to live off. Betty had had a new bed and sofa delivered yesterday when she'd moved in, and Nick had helped her transport her stuff from Dee's, her books and clothes, her clock, and odd bits that she'd accumulated for the move, a dustpan and brush, a Ewbank, a kettle, coffee mugs.

She needed other basics, a table and chairs, bedroom furniture, rugs. There was an auction house on the New King's Road and Dee had taken the afternoon off to go with her. 'Leave the bidding to me,' she'd said, pulling her face into a knowing wink. 'I'm a past master at it.' Nick said he could get hold of a van if she needed to shift anything.

Betty drained her mug and went back into the kitchen, picking up the post as she went. The flat needed decorating. She'd watched Barry Bucknell on Dee's television, DIY every Tuesday evening. Painting, papering. It looked simple enough.

She tucked the letters into her dressing gown pocket and wandered back into the sitting room. It faced south-east, caught the morning sun, was bright and airy. It could take a bold colour. There was a fireplace in the corner with an old-fashioned mantelpiece which she'd rip out in due course, put in something sleek and modern. She put the clock on it for the moment. It still kept perfect time. It wasn't much, but it was a link. Blue. Perhaps the sitting room could be painted blue, to show off the chrome frame and smoked glass of the clock's face.

The flat looked out over Fortune Green. It lifted her spirits to see the trees and grass, and she could send the boys out to play there when Dee and Kevin came over. She pulled the envelopes out from her pocket. One had a London postmark, official-looking, with a typed address, the other was handwritten, the postmark indistinct.

She slit open the official-looking letter with her finger, pulled out the contents, opening it up, staring at its letterhead, *The Daily*

Herald, skimming to the signature, *Yours sincerely, Douglas Machray, Editor.*

Dear Miss Fisher. The letter was fluttering in her fingers as she read to the end, then back to the beginning, taking it in. *I have read with interest your features in* Peace News, *in particular your articles on the recent march from Aldermaston, which in my view captured the fervour and the fun of the enterprise in ways which were both novel and enchanting. I wondered whether you would consider submitting some articles to the* Daily Herald? *We would be looking to publish a weekly column. As you may know, we have recently adopted a unilateralist stance on nuclear disarmament, and would be interested in what you have to say about issues relating to war* and *peace. We pay one guinea per 100 words, and would be looking for articles of approximately 500 words. If you are interested please contact my secretary on Fleet 6001.*

Interested? A personal invitation from the editor? She wanted to pinch herself, scream with excitement. The *Daily Herald* too. A respectable paper, with an independent line. She'd ring him straight away. There was a telephone box on the corner. A weekly column would pay more than she earned as a typist. She squeezed her eyes, opened them, checked the letter one more time. She'd add a desk to the list of basics needed at the auction. And a typewriter. She couldn't wait to tell Dee.

She put the letter in her pocket and pulled out the other, turning it over in her hand, looking at the handwriting, the unfamiliar address. It had been sent to her work, and they had forwarded it to her.

Dear Bette. He used her German name. *This is by way of an olive branch, an apology, an excuse.* She breathed out, unsure of herself. *I was a small man caught up in large events. And I was as surprised as I am sure you must have been at the decision not to investigate your father's death. I thought of you then.*

I am now head of a modern language department in a grammar school in mid-Wales, and have bought a run-down cottage where I live with a border collie called Bess, a rooster and five laying hens, Eins, Zwei, Drei, Vier and Fünf.

She tried not to smile, but the chickens' names were too absurd. *If you have read this far, I consider myself a lucky man. I plan to modernise the cottage over the summer (by which I mean plumb in the water and put in a proper, indoor lavatory and bathroom). The countryside round here is beautiful. It would be presumptuous to offer you an invitation, but you know you would be welcome. More immediately, a post has come up for a secretary at the school and I wondered whether you would be interested? It is a step up from the typing pool. Also, there is a vacancy for an English teacher. A step up from secretary.*

Will you ever forgive me?

Yours ever, John.

Perhaps she had been too harsh on him. Would she have been strong in the storm of history? She could see him in the countryside, with an old tweed jacket and wellington boots, the dog at his heel. She was a city girl, needed pavements to feel secure, but she could see the attraction of the countryside. It had been a terrible year, a roller coaster of unimaginable highs and lows. She'd sunk into her bed each night exhausted.

'You need a damn good holiday,' Dee said to her. 'When all this is over. Check yourself into a nice hotel in Bournemouth. You've got the money. Or go to Cornwall. Walk in the moors, along the coast. Swim. Work off those Cornish teas.'

She had to give a week's notice at work. She could take a few days off before she started with the *Daily Herald*. Go to Wales. Put up with an outside privy and no running water. She'd survived Berlin, after all. Could new love ever glow from the embers of the old?

She folded the letter, returned it to its envelope, and placed it on the mantelpiece behind the Kienzle clock.

SOURCES

The following sources were used when researching for the novel:

Books:

Anonymous (Hillers, M.). *A Woman in Berlin* (Virago, 2005)

Baruma, I. *Year Zero: A History of 1945* (Atlantic Books, 2013)

Beevor, A. *Berlin: The Downfall: 1945* (Viking, 2002)

Berlin, M. *The Partisan Coffee House 1958–1963* (Catalogue to the Four Corners Gallery exhibition on the Partisan Coffee House, 2017)

Caplan, J. *Nazi Germany: A Very Short Introduction* (Oxford University Press, 2019)

Duff, P. *Left, Left, Left: A Personal Account of Six Protest Campaigns, 1945–65* (Allison and Busby, 1971)

Huber, F. *Promise Me You'll Shoot Yourself: The Downfall of Ordinary Germans in 1945* (Allen Lane, 2019)

Gatrell, P. *The Unsettling of Europe: The Great Migration, 1945 to the Present* (Allen Lane, 2019)

Judt, T. *Postwar: A History of Europe Since 1945* (Vintage Books, 2010)

Longden, S. *T-Force: The Forgotten Heroes of 1945* (Constable, 2009)

Mazower, M. *Dark Continent: Europe's Twentieth Century* (Penguin Books, 1999)

West, R. *A Train of Powder* (Virago, 1984)

Peace News (selected editions, February 1958 – May 1959)

Films:

March to Aldermaston (dir. Lindsay Anderson, 1959)

The Downfall of Berlin: Anonyma (dir. Max Färberböck, 2008)

ACKNOWLEDGEMENTS

As always, many thanks are due to my agent, Juliet Mushens, and to my editor, Jenny Parrott, for her wise suggestions, and to the team at Oneworld who have done so much to produce this novel: Molly Scull, Margot Weale, Ben Summers, Lucy Cooper, Laura McFarlane and Paul Nash.

My husband, Stein Ringen, planted the seed of this story when he suggested exploring the 'evacuation' of German scientists and science after World War II, and I am hugely grateful to him.

My dear friend, the late Raphael Samuel, an inspirational historian and intellectual entrepreneur, founded the Partisan Coffee House as 'the first socialist coffee house in the country' and 'an anti-espresso bar' in 1958. It closed in 1963, but in its short life it was the epicentre of radical and progressive thought and debate in politics, art, music, film, literature and design. The menu was eclectic, the coffee undrinkable, its influence on postwar cultural and socialist politics and thought immense.

Many friends, acquaintances and strangers shared their memories of the Partisan Coffee House and the early days of the Campaign for Nuclear Disarmament, or gave me insights into the world of spooks, spies and Special Branch. This is a work of fiction, and some may find their insights or memories transposed in time and place. I hope, however, I have kept to the spirit of their words if not the letter, but any errors are entirely mine. Huge thanks therefore to: Anna Davin, Brigid Davin, Nick Henson, Tricia Leman, Jo Stanley, Mike Warburton, Andrew Whitehead, Nigel Young and from the shadows, as befits their craft, 'X' and 'Z'. And for the introductions, Anna Davin, Guy de Jonquières and Richard Ralph.

A special thank you to Peter Huhne for his memories of postwar Berlin. I also owe posthumous thanks to my father, Arthur Chamberlain, for his stories of North Germany and Berlin in 1945 – and for the Kienzle clock acquired at that time.

Cecilia Ekbäck, Viv Graveson, Rosie Laurence, Laura McClelland, Sara Sarre, Saskia Sarginson, Gill Marshall-Andrews and Bob Marshall-Andrews read parts, or entire drafts, of this novel and gave me invaluable feedback, so many grateful thanks to them.

Throughout the writing of this book (during lockdown) I met (via Zoom) with my dear friends Sally Alexander and Ursula Owen, whose conversations on the war and postwar were invaluable in shaping my thinking, so a special thanks to them. And Bill Schwarz deserves a particular mention, too. He'll know what for. (A small in-joke. Sorry.)

Sylvia and Hans-Joachim Kieling helped with my German, so continuing thanks to them.

Finally, of course, my wonderful family for all their love and support and for delivering, with impeccable timing, a new grandchild as I delivered the manuscript of *The Forgotten* to Oneworld.